TORMENTED

TORMENTED

ELLE CHARLES

TORMENTED

Cover design by Rachelle Gould-Harris of Designs by Rachelle
https://www.designsbyrachelle.com

For all enquiries, please email: elle@ellecharles.com
www.ellecharles.com

ISBN: 978-1-69-586701-7

First publication: 7 October 2014

First Edition
Version 1.5
December 2019

Contents

Chapter 1

"HAS HER NEXT of kin been contacted?"

A soft, female voice penetrates my tender hearing. My head feels full of water, and my eyes refuse to do anything other than remain closed. My body is sore in multiple places, while my limbs carry a certain heaviness that I know is a culmination of being unduly assaulted, and being laid in a static position for an undisclosed amount of time.

"The police were called as soon as she came in. Miss Petersen is a family friend, and as such, I personally called her mother to inform her of her daughter's injuries. I appreciate it isn't usual policy, but I felt it necessary due to her history." A familiar, male voice responds firmly. "I've also called her boyfriend."

"Stuart, whilst I appreciate she is a family friend, and forgive me if I am being intrusive, but is there any reason to suspect the boyfriend is the one responsible for her present condition?"

A loud snort escapes him, but he doesn't answer.

"Fine! I will take your word as gospel, but as my patient, it's my responsibility to consider all the possibilities," the woman replies firmly. A pair of heels then click sharply out of the room, followed by the closing of a door.

A sigh ripples through my hearing, then something scrapes across the floor. A warm hand takes mine and starts to rub gently. Fire garners prominence inside, but in my current, inert condition, I am unable to give credence to my inability to snatch it back.

"God, I didn't think I'd be seeing you hurt like this again. Marie's on her way over. You're probably going to kill me when you wake up, but I called Sloan. He'll be here shortly. He's been off the rails these last few months without you. Please forgive him; he's lost. He has been for a long time until he found you." A gentle hand strokes my forehead. "Your old flatmate brought you in and then she vanished. When you wake, I hope you can give us some insight into what brought you here." He sighs. "What did she do to you, Kara?"

My mind floats back into the darkness, carrying me away, causing Stuart's voice to become barely audible. My brain starts to filter through the blackened haze, until it plucks out Sam's memory.

Looking back, as an outsider looking in, I should've known she was up to no good. I should've known she would never show up at Marie's house alone.

But the absolute truth of the matter is, Sam didn't do anything other than stand by and watch in glee.

"Hi, Kara." She grins, smug and coy.

I can feel my body harden once more in my subconscious state as she asks me pointless questions - ones she already knows the answers to. I look into her eyes again as a bystander, knowing I have to get away from this potentially volatile situation. I know nothing good is going to come out of this little meet and greet.

"Well, I wanted to talk yesterday, but you didn't answer the door last night."

"I was asleep." I mentally laugh at myself for saying the first thing that came into my head. It was such a pathetic attempt at a response, even I wouldn't have believed me. How I ever thought I could lie to her and she would believe it, was a wasted effort.

"No, no, no! You're lying!" She continues to spew shit from her mouth, but I was too lost looking at what she had finally become.

Then he made his grand entrance.

The devil incarnate himself.

I barely have time to scream out, as he launches his body towards mine. Something hard digs into my back, and I'm not sure if it's a gun or a knife, but my breathing starts to leave my lungs in heavy, laboured breaths. He forces my head and then his large fist lands on my cheek, directly aligned against my nose. As I taste my own blood, I register that my body has already given up and is sagging beneath me.

I pray for God to either save me or take me, when my nightmare becomes reality and Deacon pulls me up, hard and unforgiving under my arms. The waters of mouth turn, and I can taste my own vomit for a second time, rising up from the confines of my stomach.

Displeased, and probably fucked off that I am finally fighting back - for whatever it's worth - he raises his large, intimidating fist again. I instantly surrender and quieten down. My respite is short-lived when he hits me again with the force of ten men. Hot tears run down my face disconcertingly. The tears mix with the blood from my nose, which feels like it is being pressured to the point of combustion.

Grabbing me hard, he all but throws me into the car, and I crawl, childlike, into the space between the back seat and the front. Clutching my knees tight to my chest, I rock lightly. My blood and tears combine and saturate me, running down my chest, carrying away any hope of salvation with them.

"Shall I call him, or do you want me to go in person again?" Sam asks her bastard of a boyfriend hopefully.

"No, change of plan."

"...what are you going to do with her?" Her tone is boarding on panic, but my hearing is giving out with each passing second.

"Anything I fucking want!"

"Deacon, no, you promised-"

"Shut the fuck up, you don't call the shots here!" The sound of him beating her, and her subsequent cries of pain, puncture the cabin of the car. I rock against my knees again, silently begging and praying.

In the darkness, my childhood fears assault me repeatedly. Perpetually bound to the horrors of my past, I'm back in my bedroom with the music cocooning the space where I hide.

It's a place I fear I will live my entire life in.

A door slowly creaks open in the dim room I'm a prisoner in. Deacon has long gone, after inflicting yet another night of damage to my tender body. I hurt in places I have no recollection of hurting in before. I turn my head to the undressed, dirty window. The moon is starting to rise again, which means I've been here for two days, possibly three. I can't remember how long it has been since I woke up.

My stomach rumbles defiantly, and I'm not so ignorant to know that at some point, I'm either going to pass out from the beatings he's interspersing periodically, or the fact my body is shutting down, since the last time I ate was hours before I left for my night out with Sophie.

I continually press my lips together, hoping my body will create some much-needed saliva to dampen my parched mouth. A few tiny drops trickle down my throat, and I swallow them quickly, in between inhaling gulps of stale air. My lungs protest at the foreign moisture trying to enter them, and I start to choke and gag. My body convulses, as I try to simultaneously cough up and regain control over my breathing. I pull my arms, needing some leverage, but they won't budge. As my choking fit starts to ease down, my eyes slowly drift up to my outstretched limbs and reality dawns that I truly am a prisoner here.

Tears flood my eyes, as I squint and see the rope binding me to the wooden bed frame. Instinctively, I rub my thighs together, concentrating on the area between my legs. I let out a sigh of relief; I'm still clothed and positive I haven't been violated at his hands.

That's if you call physical assault not being violated. Nevertheless, it has to be better than being assaulted in a different way.

Footsteps resound and stop outside. The door pulls back, and a shadow enters. It makes quick work of putting a torn piece of fabric over some nails in the top of the window frame, and the hideous material falls down, disguising what's really happening in this soulless room.

The light flickers on, and I sharply twist away, trying to avoid looking into the piercing, white light. My eyelids move rapidly against the bright intrusion, and eventually, I'm able to see who is sitting next to me.

Sam smiles sadly, but she doesn't speak or make any gesture as to give me a reason why she is helping to keep me hostage. Standing, she leans over and quickly unties the ropes. Massaging my wrists, she moves to the side of the bed and carefully helps me to sit upright.

"I'm sorry," she whispers. Tears fall from her eyes, and light sobs fill the room to capacity. Horrified that I'm breaking down in front of her, I turn to gauge her expression. Her face is distraught, and I realise it isn't my heartbreak devouring the silence, it's hers.

"Here, drink this," she says, unscrewing a bottle of water and holding it to my mouth. The liquid pours over my lips and down my chin as I gulp it down, but I don't care. My body is at the point of shutting down, and I'm starving. I finish the water in record time, and she throws the empty bottle on the floor.

She then brings a bowl of steaming hot soup towards me and starts to feed it to me slowly. I blow the spoon before allowing it entry. It's force of habit, but in all honesty, it could scold me to death, because right now, I need it. I need it to survive.

After only a few mouthfuls, I refuse any more. I haven't consumed hardly any of it, and because I've been forcibly starved - for what I gather is probably days - my stomach is already aching from the little I have managed to swallow.

She starts to open her mouth, but stops when shouting erupts from somewhere in the confines of this murky place.

"Where the fuck are you, you little bitch?!" Running commences, and then the door slams open. Deacon's menacing stature fills the frame.

"Deacon, no more, please! This isn't what he wants! Please, just let her go!" Sam begs.

Deacon slides his finger down her temple, then grunts and smiles demonically, before picking her up and throwing her like a rag doll to the other side of the room. Her body smacks hard against the wall, and she wails out in the aftermath of the impact. He storms over to her, picks her up, and whacks her hard across the face. Her head is slammed to the side under the beating, and a small spray of blood leaves her nose.

"Please, stop!" I croak out, my arm outstretched. I will plead and beg.

I'm not above doing something that makes me feel physically sick, not if it means I will live to see another day – and so will she.

"What the fuck did you say? You have no power here; I do!" He stalks towards me, stopping at the foot of the bed. He grabs my ankles and drags me towards him. Hauling me up, he shakes me as though I weigh nothing, and turns and pins me up against the opposite wall. With one hand on my forehead, he slams it against the wall repeatedly, until pain reverberates through my skull. Smiling cruelly, he throws me back onto the bed and climbs on top of me. I claw and scratch at him.

I will not be a fucking victim again! Especially not his! I will fight until my last breath, if that's what it takes.

"No, no, no," he clucks. He drags my arms back over my head and refastens the ropes around them. "We're gonna play a little game, and I'm gonna win! You ready?"

I shake my head and start to cry. "Please, please, leave me alone!" I beg.

Not good enough.

His arm pulls back, and he fists me across the face. My breath is exhausted, and I gasp in the aftershock. He doesn't leave me enough time to recover before he does it again. And again. And again.

"That's enough of that! I can't have pretty boy ashamed to be seen with his pretty little bitch, can I? Let's see what else I can do!" He rips my clothes away, and his fists beat me raw. Pounding at my chest with such malevolence, my breasts feel like they are going to explode under the pressure of his balled hands.

Methodically, he slowly tortures his way down my small frame. The pain is too much, as he levels more hits to my hips and thighs. My body is giving out and falling away from me. My wrists chafe as he starts to tighten the ropes around them once more. It's a pointless act - I can no longer move my arms anyway. I stare up at him through bloodshot eyes, and he smiles, one last time, before delivering the final blow to my abdomen. My belly churns loudly, and I bolt upright, as far as my binds will allow, and empty the minuscule contents of my stomach over the side of the bed.

I stare blindly at the ceiling, as the darkness turns to light, and then back to dark again. I've been here for hours, days, or maybe weeks, who knows.

Does anyone know I'm here?

Are Marie and Sloan looking for me?

My own tears burn the tender, inflamed skin surrounding my eyes. A murmur in the room rouses me, but I'm unable to see who is there now. A shot of pain, combined with prickly fire startles me, as I'm lifted, and something is then wrapped around my body.

"Jer, be fucking careful with her!"

"I'm trying!"

I whimper as the material is pulled tighter over my torso.

"You're hurting her!"

The man snorts. "Me? You led her like a lamb to the fucking slaughter!"

"I know, but it's too late now."

My body is then raised further, and something is pulled up my legs. "I warned you, but you didn't listen. I warned you after he raped and battered you in the hotel."

"He didn't rape me," Sam mutters quickly, as they continue to bicker between themselves, unaware I can hear every word they're saying.

"Did you say no?" Silence. "Did you beg him to stop?" Silence. "Yeah, that's called rape, Sam."

"I didn't think he'd hurt her."

"You thought wrong."

"I thought they were just empty words."

"Samantha, as far as this girl is concerned, there's no such thing."

"What do you mean? I don't understand."

"You don't need to. Just know this, the next time you orchestrate shit against her, I'll kill you myself," the man says with a warning tone.

Sam's dingy blonde hair falls in front of my face, and she gives me a sorrow-filled smile again as I look up at her, insofar as I'm able to.

"Put your arms around me, Kara," the male requests.

"I can't," I whisper, as my head falls back against the bed.

A pair of strong arms pick me up, and I drift away into the perpetual darkness, with the feeling of fire eviscerating me from the outside in.

I'm shocked back into reality, as the sound of a door opens and then closes with a slam. Even in my drug-induced state, the atmosphere is thick and full of tension.

Soft lips touch my forehead delicately. "Marie's here. You're safe now, Kara," Stuart says gently. "You're safe."

The click of the door mechanism spells out that I'm back to being what is an undeniable constant in my life.

I am alone.

Chapter 2

MY EYES FEEL like lead, and the light taunts my sensitive irises. I slowly open them, considering for a moment if this is what heaven looks like. The walls are sterile white, and the smell of disinfectant lodges in my throat.

What the hell!?

I'm in hospital.

Again.

I despise hospitals!

The first and only time I've ever been in one - excluding my birth, of course - was eight years ago. I never wish to relive that experience ever again. But unfortunately, my current situation is ensuring that I am.

My body is prone and stiff. I attempt to lift myself up from the hard, unforgiving mattress, but I can't hold my own weight. My inability to perform such in an innocuous task is both futile and painful – and it pisses me off royally.

Forcing myself up abruptly, I cry out at the shooting pain coursing through my arm and stare mesmerised at my side. In my haste, the intravenous drip has dislodged, and blood is now seeping over the back of my hand and staining the sheets. I barely hear the constant warning beep of the monitor next to me, until a nurse comes rushing through the door, with an exhausted-looking Marie hot on her heels.

"I have told you before Mrs Dawson, you're not supposed to be in here! Family only outside visitation hours!" the nurse states, in a very matter of fact tone.

"It's *Miss* Dawson, and I am family. I'm her mother," she responds curtly, with a quick roll of her eyes, brushing by the nurse to get to me.

Shifting up in the bed with Marie's assistance, the nurse dutifully reinserts the needle and resets the monitor, giving me a pointed look. It's patronising, and one that tells me not to do it again.

"Hi," is all I can manage. My mouth is so dry; I feel like I've swallowed sand.

"Oh, honey, I'm so happy you're finally awake," she breathes out. The tears in her eyes make her look weathered, suddenly old before her time. She sits tentatively on the bed and embraces me tightly. I stiffen, then relax.

I open my mouth to try to speak again, but I can scarcely verbalise a hum. Marie cups my cheeks, and a wave of concern washes over her. She quickly looks around and locates a jug of water on a nearby table. She pours a small glass, drops in a straw, and lifts it to my mouth. I suck it down in seconds. It's refreshing and moisturises my palette instantly. I swear water has never tasted so good. She takes back the glass and refills it, but I wave my hand at her to leave it on the table, since my stomach feels undecidedly delicate.

Searching her eyes, she appears fretful. I sigh, realising something is terribly wrong. "How long have I been here?" I enquire in a whisper. It's the most logical question in my mind, which is currently bursting to capacity with them. She gives me a weak smile, and it isn't one that fills me with hope.

"Five days, honey."

"In the hospital? How many days in total from the night at the club?" I ask, knowing that I had spent at least two, maybe three, at the mercy of evil.

"Nine." The word carries over the atmosphere in a ghostly whisper, and I blink, not quite sure if I've heard her correctly.

"*Nine?* I don't understand. I mean, I don't remember anything. All I can remember is being thrown into the car by Deacon." My heart sinks as I conceal the truth from she who loves me the most. But I can't allow her to share this pain with me, because I remember everything he did… *Smashing my head against the wall, beating my body black and blue under him...* I remember, but I know I also have to forget. I did it before, and I will again.

Marie's eyes snap open fully, and she's verging on shock. "*What?* I reported you missing after Sophie called, asking if you were okay. I thought you'd decided to stay with her a bit longer. You'd been gone nearly two days before we realised you were missing. It had taken another two before I got a call to say you were here. They said another woman had brought you in. It was Sam, and as soon as they admitted you, she ran before the police could question her."

I let my eyes close, trying to forget the night. I'm frustrated when nothing I try eradicates it from my memory, and each part stands out vividly; taunting me, mocking me, mitigating the foundation, ensuring it remains.

Marie touches my cheek again. She bends down and kisses my forehead, and my body involuntarily clenches. She shakes her head, understanding I'm taking two steps back from what I had almost broken free of.

"Look, I need to go, I've got a meeting, but if you need anything, anything at all, call me." She turns to leave, and I know if I don't ask now I never will.

"Does *he* know I'm here?" She sighs. "Actually, no, don't answer that. He probably doesn't care. He probably thinks I got what I deserved, since I'm actually one of Deacon's sluts anyway. I know he's with Christy now; I saw them together at his club." I hold back my tears, praying for her to leave so I can cry pathetically in private once more.

Marie turns around, her lips a tight line, her features pained. "Honey, he's not with Christy, and he never was. He's been here every day since the police called. From what the nurses have said, he's driving everyone into the depths of despair. And since he's unhappy, he's making sure everyone else is, too!"

My lips tug up at the corners inconspicuously. Hope blooms pitifully in my heart, and I want to laugh at the visual, but I don't dare to hope. He's no longer mine, maybe he never really was, and the sooner I absorb that fact, the stronger I will be for it.

"Apparently, he refuses to leave the room, and he's been sitting with you all night. He looks terrible." I nod a little, thinking about everything that has happened.

The negated fissure in my heart cracks a little deeper, and I look towards the chair she has just vacated. I can clearly see him sitting there. But I can't go there, not again. Not when I'm so fragile and broken like this, that just the slightest push could take me into the void completely with no hope of return.

"Tell him not to come back; I don't want to see him." They're complete lies, but necessary to ensure I survive him.

She huffs out, pissed off. "Kara, I've never once questioned your judgement, but this time, I'm afraid I have to. He loves you, he just listened to the wrong person, and somewhere, he became lost. He has his reasons for what he did. I'm not saying it was right; it wasn't. I was livid that day at the hotel, and John was ready to kill him." She's so sincere, but I can't fathom who she's actually trying to convince here; me or her.

She starts to speak again, but I cut her off. "Who's John?" I cross my eyes, wondering who else has entered the fold in the last few months that I don't know about.

Marie smiles knowingly. "Walker," she replies with a mirthless laugh. All this time and I didn't even know his first name. "God, that man has never told you anything, has he?"

"No," I whisper, feeling pathetic and embarrassed.

I stare down at the sheets, which are now tainted red. I grimace; it wouldn't be the first time I've slept in my own blood, or rather woken up in it. I can only hope the nurse comes back in soon and changes them.

"You know, Sam might not be very popular right now, but she did you a favour; she saved you - both of you. Sloan realised he was completely in love with you, regardless of whatever he was led to believe, and you're still here." My heart skips a beat, and my fortitude diminishes. She quickly bends down to kiss my cheek. "Get some sleep, honey, we'll talk more tomorrow."

On the verge of tears at hearing her say his name again, I nod and tell her okay. It's ignorant, but I want her to leave so I can mull over my hurt and indecision.

She opens the door and pauses. "Do you still want me to tell him to stay away?" Her face is a vision of hope, confirming she has more than enough optimism for both of us. I just hope my next decision isn't the wrong one.

"No, I need to see him, even if it is for the last time." I remain defiant. I need to hear his feelings from his own mouth. I don't want some convoluted, twisted, second-hand version, even if it was from someone who loves me unequivocally.

With a roll of her eyes and a defeated nod, she closes the door behind her.

Staring at the off-white wall in front of me, yet again, I've been left alone.

Attempting to improve my comfort level is a pretty hard feat, especially when the mattress feels like it's padded with rocks. Even the tiniest movement results in some degree of pain. I breathe in, and eventually accomplish a relatively comfortable position. Ignoring the intermittent discomfort, the old adage of mind over matter prevails, and I descend into a deep sleep.

"I love you," Sloan whispers to me.

Frustrated, I thump my fist against the pillow. Ugh, I can't even escape him inside my dreams. I'm back to where I was when I first met him – he's taking up residence in my subconscious bed again.

It has been two days since I woke up, and I still haven't seen head or tail of him. I figured Marie had told him I initially didn't want him here, until she endeavoured to right a few wrongs.

How wrong she was.

I braced myself for his arrival, expecting him to come thundering through the door, shouting the odds, not long after she had left, but he never did. I have since refused all visitors for the last thirty-something hours. No one needs to see my bright red eyes and watery nose, brought on by the pain of unrequited love – regardless if Marie said it was the exact opposite.

The only thing that has kept me together are the nurses coming and going with magazines and mindless gossip. Oh, and the police, who want to know precisely what I remember. I'd like to say I confessed my pain, but I didn't. To confess means I bring Sloan into the fray, and unfortunately, until I know what his connection to Deacon is, it isn't a viable option.

Needless to say, everything I've been fretting over was completely forgotten when I was finally strong enough to look upon my own face yesterday. I knew it would bad, but I still wasn't ready for the reality. Ugly, purple bruises mar my pale skin, and my heart almost stopped in shock at first sight. Chancing a peek down my top, seeing my breasts and stomach more openly, I threw up. They are virtually unrecognisable. The result of what Deacon did while I was captive is clear to see in my reflection.

After being momentarily catatonic as I was finally told of my injuries, I had been generously offered a valuation of the psych kind. My lungs failed to operate correctly with each word that came out of the doctor's mouth. Although I was told that I'm healing well, and I might even be discharged in a few days, my body flourishes with hope and simultaneously wilts with fear.

I'm safer in here than I am out there, especially with *him* and Sam still on the rampage.

"I love you." Dream Sloan confides again, before he smiles and turns on his heel into a jog.

I'm running after him, unable to catch him up, down a long corridor that has no end in sight. In my dream, he's leaving me, rather than him telling me to go. I'm not quite sure what significance my mind is trying to impart, but it's painful to watch him turn away.

The muffled sound of a door closing resonates in my head, and I wake groggily. Turning sleepily, one side of my body burns like fire under the bruises. I roll over to the other, and come face to face with the man who has invaded my life in every waking moment, and every sleeping one, too.

"*Sloan...*" I sigh out. He *has* come to see me; I just wasn't conscious to see him.

"Shush...go back to sleep, my love."

Electricity surges through every nerve ending as he touches me for the first time in months. He places his finger over my lips and traces them gently. Raising his hand, he strokes my forehead, and with a touch as soft as velvet, he drifts over my cheek. I have a visible bruise there from the force of the punch that Deacon knocked me out with. With his forehead creasing, I know he sees it clearly in the night shadow.

"Will you be here when I wake up?" I ask softly, my heart and brain unengaged, going against everything I attempted to make Marie believe.

He squeezes his eyes shut and nods. When he opens them again, a solitary tear forms, and falls away just as quick. He draws me closer and allows his arm to envelop my waist, while his fingers repeatedly graze over the soft skin of my stomach.

"I'll always be here; whether you want me to be or not." I close my eyes at the context of his statement. "I've got you. I've always got you."

Chapter 3

A THROAT CLEARING wakes me. I rub the sleep from my eyes, happy that the deadweight sensation in my limbs is finally subsiding.

Sloan's large frame is holding me down, and I nudge his arm to rouse him, as Stuart stands at the end of the bed, watching unimpressed. Albeit, he does appear to be a little amused, too.

"Foster, wake up!" he shouts to no avail. I quickly glance at the door; positive the nurses are going to come rushing in due to the commotion. "Don't worry, Kara. They know he sleeps in here every night. They gave up trying to get him out after the first night." He chuckles.

I squirm a little. *Every night?!*

"Trust me, it makes life hard when they swoon and fuss all over him! I don't know why, but they seem to find it especially attractive when he becomes confrontational due to your welfare. He's also the reason why you have a separate room and not one on the ward." He holds his stethoscope, and gives me a perceptive smile. "It's nice to see you again, although I would've preferred it under better circumstances, of course. When I told you not to be a stranger, I didn't think you'd take up occupation in my place of employment. It's pretty damn grim seeing you in this bed, if I'm honest," he says sadly. I muster up a smile, knowing that neither of us wants me here. He places the clipboard back in its holder and walks round to Sloan's side, who is still very much asleep.

"He hasn't been sleeping well lately. Hopefully, now he'll be better." He gives me a sly look. "Normally, I would leave him, but Dr Peters will be making his rounds shortly. Under the current circumstances, he won't take too kindly to your bed guest. Let's just say they have agreed to disagree over the last week. And as we both already know, what he wants, he usually gets!" He rolls his eyes, before pinching Sloan's nose, holding it until a gasp escapes his mouth and his eyes shoot open.

Unable to suppress my laugh, Sloan staggers ungracefully to his feet, still half asleep, and veers around the bed with purpose, glaring at Dr Andrews.

"*Stuart...*" he says sternly.

"Oh, so it's Doc on a good day - or whenever you are in need of my medical services - and Stuart when you're pissed off?"

"Welcome to my world, I'm *Ms Petersen* when I transgress." I bite my lip the instant unimpressed midnight blues transition from me to Stuart, and then back again.

"Ah, well...very interesting." Stuart straightens up, his full height isn't much smaller than Sloan's. His dirty blond hair is neatly cut and styled. His frame is almost as large as Walker's, but whereas he carries a certain menacing quality, Stuart is pure charm. This, I hadn't noticed previously.

Doc's eyes fix on Sloan, and he gives his friend a once over. "Good to see you finally had a shower, you smelt like shit the last time I was in here. No wonder why she didn't want to wake up!" He winks at me. "I'll be back later, Kara. I just wanted to see how you were doing." Stuart takes his leave, but a look of *need to know* flits between them, and I get that grating feeling in my chest again that I'm being forcibly kept out of the loop - one which I'm currently floundering in the middle of.

Sloan's features mar with frown lines when he turns back to me. I stare at him, waiting. I sigh as he starts to pace the floor.

"Fuck! I'm sorry, for everything. But mainly because I believed her lies."

I stare at him, not really sure what to say or how to react. Actually, I know exactly what to say, and the time for my procrastinating and tiptoeing around him is over.

"Well, you should have listened before you kicked me out, but you didn't. You left me to walk the streets alone. If it wasn't for Marie and Walker's impeccable timing, that's exactly what I would've done!"

He turns away, the unmistakable look of shame is clearly etched on his face. "I know, I-"

"No, you don't know!" I cry out, then sigh as I shake my head. "You have absolutely no fucking idea what I went through that day! I just don't understand why you would believe her in the first place. She's not exactly the paradigm of truth and virtue, is she? I especially can't believe it, considering I had called you when *he* was loitering at the front of my building. Surely Walker would have picked up on anything untoward I was supposedly doing."

"Yes and no. God, I didn't know what to think, okay! I had spent most of the afternoon sparring with Devlin, and he just kept riling me up, until I snapped! Then Tom was calling to say the phone and the car signals were transmitting from your old flat, and I knew it was either Sam or your parents, and then I couldn't get in touch with John. I wasn't fucking thinking straight!"

"That's no excuse, and you know it!"

"No, it isn't! I was fucking blind and the biggest arsehole in the world. I swear I didn't know John was there with you until he told me, right after he took me down for kicking you out. He said you were ashamed of your father, and that was the true reason why you didn't call me."

I nod, but I am far from placated.

"Kara, I believed it because I guess, deep down, I thought it was a miracle you were finally mine. That I finally had something good and pure. I will always be ashamed of how I treated you. I wouldn't blame you if you choose to walk away once and for all. Believe me, I never wanted to hurt you. I was just so blindsided by what I'd been told, I couldn't see beyond it. Then the night I saw you in my club...the way that Carl looked at you again..."

My eyes narrow into slits at his assumption, and I breathe out, pissed off. "*Me?* How dare you! You were with Christy at the club. She was sat in your fucking lap, with her tongue in your ear! You had your arm around her! I didn't do anything with Carl. I barely said hello to him, unlike you." He opens his mouth to try and cut me off, but I don't give him an inch.

"Not only that, I heard her - taking her to the May function at your hotel, planning a goddamn jolly, fucking holiday! For all I know, you were seeing her the whole time we were together. God knows there are enough things you haven't told me. I know you have secrets, and it's not fair. I've told you stuff...things about me..." My lungs gasp for air, and my chest seizes up painfully, because I have my own guilt to conceal.

Factually, I might not have told him *everything*, but it's a damn sight more than I thought I'd ever be able to do, and a hell of a lot more than he has given me.

"Kara, I'm many things; a bastard, an arsehole, an idiot, but I'm not now, nor have I ever been, a goddamn cheat! I promise I didn't do anything with her. We were both at the event, but I went alone, and I left alone. She said it to rile you up because she's jealous of you. Trust me, the only move that was made was her trying to stick her tongue in my ear, and me leaning in to tell her to politely fuck off! Anything out of her mouth is bullshit!"

He cradles my cheeks, his hands are light, enabling me to turn away if I wish. But I don't. I want him to see how much he's hurt me. I want the pain on my face to have his name written all over it.

"There's only been you since the night we met." His eyes reflect the truth and sincerity of his statement, and I may currently be a drug-induced fool, but I believe him. I love him, so how can I not? But I still have to protect myself. I push back from him, but his hands remain fixed in exactly the same place.

"Why didn't you come and see me in the weeks after?"

He drops his head down. "Because you hated me. I know I would've. I swear I sat alone in the house every single day and only left to go to work. Charlotte refused to speak to me for weeks. Even Jake and Doc were off. Everyone took a side..." he stops and looks at me. "And it wasn't mine. I promise you, there's been no one, but you, since the night you blustered into my suite back in March."

I turn away from him because, emotionally, he's breaking me. "No, I can't do this any longer. I'm sorry. Please leave and never come back!"

"Kara, I need you!"

I scoff, unable to control my pain. *"You need me?* Why? Do you need someone to look after all the battered women your hotel churns out? Or just someone to flaunt in front of the redheaded bitch who doesn't know when to quit!"

He throws his hands on his hips, displaying that thoroughly annoyed look he executes perfectly when he is faced with hearing something he doesn't like. I stare at him patiently, waiting for him to rebuke my outburst, but strangely, he doesn't.

"Baby, don't do that. You're better than that! Please let me make us right," he pleads. "Let me fix us!"

"You can't fix this!" I cry out, pressing my hand to my chest, holding it over my heart, showing him what he has damaged. "You broke us; you broke me! You destroyed my spirit, my faith. You shattered my heart. How can you ever expect me to trust you not to do it again? It doesn't matter how I feel about you; you can't keep doing this to me every time someone tells you crap! You didn't want the truth. You just want to believe the lies because it's easier!"

"So tell me, tell me what is true! Tell me what to do to make it right. I'll do anything to put us back together again!"

The door swings open, and Nurse Smith walks in. She halts,

looking aggravated at seeing Sloan in my room at such an ungodly hour. She judges our expressions perfectly, before politely excusing herself, saying she'll come back later.

He stands and gazes out of the window. "I love you. It took seeing you in this bed, fighting for your life, to make me admit just how much I always have. That's what hurt so much when Sam told me. I didn't believe her at first, I couldn't, but she was so convincing. Forcing you to leave that day killed me, but I have to protect my family. I can't have him back in our lives again. Not after what happened!"

I scrub my hand over my face. "What are you talking about? *Who are you talking about?*"

"Kara, don't!"

"Don't, what? Ask questions that you seem to want to avoid? Who?" I scream. He turns and faces away from me, before he huffs out and spins around abruptly.

"*Deacon!*" he spits out, slumping into the chair next to me. Taking my hand in his, his warmth spreads through me like red-hot lava. "We grew up together, Kara. He knows everything about Charlie and me."

My breathing hitches in my throat, but surprisingly, I'm not actually shocked to hear of his connection with him. Somewhere deep inside, I knew they had a shared history. I identified it the moment he confessed he knew him months ago. Just how deep that history went, I still had to question. Although I'm more concerned about why Deacon is now using me as a pawn to get to him.

"He did things... Things to us, *to Charlie,* that can never be forgiven. I..." I turn my hand in his and squeeze lightly.

"No, don't. I can guess what he did, but like you said before, it's not your story to tell. If she wants to tell me, she will." Exactly as I thought the first time I saw the loneliness in her eyes at the March function, Charlie had been hurt in her past, and Deacon was the reason behind it. Her concealed pain was of his creation, the same way that mine currently is.

He leans forward and levels his look on me. "Take me back, I'm begging you. *Please.* Please make us right again."

"You don't like begging, remember?" He raises his brows, unimpressed. I lean back, defeated. "You hurt me, more than you could ever imagine. Maybe more than anyone else has in my whole life. I'm not over exaggerating to make you feel guilty, it's the truth."

His face hardens in pain, and he paces towards the door. "I've never told any woman that I love her, except you. I appreciate you need time and I'm willing to wait, but I won't wait forever." The door slams shut behind him.

And just like that, he's gone.

Chapter 4

WELL, IT'S BEEN nearly two days since my talk with Sloan. He's not been by during visitation hours, and I don't know whether or not he still shows up when I'm asleep. My heart is barely functioning correctly, and I wonder how long it will be before it cracks and kills me completely. I'm starting to believe you can die of a broken heart.

He said he would give me time, but I didn't think it would be days before I saw him again. In the last forty-eight hours, my heart has performed on both ends of the emotional spectrum; thudding faintly inside my rib cage, and then skipping a beat each time the door opens, anticipating it's him.

It never is.

My dilemma has forced me to spend, and subsequently waste, two days deliberating whether or not I should give us - or more him - a second chance. My brain has virtually seized up, going through every possible scenario imaginable, as to why I should and shouldn't rekindle this. A roaring headache - that no amount of paracetamol or ibuprofen can seem to eradicate - spells out I need to stop thinking about it so much and let my heart decide.

And that is the most problematic issue I'm facing; my heart has already made its choice, and as far as it is concerned, we belong together. My logic, on the other hand, can always be relied upon to sensibly point out so many things that will have to change if I do take him back. Namely, the lack of communication and understanding.

I nibble on the banana from lunch, questioning my prudence and reasoning all over again, when the door opens. I twist to see who is visiting now, and unknowingly disrupting my solitary reverie. I hope it might be Marie or, please God, Sloan, but my mouth gapes open when Sam enters.

Almost immediately, I'm on high alert. My senses are assaulted with visions of her frail, drug-ravaged body slamming against the wall, followed in quick succession by my own. The smell of Deacon's breath on my face feels so real, I can almost taste it. The memory of his damning actions resurface, and it's like being back in that awful room again, with only him and my own determination to survive for company.

"I'm so sorry, Kara. Please forgive me," she whispers, closing the door and dropping down the hoodie.

She dawdles just inside the room, and I gesture for her to take the seat beside me. She rounds the bed slowly, but I don't fail to see the limp in her right leg. I scrutinise her body suspiciously, wondering what other damage he has inflicted since she dropped me off here more than a week ago. Seeing I have noticed, she raises her shoulders with an uncaring shrug.

"Are you okay?"

"I'm fine. I just came by to see how you are...and to let you know that I'm leaving. I'm going back up north. It's not safe for me here anymore," she says, lowering her eyes, and rubbing her hands together in a way that would make you believe it was the middle of winter and not June.

"What about the flat?" I ask. "The rent is still paid up for another couple of months." As I suspect, she lifts her brows noncommittally, but I appreciate it's the least of her worries right now. Her eyes are full of sorrow, as she wraps her arms around herself and shivers.

"Cold?" Except, I know it isn't cold. It's a standout symptom of addiction and withdrawal. It's something I had witnessed more than once growing up.

"A little, but I'll be okay. Kara, I'm sorry I brought Deacon to Marie's house. He said he just wanted to frighten you and get to Sloan. To send him a message. He said he wouldn't hurt you... Oh, my God...why did I believe him?" she cries out.

"Hey, Sam, it's okay. We're alive, that's what's important, right?" I try to sound as upbeat as possible, but fail drastically. I know she's stuck between a rock and a hard place, as far as that bastard is concerned. I shouldn't care after all of her indiscretions, and the fact she ripped my world to shreds - twice, but I do. You can't just turn feelings on and off at will.

That, I am finding out fast in other aspects of my life, too.

"No, it's not okay, you didn't see what he did to you!"

"No, but I felt it, and I see it now. Each time I look at my arms or legs, he's still here. Each time I look at my wrists, I see the red welts of the ropes over my old scars. I do see what he did to me."

"But it wasn't what he wanted to do; what he planned to do. He beat you, Kara. All those bruises on your body, they're because I wasn't strong enough to walk away from him. They might be of his doing, but they are of my making. They're all because of me… I never thought he'd do that." She quickly wipes her eyes. "I haven't seen him since, but I'm terrified, because when he finds me…"

"You have to go to the police, Sam. You have to tell them-"

"Tell them what? That my pimp beat my best friend and planned to rape her?" Her eyes are wide and wild in both anger and fear.

My body recoils at her words. My reoccurring recollections and numerous talks with the doctors over the past few days have confirmed what he had done to me. I have both the scars and full-body bruising, plus the medical descriptions to prove it. Not to mention the memories I'm hiding. But hearing it from her, out loud, brings on a whole new level of realisation.

She gets up to leave and bends down to me. Her lips lightly brush my shivering cheek. "Remember, never forget. Ever." These are words she had whispered to me as we grew up; each time I was suffering. She hasn't uttered them in years, and so I don't quite understand why she is rehashing them again now. She then quickly turns to leave the room.

"Sam? Please let Marie know where you're going. I'll always care about you, you know. I love you."

She wipes her hand over her eyes. Giving me a pitiful smile, she pulls the hood up and leaves. The sound of the door closing is indicative this is the end for us.

I stare long and hard at the wood for an infinite amount of time, willing myself to never, ever forget.

Whatever that may mean.

The sound of familiar girly giggles drowns out the relative quiet of the surrounding area, making my eyes flutter wide. My room door swings open, and Sophie blusters in with a nurse.

"Oh, shit, she's asleep!" Her voice carries over me as the door closes, and the back of a nurse disappears down the corridor through the glass observation window.

"No, no, I'm awake," I reply sleepily. I lift up on the unforgivingly hard mattress, which hasn't improved during the time I've been incarcerated under medical supervision. It really is a wonder I've managed to get an ounce of shut-eye at all on the damn thing.

"I'm sorry; I wouldn't have come if I'd have known you were sleeping. You look really tired and exhausted. No offence, chick!"

I shake my head at her kindness. "None taken, I'm just so tired of being here. I'm itching to get home. Did you come alone? Marie's meant to be dropping by soon."

"Oh, she's already here. She's downstairs in the canteen getting sandwiches and coffee." Sophie comes around and starts fussing with the sheets, before making herself comfy on the bed.

I hesitate, wondering if I should tell her about my shock visitor. She looks at me with narrow eyes, realising I have something to get off my chest.

"Sam finally showed up. She said she was sorry. I guess I shouldn't expect anything more from her, probably quite lucky I even got that."

"No fucking way! She doesn't know where she's not wanted, does she?"

"Sophie…" I shake my head. She has disliked Sam from the word go, and there's definitely no love lost between them. Soph tolerated her when she first came back into my life, but she has never gone out of her way to be endearing or welcoming.

"No! I've held my tongue for years, but after what she did, the part she played, she has no right to waltz in here and expect your forgiveness. Look at you!" Her tone gets higher. "She may not have laid a finger on you, but this is all on her!"

The door opens, and Marie hurries in. "Christ, Sophie, I can hear your shrieking outside!"

Sophie looks forlorn, being reprimanded by Mum. "Sorry, I'm just so fucking angry!" she says, almost tearful. "I should never have let you run from the club."

And there is the truth behind her anger; her own guilt over proceedings that night. She blames herself, however unnecessary, unwarranted, and most definitely, unfounded. I want to reach out and touch her, but don't feel strong enough to. My aversion is still back in full force.

Watching Soph dab her eyes, what I wouldn't give to be able to turn back time and heed her advice. I should have listened when she told me to talk to Sloan. If I had, this precise moment might have been very different. In some warped, parallel universe, I might be wrapped up in him, as opposed to waiting for him to walk through the door and secretly complete me again.

Marie sighs, and puts a ham and cheese and a latte on the bedside table. I give her a small shake of my head. Everyone seems to want to blame themselves for my current condition, but the sad fact is, I choose to walk away from the club. I choose to leave Sloan standing on the kerb incensed, and I choose to get in that taxi alone. I thought I knew Sam, but the woman waiting with intent on Marie's driveway, assisting in a sordid part of my fate... Well, I didn't know her at all.

"Soph, it's not your fault, darling, and if I hear you saying otherwise, you and I will be having serious words about it. All we can do is be vigilant and careful. Be mindful of what's happening around you and just be aware," Marie executes perfectly, almost like she has been conditioned to say it. I stare at her from under my lashes, wondering how long it has taken Walker to train her to perfect it.

As I take long swallows of my latte, listening to Soph and Marie babble on, my eyes drift shut again. There isn't much to do here other than watch mind-numbing daytime television, namely consisting of re-runs and chat shows, or sleep.

A sharp knock comes to my door, and Stuart pops his head around the wooden spine. His smile drops a little when he sees Sophie sat cross-legged on the end of my bed, a book in her hand.

"Hey, I just came by to see how you are today. Are you still experiencing some pain?" he asks, approaching me with caution. "Marie, Sophie." Marie gives him a beaming smile, while Sophie quickly lifts the smut book up to her face. I doubt she even realises what that cover looks like.

"Erm, not so much pain, just unable to sleep," I whine a little.

"I can give you something to assist if you want? Eyes wide." He pulls out his light pen thing and starts shining it in my eyes. I note he makes a conscious effort not to touch me at all.

"Actually, it's not sleep, per se, more like the mattress is stuffed with rocks and concrete!"

He chuckles and folds his arms. "Well, there's nothing I can do about that, unfortunately. Complain to the NHS!" he jokes. "I'll leave you since you have company, but if you need anything, get Nurse Smith to find me. I'll drop by again later." He heads towards the door, but stops and turns. "Sophie, can I talk to you?" He looks hopeful and walks outside. Sophie huffs out, throws the book down and follows him out sheepishly.

Marie turns to me and gives me a shrug. "What's going on with her?"

"I don't know," I answer, as we both watch Stuart and Sophie, unashamedly, outside the window.

"What's going on with you? You and Sloan?" she asks. "He told me you'd talked."

I sigh out. "I definitely don't know. I haven't seen him since he left two days ago, and it's killing me, if you really want the truth. I love him, but I just don't know if I can give him all my trust again. I'm scared that if I do, he will rip my heart out for the second time."

"Oh, honey, he's not perfect. I know you think he is, but he isn't. We all make mistakes; it's how we learn to live, how we learn to love. If we never experience the bad stuff, how do we know what's good?" I lean into her and smile.

"I wish I could be as optimistic as you. There's nothing other than black and white in my world, and various levels of shit in between!" I laugh out, not because it's funny, but because Marie always looks on the bright side, the side that deserted me years ago.

"Marie, I need you to do something for me," I say in all seriousness, and she looks at me dubiously. "My desk drawer at the office, there's an A4 notebook hidden underneath everything. Can you bring it in for me?"

She looks at me with acute concern. "Of course I will, but I'm too scare to even ask."

"It's my memories, things that I have started to remember. Things that have begun to come back to me since I've been with Sloan. I don't understand why he's the trigger for them. I guess it remains to be seen whether it's a good thing or not."

She's about to answer, when the door creaks open, and Sophie sneaks back in. We both turn to her. She's trying to play dumb, and that is mildly insulting to all of us.

"So, what did the handsome doc want, dear?" Marie tugs her hand. Sophie shakes out of her hold and takes her place back on the end of the bed.

"Nothing, he just wanted to say hi," she says, lifting the book back up.

I let out an irritated groan. "God, Soph! You and I do have something in common – we're both pathetic liars!"

With a glare that could set me alight instantly, she tosses down the suspicious looking book. I know she's angry, but she's making my mistakes all over again. She is letting a good man go because of her own impaired reasoning. I know her standoffish conduct towards him has something to do with what has happened over the last couple of weeks.

I reach for the book and almost choke when I see the cover properly. "Seriously, is it really that bad?"

"They didn't have anything else in the shop downstairs!" Embarrassed, she defends herself.

"No, of course they didn't!" Marie chimes in. We smirk at each other when she starts to shift uncomfortably.

"Look, whatever you two have to say, just spill it!" she virtually shouts out. She's pissed at us both.

"Why are you ignoring Stuart? It's clear as day that you're both attracted to each other! What's going on with you? He looked gutted when he left."

She drops her head down, refusing to look at me. "Kara, he's Sloan's best friend - or one of them. He hurt you, and I won't betray you with his friend."

"My God, have you heard yourself? We all know Kara can be ridiculously stubborn, but you are pure ludicrous at times. You two have gotten worse over the years. Between you both, I get more strife now than when you were teenagers!"

"Hey!" I snap.

"Oh, be quiet! You know it's true," Marie snaps back. I tuck my chin into my neck and pout. There is nothing quite like being lambasted with the truth to make you speechless.

"I don't care how ludicrous I sound, if it's not okay with Kara, then it's not okay with me."

I sigh. "You're not betraying me. I love Sloan; I really do. I just need some breathing space from him. Don't let my life and it's non-stop trouble dispel any chance you might have at happiness. Stuart's a good man, and you would be a fool to let him slip away from you." She gives me a timid smile, silently considering my words.

If only I could absorb my own advice when it comes to allowing good men to slip away.

I lean forward and reach for her. She allows me to take her hand, and as much as it itches my skin incessantly, she needs to hear this. "Go and find him." I pick up the smut book and throw it at her. "Tell him you want to read to him!"

Sophie huffs, grabs her bag and heads to the door. "I'll see you later, babe."

"Hey, you better go find that man before you leave, because I'll find out if you don't. By the way, for future reference, next time bring me the classics, or Mr King!" I laugh as she flips me the middle finger.

Marie stands, equally amused. "Get some sleep, honey. I'll come by with a bag of clean stuff, and I'll put your notebook inside. I promise I won't look. We'll talk about what Sam said later."

"Thank you," I say, picking up the smut read left languishing on the bed.

Starting at the first page, I shake my head, knowing if I read this, it's going to leave me either incredibly frustrated, or borderline suicidal.

An hour or so later, I'm still completely immersed in the novel of graphic sex and very little else. Just like the disaster that has been my life for years, I'm unable to turn away.

As I flick to the next page, with wide, curious eyes, butterflies drift lower in my abdomen. I'm unable to rein in the sensations running rampant, induced by him who is giving me far too much time to procrastinate.

Chapter 5

"HEY, MISS P, guess who's going home today?" Nurse Smith comes in all jovial and smiley.

I'm counting down the days lately; six since I have regained consciousness, four since I have last seen Sloan, and two since Sam had departed.

Marie visits daily, and has even brought Walker with her a couple of times.

I really expected, and wanted, Charlie to show up and make me smile, but she, just like her brother, has chosen to stay away. When I finally plucked up the courage to ask Walker why, he told me she felt responsible in some way, and thought I would blame her.

She couldn't be more wrong.

We've both walked the same path of pain at some point in our lives. We have more in common than she presently knew.

As promised, Marie and I had spoken briefly about Sam's words of remembering, and Marie shook her head at it, also not understanding why she had brought them up again. We discussed Sam's plans to leave in depth, and Marie thought it was for the best, considering the recent tide of bad events. Especially since Deacon had gone AWOL, and not even Walker, with all his glorious technology and connections, could locate him.

By his own admission, I now know a little more about what Walker and the guys actually do. As I already knew, he runs his own security company, with Sloan as the silent benefactor. They deal with state of the art security systems for commercial businesses and the obscenely wealthy, as well as personal security.

As a side-line niche, they are also apparently very good at finding people that want to stay hidden - whenever the situation arises. I must admit, that makes me nervous, and very wary of how much he is also hiding from Marie. Although the words *bounty hunters for hire* were never mentioned, I imagine it isn't too far from the truth.

A cluck of a tongue makes me turn, and I stare at Nurse Smith, who looks anxious since I still haven't answered her yet. "Who? Me?" I point to myself and smile innocently.

"I'm gonna miss you, Kara. Especially that sexy, handsome, virile man who is adamant he doesn't want to leave you!" She fans her hand in front of her face, and I burst out laughing.

"You are terrible! I'll ask him to come and visit you personally," I chuckle, keeping with the spirit of the conversation.

"Doctor Peters approved your release, but he's been called into theatre, so Doctor Andrews will be by shortly to sign your forms. Oh, and these were dropped off for you a little while ago," she says, placing down the bag of clean clothes and underwear that Marie promised she would bring in for my imminent departure.

"Where's Marie?" I query.

"Mrs Dawson said to tell you that she double booked and has an appointment with someone. Something about a banquet and food? Anyway, she said someone else would be taking you home today."

Double booked, my arse! We've been counting down to this moment for days.

I inhale sharply. I'm about to ask the most stupid question that doesn't require an answer.

"*Who?* Who is taking me home?"

"Your boyfriend. She said he'll be here before lunch." She extracts a few clean towels from the trolley and lays them on the bed.

I quickly glance at the clock, realising I don't have much time. I'm about to ask for a doctor - *any doctor*- to release me immediately, when the sound of collective, girly swooning from outside snags my attention. I clench my fists and curse under my breath.

Sloan marches into the room, and I swear all the air is sucked out in the same instant. His body has a certain swagger and confidence to it. He pauses, and his beautiful blues spear me into submission. I swallow audibly at the sight of him, leaning against the architrave. God, he really is the embodiment of masculinity. Testosterone fills the room to capacity, and I push as far back into the headboard as possible, just to be able to breathe normally.

His presence is tangible, as he resumes his pace and picks up the clean towels. He greets Nurse Smith, who in turn nods and quickly escapes. She's beet red, both flustered and embarrassed. I smile when I see her fanning her face in the corridor animatedly.

"Let's take a shower, shall we?" His arm darts out to me, and I insolently fold mine across my chest.

I drink him in; his dark, messy styled hair, those broad sexy shoulders, the fitted jacket and shirt that cover his toned torso perfectly, all the way to his worn jeans, which sit on his hips effortlessly.

He is mouth-wateringly beautiful, and exactly what Nurse Smith had just described; sexy, handsome, and extremely virile.

I'm just not sure I can still call him mine at this moment in time.

"You are not helping me shower, Sloan! I need distance, and you need to go back to work! There was no need to go out of your way for me. I shall get a taxi home!" I spout out, getting off the bed and grabbing the towels from him. His nose creases, and he snatches them back.

"No way in hell, gorgeous! I'm taking you to shower, then I'm taking you home. To *our* home," he states firmly. He takes off his jacket, unbuttons his shirt, and then loosens his belt.

God, please don't let him stop, is the one and only thought running riot through my head. That is until the voice of reason sings out loud and clear. I raise my hand to my temple, desperate to eliminate my wayward thoughts that are anxious to be silently heard over each other.

"It's *your* home, *gorgeous*. It has never been *our* home! Give me those!" I reach out for the towels, but he moves them away from me. A sly grin forms on his face, and my determination is quickly disintegrating from it.

"Shower and home. Come," he commands. His rich voice ripples through me desirously, and my body betrays me in more ways than one when my centre flushes liberally.

Time stands still as we glare at each other. I breathe a sigh of relief the moment Stuart pushes the door open with my release forms in his hand. I quickly sign them off, seizing my opportunity to escape as Sloan pulls him aside for a chat.

I lock myself in the small, ward bathroom, and run the shower. The water is more than welcoming as I stand under the hot spray, loving how it feels to finally be able to wash alone, rather than having assistance. Suddenly, the curtain opens with a snap, and I shriek loudly, when Sloan steps in behind me, completely naked.

So much for being alone!

"Jesus, this is tiny!"

"How the hell did you get in here?" I demand, trying to cover the essentials. He drops a key to the floor before he entwines our hands and stretches my arms apart.

"Beautiful," he murmurs, leaning his head to mine, touching my lips briefly. I mentally curse myself for groaning the loss of him when he pulls back. My head is screaming, demanding he kiss me again, until he speaks.

"I'm through waiting. If you won't make us right, then I will. Starting right now."

"Get out! I mean it! If someone comes in here and sees you-"

"The door is locked, my love. No one is getting in here, except you and me."

"Sloan, I swear to God, get out! If you don't, I am going to pull that red flipping cord over there, and I'll make Stuart get you out!" I start twisting my arms and body, trying to break free.

"Go ahead! Stuart gave me the key, my gorgeous girl, plus the nurses already know I'm in here. Now stop fighting this. Quit wiggling!"

I scowl furiously at him. My arms are still splayed wide, and his eyes crease when they drift over the first of my bruises, thoroughly capturing his attention. His nostrils flare disproportionately, and he frowns. I look up to the ceiling as his fingers lightly touch the tender parts of me that are starting to heal.

"This is all my fault. *I* did this to you," he whispers sadly. "I didn't protect you from him. I didn't do enough."

Sighing, I can't even begin to imagine just how much Deacon has truly affected the lives of him and his family, that he feels he is to blame for this.

I slowly lower my eyes to his. They are mournful, full of regret and glassed over with pain. He releases my arms and lowers them, rubbing the circulation back into them slowly. Premature frown lines wrinkle his brow, when he sees the fading red abrasions the ropes have left behind.

"Sloan," I breathe out softly. "You didn't do this to me. You have no reason to blame yourself."

"But I did. I did all of it." He stares down at the shower floor, and my heart spasms painfully from his admission. I tilt his chin up, forcing him to look at me.

"Don't leave me," he pleads, and the barrier protecting my heart is breached and falling, as the last word fills the void.

I shiver under the flow of the hot water, as he runs his hand over my skin, across my bruises. He's gentle and soft, but it still hurts. It hurts because he has all the power. He has the power to help me overcome, and to bring me to my knees. He has the power to irrevocably hurt me, and to undeniably love me.

He owns me; body, heart, and soul.

He is elemental to my existence.

Picking up my body wash, he doesn't make eye contact with me. Instead, he concentrates on every limb and body part efficiently, taking extra care not to cause me any further undue discomfort.

Silence thickly consumes the small cubical, except for the sharp whistles of breath each time he discovers another dark mark. His sporadic muttering of expletives tells me I won't be impressed with my healing progress when I'm finally able to see my naked self from head to toe properly.

After holding me for an unknown amount of time, he finally shuts off the water and exits first, returning with a towel wrapped around his hips. He holds one open in front of me, and I inch forward. His hands curl around me protectively, and I surrender in his arms. His body is hot against mine, and it warms me through the cloth. My skin tingles as blood pumps just under the surface, heightened by the friction of him drying me painstakingly slow.

Falling deeper into him, I concede I'll never stop loving him, regardless of where the future takes us.

Inside his arms is where I belong.

He is home.

After growling his disapproval at my protesting, he carries me back to the room, much to my own mortification, and the amusement of the nurses, who are openly gazing and swooning at his display of definitive love and affection.

Not to mention he's half-naked.

Stuart, who is still on duty, looks positively horrified when he sees his friend carrying me down the corridor. Whether it's because Sloan treats me like glass, or the fact we're only wearing three towels between us, in full public view, I have no idea.

Inside the room, he pulls me close; his hands glide over my face and his lips warm mine. He slowly reaches down my back, dislodging the towel which starts to fall away. I'm thoroughly consumed by him, not wanting to let him go. Inside, I need to reach that indescribable level of love you read about, but never believe you will experience.

Lost in the moment, the door opens unexpectedly. "Kara, I just need to give you your prescription before you leave. Oh, shit, I'm sorry!"

Sloan stops instantly, and we both turn to see Doc standing there looking very embarrassed and sheepish. He turns his back to us, as Sloan mutters and quickly starts to cover me again.

"For fuck sake, Andrews! Don't you fucking knock?" He hides me completely with his body, ensuring I am out of Stuart's sight.

"It's a hospital, Foster. We have an open-door policy. Trust me, the last thing I want to see is you two almost fornicating! Next time lock the goddamn door!" he says with his back to us.

"It's okay, Stuart. You can turn around now," I tell him, ignoring Sloan's infuriated glare.

"Sorry, I'll just leave the script for your painkiller." He turns on his heel, but stops. "I trust you are both aware you'll need to take *extra precautions* whilst you're taking them?" I drop my head down, feeling my face turn red and nod. "Good. I'll see you later, but don't hesitate to call if you need anything." Stuart then literally runs out of the door.

With a growl, Sloan quickly locks it behind him, closes the blinds, and picks up another towel. Coming back and positioning himself in front of me, he begins to gently dry my hair.

"Come home with me, I can protect you there. *Please.*" His voice falters a little; the slight distress in his tone currently matches that deepening inside my chest.

"Marie can look after me, and Walker will be there. I'll be fine."

I stare blankly at the drawn blinds. I can't look at him, because looking means I'll give in. I can't consent, not yet, not when there's so much left unsaid between us.

"John sees more of you than I do," he mutters to himself. He's baiting me, whether he knows it or not.

"You'd see me a lot more if you hadn't kicked me out." His hands freeze instantly, and he levels with me.

Yes, it's a low blow, and although I don't mean to be unduly nasty, I just can't forget how much I've suffered because of it.

"How many times do I have to say I'm sorry? I am. I truly am. If I could go back and change it, I would. I was a fucking idiot to listen to her!"

Staring at him, I wonder if I really have what it takes to truly absolve him. Still, there's no point over-analysing it, because my decision is already final, but he doesn't have to be privy to it, yet.

"I just need time. I never expected to fall for you so hard, so fast, but I did. That day you ripped my heart out and left it dying on the floor. You can't expect me to forget that in a hurry."

He lets out a frustrated huff and picks up my bag. He rummages through it, pulling out a pair of beige linen trousers, a dark t-shirt, and some white cotton underwear, and places them on the bed. He seems distracted, as he drops the bag and lifts his jacket and puts it over my clothing.

My eyes have died and gone to heaven when he unexpectedly discards his own towel and lazily dresses. Shamelessly, there's not much else I can do other than watch. He's doing this on purpose. He's well aware he's being juvenile, while I'm well aware that I'm salivating amply, never wanting this private show to end. He zips up his jeans, leaving the button and belt hanging open, and then slides into his shirt, which he also leaves open, exposing his gorgeous chest muscles.

He peers up at me intermittently to see if I'm paying attention.
Yes, the intelligent man knows exactly what he's bloody doing!

My body temperature soars through the proverbial roof. I fear any moment I might do a Nurse Smith, and start fanning myself from the heat he's directing straight into my private parts.

He stands in front of me, and instinctively, I reach out to him, but he moves away, still smirking. Casually reaching into his jacket pocket, he pulls something out, shielding it from me.

My heart stops, because it's obvious whatever is in that box is going to be making an appearance whether I like it or not.

Slowly and deliberately, he gets down on one knee.
No, he better hadn't dare!

This has to be the most ridiculous idea ever. He really has lost his mind. He can't honestly think anyone would marry someone after only knowing them for four months or so, especially with all the unaddressed issues hanging precariously in the air between us right now.

I battle with my inner thoughts, everything bombarding my mind all at once. The devil and angel take residence upon my shoulders and start a war between themselves. My eyes flit to him when he clears his throat.

He grins at me, then eventually breaks out into a smile. "Baby, the next time I get down on this knee, it will be in a better place than a damn hospital room. Relax, it is, and isn't, what you think." He holds my hand, while the other is open in front of me. A black box sits neatly in his large palm. "Open it," he urges.

I inch forward prudently; a look of suspense plagues his handsome face. Touching the box with my free hand, he lets go of my other. My attention is centred, and I question whether or not it's such a good idea to open Pandora's Box. Whatever occurs in the next few minutes, as a result, is going to change everything between us.

Forever.

The bed creaks as he climbs on behind me and shuffles me between his legs. Settling himself back against the headboard, he influences me to rest against him, so we are back to chest. Like good times gone by, it feels natural to be in his embrace again, but I can't let him overpower me. He tugs on the towel, covering up my exposed upper thigh. I grin at his imperious demeanour, especially considering it's just us inside this locked room.

My hand glides over the box, and I lift the top off. Another black velvet box is nested inside, and I upend it. Timidly, I press the button to release the lid. My eyes broaden when I see the lights glint over whatever is inside. Sloan's chest moves behind me, indicating he is either holding his breath for my response, or silently laughing at my hesitancy.

With the lid fully open, I lovingly admire the bracelet nestled against the bed of black silk. It's beautiful and timeless; gold with a multitude of diamonds adorning its length. I raise my head and attempt to turn back to him, but he brings his hand to my cheek to stop me.

Resting his chin on my shoulder, he says, "It belonged to my mother. My father bought it for her after I was born. Years after he died, she gave it to me. She told me I was only allowed to give it to the woman who owned my heart, the way that she had once owned his." Tears form in my eyes at his beautiful words, and my resolve dissipates on the spot. "That woman is you, Kara Petersen. There will never be anyone else for me, only you." His hand traces down my arm and strokes my wrist gently; his thumb pausing on my scar. Removing the bracelet from its box, he secures it on my left wrist. "Not a ring, but it stays right here. It's a promise of forever."

I angle my arm, and he tangles his fingers with mine, holding them higher. I'm mesmerised by the twinkle of the diamonds under the harsh hospital lighting. I turn around, kneeling between his thighs.

"It's beautiful, but I-"

Shaking his head, he doesn't allow me to finish. "I will give you what you want. As much time as you need, but I'm not letting you go. *Ever*. This…" he touches the bracelet gently. "This tells me that you're mine. If you weren't, you wouldn't have let me put it on you. That much I do know." His hands frame my face, and I wince when he catches a sore spot on my temple. "Sorry," he mumbles.

"I'm yours. The truth is, I'm positive I always will be. I love you, but I just need time to adjust to…to everything. There's so much we still need to discuss. We need to talk about what happened to me when-" He cuts me off with a finger to my lips.

"Say it again, my love. I like hearing you say it." I curl up against his partially exposed chest. His heart is beating so fiercely, it resonates against my cheek.

"I'm yours?" I say innocently, knowing that isn't it.

"Nice try, but try again."

"I love you?" I say, as equally innocent, placing a light kiss on his chest, just over his heart. He returns it with one on my crown.

"I love you too, *Ms Petersen*," I smirk against his skin.

His irony isn't lost on me.

Chapter 6

AN ALMIGHTY SIGH breaks free from the confines of my throat.

Awkwardly settling into the 4x4, I pull the seat belt around myself and fold my hands in my lap. I quickly look around the large space. I'm so used to seeing him driving the Aston, that this was a surprise for me. My personal safety has obviously won the battle with his need for speed. I had seen this parked in his driveway all those months ago, and again, when he left me high and dry at the pub, but I've not seen it since.

Sloan opens the rear passenger door and places my bag on the back seat, followed by his jacket. He watches me closely, as he shuts the door and effortlessly slides into the driver's seat.

"Where's your baby?" I ask, the same moment the engine roars to life.

"I'm looking at her."

I purse my lips. "Very funny! I'm being serious, where's your Aston?" He turns to me, an expression boarding on painful creeps over his features.

"It's at the house. I didn't know if you would still be experiencing some pain or discomfort, so I thought it more sensible to bring this. Sorry, I forgot how small you are in comparison."

He quickly checks his mirrors as he reverses the car out of the space. I watch him as he glides the vehicle towards the give way sign, and then onto the main road. I smile to myself at his thoughtful consideration - even if I did need his assistance to climb in.

"...Hungry?" I do a double take when he asks me the question again. "Baby, are you hungry?" He narrows his eyes in confusion, awaiting my response.

"Erm, no, thank you." I shake my head and go back to gazing out of the window. I'm borderline ravenous, but the need to be alone is greater than my need to nourish.

A frustrated huff resounds in the car, and I grimace in my seat. The temptation to turn and tell him how much I love him, how much I desire and want him, is profound inside my heart. The truth is, loving him and wanting him will never be a problem for me. They are as central as breathing for me.

Trust, however... Trusting him is far easier said than done.

It also doesn't help that the dark cloud in the shape of Deacon is still out there, still able to get to me again. It's his own game of cat and mouse, in which he satisfies his morbid fascination with Sloan by hurting me and everyone else that he cares about.

A warning sign for horses and pedestrians yanks me back from the blackened caverns inside my mind. I snap my head around at the thick, green countryside, and the dry-stone walls edging the farmers' fields. I've been so preoccupied with my own thoughts, that I haven't paid one jot of attention as to where he is driving to.

"Where are we going? This isn't the way to Marie's house," I state, recognising exactly where we're heading. We are going home. To his home. He pulls off the main country road, and into the private lane that marks the start of his property.

"I told you at the hospital, we're going home." His concentration is fixed on the road ahead, but I can tell by his nervous tapping on the steering wheel he knows I'm unimpressed with his deceit.

"Sloan, we've already been through this - umpteen times - it is *your* house, not *our* home. My home is at Marie's. If you have any ounce of respect, or really care about what I want, you will take me there, so if you please." I cross my arms over my chest and wait.

"No," he whispers the one word he hates most in the world. Although, I'm strongly convinced the name of his ex-friend and foe is making rapid progress behind it.

He inches the car up to the large, locked gates. The guard on duty acknowledges him, but Sloan motions to him, indicating not to grant us entrance.

"Kara, what do I have to do? Tell me?" he speak-shouts at me.

Pursing my lips together, I don't respond. Not because I'm unable to, but because I don't have a reason that is honest enough, or good enough, to impart that will break through his overbearing disposition.

"It's not that I don't want to, I do, but I need to learn how to protect myself all over again. These last few months have been hard; too hard. Once upon a time, I would've been able to pick myself up and brush it off, but I don't have the strength to do that now. I don't think you understand that you possess the power to cause me real pain. Not physically, but mentally and emotionally. You could easily destroy me if you so wished. You wouldn't even have to try hard to achieve it." I turn to him, and his face is drawing premature frown lines.

"Look, I'm not saying it's never going to happen, it is, we both know it is, but this is more than either of us ever expected it would be." I sigh. "I need to rediscover myself and find that strong girl inside once again. I need to find her and bring her back before she is lost completely. Surely, you of all people should understand and respect that."

He nods slowly. "Baby, I do, it just hurts that I won't have you close to me." He touches my cheek. "That I won't be able to see you first thing on a morning, to touch you, or kiss you awake. God, I'm so in love with you, I-"

"I know, but we need this time apart from each other. We'll both be stronger for it in the end."

He breathes out a sharp, fast breath - one that would tell me I'm wrong if it could formulate words.

"We've had enough time apart," he states firmly.

My body aches for him; hurts for him, but I have to keep my guard up. "Baby..." The little-used endearment still feels foreign rolling off my tongue, not because it's not felt, but because he's the only one I have ever said it to. I touch his hand delicately. "Please take me to Marie's."

"You mean home."

Oh, shit, his face is unfathomable and irreproachable. The sadness slowly creeps in, and my determination starts to falter. I grab his shirt collar and force him to look at me.

"No, *that's* where I will live, eventually." I tilt his face towards the house, "and *this* is where my home is." I press my hand to his chest, directly over his heart. "I just have to find and reaffirm my place within it again. The words from your mouth don't mean a thing if I don't believe in them."

He leans in and kisses me, and our eyes remain open, staring sadly at each other. He gently shakes his head from my hands and rests back into his seat.

"Fine, I'll give you want you want. I'll take you home," he says emotionless. He starts the car, and the house begins to meld back into the countryside behind us.

Marie's small, quaint, semi comes into view on the tree-lined street. Sloan slowly turns into her driveway and kills the engine.

He makes it look so easy, when he jumps out of the car and grabs my bag from the backseat. Coming around to my door, he swings the bag over his shoulder and lifts me out with genuine ease.

I lean in to kiss him. "Thank you." He holds my cheeks, reciprocating my affection, until he reluctantly pulls away and grabs his phone and wallet from the dash.

Staring down, my mind drags me back to the last time I had stood on this exact spot of concrete, whimpering in pain as Deacon hauled me to my clandestine fate. Tears drip over my cheeks, and I quickly wipe them away.

"Baby?" The confusion in his voice validates that nobody knows this is the place of my abduction, and the cause of what might become my newest, reoccurring nightmare.

"He was here. Right here. Sam stood there." I point a few feet in front of me. "And Deacon was behind me." I turn slowly, seeing his image clearly over my shoulder. My legs give out, and I drop to the floor like a sack of potatoes. Curling my arms around my knees, I slowly rock back and forth in the middle of the driveway, partially obscured by the large vehicle.

The sound of my bag hitting the pavement, and feet rushing towards me, rings out in my ears. Strong arms pick me up from the cold concrete, but my body is lax, languishing in the pit of misery and despair I never seem to be able to claw my way out of.

"No, don't do this! Come on, stand for me. If you don't, I'll throw you over my goddamn shoulder, and take you back to the house kicking and screaming if I have to!" He pulls me up, forcing me to face him. "Prove to me your decision to stay here in the short term is the right one. Don't allow him to have this kind of power of you. Kara, you're stronger than this!"

I let his words worm their way into my head. I am strong. I am resilient. I am many things, but I'm not, and never will be, a fighter. And I know what Deacon did was just the beginning. I will be fighting every day for the rest of my life, endeavouring to escape this cycle of pain that has lurked inside for far too long.

Sloan presses my head into his chest and kisses my crown. My legs feel undecidedly numb as I tuck myself tight into his side, grasping him with all I have, as he leads us up the driveway.

He pulls a set of keys from his pocket and unlocks the door. He gives me a pout of concern and pushes it open, standing aside for me to enter first.

The familiar scents of Marie's rare home baking assault my senses, while the sound of Sloan shuffling behind me compels me to turn. He brushes the back of his hand over my face reverently. He sighs out in a mixture of annoyance and concern, and I let my head lean into his much-wanted touch.

"You've been here before, right?" I mumble rhetorically, remembering all of my personal effects that he'd ordered to be moved into his hotel suite months back – the majority of which are still there.

"No, actually, just Walker. Marie gave me these keys a few days ago." He gives me a pointed look, one that tells me I'm trying his patience, amongst other things.

"Oh," I say, as he goes to close the door, but a gust of wind from outside slams it shut, forcing me to jump. The sound of the key and the single deadbolt locking into position fills the small hallway.

I stare at my very familiar, and bizarrely, now very foreign surroundings. This was my home away from home. My home throughout my teens and into my early twenties. It was my go-to place when Sam was proving difficult to co-habit with, but now I feel like an intruder. An outsider.

Long, uncomfortable minutes pass by, with the sound of nothingness swirling around me. I turn back to see what Sloan is doing. I drop my chin when I realise he's examining the back of the door, or more notably, the lack of additional locks and bolts on it, to be precise.

"Sloan, stop it!" I shout, scrubbing my hand down my face and neck, feeling the atmosphere thicken further around us.

"What?" He faces me head-on with a hard look.

"Staring with furious intent at the non-existent bolts! There has never been any reason to invest in extra security, and there's definitely no need to start now!"

He stands up from his crouched down position by the door and stomps over to me. "You don't think so? Well, I do! Look at you. Look at what happened outside. Not to mention, I'm only just finding out that *he* took you from *here*. So you be fucking reasonable for once!"

"I am being reasonable! You standing here is proof of it!"

He throws his hands on his hips and jerks his head. "Baby, this isn't about us, this is about making sure I can sleep at night knowing I will see your lovely face in the morning." And just like that, my fight is gone. "I just think you ladies need more security, especially considering you're both as stubborn as each other. Trust me,

Walker's already been shut down on this subject more than once."

"Good, I don't doubt that for a second, but more security? Seriously? Do you honestly think a few more locks will keep the bad element out? Glass windows break, remember? Or were you thinking something more extreme? I don't know, maybe bars on the doors and windows? Would prison standard be secure enough for you? Would they be strong enough to keep that lovely ex-friend of yours out?"

"That's uncalled for!" His nostrils flare with rage, and his eyes penetrate into mine.

I turn away feeling ashamed. "I know; I'm sorry. I just can't stand this!"

He reaches for me and embraces me tightly, and I slouch against him. His unwavering arms hold me safe and secure, and I feel my body acquiescing, giving up the battle to keep him on the outside of my forgiveness.

I pull away, peeking into his eyes. "Baby," I whisper, as his pools dilate and deepen into a darker shade of night.

He pulls me back into him and slants my head to the side. His mouth slams over mine and I respond easily. The warmth of his tongue ignites the passion inside - not that it has actually died down from our water-saving shower earlier today.

Falling deeper, I can feel my lungs constrict from his current position of power, and I moan against him. He bends down, his mouth still covering mine, and grabs behind my thighs. Picking me up, he walks us up the stairs. Stopping at the top, his lips start to slow down, and I open my eyes to find him looking at me in question. I point towards my bedroom door, and he resumes his pace again. My legs slide down his body, as he puts me back on my feet and opens the door.

His eyes widen when he looks around my teenage bedroom. "Nice," he says, tugging at my waist, reeling me in slowly.

"Sloan, please..." I whimper. The heat of him envelops me swiftly and completely.

"Please don't ask me to stop," he says, sliding my cardigan down my arms. "Please don't refuse me this. I need to feel your flesh against mine, it's been too long," he confesses, lifting the hem of my t-shirt. His eyes plead with mine, and I nod, shakily, at his request.

Without further hesitation, he pulls the t-shirt over my head. His hands slide down my waist and tighten, then he slowly, painfully, rides them up my bare sides to my breasts, squeezing them hard through the cotton. He moves around me and sits on the edge of my bed, guiding me to stand between his thighs.

He pushes the fabric cup aside and rolls my exposed nipple between his fingers. I groan out, betraying my steadfastness. Except, I betrayed any good intentions I had as soon as I let him carry me up the stairs. I knew precisely what would happen the moment I let him reclaim his beloved control.

My head falls back as he takes my nipple deep into his mouth. Rolling and sucking my hardened peak between his teeth, my hands rake through his strands, while my breathing comes out in pants - long, deep, body defying pants. I run my fingers over his scalp until they rest comfortably on the back of his neck, and he groans out as I stroke and twist the short hair at his nape.

He pulls away from my chest, and instinctively, I look down at him with concern. His hair is ruffled and sticking out all over, due to my need to feel him closer. His eyes are large and dark, iridescent, tantalising and scintillating, inducing me to submit with just one look.

He adjusts our position and reaches around my back to unclip my bra. The natural chill of the room hits my other nipple, and it puckers the instant the remaining cotton is removed. Grinning, he covers my neglected tip with his mouth. He pinches and rolls my other well-loved peak between his fingers, making me mindless and ready to beg for more.

His hand leaves my breast cold as he drags them down my waist, coming around my lower back, until he's pressing me into him. I secure my hands on his shoulders, as he leans further and falls back onto the mattress. I land on top of him, his mouth still on my tight bud, lavishing it to the point where I feel I might shatter into pieces.

It's been far too long since I felt him in such an intimate way. I know it won't be long as a flurry of sensation builds stronger inside me, and in a bid to reach the finish line faster, I rub myself against him. In response, his erection elongates further against my lower abdomen.

"Oh, God, baby," he groans out.

Frantically grabbing between us, he makes quick work of my trousers, and already has his hands over my arse, sliding the intrusive garment down my backside. Unable to move them any further than my mid-thighs, he flips us over and stands. In a single, well-practised move, he whips them off my legs, leaving me heady and my body silently screaming for him to hurry up and complete me.

I wiggle uncontrollably, practically naked under his sensual, brooding gaze. I can't ever remember him looking as dangerous as this, but I guess this is what months apart will do for your better judgement. He licks his lips deliciously, and I find myself running my own tongue over my lip, emulating him, showing him.

He grins, before tugging and devouring my bottom lip. He drops to his haunches in front of me and runs his palms up the backs of my legs, stopping just behind my knees. He gazes like he's seeing me for the first time again.

Suddenly, he yanks me forward and simultaneously leans into me. My heart starts beating rapidly the moment he plants his face firmly between my legs - high between my legs. We might have done this plenty of times before, but it still makes me self-conscious. He breathes in deeply and grunts, running his nose up and down the length of my aching sex, learning my unique scent for the second time.

My eyes roll as I feel the tip of his tongue exploring me. My lungs are on the verge of failing, and I start to press my legs back together, inadvertently crushing his head.

"Hey, I break you know!" He flicks my clit sharply, admonishing me playfully from between my thighs.

I loosen my grip, but my muscles spasm seconds later as he lazily drags his tongue through my folds. I moan out incoherently, something that sounds like a cross between *sorry* and *more*. He chuckles, and the sound passes over his lips and reverberates against my flesh, raising me higher. His hands then enter the foray, and he pushes my knickers further aside, as a single, talented finger breaches me beautifully.

"Fuck! So fucking wet and tight for me. God, I missed you so much," he murmurs, kissing the inside of my thigh, while he pumps into me a few times. He gives my skin a little nip; it's only a mediocre, but still enough to make me cry out loud.

I gaze down as the thrusting to my core slows, stills, and then stops completely. "No, don't stop!"

He circles my opening with a thoughtful expression. "Two?"

"Oh, God, yes!" I cry out, immediately transforming into that wanton, sexually deprived girl he had unleashed from deep within me months ago.

He pushes two fingers inside, and works me up into a frenzied, human ball of need and release. My internal muscles clamp down on him, and I can sense his need to extract them as I hold my breath, my body contracting and letting go beautifully.

I cry out, milking him with all I am, giving him everything I've got. I squeeze my thighs together, momentarily forgetting his head, which is still taking up residence between them. I relax my legs when he pinches my arse to stop, and I fist my hands into the sheets in frustration.

"Come for me. Scream my name, baby." I honour his wish, as I unravel spectacularly beneath him.

"Oh, my God! That feels so good. Don't stop!" I call out, my body soaring higher and higher, fearing I may splinter and shatter into a thousand pieces before he is done with me.

He carefully slides his gifted fingers out and stands. Smirking wickedly, he slowly raises his hand up, studies them intently, before sucking them into his mouth, each one emerging clean

"Sloan, I want…"

"That's it, baby, tell me what you want." He leans back down, fixing an arm under my back. His knees lodge on the edge of the bed, and he effortlessly begins to crawl up the mattress to me, until my head falls back onto the softness of the pillows and he stares down, rapt. "What do you want, my love?"

He holds my neck gently in one hand, while his other drifts down my body, stopping on my hip. He spreads my legs apart with his own and continues to stare, long and hard, until he lifts one knee higher, and rubs it against my sensitive flesh. His hands start to move again, following the line of my hip and the curve of my arse. His fingers glide between my cheeks, and he strokes his finger over the area.

"I don't know if-"

He puts his hand over my mouth gently. "Not today, my love, but there are two places on this beautiful body that will be mine, and mine alone. They will never, ever, be touched by anyone other than me."

"Oh, God…" I'm close to weeping tears of joy. He still loves me. In my heart of hearts, I never had reason to doubt him, but thinking it and hearing it are two different things entirely.

"Close your eyes, my gorgeous girl, and just feel me. Feel what I can do and how you respond so easily to it. Remember our first time? Tell me what you want…" My body clenches as the image of him in front of the suite fire consumes me.

"I want you…so much. I want to feel you slide inside me and never leave. Never let me go." I admit, unashamed. It's the honest wish of a woman on the climatic edge.

Except, it isn't the impending beauty of my body releasing, it's a true confession of the heart. My heart. The one he shattered, and the one he now has to piece back together again.

"Good, keep going." He grunts and fumbles, removing his shirt. He rips open the button of his jeans and kicks them off behind him. The soft material of his shorts grazes my overly sensitised, sexually charged skin.

"I can't wait any longer. I need you; I'll always need you." I whisper. He holds up a silver square, it glints under the light.

"Well, you did come prepared today," I say breathless, desire coursing through me.

"Absolutely! As much as I would love to see this belly swelling with our firstborn, I'm selfish. I don't want anything, but you, for as long as possible. Unless that's what you want? You know I would give you anything." He arches his brows up and down a few times, and grins.

I shake my head. "Too young. Right now…I just want you to make me feel…and come…hard," I confess, hesitantly. "*Please?*" I beg. He hisses his disapproval, but smiles, so I know it isn't all bad.

"You know, as much as I hate that begging tone you seem to have down pat, I do like that you're more confident in telling me what you want these days. I like it even more that I'm the only man who will ever hear it."

I sense myself flushing a darker shade of pink. I'm abundantly aware it doesn't take much to coax out who I really am from under the veil of ambiguity. I still find it amazing how fast my personality can change when faced with a man who inadvertently intoxicates me with just a simple touch or smile.

I barely have time to work up a response, before he slams into me hard. I yelp out in shock and delight at the steel force of him thrusting into me, throbbing in synchronised precision. Finding his rhythm, he rotates his hips in a figure of eight shape, driving harder and deeper into my aching softness. His face is consumed with euphoria, as he lessens his speed and gently starts to plough in and out. My body liquefies further, and I can feel my wetness escaping with each rotation and lunge. He groans and grabs my thigh, bringing it up to his shoulder. Holding it in place, forcing me to open wider, he closes his eyes as he rides my body reverently. Testing my sexual limits, he grunts out his passion and will, making me feel whole and complete. My skin glides upon contact with his, but I'm a hot, slick mess, unable to make purchase.

"God, baby, I can't hold back any longer! Come with me," he breathes into my mouth, sucking on my bottom lip, nipping it gently.

"Yes!" I cry out. "More, *please*." Again, I don't recognise my own voice, as I request something that would have horrified me only months ago.

We cry out together; at each other, as we soar to new heights that are foreign to both of us. It's a feeling that is burning a red-hot path inside my soul. It's a power that I've never felt in his embrace previously.

He pumps himself inside for the final time, as the last vestiges of pleasure jolt and bounce around my body. Roaring above me, he collapses in a heap on top of me, breathing hot and hard into my neck. Our combined breathing is staccato, and ripples around the room.

"Wow! That was..." *Amazing.* "I can't even..." *Verbalise.* I stare at the ceiling, unable to speak the right words. They are lodged in my throat, but I know words will never express the love we share for each other.

"I know...I feel it, too." He kisses my neck with sloppy, wet kisses while rocking me.

He shifts, gently lifting me, his beautiful length still firmly embedded. He rubs my outer thigh and drapes it over his hip. He holds me close, rubbing his nose against mine, his fingers lave my nipples, and he palms my breasts in his large hands.

"Sloan, we need to talk abo-"

"No, we don't. Just let me hold you. I know what you want to say, and I'm going to be a complete bastard. I don't want anything to mess this up. I just want to hold you, learn your contours again, cement your scent back into my memory, have your taste consume me fully." I stroke his face lightly, falling in love with him all over again – if that is even possible.

Time passes by slowly in a labyrinth of passionate kisses, tender touches, and welcoming embraces. Eventually, I feel him becoming flaccid inside me. He gives me a little grin, before sliding out and off me. Lounging on his side, he looks confused as he does a cursory glance around the room. Knowing what he's looking for, I sigh out.

"No en-suite here. Second door on the left." I point towards my door and the landing. "Just make sure you don't leave it in the bin where Marie can find it." I raise my brows; she will blow up like a rocket if she finds out I've had sex under her roof. It doesn't matter that I'm twenty-three or that she adores him; her house, her rules regardless.

He gives me a nervous look, before he kisses my hand and gets off the bed to deal with the condom. He strolls out of my room, and I wish I could say that I refrain from openly staring at that ripped body of his, but I can't. I admit I'm almost ready to rugby tackle him to the ground, but my own body, as satisfied and content as it is, refuses to budge.

Minutes later, my sexy boy approaches me, and all but throws himself back on my bed. Using his middle finger, he pushes the hair from my face. He tilts his head around my room, which hasn't changed since Marie and I had first decorated it when it was clear I didn't want to leave, and she wanted me to stay.

"It's nice." He smiles, distracting me with his maddening touch and the invisible electricity stemming from his tips.

"Thanks. This is another first for me, you know." I chew my lip shyly. Why I'm shy, I'm not really sure. It's not like he doesn't already know he's technically my first everything. His brow quirks, wondering what I'm talking about.

"The first time I've ever had a boy in my room," I giggle as it leaves my mouth.

"Good. I'll be the only boy ever to grace this room, or any room that you're naked in, as a matter of fact!" he says, full of dominance.

"Your confidence really knows no bounds, does it?" I query, faking my exasperation.

He chuckles. "Nope, not when it comes to you, my love." He lies on his back and pulls me over him. I trace my fingers up and down his chest, between the muscle definition and around his nipples.

"Look, I know you want time. As much as it kills me, I respect you immensely and will abide by what you ask of me. I have no right to make demands of you, not when I treated you so despicably. I know that isn't something either of us will forget in a hurry."

"No, it isn't," I murmur against his hard chest.

He huffs out, but it's not a pissed off sound, it's more defeated. "Baby-"

"I'm not doing this to hurt you; I'm doing this to protect myself."

"From whom?" His forehead creases.

Tilting my head, I stare straight into his eyes. "From you. I've already told you; you have the ability to hurt me like no one else ever has. Please, I need you to understand that I have spent many years, too many, living inside a world of my own making. I don't want to fight or argue about this, but I think it will do us both a lot of good to have a little space. I appreciate we have already suffered and spent a lot of time apart recently, but this is different, this is my request. Rather than jump straight back in, like we did the first time we met, I want to do this slowly, and maybe just see each other..." I inhale and brace myself. "...Twice a week." I breathe out optimistically, having made my case, and a good one at that.

I suck in my lips and innocently rake my gaze up to his, knowing this is definitely not what he expected to hear from me. Except, this is what I want – *for now*. I look into his eyes again, realising my optimism is about to be blown out of the water.

"Twice a week?" His eyes are wide, horrified. "Tell me you're joking! I was thinking every day, and possibly a night or two together. Twice a fucking week isn't going to cut it with me, baby! I'm going to go out of my goddamn mind if I can't see you every day. Why are you doing this to me?" He swipes his hand over his face, and I fear I may have just splintered a small part of him I cannot see.

"It's twice or nothing at all." My voice falters. "I won't yield, and I don't want to rush back into this. Twice is the only offer I can give you right now."

"No!" he spits out in frustration.

I cock my brow at him; I don't want to fight, but I'll fight for what I believe in. *This,* I more than believe in. I wait for it, as he stares at me and sighs.

His jaw tightens and grinds. "Fine! But don't think for one minute this twice a week shit is going to be carrying on for more than a fortnight. Trust me when I say we *will* be discussing this again!"

I have no doubt.

I sigh subtly, and wrap the sheet around myself tighter as he starts to get dressed. He's suddenly clumsy and uncoordinated, and I know it's because anger is undulating through him in light of the last ten minutes. Locating and tugging on his clothes, he makes plenty of intermittent huffing and puffing noises as he moves, and I'm trying hard not to laugh – and not to give in and allow him more.

He grabs his wallet and keys from the dresser, and stomps back over to me. He kisses me deeply, removing any last shred of lingering doubt fluctuating inside my mind. I open my mouth to permit him access, the same time he pulls me forward and my hips gyrate against him. I boldly swipe my tongue along his, not really wanting him to leave just yet. He gives me a devilish grin and drags himself back.

"Oh, no, no, no!" He clucks his tongue. "You don't get any more of that from me until I get my seven days and seven nights!"

I reach out to him again, and he sidesteps away. "That's a little unreasonable and childish, even for you!"

"No, denying me the right to love and protect you is unreasonable and childish!"

My heart is ridiculously full and overflowing with love for him. Anyone can see how much I feel. I wear my heart on my sleeve as far as he is concerned. I admit, I love he has kicked up a shit storm about this. I love that twice a week - or more realistically, a few hours, twice a week - isn't enough for him. He may be ready to forgive and forget, but a small part of me isn't so willing.

I need to find myself again, and it's something I won't achieve if he is breathing down my neck and wrapping me up in invisible cotton wool. He's trying his hardest to shield me from the big, bad world, and whilst it's admirable, he's too late, because I already know it exists.

He slides his effects into his pocket and puts his hands on those incredible hips of his. "I'll be back tomorrow for the first of our fortnight, bi-weekly visits!" On that note, he turns, walks out, and slams the door behind him.

With my sight trained on the floor, I listen carefully as he stomps down the stairs until the front door opens and closes. The sound of the key turning echoes clearly through the empty house.

The car roars loudly outside, and I cuddle into the duvet, as my angry, first love, leaves me wanting more in my teenage bedroom, for the very first time.

Chapter 7

RUSHING FROM THE bathroom, I take another glance at the clock – almost nine.

I'm going to be late.

No, I'm already late.

Brusquely rubbing the towel over my head, I dry off my hair as thoroughly as I can and tie it up. Standing in front of the dresser, I pull out my make-up bag and dig around for the tube of concealer I definitely know I have. Chances are it might be rather off by now through seldom use, but this morning, I need it.

Finding the little tube, I sit cross-legged in front of the large mirror behind the door. My fingers lightly drift over my face; examining, probing, wondering if my limited ability with this stick of slap will be enough to cover the signs of assault and battery.

I guess I'll soon find out.

Sighing out, I hold up the wand and begin.

With my face looking half-normal again, I pull out a white blouse and black skirt. Slipping into them, my mobile rings inside my bag, and I pick it out to find a message from Sloan.

Good morning, my love. Lunch today?

I hesitate in my reply. I'm not meant to be going to work today – or any day, apparently - but if I get there, I know there's no way Marie will send me home. Or at least I don't think she will. I guess it all depends on how brainwashed these two have gotten her lately.

I quickly return the message, saying I'm extremely tired and will probably sleep through past lunchtime. I know he isn't stupid and he will see through it easily, but I just need to get out of this house. I spent enough time heartbroken here after what happened in May, I really don't need to be here alone after what happened two weeks ago.

"He'll be there in ten minutes, love." The taxi firm telephonist hangs up, and I hold the handset tight. Putting it back on the cradle, I collect up my bag and jacket. Fishing out my phone, another message has come through from Sloan. I refuse to look at it, since there's an ominous feeling in my gut that tells me he knows exactly what I'm devising today.

I pace the small hallway, until a car horn beeps from outside.

Locking the door, I stride towards the taxi, check his ID hanging from the rear-view, then climb inside. Informing the driver of my destination, I ease back into the seat, and watch the familiar paths and roads drift by.

As we stop at a set of lights opposite a used car dealership, at some point in the future, I'm going to have to invest in another cheap run-around. I haven't dared ask Sloan what he's done with the BMW he kindly bought me. Although, it wouldn't surprise me if he'd gotten rid of it minutes after I ran out of the suite devastated.

I sigh, louder than intended, and catch sight of the driver. "Mondays!" I say, not needing to extenuate further.

He chuckles and nods. "Every day ending with day, sweetheart!" I smile and laugh. He's right about that.

He brings the car to a stop outside the car park, and I hand over fifteen quid. "Keep the change," I murmur absentmindedly, looking over the office block, as though I'm seeing it for the first time again. It's been a while since I've been here.

As I march across the car park, the bays allocated to us are all empty but one, which means Marie is either still at Walker's place – she didn't come home last night – or she's probably at a meeting. I stare at the Mercedes parked in the end bay and blow out my breath, remembering.

The last time I had seen a car similar, it had been when Sam had invited Deacon and Remy into the flat and broke golden rule number one. I purse my lips together, thinking of that disastrous day, and the fact it altered the path I was walking on alone. I shake my head, trying to forget the insinuations I had levelled at Sloan the very same night, upon seeing Sam's battered body, and him clearly being repulsed by my allusions.

Finally, I understand why.

Snapping back out of it, I pull out my security card and flash it at the door release panel. It clicks open, and I start the two-minute jog up to the office. My thighs feel the burn as I enter and turn on the lights. Heading towards my desk, my mouth falls open when I see the two stacks of paperwork that Marie has just left to fester. I could seriously kill the woman at times.

Picking up the first pile, I shake my head. Disheartened, I drop it to the floor, causing invoices and letters to fly in all directions, and then go off to make some tea. Bizarrely, acting immature for a minute actually feels good - even if I will be scrambling around on my hands and knees collecting them up shortly.

Placing the last of the invoices in order on top of the pile, I smile with satisfaction at what I have achieved. It has been two hours since I dropped the first stack, and an hour since I put my hands on the second. Sitting with my hands folded over my middle, the office line rings. I stare at the handset as it goes to voicemail, but instantly wish I hadn't.

"Marie, it's Sloan, call me back. I've just been to your house, and Kara isn't there. She also isn't answering her phone. I'm on my way over, but call me if you get this before I get there."

He hangs up abruptly.

"Shit!" I mutter, picking up the piles and putting them back on my desk. I slip into my jacket and shoes and reach for my bag. It starts to vibrate, and I pull out my mobile. There are numerous missed calls over the last few hours, and unfortunately, he is calling again.

I look out over the car park, and whilst the Mercedes is still parked in one of our bays, there isn't a Range Rover or Aston in sight. I breathe out, relieved, but I wonder. Locking up the office, I virtually run down the stairs and out of the front door.

"I was wondering how long it would take you to scarper." I spin around instantly to find Sloan leaning against the wall, his hands on his hips, stretching his shirt and waistcoat. Stepping closer, my image begins to fill his aviators.

"Sloan..." I don't finish, because there's nothing I can say to defend myself. I know being fed up of looking at the same four walls won't cut it.

"Shush," he says, cradling my head, his fingers drifting over my half-arsed concealed bruises. "You've done well with these."

"Why, thank you, Max Factor," I reply sarcastically.

He snorts. "Baby, what are you doing here?"

"Working, genius, what else?" I stare past him and start to scan the car park, trying to find his other baby.

"You know you don't need to, smart-arse,"

I sigh loudly, making sure he hears it. "No, we've already had this conversation, and as per usual, you refuse to listen to me. I won't have anyone thinking I'm with you for your money. I won't!"

"No one thinks that!"

"*She* thinks it," I mumble, scared of what his reaction will be that

I have raised the old topic of the ex who won't quit. He breathes out and crooks his finger. I take tiny steps until my feet almost touch his.

"I don't care what *she* thinks. I care about *you*, and what *you* think. I appreciate you don't want to stay at home, but you're still healing. Come on," he coaxes me.

"Is that your Merc?" He turns and looks at it, his eyes dropping down to the plates.

"No, but Rem has one like that. I don't know, maybe John told him to keep an eye on Marie. I wouldn't worry, come on." He wraps my arm in his, but I stare back at the empty vehicle, silently stipulating.

"Where's your car?" I ask suspiciously, still not seeing it in the car park.

"Do you think I'm stupid enough to park it here when I know you would be looking for it? It's further down the street, probably being thoroughly appreciated by a traffic warden as we speak!" He gives me a big smile and pulls me into his side. "Let's have some lunch, my love. I've left Ken in charge, so I'm all yours for the rest of the day."

I stop. Pressing my lips together, I stare up at him. "This counts as one bi-weekly visit, you know," I manage to say with a straight face.

He quickly slides my body to his, so fast, I yelp. Running his hands up my waist, under my jacket, his fingers massage the sides of my already heavy breasts.

"Baby, we both know these so-called visits of yours are a complete pile of shit to prove you have some power and to piss me off! So whilst I'll play ball, this isn't counting as a visit. Now, let's go have lunch, and then maybe we'll catch a film or something."

He opens the car door, and I climb in, revelling in the scent of him drowning me. His door slams shut, and I turn my head towards him.

"I love you, Sloan Foster. You drive me batshit crazy, but I do." The words flow from me effortlessly.

He leans forward and presses me into him. "And I love you, but you've driven me crazy for far longer," he replies. I can feel my expression change, but he kisses me lightly. "One day. Trust me?"

Do I?

I have to.

Cupping his face in my hands, I reciprocate his affection and pull back. "I trust you."

My legs are stiff as we exit the cinema. Standing behind Sloan, I stretch them a little, still clutching the leftover popcorn. He takes it from me and throws it in the bin.

"My bum feels numb," I grumble rhetorically.

A film seemed like a good idea at the time. If only I'd have paid more attention to the timings and saw it was hours long. Hours, in which I've gone through every emotion conceivable, due to the fact he has a problem of not being able to keep his hands to himself. Even more so in a relatively empty, darkened room.

"Really?" He grabs me and shifts us into a less congested area. With my back to the wall, his hands knead either cheek firmly. "I have plenty of ideas to snap some life back into it. Let's go!" Excited, he grabs my hand and leads us out of the cinema.

Throwing his keys to one of the porters on duty this evening, he tugs me into the hotel and towards the lifts. He smiles gloriously at everyone who passes by, and even James, the formerly rude reception manager, gives us a smile and a salute.

The lift doors open, and I falter as I step inside. This is my first time back here, and the fine hair on the back of neck stands on end. Sloan's hands fix on my waist, grounding me. He encourages me to move inside the box and turns me in his arms. I wrap myself around him as the numbers ascend on the mirrored panel, along with my anxiety, until it slows to a stop and chimes our arrival.

Entering the suite first, I grimace. The memory of standing on this very spot, begging him to want me as my heart shattered, comes back to assault me unforgivingly.

A hand comes around my arm, and I turn. Tears spike my lashes, and I fight hard to try to keep them concealed. His sad eyes flit around, remembering the day the house of cards came tumbling down in spectacular fashion. A sigh emanates from him, and he wraps his arms around me.

"We need to make a new memory here," he whispers. I pull back, wiping the wetness from my cheek. His thumbs gently replace my fingers, and he tenderly strokes under my eyes.

"No, we don't. Trying to erase it won't work, it needs to remain, so we'll always know how easy it is to hurt each other." He nods, appreciating that some part of me is willing to move on, even if it does still cause me pain.

"Let's have some dinner brought up. I'll even pretend I cooked it, just for you," he says with a grin.

"I've had nearly a full tub of popcorn! I'm really not that hungry." I slowly walk into the open plan living room. Doing a complete turn, I stop and walk towards the glass, watching the city fall into darkness below.

"Or maybe we can re-enact an old memory," he says, spinning me around and pressing my back into the glass. "I think I might have a bottle of something knocking around."

"Can I just...hold you?" My voice sounds fragile and unsure.

His hands reach under my thighs, and he picks me up and carries me to the sofa. Laying me down, he shuffles beside me and softly places his arm across my middle. My head lulls against his chest, and he breathes in slowly.

The room gradually dims as the night steals away the day. Eventually, the tiny path of air being exhaled over my face softens, and the sound of a low, content snore escapes him. I close my eyes, wondering if I've grown too complacent since he's been in my life. My name is murmured incoherently from the sleeping man beside me, and I squeeze his hand.

Drifting off, the shadows wash over the room, and once more, I am forsaken.

My leg bounces up and down as my foot taps with nerves. I keep my hand on the handle, pressuring it to stay shut. The sound of my mother and father arguing is louder than usual. I lean my head against the wall and stare into the impenetrable darkness. Heavy steps move in front of the door concealing my whereabouts, then stop.

"Please don't do it!" my mother begs, in that simpering tone I have become accustomed to hearing over the last few years.

"Lorraine, I have no choice," my father replies. The doorknob rattles, and it slips from my hand as it swings open.

"Come here, sweets," he says to me. "Big thirteen tomorrow." I smile a little, dragging ted by his leg. "Frankie is here with a gift for you, come on."

I turn to my mother, whose teary eyes are bright red. She holds her hand out to me, but my father pulls me away and leads me out of the room.

Slowly hitching up my worn jammy bottoms, I rub my eyes as the light in the landing hits them. Following dutifully, as I have always been taught, I stop and look back. My mum is silently crying into her hand, and I wonder what's wrong with her. Ushering me into the living room, I stare up at my father, towering over me with Uncle Franklin.

"Hello, Kara, I'd like you to meet my boy." I turn around to see a figure of a teenage boy stood in the shaded corner of the living room. He grins at me, and a chill makes my skin prickle.

"How old are you?" The boy asks me coyly.

I cower into my father's side, but his hand pushes me slightly to stand upright. "Kara..."

"Twelve. I'm thirteen tomorrow," I say scared. He walks towards me, still partially shaded, and looks down.

"Unlucky for some."

I gasp out and instantly cover my mouth. My tears become audible and louder, and I breathe deep, trying to regain composure. Sloan shifts and his hand tightens over my stomach again.

"Don't be upset, baby. Just fourteen more days," he sighs out behind me, referring to the end of the fortnight in which the bi-weekly visits will stop.

"Thirteen," I counter quietly, the number having a completely different meaning to me. He kisses my neck and brings me closer.

"Unlucky for some."

Chapter 8

THE CLOUDS RUBBLE and resound overhead, until a sheet of lightning covers the sky, brightening and blackening in succession.

"How many times are we going to have this conversation? You're like a broken record! If you have nothing new to say, then don't say anything and just leave!" I throw my hands in the air and quickly run into the one and only bathroom the house offers, with a mercurial man hot on my tail.

Locking the door behind me, I climb into the empty bath and pull Walker's old, oversized t-shirt over my knees. Sloan's fist hits the door, and I rock a little, the cold of the metal chilling my extremities.

"Kara, I'm going to sit out here all day if I have to! I have the laptop here. I have my phone. I'll conduct business outside this fucking door! Makes no never mind to me, baby!"

"Sloan, go home! I mean it, if you don't move, I'll call Walker!" I shout at nothing in particular in front of me.

We are currently on day fifteen, needless to say, day fourteen took a turn for the worse. Our little showdown yesterday didn't go too well, and my bedroom door is suffering. After I had locked him out last night, the sulky sod rooted around Marie's garage until he found something to open it. Safe to say, Marie was on the verge of GBH when she came home to find the wood surrounding the handle peppered with drill holes, and I was still locked in on the other side.

So now, due to Mr Overbearing's less than desirable carpentry skills, I have a new door to pay for and organise fitting of, plus a very heartfelt apology to give to Marie, especially considering he pelted her with a tirade of foul obscenities, and I'm positive I heard her slap him. *Hard.*

"Fucking call him, then maybe this bastard can finally catch a break with you! We also need to discuss why the fuck you're wearing his t-shirt in the first place!" He starts pacing up and down outside the door, and I slam my fist down on the bath base. The pain is irrelevant; I've already shot myself in the foot. I waltzed in here in an almost threadbare t-shirt that was on the charity pile, a pair of tiny shorts, and no flaming phone. I really know how to orchestrate an intervention for myself.

"Sloan, just go home! You're not needed here!" I carry on, knowing he won't take the hint, but hoping it will be enough to piss him off so he'll leave.

"Kara," he says softly. "I'm not leaving, so you can stop acting like a child!"

The sound of a phone ringing leaks into the cold, small, locked bathroom.

"Hi, Gloria. No, I'm not coming in today. I'll be working from home." Pause. "No, I'm at Kara's house. Just email me anything important, everything else can wait. Yeah, bye. Sorry, what was that?" Another pause. "I would, but she's locked herself in the bathroom. She can be quite ridiculous at times!" he chuckles loudly.

My blood boils at his audacity.

"If I'm fucking ridiculous, it's because you don't listen. You've never listened!" I shout, breathing through my nose like a raging bull. "There are times I could hate you!" I scrape the bottom of the barrel and instantly feel guilty. Simmering down, I hug my knees to my chest.

"You fucking hate me, do you?" Shit, he's furious. "Do you?"

"No, I said '*could*'!" I feel a little better, slightly.

"Kara, open this goddamn door!"

"No! You promised me you would give me time. You're not giving me shit!"

"I told you two weeks, and it's been and gone! You want to beat around the bush? Fine! I guarantee you will be out of that room within the next hour."

His feet play heavily on the stairs, descending, fading. Time passes by, but I can hear him speaking to someone in the distance. I narrow my eyes, wondering what new tricks he has up his sleeve. I crane my neck when I hear him come back up, two rungs at a time.

He knocks on the door once.

"Yes?" I ask, clambering out of the bath.

Wandering to the cupboard, I grab the cleaner. I figure I'm going to be here a while, so I might as well do something productive with my borrowed alone time. I know full well that when he finally gets me out of here, every door in the house will be without its handle.

His phone starts to ring again, and I turn slightly, suspicion ensnaring me.

"Ah, John Walker! Very nice of you to call back at long last! I have a security issue," he says, over-exaggerating, before murmuring something I can't quite make out. "Actually, no, I have a security issue at your woman's house. I suggest you get over here before I get the drill out again or take the fucking door down! I haven't decided which."

The manipulative son of a bitch!

I rush to the door and open it, just as Sloan says, "Oh, and another thing? Why the fuck is she wearing your t-shirt, sunshine?"

I lob the spray cleaner at him, and he throws the phone down and snatches my wrist in his grip. We struggle against each other, and he starts to laugh. I feel his foot hook behind my calf, and then I'm falling to earth, onto the hard floor behind me. Straddling my waist, he holds me down painfully by my wrists.

Eight years of survival are cruelly torn away, as the faceless, nameless man appears in front of me, and then moulds into the face of Deacon, beating me into submission, in that dirty, dank room. I scream in shock and start kicking out.

"Get off me! Get off me!" I scream; I whimper; I kick out. I forget that I'm actually safe, and this man is not *that* man - *either* of those men.

"Christ, Kara!" Sloan whispers, as a look of pure horror takes over his features. He instantly loosens his hold, and I'm being pulled up and enveloped by him. His arms hold my slack body and rock me slowly.

The sound of Walker shouting from the phone induces me to open my eyes, as Sloan picks it up.

"Seriously, get the fuck over here right now," he says, then listens. "Is Marie with you?" Silence again. "Good, bring her with you." He disconnects the call, tosses the phone back down and lifts me up.

My back touches down on the duvet, and he slides onto the bed beside me. He gently strokes my head, my cheeks, and my neck. His touch is soothing, whereas the images refusing to leave my head are savage.

"Kara, we need to talk about this. The past consumes so much of you, I fear you'll become lost within it, and that I'll always be on the outside, fighting my way to get in."

I'm with him in body, but not in mind. The sound of tears racks me to my core. He whispers to me, words that I don't understand. Words that I don't really hear.

"Baby, I'm sorry. I didn't mean to push you over the edge. I'm just so tired. I don't do well without you. I need you. I've needed you for a long time. I feel shattered, empty and alone. You make me whole, complete. You're a part of me here." He touches his hand to his chest.

I reach up to him and run my hand over his face. He shudders the instant my fingertips connect with his skin. His five o'clock shadow is darker than it was yesterday, and I scratch my nails over it, before grazing them over his lips - his amazing, full, perfect lips.

"I'm not ridiculous," I mutter against him through my tears.

"No, you're just ridiculously easy to wind up. Gloria had already hung up when I said bye." The silence beckons, and I quieten down to the sound of our individual breathing.

I close my eyes, knowing he's right. He will always be on the outside, because of what lurks inside. Deep in my heart, I know what I have to do to make us right.

"I'm ready." The words are a whisper from my lips. I can barely believe my own ears, realising that hell has finally frozen over, and I'm going to do something that used to revolt me.

"Ready for what?" His confused tone is discernible.

"I'm ready to talk to someone again. I can't live like this anymore. I just want to be able to go to sleep and not have to see the horrors of my past." I grasp him, pulling myself as close as I can. My sight lulls, and I doze off, but I'm still aware of my surroundings.

Waking a little, he pulls me closer as the sound of multiple feet running up the stairs kills the beautiful silence. I groan out, then panic.

"Please don't let them in! I can't let Marie see me like this!" I try to get off the bed, but he holds me back.

"What are you talking about?"

"Seriously, don't let her in! She thinks I'm better; she has for a long time. She doesn't know I still have nightmares, only you do!"

"How is that possible?"

"*Please!*"

"Okay my love, I'll take care of it." He turns us over and covers my body with his.

"Kara?" Marie calls out, and my door flies open.

"It's okay, Marie, just a little misunderstanding. She's sleeping."

"Move your arse, Sloan. Let me see her!"

"I said, she's sleeping!" he snaps viciously, and tightens his hold. "Marie, leave her alone, she's fine."

"Everything okay, kid?" Walker's voice edges on suspicion, resounding in my room.

"Yeah, we're good."

"Come on, let's leave them. She's sleeping. Come on, angel." Marie puffs out repeatedly as Walker coaxes her away. Their steps retreat back down the landing and fade into the sounds of the house.

Sloan pulls away from me, lifting my face up. "I'll get Gloria to look for the best doctors to help you. I promise it won't always be like this for us."

"No, I don't want her to know." I start to cry.

"Baby, she's worked for me for years, and my dad before me. She's the epitome of discretion. I trust her, so please, trust me."

I stare up at him. "Okay, but I don't want anyone else to know." He rocks me repeatedly, comforting me into a deep sleep.

"I love you, my gorgeous girl. Stay strong for me; *for us*. Don't let him do this again," he whispers in my ear.

I turn over, and my eyes drift from his bare chest to his beautiful face. He smiles, but it's guarded, and I know I've had yet another nightmare - one I cannot remember - inside his arms. I attempt to get up, but he pulls me back again.

"Gloria emailed me some names of a few psychologists while you were asleep, although I know one who helped Charlie when I moved back here from uni."

I stare at him wide-eyed. *He really doesn't waste time, does he?*

Two shrinks in the space of eight weeks. I should be proud I'm doing exceptionally well.

"Okay," I reply, defeated.

"Baby, I know that look. I want you to see someone for you, not because I've asked you to. You don't have to make a final decision now, but just consider it, okay?" I nod.

"Was Marie really pissed that she couldn't mother me when she got in?" I ask, walking my fingers up and down his chest.

"She was, but again, all I care about is you, and if that's an issue for her, tough. If she wants someone to whine to, she can do it to John. She's not my concern, you are. Never forget that."

"I won't, but we need to talk about where we go from here. I know you wanted more after two weeks. You put a smile on your face and pretend you're happy, but that's all just a show to make me feel better. You deserve to have everything; more than I'm currently willing to give you. I wish I could tell you something different, but I don't feel strong enough to rush headfirst back into this."

"I know-"

"No, please, I need to say this. There's a huge void in my heart that only you can fill, but there are some massive obstacles in our way. To make this work, we have to be one, except we're not one. It's abundantly clear we never were. You have secrets, and so I do, and I'm not ashamed to admit that. The day we become one, is the day we speak truths that we both want to bury and never dig up again. The only promise I can give you, is that I'll try. I swear to God I will." I breathe out a huge sigh of relief. I might not be prepared to disclose my fears fully, but at least I've absolved myself of the truths I dared not speak weeks ago when I should have, at a time when it mattered.

"I promise I'll try, too." He kisses me, and my body quivers and relaxes. I expected him to push for more; I know I would've done.

He grips my shoulders and pushes me back; his expression is thoughtful and compassionate. "So, what are we going to do about these bi-weekly visits? I have no reservations in throwing you over my shoulder and carrying you out of here right now. I want you home with me, and that is not a secret I wish to conceal." He bites his lip, deeper in thought. "How about we take it slow and make it three days a week. We'll go out, watch films and have dinner, like we did the other week. We'll do the dating thing that we never really did before. Hopefully, we can build it up a day at a time, however long it takes. You have to learn to trust me again."

I stare at him vacantly. I want to smile at how much he has changed in the past couple of weeks. I climb onto his lap and cradle his face. I can't quite work him out sometimes. The way he is with me and then everyone else. Sometimes it's hard to fathom. I know underlying anger threads through him, holding him together. No one else sees it, but I do. I saw some of it fall away at the hospital when he saw my bruises, but just as quickly, in front of everyone else, that disguise came back up, harder than ever. Yet I have no right to judge, because I know how much it hurts to have deep-rooted fears eat away at you until you can no longer see straight, and there is only black and white.

"What's that look for?" His eyes narrow.

"I was just thinking about the subtle changes in you. With me - most of the time - you're so gentle and loving, attentive, easy-going…" He smirks. "I said sometimes. Then with everyone else, as soon as someone questions your decisions or authority, your personality does a full one-eighty, and you turn into a completely different man."

"Is that a bad thing?" His eyes soften, and he lifts his brow.

"No, but do you realise you just compromised? You negotiated with yourself. I never thought I would see the day." He rubs his hands up and down my back lovingly.

"I won't lie, it's hard for me. But as I've already said, you've always held the power in this relationship. I know you don't see it, but it's true. Everything I do is with you in mind."

I hiss out when he touches a sensitive part of my skin. Pleasure burns through me rapidly, heating me euphorically. He drags his lips over mine, and I sigh loudly into his mouth, before pulling away.

"I think I just fell in love with you all over again."

"That's my whole mission in life, my love, to keep you so madly in love with me, that you don't know where you start and I end." He kisses down my neck, and I let out another desirous moan.

"I think you already do that. Some days, I don't know my own mind or my own thoughts…and you clearly know my body better than I do. All of it, every part, right down to the places we can't see." His hands run over me, and I feel my centre heating.

"Baby, not the best time to bring it up again, and I really don't want to, but you're more compliant when you're wanting." He smirks, and I feel my abdomen squeeze. "Psychologist…"

"Sloan…" I barely manage to breathe out. My voice is husky, and I am indeed wanting. I'm also aware of what he wants to discuss at this very inconvenient time.

"Would you go with me to see somebody? I mean, I'm not going to invite you to sit in the room and listen to every wretched detail, but to wait for me; be there when I need you to. I can tell you from past experience that the aftermath and fallout from these sessions might not be pretty, but I'll need you."

"Of course, I'll always be there, whenever you need me. Always."

I lean forward and kiss him, forgetting the momentary pleasure. My heart is so full of hope that we will have a future together. A future that includes more than just us. It involves something I never thought I would ever be entitled to. *A family.*

"Come on, let's go freshen up. Marie's making dinner."

Chapter 9

AUGUST.

A new day of sunshine starts to ascend through the panes of glass.

Nearly two months have passed since I was discharged from the hospital.

Two months that I have spent convalescing on the sofa, very bored, I have to confess. The only highlight and remotely interesting thing that has happened, was on day fourteen when Sloan went on the rampage and put peepholes in Marie's doors.

Marie - God bless her - continually refuses to let me return to work, even though there is nothing physically wrong with me. I guess she's playing protective mother, and she is frightened in case some bad befalls me again. She seems to be walking around on tenterhooks, as though any moment Sam or Deacon will re-emerge from the darkness and come back to finish what they started. It also doesn't help the situation that Walker poisons her mind with chapter and verse of all the bad shit that could possibly become a reality.

And then there is Mr Foster.

Uncharacteristically, he has also stayed true to his word, and given me what I asked for: time.

He reluctantly kept his promise after the whole ridiculous bathroom and bedroom door debacle. One extra day at a time proved to be a good solution; only seeing me two or three times per week. Lately, he drops by every day to see me, and to give me details of the different psychiatrists he and Gloria have managed to unearth, and to try to convince me to move back in with him. My objection, that I'd never officially moved in with him per se, and that he's backtracking on his promise to allow us to redevelop naturally, evaporates each time his lips chastely taste mine.

This is his defence mechanism – it means he doesn't have to listen, and I will ultimately be unable to say things he doesn't want to hear.

He isn't imprudent when it comes to getting what he wants.

Last night, he told me that time was fleeting, and I wholly agreed. The powerful, departing kiss I allowed him to take freely provided all the confirmation I needed. It's the first time he has made such a bold move towards me since my mental breakdown on the landing.

I have spent the majority of these last two months trying to find reasons why I should not be with him. Each time I come up empty. While I know he can be a tad possessive and maybe a little unreasonable, he has a genuine reason to be; my beating and unknown would-be attempted rape at the hands of Deacon - if what Sam had said was remotely true - attested to this.

My unremitting, dream-like trance is broken, as Walker clears his throat, and I peek up shyly at him. Whereas Marie has skirted the subject of my relationship with Sloan, unless we are alone – of which she is vociferous - Walker has no qualms and calls it as he sees it.

And one night over dinner, not so long back, he gave it to me straight.

"You see, honey, when the kid called me, I thought you were just another one of Deacon's whores, especially when we found Sam floating down the corridor, high as a kite. I didn't think anything of it and just did what he asked." His eyes shift nervously.

"Anyway, after we found Emily banged up, I was more than surprised when I saw you in his suite. I've known him for a lot of years, and you pull his strings like no one else ever has. He's normally a love and leave them type, but you're under his skin in a big way."

He pours himself a glass of wine and tilts the bottle towards me. I shake my head and sip my water. I'm already three sheets to the wind on the strong hospital meds, I don't need alcohol in my system to assist with my ramblings and indecision. He grins at me, and I narrow my eyes suspiciously. I'm not quite sure if I want to hear any more of his wild theories.

"I think it's safe to assume the feeling is mutual," he smiles gloriously.

I scowl, annoyed.

"John! Just leave her be!" Marie chimes in, when she notices my discomfort.

"All I'm saying is, the kid loves her, and she loves him. Damn, he's never loved anyone! He's never allowed anyone close enough to love him, but shit, he has it for you in spades. Just give him a chance. One day he'll tell you everything you need to know, but now isn't a good time. Things are complicated." He shifts his eyes again.

Well, that's nothing new.

Things would always be complicated with Sloan Foster.

"Earth to Kara! Where were you just now?" A hand waves in front of my face.

"Just thinking."

"Hmm, hmm, that can be dangerous," Marie says, with a knowing grin.

She sets down a bottle of wine and four glasses. I rub my eyes, wanting to make sure I'm not seeing things. Having been off the drugs for almost a week, I'm positive the effects have left my body, although I still can't be too sure.

"Four glasses? Are we expecting company?" I ask flatly, as Walker puts an empty plate on the placemat beside mine and my heart flutters in anticipation.

"Sloan's coming by when his meeting finishes, hence why dinner is a little late tonight. And speaking of late, so is he!" she utters, searching through her handbag. She pulls out her phone, just as the front door opens and subsequently closes.

Walker is asking me something, but I consciously pretend not to hear him. I know it's ignorant, but the impending presence of Sloan fills the air, and I smell him before I actually see him. He's still dressed in his suit; the jacket is thrown over his arm, his tie is slack around his neck, and his shirt is open at the collar.

Perfect is nowhere near good enough to describe him; edible might be more appropriate.

Marie greets him with open arms and kisses his cheek. In the last few months, she has become the voice of reason and is doing everything in her power to get us back together.

Funnily enough, the biggest unanswered question is whether or not we were ever really apart? Notwithstanding he threw me to the wolves unceremoniously, allowed Christy to maul him like a dog on heat, and I spent six weeks breaking my own heart over it, was there ever a day that went by when we still didn't belong to each other?

"Hey," he whispers, bending down to kiss me. The warmth of his breath drifts into my mouth, intoxicating me, until a small whimper escapes my throat.

Oh hell, it doesn't matter that we are in polite company, or in the middle of dinner, I want him. *Now.*

Walker grins at me, rests his chin on his hand, and then greets Sloan loudly. Purposely interrupting my reverie, he winks at me - and I want to absolutely kill him! It has taken me this long to openly show in front of those who love us that Sloan holds my heart completely. I acknowledge, regardless of whatever happens, he always will. Now the moment is bloody ruined for me.

"Hey, man," Sloan replies, carelessly throwing his jacket on the sofa at the other side of the room. He folds himself into the seat and reaches for one of the various bowls of food. He serves me first and then himself. Touched by the gesture, he's putting my needs before his own.

His hand clasps mine under the table, and he continuously strokes over my scar and the diamond bracelet - which I only take off to shower and sleep. My body turns boneless at the contact, weakened by the strength of the electricity treading a slow-burning trail through me, and the immersive love I will gladly allow to drown me, if it so pleases.

I watch him carefully through a haze of intent, while he talks to Marie and Walker. He is discussing some hotel takeover he's interested in. I catch titbits here and there, but since I have no clue about corporate acquisitions and property formalities, I keep shut.

"What do you think, my love?" I snap my head around. My vacant expression is more than obvious.

"Sorry, I wasn't listening."

Except, I *was* listening - *to him*. Only I'm more interested in the way his velvet tones sing to me on a visceral level, rather than the deal he now begins to describe in detail once more. I nod in agreement, still not fully understanding, but he is satisfied, nonetheless.

Dinner sees us ease back into normality with each other. Marie bestows chaste smiles upon me and watches him diligently. He constantly touches me; raising my hand and kissing my fingers, circling the bracelet on my wrist. All signs of love and tenderness I can't ignore any longer. Not that I could ignore them in the first place, irrespective of how hard I tried.

"Have you given any thought to coming back home?"

I'm curled up on the sofa, with my head resting on his lap. He is holding me close, brushing one hand up and down my side, causing my skin to goosebump under my clothing. Marie and Walker are cleaning up in the kitchen, no doubt having a little alone time of their own.

"I... I-" I pause, staring up at him, thinking of the best way to tell him I want everything he's willing to give me. That I don't want to spend another day apart from him, but the panic on his face stops me.

"How about five days a week now? No, four - four to start!" he says in desperation.

I'm stunned.

He's compromising again.

He's business in every aspect of his life, but over the last two months or so, he has conceded more times than even Walker could recall.

I let out a laugh, and he looks down at me, upset. I raise my finger to his lips. "I was going to say - before you interrupted me - that I want to be back with you. I've spent a lot of time, right here on this sofa, evaluating every rational emotion running through me."

He frowns. "And what did you come up with?"

"That I love you more than I will ever be able to express. That I physically ache without you. That I want to be with you, always." And just like that, another one of the bricks that form the invisible shield surrounding my heart falls to earth and shatters.

A smile immediately replaces his frown, and he reaches for me. He lifts me up, slides his legs onto the sofa, and rolls us. His body covers mine, and he plays with a loose strand of my hair.

"You're amazing," he says reverently, cupping my chin and cheeks. "You're beautiful and smart, incredibly sexy, and you fit me perfectly." I bite my bottom lip as my heart swells to epic proportions.

"So, when can I get you back home – to *our* home? There are unspeakable things I really want to do to you, and I'm afraid I don't want your mother, or my best friend, overhearing us." The heat creeps into my cheeks, but he leans down to kiss me before I can feel embarrassed.

His distraction method is impeccable.

"Right this goddamn instant, if I have anything to do with it!" Walker answers for me, confidently striding into the living room with Marie attached to his hip.

Sloan grins and pulls me up. His happiness is infectious, and I ease into him, thoroughly content again at long last.

"Seriously, Kara, I'm going to go upstairs and pack all your shit up again right now! I need alone time with my own woman. I'm tired of having to sneak around like a teenager. Come to think of it, I didn't sneak around when I *was* a teenager!" He squeezes Marie's thigh, who in turn colours crimson and bats his hand away.

"Don't listen to his crap, honey. Move out whenever you feel up to it, or not at all!" Marie says, slapping his chest playfully. Walker manages a pitiful pout, and she nuzzles closer, before whispering something to him. Whatever she says, we aren't privy to it, but Walker is clearly elated.

I look between the three of them, and make my decision final. I turn to Sloan in question. "Danny called last week, asking what I wanted to do with the flat since the rent is still paid. He hasn't heard from Sam, and all my stuff is still in there."

"Pick a day, and I'll get the guys to help," Walker says, popping a crisp into his mouth. "Hell, those boys need something to do at the moment since we aren't having much luck with the other thing." His eyes flash to Sloan, whereas mine narrow at their secrecy. "I'll get Devlin over. I know he'll have a soft spot for little Kara here." He winks at me, and all the muscles in my face tighten.

Sloan shifts under me. "Fine, but just warn the little bastard to keep his attitude in check!" he tells him, bringing me closer. I expect him to be angry at the implication, but he is completely relaxed – if that's what you can call that little outburst.

"Will you be there to help?" I turn and ask him. "And you'll have to make room for some of my things, you know." Not that I'm worried, two of his spare bedrooms combined have nearly the same floor space as my old flat.

"Of course I will; the house is big enough for everything you have. I will do anything for you, you should know that by now. Bring whatever you want. I want you to start making it your home, too. You can redecorate and change whatever you want to, no matter if it works or not, we'll make it work." He drops a kiss to the tip of my nose and my eyes close under it.

God, how I want this to work.

I hear Marie's content sigh. "If there's anyone in this world who deserves happiness, it's you, my girl," she says, and I grin happily.

"So, I guess the big unanswered question is, are you staying here tonight, or are you coming home…with me?" His tone radiates hope and anticipation.

"I want to go home," I whisper. "With you."

Unable to contain his delight, he picks me up off the sofa, and carries me straight upstairs to my room. He pauses outside my door and grins at the handle, clearly remembering his handiwork with the drill prior to the new door being fitted.

Delicately sitting me on my bed, he heads straight to the drawers. Fumbling through them with determination, he picks up a black lace thong - which is very similar to the one he shredded – and twirls it on his finger, swinging it around incessantly.

"This is the only thing we're taking!"

I smile at his brashness and wiggle my finger for him to come to me. He swaggers towards me, a man full of confidence and power, aware of his presence, and the way it calls to me like a siren. He drops to his knees, and my mouth runs dry, recalling the last time he was in this position at the hospital. My fingers run over the bracelet that has become such a beacon of love for me. He stares at my wrist, watching my action reflectively.

"One day, my gorgeous girl, but not today. The day you know everything about me, will be the day I do that." He stands, tugging my arm gently, until we are chest to chest.

"I love you more than anything else in this world. I have since the first moment I ever saw you."

"Well, Sam's drugged up condition didn't exactly leave me much choice, did it?"

He closes his eyes momentarily and breathes deeply. "That wasn't the first time I ever saw you, Kara."

I shift slightly from his revelation, but this isn't the first time I have identified his innuendoes. The first time was when he asked Walker to do a full report on my father. There have also been lots of other unmistakable moments, such as knowing my number, and things that should have shocked him, but didn't.

He cradles my head and kisses me tenderly, then pulls back. "Eventually, but not right now. Do you trust me?"

Can I really trust him?

Again, this is a huge leap of faith for me. Another one of his secrets has just come to light, and although I should be worried and frustrated as hell, I'm not. It wasn't a Freudian slip of the tongue, he was being honest, and I shall hold him to it. He trusts me not to delve further, and starting from now, I will trust him to love and protect me, regardless if I like the consequential truth or not.

My life is already tumultuous. It can't get any more complex than it presently is.

"I trust you *and* your secrets," I tell him coyly. He tucks my knickers into his pocket and leads me to the door. Marie kisses me goodbye, while Sloan and Walker discuss tightening up security.

"Kara, how do you feel about having Devlin hanging around?" Walker enquires.

I shrug uncomfortably because I'm not entirely sure how I feel, especially considering his insinuation. "I don't know. I guess it'll be okay, if it makes you two feel better."

"It does. It *really* does," Sloan says with relief, wrapping his arm around my shoulder. "Devlin's a good guy. A little hot-headed at times, but he would fight to the end to protect you."

I hide the shudder that runs through me, realising that Devlin is about to become my permanent shadow, because of he who lurks in them for reasons unknown.

Walker approaches us. "Honey, what I said earlier? I didn't mean to make you feel embarrassed, it was just a bit of fun. I'm sorry." Sloan pats his shoulder.

"You didn't, but thank you anyway," I lie. He bends down and pecks my cheek. I touch over the part of my skin that is tingling with awareness as he steps back to Marie, gesturing for us to leave.

"Don't call us unless the world is ending!" Sloan shouts to Walker, who salutes animatedly.

I stifle a laugh. They are such polar opposites, yet they complement each other perfectly, both in business and in the brotherly affection they share. Although something tells me that Sloan looks upon him more like a father figure he never really had growing up, even though there isn't more than ten years between them.

"Are you going to work tomorrow?" Walker shouts at him.

Sloan looks at me thoughtfully, tilting my chin, searching me for his answer. "I haven't decided yet. Have a good night."

I walk down the driveway, and nearly stumble when I see the BMW parked. Sloan smiles sweetly, and I swear my heart might have just stopped beating momentarily.

"You kept it?" I'm only a few octaves away from squealing in delight.

He hands me the key, folding it inside my palm. "Of course, it's yours. The first time I got in it after... Well, it smelt like you. I knew you hated me and that I might never get you back, so I actually started driving it, just so I had something of you with me, even if it was only the faint aroma of your perfume." I raise my hand to my chest and battle with myself not to cry, even if they are tears borne of happiness.

Deactivating the locks, I manoeuvre to the driver's side. I climb in and begin repositioning the seat and mirrors. My hands rim around the wheel, and I feel anxious that everything has changed, and yet everything is still the same.

I twist to watch him slide in, and his body fills the passenger side. He rests his hand on my thigh and squeezes.

"Take us home, baby."

I stare lovingly into his eyes and smile.

I am home.

Chapter 10

THE LOW, MORNING sun is unforgiving as it hits my eyes through the partially open curtains, causing me to squint rapidly. Aggravated by nature's intrusion, I roll onto my side to find my reflection looking back at me inside beautiful glossy, midnight blues.

My eyes expand desirously, and I explore him with intent. Mentally checking myself for not having the courage to do this previously when we have woken up together, I realise, until recently, those days have been few and far between.

"Good morning." The words roll off Sloan's tongue fluidly, sounding both effortless and erotic.

"Morning," I purr, deciding to take control. I close in and stretch across his body. Straddling his hips wantonly, I position myself over him, effectively immobilising him as I rock against his growing hardness.

Since it was a little too late when we arrived home last night, and considering he hasn't touched me intimately in months, he had been a complete gentleman when he declared it wasn't the right time. Instead, he tortured me by undressing, then redressing me in one of his tailored shirts and the knickers he had in his pocket. He didn't make any attempt to touch me intimately, except for pulling me in close and wrapping himself around me.

All I know is that, aside from the day he brought me home, I have waited nearly four months to get him back with me completely, and I'm not going to waste another second.

Grinding myself against him, an hiss escapes his throat. His fingers move laboriously up and under the fabric of the shirt, sensitising and heating my lonely flesh.

"Baby, what are you doing?" he growls out breathless. I slyly tilt my hips over his now fully engorged length.

"What I should have done weeks ago. I want you so much it hurts. Please, don't make me beg."

"Never," he replies roughly with a smile. He leisurely unbuttons the shirt and exerts pressure down my sternum. "I love you in my shirts. Incredibly sexy." He opens the fabric and his eyes hood. Never breaking visual contact, he pulls it down my arms, balls it up and tosses it aside. His hands roam over my shoulders, then my breasts, and he regards me with a hungry expression, like a man being denied the basic essentials of living.

Somewhere, the voice of reason is telling me to be cautious and restrained, but I need this. *I need him.* For, I too, feel like I'm being denied something vital deep inside.

Pushing up against me, until we are nose to nose, he kisses me until I have difficulty breathing. I press him back down on the bed and reciprocate. First his full lips, then his neck. I kiss my way down to his chest, and then over his flat nipples, licking and sucking as I go. His breathing is arduous, and his chest pumps wildly. I glide my hands over his hard stomach, tracing over his muscles, until I reach the fine, dark line running down his abdomen.

He slips his hands into my hair and tugs gently. "Oh, Christ!" he gasps out. I smile against him, loving how easily I can turn him on.

I lift up, and the tip of his hard penis tickles my throat. My pulse quickens, the anticipation and anxiety of what I plan to do for the very first time rushes through me like liquid fire, burning everything in its path.

"Baby?" He looks at me with concern. I shake my head, but he pulls me up and holds me, so I can't conceal my embarrassment and fear. Identifying my worry instantly, he stares straight at me and strokes my cheek. "There's no rush and no pressure. Just do what you're comfortable with, but slowly, okay?"

"What if you don't…What if I'm no good?"

"Baby, anything you do will always be amazing." He strokes my cheek. "I love you. You couldn't disappoint me if you tried." His finger outlines my lip tenderly.

Lust pours from every cell, as I see his crown glisten. Lowering back down, I lick my lips and my tongue darts out and touches the head, testing the waters, as such. He jerks harshly, and a loud moan rumbles from deep within him. I peer up, and his face is clouded over with desire; his eyes are dark, penetrating with ecstasy. My lips cover him, and I take him in slowly, little by little, my mouth acclimatising and accommodating him. The hand in my hair tightens, as I timidly move my lips up and down his length. My hand circles his base, and I pump him slowly, copying the movement of my mouth. I swirl my tongue around him, pulling back to the tip, and let my teeth graze him ever so slightly. I'm not quite sure what I'm doing, or if I'm doing it right, but I'm satisfied nonetheless when I hear him verbalise.

"Fuck," he hisses. "God, that feels good!"

Pleased with myself, I move over him with more confidence. His length hardens further and pulsates on my tongue. I pull back fast, just as my gag reflex almost kicks in, and slap a hand over my mouth. I don't think vomiting would be attractive at this moment. Continuing to shift my other hand up and down at his base, his fingers leave my hair. He grins at me, and suddenly, I'm being lifted back up his body and flipped underneath him.

"Hey!" I manage to get out, the same instant my thong is slid down my legs, as opposed to being shredded this time.

He parts my thighs and looks down between us. "Beautiful," he says, dropping a kiss to my aching sex, causing my back to arch off the bed instantly. He comes back up, and his mouth covers mine fully, as I concentrate on the place desperate for his immediate attention.

He enters me in one fast thrust, and it feels like the first time all over again. I gasp as he touches me deep inside. He gives me a look of concern and pulls out a little.

"Sorry," he whispers, but I shake my head and kiss him until he moves forward again.

Tightening my internal hold, his guttural moan echoes through the room. My hands grip his neck for leverage, and I wrap my legs around his hips, digging my heels into the top of his buttocks.

"I want to come inside you. I need to," he says with determination, as he begins to move fluidly.

Rolling me over, I'm now sitting astride his groin. His hands glide down my back and cup my arse. I slide up and down on him, throwing my head back, as carnal pleasure begins to catapult me to heaven. His fingers slide between my cheeks and lovingly stroke my rear entrance. I tighten up slightly, but he gives me a look of sincerity; I trust him not to hurt me this way. I nod, hoping he understands, and his returning look gives me the validation I need.

His hand drags around my front, and he rubs it over my nub. I moan as he stimulates me beautifully. Trailing a finger up my body, he presses the pad against my full, bottom lip.

"Suck." Slipping his finger into my mouth, I do as I'm told, imagining it's something else, wanting to finish what I started only moments earlier.

He withdraws his finger from my mouth and skims his hand down to my arse. He allows it to linger at my entrance again, before the sensation of his intrusion spikes, and he gently penetrates me. I instinctively tense against the foreign entity, and then begin to relax, my body on the verge of shattering. I continue to move up and down on his length, taking him to the hilt and back up again. His finger replicates my movements, and I mellow in the feeling that is so forbidden, yet so amazing.

Kissing him to the point of numbness, his tongue breaches my mouth the moment he finds an opening. The feeling is too much; him inside me, his finger pumping my behind, and his tongue against mine, rounding off the overarching sensation of being completely invaded.

My rapturous cries are swallowed by his mouth the moment we simultaneously climax. It's the headiest feeling I've ever had in his embrace. He glides his finger back inside one last time as the last of his orgasm flows from him, then he eases out and flips us over. Putting his weight on his elbows, he stares down, a man fully sated.

"Did I hurt you?"

"No," I shake my head, and he suspiciously tilts his brow. "Maybe a little, but that was wonderful and perfect. Thank you." I rise up and kiss him. His lips slowly move with mine, and I start to think of ways to convince him to do it again.

"You know, you display so much emotion facially, my love. I'll never tire of reading you." He gathers my hair to one side, and I shiver. He rubs my arms and covers his warm body with mine. I curve my legs around his hips, bringing him closer.

"You want to do that again?" he asks. I quickly nod, because I don't need to fake my enthusiasm, what he just did was mind-blowing.

"Good. I want all of you, forever." He tucks my head into the crook of his neck and rocks me. We're so close, connected on such a physical and emotional level, that I know I will never be able to let him go.

"I love you, Mr Foster."

"I love you too, Miss Petersen."

Just as I ease into his shoulder, he flips me over, so I am back on top, and he smiles devilishly. His hands cling to my hips as he tilts them back and forth, his length gliding through my wetness.

"You know what to do, baby," he says, relaxing back.

I turn on all the jets and allow the water to fall; over my head, down my torso, over my backside, and finally, down my legs. The flow of nature cleans away the smell of him from my skin. I stand, unmoving, close my eyes, then place my palms on the glass. My hands cause the condensation and droplets of water to run down and around them.

The sound of the door latch clicking forces me to open my eyes. Sloan is on the other side of the glass, his palms perfectly aligned with mine. His bare body shines with a visible sheen from our lovemaking, his chest heaves with evident desire, while his eyes are glazed and dark.

My eyes drift down to his feet, and I leisurely work them back up his body, my vision partially distorted due to the billowing heat and the flow of the water catching in my lashes. I press further into the glass, until my lips are mere millimetres from him. A ghost of a smile begins to form, and he sidesteps to the door.

The steam in the large cubicle escapes as he enters. He stands in front of me, and brings his hand to his mouth, running his finger over his lips. I cross my arms over myself and turn, so that my side is to him. I push my face under the flow of water, at the same instant his hand slides over my wet skin.

His hard length presses into my hip, and he spins me around effortlessly. My hard nipples glide against his equally hard chest on the turn. His hands are fast, and in seconds, they are both flat against my shoulder blades. My body moulds into his, as he throbs against me, and I let out a small, raspy moan, unable to control myself. He grunts into my neck, sucking on my tender flesh.

"Oh, God…" I sigh out as he positions us under the showerhead. Picking up my bottle of shampoo, he squeezes it into his palm and starts to wash my hair carefully. Euphoria spreads through me, not that it has disseminated in the first place. I slam my hand onto the tiles, feeling distinctly unsteady and weak.

He pulls me into him, still massaging my scalp. Seconds later, he braces his arm around my back, and tips my head under the stream of water. My chest starts to rise in a panic that I am, once again, momentarily not in control.

"Trust me?"

I nod quickly, uneasily, and close my eyes in fear.

"Don't do that with me; never be frightened. Open your eyes, baby. Let me see those beautiful green gems I love so much," he requests reverently. I open and smile at him, fighting my discomfort.

The water runs over me, and he's extra careful not to allow it to run into my eyes, which are still wide, staring at him.

He finishes washing the lather from my hair and then reaches for my body wash. Again, in meticulous fashion, he gently starts to bathe my skin. His eyes rake over my body, causing it to ignite, and it isn't the heat of the water making me hyper-aware, it's him. It's always him.

His hands glide down my arms and over my chest; lathering me, inflaming me. He stops his attentiveness when he reaches my apex. He leans in close and cups me, as one hand washes up and down my limbs assiduously. My head falls back against the tiles, as a low, scratchy moan, flies from my mouth.

"Hands on my shoulders," he whispers, low against my core. I oblige eagerly, and stroke my hands down his wet hair, over his cheeks, and onto his shoulders.

Peppering my inner thigh with kisses so soft, he presses his face deeper into my centre. His rough chin grazes my softness, and I moan incoherently, as his tongue confidently swipes over me. I close my eyes and rock my body against his, desiring him in ways I don't think I'll ever be able to vocalise. I fantasise behind my closed lids, furrowing my brow, desperate to have him devour me completely yet again.

A strong palm reaches down to my ankle, encouraging me to lift my leg as he simultaneously slides his hand up, hooking my limb over his shoulder. I lift my hand, unsure what to do with it, until he grips it in his, entwines our fingers, and rests them on my raised thigh.

His talented tongue slides inside my wet heat, and I cry out in pleasure as he starts prepping me for round two. My free hand slaps against the glass, feeling for the top of the enclosure. Clasping it tightly, my fingers curl around it for leverage. Sloan groans out from between my legs, and his hand reaches for my wet nipple, twirling and rolling it between his fingers. My head falls back against the wall, causing my torso to arch and my breast to fill his hand perfectly.

The ache developing inside my body is maddening, longing for him to devour me senselessly. I shift my hand from under his on my thigh, and he grunts annoyed, until I look into his dark eyes and slowly drag my hand up my body, stopping at my lonely, neglected nipple. I continue to stare at him, awaiting his permission to touch myself. He nods, and a fierce need to release overwhelms me. I squeeze my areola and peak in my hand, never breaking the precious eye contact I need - that I will always need.

His mouth smothers me, while his tongue continues to thrust repeatedly. He carries me to the edge of reason and common sense, and I long to fall over the edge with him.

Unable to look at his beautiful, sexually induced features, I rock back and close my eyes. Dissatisfied, he nips my ultra-sensitive skin, and I yelp loudly. He grunts, his nose scrunching slightly and sucks my brutalised area.

"Oh, God, I need to come..." I whimper. He slides my leg off his shoulder, rises, and kisses me. His tongue dances with mine, and I taste myself all over it, while he cups me, pressing two fingers inside my ready core.

"So ready and wet." He slides his hand over my face. "So beautiful and amazing."

He quickly twists me, until my front is pressed against the wall. My hands brace on the slippery tiles, seeking ballast that actually isn't there. Strong hands glide down my back with a definitive hardness I've never felt from him before. Whether it's remembering the way my skin looked while I was hospitalised, or something else, I'm undecided.

His warm breath blows over my tailbone, as he starts to massage my backside. My breathing hitches and speeds up frantically. A kiss is placed on either cheek, before he pulls back, and I glance to my side and look down at him.

"Open," he says gently against my hip, smothering it with wet kisses.

Pressing my hands harder on the slippery marble, I spread my legs slowly as his fingers rub against my folds. I cry out the moment he claims me, thrusting into me hard and unforgiving. He moans low and continuous behind me. I mellow with each thrust, and press myself against the wall further, knowing the surface will not give me support, but I need something as he re-stakes his claim. My inner muscles contract, and I can feel my body change, readying itself for the onslaught of climax. I breathe out, feeling the silky smooth flow of ecstasy rising steadily, coming in full force from the actions of his steel hardness. His motions become deeper, harder; he's aware I'm hanging on by a thread.

"Let go, my love," he whispers.

And I do – with pleasure.

I let the pent-up sensations flow from me in a chorus of guttural moans and cries of joy, all interspersed with his name. His hips grind against mine, rotating himself deeper inside me, wringing out the last of my passion for him.

My body eases down naturally, until only the sound of our heavy pants, and the stream of water hitting the marble floor, are the only noises filling the room. I squeal out when he bites my shoulder spiritedly and spins me around.

He pulls me into him, and his still extremely hard erection digs into my stomach, almost to the point of pain. Resentfully, I slide myself away, until the power of him is barely grazing my flesh. I stroke my hand down his face as he starts to wash my body all over again, paying particular attention to my sensitive sex.

"You know that was highly dangerous and highly pleasing." I smile shyly at him.

"Well, I do like to live on the edge, especially if I'm living on it with you." He kisses my collarbone and lobs the body puff to the base.

"Noted," I say, kissing him lovingly. "Want me to scrub your back?" I flutter my wet lashes at him, and he chuckles as he ducks under the hot spray.

"Baby, we both know we won't be getting out of here anytime soon if you do. Go on, go," he says, kissing me one last time, before slapping my arse as I exit with my marching orders.

Entering the bedroom, my eyes skim over the floor, and I let out a loud laugh. I shouldn't have expected anything less, but the clothes that were scattered over it before I went into the bathroom for the best shower of my life, are now gone.

I guess some things never change.

I linger in the doorway of the walk-in. As per usual, everything is methodically organised and nothing out of place. A deep throat clears behind me, and I rotate to find Sloan leaning lazily against the frame, looking like pure sin and sex combined.

"You have that look again. What's on your mind?" he asks, moving towards me, rubbing towel against towel.

"What look?" I ask inquisitively. "I'm not aware that I have a *look*." I step towards the island and run my hand over it, my memory rehashing the first time.

"Well, you do, and it's one that makes me want to run for cover.

When you're wondering, you wear the look. When you're annoyed, you wear the look. If you're pissed, it's the same one. It's your *look*." He turns me and holds my head up. "Trust me, baby, I love that look, I really do. Especially, when it's staring up from under me, all wanton and compliant, requesting more." He smiles, and I shake my head, digging my palms into his chest.

"Okay. Well, today it's the *look* of where have my dirty clothes vanished to?" I query sarcastically.

"They're in the same place they are every day – the laundry bin, where I usually put them. How do you think they normally get there?" He smirks, as though I should already know this.

"I don't know, maid or something? In all the time we've been together, I've never once seen anyone up here cleaning," I comment, pulling away and walking to my side of the room.

Choosing a pair of slim fit jeans, a black top and calf-length boots, which still have the shamefully expensive price tags on, I wait. He remains mute, and I shuffle to the drawers in the island, pulling out a set of black matching lingerie.

Long minutes tick by, and I turn to see him dawdling on his side, looking completely confused, until he senses he is being watched.

"Well, obviously the hotel staff do come up and clean a few days a week, but it's not a permanent arrangement. Kara, it may come as a shock to you, but I'm more than capable of tidying up after myself. Now, the house, well that's a different kettle of fish entirely," he says, turning away and pulling out one of his usual suits, complete with waistcoat.

"That explains it then," I say, shimmying into my jeans. I slap my hands on my denim-clad hips, inadvertently pushing out my silk and lace-covered breasts.

He licks his lips and starts a slow, predatory approach towards me. "Explains, what?" He bends down, and puts his open mouth over my nipple, gripping it moderately hard.

"This obsessive-compulsive disorder you seem to have, but don't seem to realise. You know you don't leave anything on the floor, not even a sock," I say with breathless, mock exaggeration, gently pushing him off. He starts retreating back to his side with a grin.

"It's not a disorder, it's about having discipline. Besides, everything has its place." He pulls on his trousers and grabs a shirt and tie.

"Well, I'll tell you what it definitely is, it's an invasion of my privacy and unauthorised touching of my personal belongings." He looks at me, surprised and open-mouthed, before stalking closer again. "And the fact there's not a single thing out of place, that has nothing to do with discipline, that's just you wanting complete control over everything and everyone," I finish proudly, the same moment he grabs and kisses the life out of me.

His lips leave mine, and he leans back, assessing me. "Everything has a place in my life, and so do you," he murmurs low, obviously hoping I won't hear him. Except, where he is concerned, I'll never miss a thing from his mouth.

He reaches for my top on the island, and I lift my arms dutifully as he pulls it over me. I watch as he pads back to his side, buttons up his shirt, and slides into his waistcoat. I study his back as he brings a tie around his neck and turns back to me with a fierce, serious look, willing me to comment.

"Well, if it makes you sleep easier at night, you keep telling yourself that." I have the last say, ending the discussion with a smile, and swagger out.

Chapter 11

I SLIP ON my jacket as the Aston roars to life. Sliding into the passenger seat, Sloan grips my hand before he releases the handbrake. Dropping it down, the car moves slowly out of the space.

"So, I made an appointment for you with someone this morning," he says quietly.

"*Someone?* A shrink?!"

My fists bunch and my forearms tighten. He's doing a Marie, circa seven years ago – he's taking away my right to choose, by dropping this on me at the last possible minute. It doesn't take a genius to guess he has already spoken to her about it.

I curse under my breath as anxiety claws at my chest. He really does know no frigging bounds. Or maybe he just likes to test me and mine.

"And when were you planning on telling me? When you frog-marched me into the office? When they call my name, and I don't understand why? Why the fuck are you just springing this on me?" I ask angrily.

There are times when life is so easy with him, and then there are times like these, when I want to scream in his face until I'm mute and crush his larynx with my fist. Why does he insist on constantly pushing my buttons? I'm already walking a fine line as it is. I don't need any more turmoil putting upon my mentally weak shoulders. Truthfully, with my history, it's a wonder I don't snap on a regular basis with some of his passive-aggressive antics. I begin to rub my forehead, trying to control the heavy breathing leaving my body.

"Kara, I was going to tell you. I know you're pissed off; I know you're pissed off with *me*, but I had to do this for us. The only way we're going to move past the shit that eats you up and haunts you, is if you start to own it." He's not looking at me, which means he knows I am incensed beyond belief.

"'*The shit that eats you up?'* Who the fuck are you right now, Foster?!" His head snaps towards me at my insolence, and the sole use of his surname for the first time in our relationship. "How dare you presume to plan my life for me? We had an agreement, we would take it slow, remember? This isn't taking it slow; this is you doing that controlling shit we were talking about earlier!"

"Kara, you're being really unreasonable-"

"Well, I'm learning from the best, aren't I!" I shout out.

I tug my bag closer to my chest and gaze out of the window. The car stops at a red light, and I notice a fairly familiar car in the wing mirror. It's black, heavily tinted, and very goddamn flaming familiar. I squint, trying to get a better view of it.

A quick glimpse at Mr Unreasonable assures me he's not noticed. Not that I expect him to, considering the raging argument brewing between us, threatening to ruin the perfect tranquillity of the last twenty-four hours.

We start to move again, and I give my full attention to the vehicle trailing behind. Sloan is mumbling beside me, but I'm so far away in the zone, my concentration in full force on the car, I haven't picked up on a word of it.

Worryingly, the car overtakes one in front of it, which now puts it three behind us. I turn to Sloan, who is still talking and gesturing with one hand animatedly. I narrow my eyes at him.

How the hell hasn't he noticed that there is someone clearly tailing us, and that I am clearly not listening? I shake my head at his failure to see anything, except his own so-called reasonability right now.

"Baby, did you just hear a single thing I said?" I turn to him with exasperation.

"No, *baby*, I'm too busy watching the car behind us that has been following for the last few miles!"

He does a quick glance in his wing mirror and huffs. "Fuck! Hold on!" he says, pulling the seat belt tighter across my body. He slams his foot onto the accelerator, and the car shoots off into the traffic. He narrowly misses another car as he weaves through those slowing down and runs the red light. My breathing is fast, and I hold on tight to the seat belt strapping me in for dear life.

"You just got flashed by a speed camera!"

"I don't give a fuck! Hold on!" He grabs the belt and yanks it hard again, until it cuts into my stomach.

"My God, you're going to kill us!" I stare at him; his face is unreadable.

"Don't worry, Walker taught me how to drive. Trust me."

He presses down hard on the accelerator again and takes a maze of one-way streets. His office comes into view, and I finally breathe a sigh of relief.

Stopping abruptly outside, he jumps out of the car and runs around to my side. Quickly unbuckling, he holds me under the arms and lifts me out. Jogging us towards the building, he throws his keys at one of the security guards and stops us at the entrance, watching to see what the car following will do. I have no idea why; we both know it's going to stop. Just the same way we both know who is probably residing behind the wheel.

Right on cue, the car slows and halts opposite us. I turn myself into Sloan's body, shielding my face from the line of sight of the driver. Sloan's arm wraps around me, and his phone starts to vibrate.

"Hey, look before you say anything, we have an issue." His voice is firm and commanding. The arm around me squeezes harder, and I look up. Impulsively, he stares down at me.

"Baby, have you ever seen that car before?" I look at the vehicle, but I don't need to because, instinctively, I know it is the same one from when I first had the misfortune of meeting the *Kray* wannabes. But in a city as populated and wealthy as this, there are probably thousands of them on the streets.

"Kara, do you recognise it?!"

Confused, I look back to him and nod. "I-I don't know. Maybe."

"Tommy, black Merc, pull the security footage from March, see if it's on there. If it is, run the plates – it might just be Jeremy. And find out where he is, too! Tell him I want to speak to him!" he hisses quietly, showing me his back, obviously hoping I don't hear. Spinning back around, he stares at me, then says, "No, we'll be next door." He hangs up and throws his arm around me; his fingers cut into the ball of my shoulder.

"What's next door?" I ask, looking past his glitzy office building to the unassuming adjacent property.

"David. Your new therapist."

I purse my lips tight. I appreciate I promised to try, but this is going a step too far. I, at least, thought I would have a few more weeks, possibly months, to come to terms with having to see someone again. I might have seen my old one a few months back, when the world came tumbling down, but let's face it, I never had any intention of going back. But now I have no bloody choice in the matter, irrespective of the fact I originally offered, in a moment of lunacy, during my post mental breakdown state.

I give him a small, unhappy nod, rather than start another fight, before walking down the steps onto the street. A strong arm wraps around me.

"Look, I know I just sprung this on you, but you don't have to go in there today if you don't want to. I don't expect you to spill your secrets right off the bat." I rotate and stare at him. Pressing my hand to his face, he leans into my touch.

"Promise me, regardless of whatever progress I make, however insignificant, that you will never, *ever*, let me down again. I don't think I could survive that a second time."

"Kara, I will never, *ever*, put you through that again. I promise."

Thirty-five steps.

Thirty-five small steps are all it takes to reach the building I fear is about to become my newly found object of fear and loathing.

Sloan presses the intercom, and a woman greets us. My footsteps resound loudly on the linoleum floor as we head up the stairs to the office.

My hands are sweating, and I rub my sticky palms over my jeans, while Sloan eyes me with concern.

"Seriously, there's nothing for you to worry about." I stop and glare at him. No doubt I'm giving him the *look* again.

"Have you ever been to see a shrink?" He cocks his brow. "No, I didn't think so. So, you've never had to sit there while someone tries to tell you how to deal with your problems. It's easier said than done. I find it absolutely insulting that you tell me there's nothing to worry about!"

With a shake of his head and a resigned look, he takes my hand and leads me into the small, yet intimate, waiting room. The receptionist greets us, and I'm forced to sign in. The pen wobbles in my hand, and for a second, I forget my own name. Sloan's hand comes over mine, and he gives me a forced smile.

"Would you like something to drink, dear?" the older lady asks.

"Please can I have a coffee? Milk and two sugars, thank you."

"Of course, sweetheart. The usual Sloan?" My eyes turn to slits at her familiarity with him. Unaware she has just piqued my curiosity, she shuffles off into another room, and the sound of a kettle starts to boil.

Sloan starts to fidget and paces the room, taking in everything. There is nothing that he misses, judging the way he's looking at the certificates on the wall and the trophies on the shelves with a smile.

A smile that says he has seen these before. He might think I'm ignorant at times, but I know how to be assertive when it matters.

"Here you go, sweetheart," the woman says, passing me a cup and saucer.

"Thank you." I take it from her. "I'm Kara, nice to meet you." I hold my hand out reflexively, without thinking.

"Margaret Walton. I'm actually David's wife," she says with a smile. A cold sweat starts to build as she is just about to take my hand, when another door at the opposite side opens, and a man enters.

I look him up and down. His features are kind and approachable. He rubs his fingers over his grey-streaked beard and motions for us to enter. Accepting his invitation, I follow him inside.

Rather than the typical clinical style room I've been subjected to over the years, this is homely. Mismatched comfy chairs, two sofas, and a couple of tables are placed in between. A tray of tea and coffee and a plate of biscuits sit on the top, challenging temptation.

Perching myself on the sofa, the man, David, I presume, sits in the seat opposite. Sloan settles next to me and places his hand over mine. I smile, but he appears nervous and reaches out for a handful of chocolate digestives. I raise my brows at him, he gives me a cheeky grin and offers me one, but I shake my head, refusing.

"Morning, Miss Petersen, I'm David Walton."

"Nice to meet you. Kara, please." My hand fidgets in my lap.

"Sloan tells me you don't really want to see a shrink, and that you just need someone to listen, someone who won't judge and won't try to psychoanalyse you – his words, not mine. In this room, we will talk about whatever you want to. It can be the weather, what type of day you've had at work, anything you want. We can keep it light, or if you want to go further, we can talk about deep-rooted things that still affect you. I will listen with an open mind, but I will never judge you." He folds his arms in his lap and smiles at me.

"Thank you, Mr Walton."

"David, please," he counters. "So, Kara, tell me about you. It doesn't have to be in-depth or personal today. It can be anything you feel comfortable with."

I bite my lip, thinking of something easy that doesn't really bother me. Noting my expression, he gives me an encouraging smile, and I shift in my seat, preparing myself to break at the seams. My eyes lift up from the table, and do a slow rotation around the room.

"Right then, I'll begin," David starts, pouring himself a cup of tea. "Let's talk about what you do for a living, Kara."

"Oh, I'm a catering manager."

"And do you enjoy it? I imagine that can be quite demanding?"

"Some days." I laugh a little.

"And friends and family? Do you enjoy their company?"

I avert my eyes to the side. What can I say about my dysfunctional family? My father who prefers to walk on the illegal side of life, dealing whatever shit Frankie is on the make with these days. And my mother, the woman who is so terrified of her own shadow, she has tolerated a half-life in the living equivalent of hell.

Do I enjoy their company? No, but I'll tolerate it - provided they stay on the other side of the country.

"Yes, they're great," I lie.

"Okay." He takes a quick glance at Sloan, before turning back to me. "I'm told you have trouble sleeping sometimes. Is it your work that causes the nightmares?" I abruptly turn to Sloan, my pupils fixated. He scrubs his face and looks away. Tears form in my eyes at his well-meant betrayal.

David looks between the both of us. "Kara, would you prefer to talk alone?"

"Please," I whisper.

Sloan rises, then leans down and kisses my head. It's light and comforting, but I know he's irritated. "I'll be outside," he says softly.

I stare straight ahead, until the door clicks, then I drop my head down, fighting back the tears.

"Kara?"

I dare to look at David. "Sorry, I don't know what to say. I'm not used to it being like this."

"Relaxed? Informal? Less clinical, maybe?"

"Yeah. And also, that you already know things about me," I whisper.

"I only know what Sloan has already told me, but I would prefer to hear it from you. Whenever you are ready, there's no rush here."

"For the last few months, I have been experiencing reoccurring nightmares. I used to have them as a teenager, and they subsided over the years...until recently." Feeling a little confident, I raise my head up further. David nods and takes a sip of tea.

"What do you think the trigger is? The reason why they're occurring again."

I turn to the closed door. "He's the trigger, but I don't know why."

"How long have you been together?"

"Five months or so." He narrows his eyes, seemingly trying to understand.

"How did you meet?"

I arch my brows. "That's a long, convoluted story. We could be here all day." I say flatly.

"Okay, that's not my concern. Do you want to talk about the nightmares from your teens?"

"I don't know. The reasons why I had them are too painful to talk about. Sometimes, I don't even remember if what caused them is real, you know? My memory is scattered when it comes to the way they were created."

I pour another coffee, strong and black. I look at David again, and he smiles. I know he is waiting for me to spill my demons in order to cleanse my darkened, permanently scarred soul.

Taking another sip, I realise if something is worth doing, it's worth doing right. This wasn't what I expected to do when I walked in here, but how many times can I sit in front of various different shrinks and flirt around the subject, hoping they will eventually drop it and sign me off as cured.

The time has come and gone.

I inhale deeply in preparation. "I was...attacked when I was fifteen. Actually on my fifteenth birthday, in my own bed, with my parent's downstairs, who never lifted a finger to stop it. They didn't even care. I was placed in social services care, but I ran away from the hospital before they could take me. It was hard, but eventually, an amazing woman found me. She gave me a life, somewhere safe to grow and try to forget. I tried to pretend, but I never did. Forget, that is. But that night is..." I sigh and wipe my lashes.

"Did you have a therapist as a teenager?" He gives me a worried look.

"I did, but I never really told her what happened. She never made me feel comfortable, and in turn, I never felt that I could be one hundred per cent truthful."

"And today, do you feel you can be truthful with me? That our time together in the future can be productive?" I look at him; study him. Judge him as to whether or not I can tell him further of my diabolical pain-filled history.

I nod quickly. "Strangely, I do feel comfortable with you. I don't know why."

"Good, how about we work up to an hour a few times a week, and just go from there?"

"I think I can cope with that. For now."

David gets up, takes my hand, and I visibly shiver. "Is this something that happens often?" he asks me tenderly, and I nod. Humming to himself, he covers my hand completely in his, much to my frustration, and guides me towards the door.

Chapter 12

AS I EXIT the room, I find Sloan laughing with Margaret. Again, they seem to be more than comfortable with each other, and I'm not reading between the lines when I come to the silent conclusion that they have already met prior to today. They both sober up as soon as they see me.

"Everything okay?" Sloan asks. I smile convincingly, as the door behind me closes and David follows me out. Walking over to my boyfriend and his wife, he pulls out an appointment book.

"Very old school," I murmur.

David laughs, and his loud bellow ripples through the soft stillness of the room. "No, just safer. These books you can take home with you each night, and they will fit in a safe. You can't do that with your fancy computers with bells on them! So, yes, I am *old school* in that respect. But as you have already seen, I like to do things a little differently."

I glance down, my cheeks flaming red with unavoidable embarrassment. Watching as he flips the pages over, he peers down, gauging me, trying to figure me out.

"Same time next week?"

"Please," I say quickly.

"Thirty minutes?" David gives me an expectant look, and I wonder if I can last longer, forty-five at the most, possibly?

"Can I book in for an hour? I mean, I don't want to run over your schedule if I need more than half."

A small, shocked gasp leaves Sloan's throat, and I turn to him and shrug my shoulders. He cocks his head in surprise and gives me a smile that makes my heart shudder in the most amazing way.

This is personal progress.

For both of us.

David picks up a post-it from a block and writes down a mobile number. "Day or night, if you need to talk, I will always be ready to listen, understand?"

I nod and study the paper, remembering the last time I had a scrap of it, with eleven numbers clearly transcribed on yellow pulp background.

"Thank you, I will." He reaches for my hand again, and I flinch. I make no gesture to hide it because I don't need to. He knows this is a problem for me. But hopefully, he might prove to be an angel in disguise.

After saying our goodbyes, and David making me promise once more to call him if I feel the need to, Sloan carefully wraps his arm around me, leads us out of the office and down the corridor. He never releases my hand as we descend the few flights in complete, yet comfortable silence.

Out on the street, he slows to a stroll, even though his office is less than fifty feet away and we could reach it in minutes – less even.

"I'm proud of you," he speaks out beside me.

I gaze up at him, unable to see his eyes through his dark aviators. I stop, and he turns around, causing my image to cast a perfect reflection on the lenses. People pass us by, some muttering we are blocking the pavement, others watching us with admiration. Or maybe they are just watching him? It doesn't matter to me because, right now, I'm the only thing in his sight.

"Thank you." I reach up on my tiptoes to place an innocent kiss on his lips. His body jolts a little in my moment of pure honesty. "Thank you for taking me to him. I'm going to do this, I am. I'm going to get better for you. I promise."

He grabs me and pulls me into his front, my feet grazing the ground. His lips drag over mine, leaving me breathless in the crowd enclosing us with amused expressions.

"No. If you're going to do it for anyone, you do it for yourself. I'm sorry I went behind your back, but you and I both know that if I hadn't, it would always be all talk and no action. David's a good man. And it's highly convenient his office is right next door to mine!"

I grin at him. "Hmm, very convenient!"

And that's not the only thing, I think, noting his warmth and first-name familiarity with Margaret.

He turns and looks at his building, before sighing out. "I want to take you somewhere today, but I have a meeting this morning. Don't worry, it isn't going to last very long."

"How do you know that? What if it runs over? I might just go home and wait for you, that way you don't have to rush on my behalf," I say, dropping back onto the soles of my feet.

"Trust me, I won't be longer than thirty minutes." He studies me, and I give him a suspicious look. "Mr Spencer is coming in to sign his company over to me. Bargain basement price. It's an offer even he can't refuse." He grins maliciously, and a shudder runs through me at the spiteful look clouding his features.

"Who's Mr Spencer?" I ask. I don't fully understand what he's so obviously trying to tell me, in not so many words.

"Christy's father." He removes his sunglasses, revealing no life inside his eyes. They are dead and hollow. I begin to back away and shake my head.

"No, please don't, Sloan," my voice pleads pathetically. I should be jumping up and down for joy that he is finally going to take that slanderous bitch down a peg or two. But I'm not. I feel nothing but sorrow.

"Kara, I don't want to hear whatever you're going to say to defend her. She hurt and insulted you, and she's angered me in doing so!"

"You think I don't know that! I was there, remember? Twice!"

"Okay, I think it's time for some home truths that are going to upset you. I had a relationship with her for years. It was never like what you and I have. All she was to me was a warm, willing body. Someone to fuck whenever I wanted it, and that's it. She wanted more; I never did."

A shiver gathers momentum and rips through me. I already knew inside my heart, long before Christy's tirade at the club, that they had some sort of *relationship,* but thinking it and hearing it are two completely different things.

My heart breaks silently, and a faint pulling inside my chest is fighting to be felt because in some regard she was right. If he ever did get bored of me, he would go running right back to her bed. He's just finally admitted what she was to him.

"I know," I whisper. "But hanging her father out to dry is not the way to get back at her!" I half yell at him.

"His company has been on its knees for years, barely scraping by. This is the reason why he accosted me at the event months ago. *He* approached *me.* Seriously, do not feel sorry for them. The lavish lifestyle that he, and the rest of his wasteful family feel they deserve, is the reason for their downfall!" he spits out vehemently. "If he'd spent more time taking care of his finances, and less time meandering to the whim of his wife and daughter, he wouldn't be in this mess! Don't go breaking your fucking heart for those people!"

His jaws grind together as he slips his sunglasses back on and takes my hand. I want to shake him off, tell him to piss off and stomp away, but I don't. We walk silently towards his building, and he stops us just inside the foyer.

"Do you hate me?"

"Yes!" I hiss out, but before I can say anything further, he leans down and kisses me. His tongue swipes over my closed mouth, and I open up automatically. Allowing him to take what he needs from me right now, I moan against his lips, suffocating on the taste and smell of him until he pulls away.

I open my eyes to find his looking murderous, and I cautiously shift in the direction they are staring. The Spencer's - including Christy - are all stood there. Whereas Mr and Mrs Spencer, I presume, appear forlorn, Christy looks like she wants to rip my head off.

Sloan's hand rides down my back and rests on my bum, and I've never felt so uncomfortable in my entire life. He knew they were going to be waiting. I don't know if I should thank him for placating me, or slap him for pissing her off.

"You're late!" he says tersely to Mr Spencer, before guiding us all towards the lifts.

My heart stops when I realise they are going to see the anguish I hide. If we get in that box together, they are going to see me fall. I rotate to him, and he gently strokes my face.

One of the lifts dings and Christy flounces into it like she is the Queen. She stands in the centre and taps her foot in annoyance, while her mother and father board, with little to no enthusiasm.

"We'll take the next one," Sloan says. The doors close, and I feel my anxiousness abating.

"Thank you," I whisper against his side.

He kisses the top of my head, tilting my chin up to look at him. "Still hate me?"

I roll my eyes and turn away. "You might have just redeemed yourself a little. Only a little, mind. Don't get any ideas that it lets you off the hook completely," I mumble out.

"Don't worry, I won't," he says, guiding me into the next lift. The doors close, and he spins me around. His finger pulls down my bottom lip slowly, while he bites his in thought. "I think this little disagreement calls for some long, outdrawn make up sex later. If I remember correctly, I think you still owe me."

My mouth opens in shock, and I screw my face up. "Oh, really? I think the events that transpired afterwards have superseded it."

He pouts, still in thought. "True, but you still owe me."

I turn my back to him. "Hmm, you keep dreaming that."

"Ah, but I do. Every damn day, and you are the epicentre each fucking time, my love!"

A grin forms on my face that I know I can't conceal. The lift whisks us up to his office, and after we get out, I turn to face him.

"Whatever happens in there, I don't care. You were right; she did hurt me. I lied to you when I said it didn't matter because it does. She was spiteful and rude, and she made me feel like I was nothing for her own personal gain."

"I know, but that doesn't change anything that is going to happen in my boardroom in the next ten minutes. This was a done deal long before she turned vindictive." I nod and follow him into his office. Gloria is sat behind her desk looking glum.

"Good morning!" Sloan says, producing a hundred-watt smile. She snorts, and it's clear she has already had a mouthful off the fiery redhead. She throws him a bunch of documents, which he rolls his eyes at.

"You owe me, young man!"

"Yes, I know! I promise I'll make it up to you. How about you and Mr Truman have a night at the theatre and then The Savoy, on me?" Gloria's scowl transforms into an amazing smile, and she gushes her thanks. I, on the other hand, give him my best pout.

Why haven't I been treated to The Savoy yet?

Smiling, he kisses my forehead. "Don't worry, you'll get your dirty weekend away. I'm already planning every significant detail!"

My cheeks flush as Gloria laughs. She comes around and gently places her hand on my arm. I flinch slightly, and she steps away, but I put my hand over hers to indicate it's fine. Giving me a warm, motherly smile - much the same way Marie does - she holds firm, much to my dismay.

Sloan crosses his arms over his chest and laughs. "Fine! Go, show her off. I won't be long."

Gloria laughs. "I never thought I'd see the day! Either of them, actually!" I narrow my eyes at her, as Sloan turns on his heel and strides confidently into the boardroom, muttering to himself.

"What do you mean?" I pick up her name plaque, and remove the tiny remnant of polish residue with my thumb. Putting it back down, I notice she's giving me a look of awe.

"Well, in all the years I've worked for the Fosters – and no, don't make me admit how long – I've never, ever, seen that boy with any girl, except for the she-devil in there." She points to the boardroom. "And today, he's waltzed in here with you on his arm again, and he's going to shoot her down in flames. Trust me, it's a good day all around, dear!"

I smile, then laugh, then feel utterly guilty. "I don't think you should be saying things like that to me." I'm worried that if Sloan hears her, then he may hang her out to dry, too.

"Nonsense! It's nothing I haven't said to his face in the past. Besides, the last time you were here, it seemed to have escaped his attention that the rooms are not particularly soundproofed." She gives me a little wink, and I blush crimson. "Tea and sympathy?" she sing-songs at me. I nod furiously, remembering every single moment of that day; his desk, his sofa, nearly his desk again...

My thoughts run away with me, while I relive each moment in vivid Technicolor in the back of my mind, until the sound of Christy's irritating shriek resounds from the boardroom. I look up just in time to see Gloria shove a mug of tea under my nose, followed by a plate.

"Hobnob?"

"Thanks," I say, picking up a biscuit, listening with morbid fascination at the sounds of a woman who is only moments away from becoming what she despises: soon to be penniless.

"Come on, we don't need to be here. Sloan asked me to show you around the building. I'll introduce you to some of his colleagues." She slowly walks in front and guides us to the lifts.

My hesitancy comes back, and she identifies my distress perfectly.

"Unfortunately, darling, I'm not able to take the stairs, my legs aren't as young as yours."

"It's okay, I just don't want you to see. I don't like small spaces; they make me...nervous."

"I already know, dear. I won't say a word."

The lift door opens, and she walks inside, and I follow sheepishly. I breathe out a sigh of relief when she presses the button for the next floor up.

"How many floors does he own?" I ask, realising I'm finally going to get a little insider information in the shape of his trusted PA.

"Well, he actually owns the whole building, but we only use five in total. The other floors are let by external companies."

The doors open within seconds, and Gloria resumes her motherly - or maybe it's grandmotherly - hold on me and guides us towards a pair of glass doors, beautifully etched with the company logo.

She then leads me down a corridor with offices lining either side. As we go, she pulls out two security cards and hands one to me. "It's registered to you, so you can come and go as you please without having to sign in downstairs. Don't lose it! If you do, I'll be forced to charge you fifteen pounds for another one. And no, I don't care who your man is!"

"Fifteen pounds!" I gasp out. "Wow, I never knew these things cost so much." I think from now on I'll take better care of the one for the office I work in. Fifteen pounds! Jesus!

"Actually, they're a fiver, but I put the rest in the social fund. It goes towards office drinks, Christmas parties, bereavements, things like that. The staff don't know I do it, but at least they get it back, albeit unknowingly at some point."

She stops outside an open door and smiles. "Anyway, this gentleman is Sloan's second-in-command, Ken. Just like me, he worked for the company when Foster Senior was at the helm."

I peer around the door, and a man in his early fifties, is scratching a pen over a notepad; his laptop open in front of him. "Piece of shit! Why does this thing never frigging work!" he yells to the not so empty room. The colour in his cheeks fades away when he sees us skulking in his doorway.

"Good morning, Ken," Gloria says warmly.

"Is it?" he snaps. I chortle, out loud, without realising. Oh, I like him. He echoes my daily sentiments perfectly.

His eyes widen, and he quickly gets up from his seat and crosses the office. "Hello, Miss Petersen. Ken Barker, very nice to meet you at long last." He holds his hand out, and I smile. I know I can't accept it, so instead, I wave like an idiot. He looks down at his hand and drops it.

"Sorry..."

"Not to worry, I'm not offended in the slightest," he says with a genuine smile, and I know he isn't.

"Ken has worked for the Foster's almost as long as I have, part of the furniture, you might say." She turns back to Ken and gives him a pointed look. "Charlotte will kill you when she sees what you've done to her accounts. I suggest you fix them before she finds out!"

I smile, remembering the times I could have done time for Marie whenever she stuffed up my spreadsheets. I dread to think what condition they will be in when she finally lets me come back to work. Any progress I made weeks ago on my single day will be worthless by now.

Exchanging goodbyes, Gloria leads me into an open-plan office, describing what each department does and the people who work in them. Eventually, we are back at the lifts and riding up to another floor.

Walking through the second large space, she points out everyone in turn by name again. Some are secretaries, in-house legal, accountants, and administration. The noise level in the office is higher than what I expected, but when I ask why - remembering Soph telling me about the morgue she works in - Gloria explains it's because Sloan prefers to keep his work environment friendly.

And speaking of the man...

Suddenly the room quietens. Anyone who was paying us an ounce of attention drops their head back down.

"Hi," Sloan says behind me, handing the signed paperwork to Gloria.

"Hello, again," I reply. Gone is the hardened look of the CEO, and in its place, is the boyish grin that induces naughty thoughts in me.

"So, what do you think?"

I look around again and smile. "It's nice. I didn't realise you had so many people working for you," I comment, as I glance at the far end of the space.

"There's room for one more, if you like?" He grins, and I laugh, shaking my head.

"I think Marie would kill you."

He laughs. "I think you're probably right. Ready to go?"

"Sure. Are you going to tell me what we're doing?"

"No." His eyes twinkle, but I know it kills him to say such an innocent word.

I lean in closer, and he copies me. "What?" he asks playfully.

"Where are the ladies?"

He twirls me around, and I identify the expressions of wonderment on the faces of his staff. I want to laugh out loud. I would love to be a fly on the wall, and to have seen what he was like before I flounced into his life. For all the glances and expressions, I'm thinking he is - or maybe was - a real hard case to work for.

He leads me into the hallway and stops outside the toilets. I turn and kiss him, then go inside.

Closing the door, a flush from an adjacent cubicle fills the void. Quickly finishing, I exit and come face to face with Christy, who is applying another layer of make-up to her already caked on face. I don't know why, but something inside me snaps. The truth is, it's long overdue.

"Are you supposed to be up here?" I ask nonchalantly, washing my hands, watching her reflection.

She scowls at me. "No, but you shouldn't be either. You should be walking the fucking streets, where cheap sluts like you belong!" I've had enough and spin round to her.

"It must kill you, to know that all the years you spent trying to gain more were wasted. All you ever were, was a warm, willing body – his words, not mine." She scrunches her face up, but something inside won't let me stop. "I'm glad, that unlike you, I have some self-respect. I'm glad that I will *never* lower myself to the level you did in order to gain some preposterous form of social rank. Yes, Christy, he told me about your *relationship*, and I must admit, I'm so happy it's not mine, and that what we have is so much more. It must really grate on you that he chose me, that he's given me more in a few short months, than whatever you had going on for years."

"He's using you! You're just too blind to see it now, you ugly, dumb slut!" Her hands fist tight in desperation.

"No, Christy, he isn't," I say with a calmness I even impress myself with.

"He'll get bored-"

"No, he won't," I counter, and having the upper hand, I do something completely unlike me, and rub salt in the wound. "One day, I'll be his wife and the mother of his children, and you will be nothing but a bad memory for both of us."

Christy's nose begins to crinkle, and unshed tears redden her eyes. She quickly dries her hands and virtually runs out of the toilets.

I sigh at my reflection, feeling disgusted. This isn't who I am. I'm not the nasty girl who uses the pain of others for her own personal enjoyment and entertainment, but there's only so much even I can take anymore.

I step outside and find Sloan leaning up against the wall, with Christy ripping strips off of him.

"How fucking dare you? It isn't enough that my father has signed his entire company away for peanuts, that you let your fucking whore talk to me like that! Who the fuck does she think is? I swear I will make you pay for what you've done, mark my words! You and your little slut are going down." With that, she marches towards the lifts and stabs her fingers into the buttons until one arrives, and then she's gone.

I fidget on the spot, while Sloan fights his amusement and scratches his chin. "Do I even want to know what you said to her?" The concealed laugh is evident in his tone.

"I don't know. You might be angry with me."

He tilts his head in encouragement. "Try me."

"Well, I might have told her a few home truths, like the ones you told me earlier," I say, edging towards him tentatively. I'm not sure if my diatribe of malice towards her will be met with his approval. Now, I'm actually scared of what he will think of me now.

"Seriously, what did you say?" he asks, throwing his arms around me tightly.

I hesitate. "Well, I might have said that she was just a body. No, no, I actually said *warm, willing body*."

He squeezes harder. "Is that all? I wouldn't have thought that would bother her," he replies, a bit confused.

"No, that's not all." I peek up at him and take a breath, while he waits to hear the rest. "Fine! What probably tipped her over the edge, was when I said that one day, I would be your wife and have your children!" I gaze at him confidently, hoping my statement wasn't too premature or romanticised. He smashes his mouth against mine, and the validity of my words are reaffirmed.

"I think I just fell in love with you all over again," he mumbles into my mouth. I draw back and gasp when his hands roam under my clothing indecently, and his tongue tries to make entry and purchase with mine.

"Cameras," I breathe out, noticing the one above us, tilting and lowering in our direction.

He shakes his head and pulls my body back to him. "Who cares? It's only John and his boys."

"All the more reason! I don't want to end up on the internet. Besides, he'll tell mother!" I say in shock.

106

Sloan looks up at the camera and waves, before slinging his arm around my shoulders. My body is rocking with unfettered emotion, but I'm too consumed with him to think about the usual dread I should be feeling.

The lift arrives, and his phone starts to ring. He pulls it out of his pocket, grins and answers.

"Yes?" he asks laughing.

I watch him while he listens to whoever is on the other end, until my phone vibrates seconds later, and I pull it out to find a text from Marie.

YOU'RE IN BIG TROUBLE WHEN I SEE YOU MISSY!!!!

Ah, shit!

I feel sick.

How the hell does she know I was making out like some hormonal, rampant teenager?

I tug Sloan's sleeve, but he's still laughing and talking. He turns and takes my phone. He shakes his head before he speaks into his mobile again.

"You're in big trouble when I see you, John!"

He's still laughing, when he puts both of our devices into his pocket, looks up to the small camera, grabs me and wraps my legs around his hips. His lips devour mine, and his hands run up my back, under my clothing.

"Now, let's see if we can get them to call back, shall we?"

Chapter 13

MY FEET ACHE, so much so, I'm dying to kick off my low-heeled boots and walk the streets barefoot. But considering what might be underfoot, I'm not *that* desperate.

Sloan nudges me, and I stop what I'm doing and gaze in awe at the four Tudor towers in front of me.

Today has been another day of firsts; new and good ones.

In my whole eight years of living in The Big Smoke, I've never done the tourist thing. Namely for two reasons; one, I've never really had the time, and two, I've never really had the money to fetter.

After leaving the office, we have spent most of the day seeing the tourist attractions. My favourites are two of the most important ones: The Natural History Museum – his childhood favourite - and lastly, The Tower of London.

"Have you enjoyed today?" He smiles down at me, slipping his phone back into his pocket. He has been fielding calls left and right for the majority of the day. Quite a lot of them from an irate Walker, and an extremely livid Marie - or so he tells me.

"I've loved today, thank you," I confirm, grinning.

I'm happy; really, really happy. More so than I have been for a long time.

Taking my hand, he leads us back to the main road as his phone rings to indicate that George has arrived. I see the car the second it pulls up and skip over to it. Sloan's heavy steps follow behind, thudding loudly in my ears, as he picks up the chase. I reach the door, pull it open and slide inside. Sloan climbs in next to me, talks low to George, and the car heads off.

The traffic around the city is busy, especially so considering it's the school holidays. After spending more time in traffic than usual, George pulls up outside Harrods. Sloan grips my hand, trying to pull me out of the car, but I sit my ground.

"Why are we here?" I sound whiny, but the truth is, I am. I have more than enough stuff to clothe a third world country. The last thing I want to do is shop for more.

"You need a dress. A special one."

"What for?" I ask. He presses his lips together, blatantly refusing to answer. "Sloan, whatever I need this new, special dress for, I'm quite sure I have more than enough in those rooms of yours! Anyway, if I did want a new one – which I don't - couldn't I just go to Debenhams, like the normal people of the world do?"

He cocks his head towards me. He's unimpressed, but I'm over it. It isn't lost on me that we will most likely be having this monetary disagreement for the rest of our lives.

"Normal people? Define *normal* people."

I worry my lip. The only way to define *normal* is to say poor people. Or specifically, those who make an okay living, but are not rolling in it like a certain person not too far away from me.

"People like me," I murmur, hopeful he might just take me to Oxford Street, and let me go anywhere except into a place that was formerly appointed by the Royal family.

"Kara, I'm not listening to this again. I know this is an issue for you, but I absolutely refuse to back down. If I want to buy you something, it's going to happen, so just deal with it. It makes me happy that in some small way, I can make you smile."

I run the back of my hand over his cheek. "Sloan, *you* make me smile. I don't need material things to put a spring in my step. Just knowing you're the first and last thing I see and think of every day, that makes me smile." Satisfied, he closes the door and tells George to take us home.

"Do you want to know what makes me smile?" He gives me a serious look and a high lift of his brows. "Knowing that you love me. Knowing that, by your own admission, one day you'll be my wife and the mother of my sons, and God forbid, any daughters!" He starts to frown, and I tap his cheek.

"What's wrong with daughters?" I laugh at him, feeling my heart expand monumentally.

"Baby, seriously, if they look like you and the boys are anything like me, then I might be doing time for anyone who shows up at our door. You can laugh, but I'm not joking."

I roll my bottom lip into my mouth and continue sniggering. I shake my head at his ridiculousness. He's completely serious, and I'm completely convinced his words are not that farfetched at all. I can absolutely see him running off any boys our future daughters may bring home. But as amusing as that image is, painting a clear, vivid picture in my mind, I also know he will be an extraordinary father.

I pause, staring at him in awe as he turns forward and frowns. *Constantly.* He's thinking about it; I can tell because he isn't hiding it particularly well.

"Stop it!"

"I'm not doing anything." He shakes his shoulders.

"You're thinking, and that's enough."

"I can't help it; the seed has been planted. Shit, what if we only have daughters?" he asks with genuine concern.

"Honestly? Are we seriously discussing this now? Is there really any need? Besides, I already told you, if you touch my pills again, there's a coil ready and waiting with my name on it!" He grabs my hand, kisses it and turns back to staring straight ahead.

As I follow his direction, I can't beat down the berserk butterflies in my stomach. Inconspicuously, I put my hand over my mouth and smile.

One day, hopefully, I'll have dark-haired, blue-eyed children running around my ankles, telling me how much they don't like the word *no*.

The hand gently running through my hair comforts me as I lie close. His interest in our unplanned future has not only planted a seed in his head, but in mine, too.

My mind has been running away with me all evening after his declaration from earlier today. My future has been set in motion by him, and as much as I detest that the men who have entered my life over the years have dictated how my future has been mapped, I could never detest the beauty he is freely offering to me.

My body, although tired, is still alive and humming from every nerve ending at his amazing attentiveness. After finally returning to the hotel after a long day, the morning of which I would rather lockdown and never unearth again, Sloan brought us to new heights, and currently, that passion is still simmering low under the surface of my skin.

"Kara?" His husky, post-sex voice filters through my ears. The hand in my hair stops, glides down the length of my side, and comes to rest on my stomach.

I've been lying here for ages, wide awake, pretending to be asleep. Honestly, I'll never admit it to him, but from this afternoon onwards, I never want this day to end.

There was little that I had to be sad about at the moment; I'm alive, loved, and happy. Yet there's still a vital part missing to complete me, and it came in the shape of two absent women: Sam and Charlie.

Months have passed by now, and no one has heard a peep from Sam. She's never returned any of my calls, and the bottomless pit in my stomach deepens further each time I wonder where she is. I can only hope she is on her mission to leave her mess of a life behind, and endeavour to get clean. And more importantly, to focus on staying clean – should she succeed.

Except, in my heart of hearts, I know that is expecting too much.

Her addiction was born of a life of dependency, and it started while in the womb. It's hereditary in a way that is unheard of. Every member of her family is addicted to something in some shape or form, and that kind of addiction can never be beaten.

And then, on the other hand, there's Charlie. Independent, fiercely loyal, and just as broken inside as I am. Trying to live under the guise of being well put together, but only marginally. Just the same way that Sam has avoided having to deal with me by fleeing to the other side of the country, Charlie has avoided having to deal with me by disappearing completely. For all the shit that Sam has orchestrated to land me where I am today, she knew when it was time to seek forgiveness and walk away. Charlie has merely chosen to sweep it under the rug and forget about it entirely because it's easier for her that way.

Tears run down my cheeks and spike on my eyelashes, as the sad realism is acknowledged inside my heart. How could I ever go back to having a normal conversation with her if we both skirted the subject of the man who had damaged us? Deacon had beaten me raw, purely because he despised Sloan on a level that is almost unimaginable, but Charlie had suffered a fate far worse due to that same hatred. Whilst we both know what it's like to be violated in the safety of our own homes, at least I walked away from whatever Deacon was planning to bestow upon me after shoving me into his car. I was lucky - Sam sacrificed herself so I could keep whatever little dignity still befitted me.

I shuffle, consciously ruffling the sheets so he won't hear my sobs that are protesting to be heard. I have one aim right now - to keep up the pretence that he's slowly waking me. I move over carefully, feeling his chest inflating and deflating evenly on my back. The hand on my stomach rocks me a little in another attempt to wake me from my fake sleep.

"I know you're awake, so you can turn over and talk to me now."

Without thinking, I sigh loudly. Why I ever thought I could trick him was an idea squandered. He knows me better than I know myself. And that fact isn't usually wasted on me. The ways he sees through me are disturbing, and yet I could never turn him out, because one day, he promised to give me the truth. When that day comes, I know I shall have to do the same. Whether it be in a moment of insanity, where I lose my mind and talk through foolishness, or a moment of pure honesty, because it's what we both deserve.

Either way, it will come.

"Talk to me. Please."

He rolls me over, and I'm instantly caught inside his arms. He manipulates me closer, and his warmth surrounds me. His hand drifts up to my cheek, pausing as soon as he touches the wetness he didn't give me time to wipe away. Leaning back, he flicks on the light, and I raise my hand the same moment he looks upon me. He bats my hand away and studies me with concern.

"Kara, you're lying here, stiff as a board, crying into the pillow, and not answering me. Talk to me, *please*."

I walk my fingers up his chest, doing whatever it takes to avoid capturing his gaze. "It's nothing, I'm just... I'm just trying to sort my thoughts out." He gives me a look to continue. I hesitate, knowing even the slightest slip of my tongue will result in dire consequences.

"What's going on inside this head of yours? What's really bothering you?" He slides his finger up and down my cheek. I sigh, there's so much going on inside my head, I'm not certain even *I* can understand. But there is one thing that's really bothering me.

"Is it something I've done?" he asks, worried, and I shake my head.

"No, this is my own doing. I'm just thinking about Sam and Charlie, and why I haven't heard from either of them."

"Sam and Charlie?" His expression tells me he doesn't understand.

"Well, Sam's avoidance is understandable and expected, but why hasn't Charlie been to see me? It's been weeks, months, and nothing." I miss her. I miss her more than I ever thought possible.

"Is that what this is about? Ah, shit, baby, why didn't you say sooner?"

I shrug my shoulders. It wasn't only just this, but how on earth I could broach the elephant in the room, was anyone's guess. We had still yet to discuss properly what had happened to me. Again, my own fault, because each time he endeavoured during the months when I was living at Marie's, I did the usual - I mentally ran. I shut myself off because it's easier than speaking the truth.

"Charlie did come and see you...and she couldn't take it. Seeing you there unconscious, barely hanging on, it hurt her. She stayed away because it broke her heart. You know she has her own demons now. Ones she clings to, ones she can't speak of, the same way you do."

"I realise that, but I just can't help feel that something has changed between us. Deacon assaulted her in ways that are unspeakable, and he hurt me. He did that to us because he hates you. What kind of person does that?"

"The evil kind." His eyes lose all emotion, and he quickly tucks my head into his chest. It's a deliberate act of avoidance.

I inhale against him, experiencing the grinding of his jaw on my skull. "So, when is my new bodyguard showing up?" I ask, blatantly switching the conversation. This is obviously a good change, considering his chest has stopped heaving, and the grinding has waned.

He tilts up my chin until our eyes meet. "Tomorrow. He didn't say what time, but he could be here at the crack of dawn knowing him. Why?"

I shake my head. "Nothing. I just want to get it over with."

"Baby, there's nothing to worry about. You'll like him," he assures me with sincerity.

"Do *you* like him?"

"That's debatable! I do like him, but he winds me up at times." And the last time being the day it all turned to shit between us, if I remember correctly.

Wrapping himself around me, he studies me hard, clearly remembering what we're both so desperate to bury. I sigh and press my lips to his, needing to placate him and soothe my inner apprehension, while forgetting the unforgettable.

"Are you going to work tomorrow?" I ask, lightening the tension. I hope he will say no, and maybe, hopefully, I might get a day of reprieve from yet another one of his friends and their inability to be reasonable.

"Why do you ask?"

"Has Walker found Deacon yet?"

His arms grip me tighter as he huffs against my head. My heart folds, and I know I'll be watching my back from here on out, until he does slip up and re-emerge, or Walker gains some miraculous insight.

"I'm guessing that's a no," I articulate. "Why is it he can't find him? Address, car, phone... Nothing?"

"He lives off the radar, always has. The cars aren't registered to him, and he lives...nomadic."

"Is he still a threat to me?" It's a stupid question, and I know the answer is yes, but again, it's something I need to hear.

"Yes. Can you promise me something?"

I arch an eyebrow. "And that would be...?"

"You listen to Devlin. I might not see eye to eye with him all the time, but please do what he asks. His orders are simple – to keep you safe, and to keep that bastard away from you. If there's something you want to do, a place you want to go to, that's fine, but if he refuses the request, you accept it. Don't put him in a position where he's forced to choose, because trust me, you will lose. I appreciate it will make you ornery, but it will be better than any potential consequences. Can you do that for me?"

Resigned, I close my eyes and nod. I twine my hand in his, bringing his fingers to my mouth. His eyes open further and light up, as I suck his fingers as deep as I can. He groans out and drags me over him. I straddle his lower belly, and he hastily tugs his shirt over my head and palms my breasts. Rolling my nipples between his fingers, my head falls back, and I moan. I rock my wet heat against his hardening length, loving the way he firmly massages my breasts inside his large, skilled hands.

"What do you want me to do?"

I place my hands over his and run them down my body, around my hips and position them on my behind. He squeezes and his fingers dip in between my cheeks. Carefully, I centre most of my weight on my thighs and walk my hands up his stomach and chest. I drop my head and lick his nipples, paying particular attention to one whilst stroking the other.

"Let's try something new. Touch yourself for me. Get yourself wet and ready." I silently baulk. We might have done this before, but it was my decision, whereas this is him ordering me to.

I pull back up on his body with uncertainty, leaving one hand lingering over the fine trail of hair leading down his abdomen.

Sitting fully upright on him, I slowly tease, as I bring one hand down my body, drifting from the curve of my neck. Slowly, I pause at my breast, unsure, and roll my nipple between my fingers. He arches his neck and presses his head harder into the pillow beneath him.

"Fuck, baby," he hisses and jerks between us. I release a breathless gasp, as a large finger traces around my hip bone and disappears into my folds.

I work my hand over my flesh, becoming more comfortable, while his finger presses deep inside me. I grind against him, sliding my body up and down. He hardens his jaw and hisses again, as his finger is removed and replaced with two.

I drag my other hand down his abdomen, until it meets the base of his hard length. Gripping my fingers tight around his thickness, I simultaneously adjust my action to coincide with the speed of his fingers inside me.

"Fuck, that's good! Who owns this, Kara? Who does this belong to?" My eyes hold his, as the edge nears deep inside. I moan out, continuing my plunge and withdrawal on his hand.

"You. You own me. All of me!" Breathless, I move faster, building momentum, pumping my body and hand in perfect synchronisation.

He lifts up, until we are almost touching chests, and the new position gives me the ability to gain leverage. He brings my finger from my centre and sucks it into his mouth. My eyes flutter shut, and I revel in the raptures.

"Eyes always on me when you come." I open as ordered and see the look of absolute ecstasy overcome him. His retreating hand leaves my core empty, then it is replaced by his hard shaft.

"Hands on my shoulders," he says into my chest, guiding me up and down, repeatedly and sinuously. My fingers cut into his skin as I hold on for dear life. The hand he was using to stimulate me quickly moves to my arse, and he presses a finger inside me. I freefall over the edge, crying out unashamed.

"Oh, God!"

"Who owns this, Kara?" I don't answer, namely, because I want to cry tears of joy at how sublimely good his body is at pleasuring mine. "Who owns it, Kara?" he asks again, this time forcing my head up.

"You do; you do!" I pant, all the while my orgasm refuses to die down.

"That's right!" he roars as he lets go. "I. Fucking. Own you. All of you!"

He shudders inside me, and I squeeze hard, conjuring up the last of my energy. He gasps and pushes me back, until my spine rolls onto the bed.

"Turn over. All fours, baby," his husky voice is menacing…and highly arousing.

No sooner have I positioned myself, he is behind me, readying himself. The fine hair surrounding his groin brushes against my skin and his tip is at my entrance. He sweeps my hair to one side and finally places his hand on my shoulder, firm and tight. The other comes around my front and starts to stroke my already wet centre.

"Oh, fuck!" He slides into me in a fluid motion. My back arches immediately as pleasure spikes, igniting every cell. He stills momentarily, before he starts to move in and out with a controlled pace.

After learning his rhythm, I press my body back to his, feeling him hard and deep. He holds me firm, his fingers digging in with each thrust, while he works me intimately with a fierce determination. I press my back down, pushing my arse up, taking him deeper, and he moans his approval.

"Baby, that feels fucking amazing. Again!" he orders, and I obey gladly.

My skin is covered in moisture, and I can feel his hand starting to slip from its death grip on me. Realising this, he slides it under my arm and holds my shoulder from underneath, pulling me harder into him.

The tingles in my body are now full-blown shocks of sensation. The deep ache rocking both sides of my lower body is extreme. "I want to come." I don't know why I'm telling him, I just am. I want him there with me. I want us groaning out in unison.

"Let go for me, baby. Give me what's mine," he commands yet again. Beyond turned on, I give him my release.

"Oh, God!" A trickle of perspiration rolls down my leg, and I call out his name over and over. I'm both lost and found, high yet tethered beneath him.

Ensuring I am thoroughly satisfied, he roars out. He continues to pump in out and, forcing semen to trickle down the inside of my thigh.

He pulls out lightning-fast and flips me over. With his fingers back in my folds and his other hand stroking himself, he sucks and bites my nipples. It's hot and erotic, and I fall apart all over again.

Crying out, eyes wide, he swallows my moans while his tongue stampedes my mouth.

"That's it, my gorgeous girl," he whispers at my lips as he withdraws. "Eyes on me when you come. *Always.*" I tilt my head back and let the last of the most amazing and powerful sensations flow from me.

He's still hard inside me, sucking my bottom lip into his mouth. "Who owns this mouth?"

"You do," I breathe out.

"And these perfect tits?"

"You."

His hand trails down my body, before reconnecting with my swollen centre. He circles his finger at my entrance, teasing me, turning me, spreading our combined arousal. I breathe out, and he gives me a questionable look.

"Yours." My voice is thick all over again.

He smiles and then puts my legs over his hips, levitating my backside off the bed. His hand languishes at my rear entrance.

"And this is definitely mine!" He grins and cages me under him. His semi-hard erection slides over my sensitive flesh, and rests on me. I wrap my arms around him and kiss his nose.

I close my eyes slowly as his hand massages my stomach, sending me into a beautiful and deep euphoric sleep.

"Can I claim you?" I whisper, sensing myself slipping away. He laughs and rolls us on to our sides.

"You already did…the first time I ever saw you."

Chapter 14

THE SOUND OF a door closing and heavy footsteps approaching, stirs me. Sloan cocoons me, wide awake, searching me like a hawk. I murmur at the soreness in my upper thighs and both parts of my core, but it's the best ache I have ever felt.

"Bath?" he suggests. I smile and kiss him vigorously, moaning with abandon.

"Half-brit? You in there?" A strange voice calls out. Sloan quickly grabs the sheets and pulls them fully over my naked body, right up to my chin, forgetting about himself.

"Don't you dare fucking come in here, Devlin!" He pecks my lips, jumps off the bed and quickly dresses in his clothes from last night. I'm amazed there are still there, to be honest. His OCD is obviously running on empty this morning. "Run a bath baby, it'll ease up any soreness. I'll be downstairs."

I stand, allowing the sheet to drop to the floor. I purposely bend over for nothing in particular, and he groans from behind me. Slowly straightening up, I turn to him and lock in on his groin, which is now flying at half-mast and growing.

"Hmm," I purr loudly as I strut into the bathroom, over-exaggerating the sway in my hips as I go.

"God, I'm still recovering from last night. You really do want to finish me off, don't you?" he says, pinching his nose and breathing deeply.

Closing the bathroom door, I laugh to myself, still hearing his deep breaths from the other side. The door opens unexpectedly, and he fills the narrow space to capacity, then he grabs me and kisses me roughly, before letting go.

"My little temptress! I shall never get enough of you. I'll be downstairs when you've finished...and clothes would be good, very good, in fact." He never looks away from my face, although I know he's dying to. He shuts the door again, and his steps retreat from the bedroom.

I duck into the shower rather than the bath, because logic tells me a bath will eat up my Sloan time, even if it will soothe me considerably, since it's been nearly four months without any, or very little sexual contact, and now I've received an abundance of it in as many days. I'm also not sure if he's going to work today, but either way, I'm getting my fill of him, whether he likes it or not.

Thinking up ways I can complete my quota, I study myself in the mirror, and for the first time, I do something I would never have before: I admire myself.

Gone is the old asexual me. The girl who shied away from life; the girl who was fearful of male touch. She is gone forever. The amazing man downstairs has ensured it. And I have to admit, I like the new Kara who is slowly crawling out from underneath her rock for the second time. She's alive and vibrant. And as much as it hurts, she's willing to have her heart broken in a bid to experience love everlasting.

I loiter in the doorway of the walk-in, a towel wrapped around my head. It still looks the same; male to one side, female to the other, but it's worryingly fuller. Now I'm actually glad I shot down a trip to Harrods yesterday. I pick out some teal underwear, skinny black jeans, and a green vintage looking t-shirt, which definitely weren't here before it all turned sour. I towel my hair until it's barely damp, brush it through and fix it into a bun.

I happily pad out of the bedroom and down to the living room. Spying my bag on the table, I dig into it for my pills. Slipping todays into my mouth, I slowly rotate as the smell of bacon, and the sound of Sloan's unique baritone, hit me. Following it trance-like, he is sat at the island, drinking coffee with one of the guys I met the night Emily was hurt all those months ago.

"Baby, this is Devlin. Devlin, Kara," he introduces us again.

"Hi," I greet brightly, offering my hand hesitantly. Devlin drops down one of the two bacon butties he is holding and smiles.

"Nice to see you again, Kara. How are you?" he asks politely, but doesn't take my offered palm.

I study him closely. His chestnut hair is neatly styled at the sides and messy on top. His thick black-framed glasses and check shirt add to the geek chic effect without fail. I can't see any visible tattoos on his fairly large, muscular arms, although I do spy the black plugs in his ears. I can't help but wonder what his story might be.

Sloan, Walker, and even Jake, while exceptionally nice guys, can come across as quite resilient and possessive at times. Devlin, on the other hand, is softly spoken, and if you threw a white coat on him, he wouldn't look out of place in a science lab.

"I'm good, thank you," I answer and shuffle to the kettle.

Stretching up on my toes to grab a mug, Sloan is instantly behind me. With his arm firmly around my waist, his hand stretches wide over my slightly exposed tum, while his fingers graze just underneath my breasts, forcing my nipples to harden.

"Here, my love," he says, handing me a mug. He sits back at the island, but positions himself on another stool, enabling him to watch my every move.

"So, what the hell are you doing here so early? You didn't get announced."

"Early? It's eight o'clock. Besides, I don't need to be announced, boss, I work for you, remember?" Devlin tells him with sass and a mouthful of bacon. I can already see the aforementioned hothead coming out to play.

I suppress my smile at Devlin's mini-tirade as I pour my drink. Standing with my back to them, I wait for my nipples to clue in this isn't the right time to be forward and centre.

Rotating back around, Devlin is grinning to himself, while Sloan is still watching my actions with a curious smirk.

"Are you going to work today?" I enquire, sitting myself down next to him. I consciously fold an arm over my chest without appearing too conspicuous.

He shrugs. "I haven't decided yet. What would *you* like to do today?" His brows shoot up and down suggestively, and I know he wants the same thing I do. Except, my soreness is now physically evident, and I know we have to take this slow, especially if we're going to stand a chance of making it work indefinitely.

"Well, I thought I might call Charlie and see if she wants to go out. I know she blames herself, but it's not her fault. I just want to clear the air, sooner rather than later." I sip my coffee and judge his expression.

"Well, in that case, I guess I'm going to work then." Pouting, he stands and tips his remaining coffee down the sink. He taps Devlin on the shoulder. "Not out of your sight for one minute. I mean it! If anything happens to her or my sister, you and Jake will be hospitalised until the end of your days." Devlin over exaggerates the roll of his eyes.

Sloan then cups my cheeks and drugs me with a passionate kiss. He lets go and swaggers from the kitchen. My expression is vacant as I watch him disappear, but I confess the man renders me speechless.

I take my time to finish my coffee and a couple of slices of toast, while Devlin watches me, obviously trying to figure me out yet again. The silence is awkward, until he gets up and puts his things in the dishwasher.

"Right then, my little charge, I'll call Jake and have him get Charlie out of bed. Hell knows they spend enough time in it, anyway!" He smirks, and my mouth opens in horror. "Don't worry, I've already said it to their faces. Go, get a jacket, and we'll head over to theirs." I nod, shocked. I know it's no longer a big secret, but he could be more tactful.

I race up the stairs and into the walk-in. Choosing a short, fitted, black jacket, I drop it on the bed on my way out. The bathroom door opens, and Sloan stands there in nothing but a towel. Chewing my lip, I allow my eyes to drift over his magnificent physique, while the water drips down his chest, inducing heat to drench my core.

"Enjoying the view?" he teases, approaching me with attitude, the challenge clear in his eyes.

"Absolutely."

He grips my shoulders, pressing a kiss to my forehead, before turning and sauntering into the walk-in. I slip into my jacket and black ballet flats. There's no way I'm wearing heels if I'm going to be traipsing around Knightsbridge and Oxford Street with his sister all day.

Sloan reappears with a black handbag, which he places on the bed. It's beautiful...and Prada. He opens it and hands me a new phone.

"Marie told me you got a pay as you go, but I bought this for you instead. It has all the numbers you need programmed in already," he says cautiously. "Needless to say, I didn't put your parents' numbers in there, or Sam's. That's your choice." He then holds up my old phone, which I haven't seen since the day it all turned on its head. "This is still exactly how you left it. I haven't snooped through the missed calls or messages, although I'll admit it damn near killed me each time it beeped or vibrated. I even charged it for you."

He digs into the bag again, and hands me a black Prada purse. He opens it and passes me a credit card. I start to shake my head, but he stops me.

"No, don't do that. We're together, and I would never deny you anything you want. I want you to be able to buy whatever you fall in love with without having to worry about the cost. I'm also positive

Jake's theory isn't correct and that you won't bankrupt me," he says amused, but I immediately go on the defensive.

"*Sloan...no.*" I begin to shake my head.

"I know, baby. I know money isn't everything to you, but get used to it, because now you have it." He pulls me into his arms and holds me, before releasing me with a resigned sigh.

"Just promise me, if your father contacts you, you'll call me. I'll do whatever I can to deal with it, but I just want you to tell me." He tugs back a little. "John told me what actually happened that day. I'm truly sorry that I made it so much more painful for you. It's obvious now why Sam showed up. I am sorry."

"Me too," I sigh out. "We both have plenty to atone for." I put my phones and purse back into the bag, and turn to the door. Pausing, I look back over my shoulder.

"You're a good man, Sloan Foster. I love you."

He smiles, and my pulse quickens. Gently closing the door behind me, I go downstairs to find Devlin.

"Ready?" he asks.

"As I'll ever be."

He precedes me to the lifts, then halts, giving me a questionable look. One which clearly confirms he's aware. "We can take the stairs, if you like?"

"No, it's not lifts, just small spaces, really. I normally count in my head until it reaches the bottom."

"Count? Knock yourself out, little lady!" His tone is boarding on amusement as the doors close behind us.

Chapter 15

THE LATE SUMMER air is thick and humid, and I have no choice but to remove my jacket as soon as we hit the street. Devlin leaves my side to ask one of the porters to retrieve his car. Rocking on my heels, I slowly move towards George, who is waiting for Sloan.

"Good morning, Kara. It's good to see him in a better mood these days." He winks.

"He'll fire you for saying that, old man!" Devlin says, approaching.

"Enough of the old man, little boy!" he replies, shutting Devlin up.

I turn back to George. "Was he not happy?"

"No, honey. He's been better these last few months, but he was withdrawn and sullen for a long time after I last took you home." I bristle at his confession, closing my eyes, reliving how distraught I had been.

"George, I'm sorry you had to see me like that," I say, meaningful and embarrassed.

"Don't be silly, we all have moments when we are less than our best. You leaving that day was probably the best - and worst - thing that has ever happened to him. It made him realise, and not a moment too soon either."

A convertible BMW slows down in front of us, and Devlin strides towards it. Taking my cue to leave, I lean into George and lightly touch his arm, shoving aside the prickle.

"Thank you."

The sound of giggling compels me to turn at the exact moment Mr Foster finally makes his presence known. Every set of female - and even a few male - eyes in the vicinity turn in his direction. Even I'm bewitched by his raw beauty and power, all perfectly presented in his usual three-piece suit.

He fixes his stare on me, and I approach him slowly, closing down the last few feet that keep us apart. I stand and gape until my mouth is as dry as the Sahara.

He removes his jacket, and passes it, along with his bag, to George, then turns back to me. His fingers trace my arm delicately. "You look beautiful, by the way. Sorry, I should have said earlier." I smile unconvinced - I'm in jeans and a t-shirt.

"That's okay. You look gorgeous, but then again, you always do," I reply, narrowing my eyes from the sunlight reflecting off the glass buildings surrounding us. I allow my fingers to drift over his shirt collar and down his waistcoat, as he pulls me in closer.

"I'll ring you later. I still owe you a proper date, too, since we've got a bit side-tracked lately. I haven't forgotten, and I *will* deliver."

"And when did we decide that?"

"We didn't, I did. I have two months to make up for."

"Actually, it's almost four," I correct him.

"You're never going to let me forget that, are you?" He smiles, running his hand down my shoulder and gripping my waist.

Pulling back, I shrug. "Maybe not. Marie tells me women are good at holding grudges in relationships. Since I have nothing to compare this to, I guess we'll eventually find out if I fit into that mould, too."

He chuckles, and the sun casts down behind him. "I'm looking forward to it. It means I have a reason to reclaim my superseded make up sex!" he states, very self-assured. He puts his lips firmly on mine, then moves away, patting my backside lightly. I blush, thinking about something else he had done with it earlier, whilst thinking of unobtrusive ways I can get him to make me hold a grudge, so said make up sex will find a way to materialise again.

Climbing into the passenger seat of the car, I watch the limo disappear into traffic. Devlin clears his throat, and I raise my brows, daring him to comment.

"What?" he asks innocently, but I don't reply.

Breathing in deeply, I pull out my old phone, dreading what I will find. Four months is a long time to not have any contact. I scrunch my nose and forehead, fearing how many texts and voicemails will be from my dad. Thinking better of it, I slip the phone back into the ridiculously oversized bag, and watch the city transform around us.

My old phone vibrates repeatedly, indicating each new, unread message and voicemail. Still, I know no good will come from them when I finally pluck up the courage to listen with impartiality.

We arrive outside a gated, newly erected, apartment building. The front of house security guard greets Devlin with warm familiarity, and it's abundantly clear he's a regular visitor here, too.

We make our way up in the lift, and his expression is curious, as I stare at the ceiling and silently count in my head. I swear he's dying to piss himself laughing. He notices me watching him, aware of what he's doing and mumbles sorry, before turning away with a smirk.

We exit on the top floor, and Devlin walks to one of four doors and knocks. Jake opens it and bumps fists with him. I move out from behind him and smile shyly.

"Shit, Kara! God, it's so great to see you. Jesus Christ, I thought he had fucked it up royally this time!" He hugs me when I'm close enough, and bizarrely, I don't experience the ghastly prickle, but I don't get it with Walker now, either. It's a realisation that gives me hope that one day, I might get past it altogether.

I glance around the apartment as I enter, taking in the eclectic styles and mismatched accessories. This is definitely Charlie's handiwork.

"So, the boss has finally got his head out of his arse then?" I hear Jake ask Devlin quietly, while I wander around the living space.

"Oh yeah, I'm thinking last night was hot. This morning, too, judging by the looks on their faces when I arrived, and they were still in bed!" Devlin replies with too much zeal for my liking. My face flushes crimson.

I spin round when I hear him begin to open his mouth again. "Quite finished? Or maybe I should call Sloan, and you can talk about it with him, instead?" I suggest calmly. Jake looks ashamed, whereas Devlin just rolls his eyes.

"Parker and Foxy were right - you're no fun, Kara."

"Happy to disappoint you all," I mutter.

"Yeah, sorry, Kara. You just have no idea how glad we all are to see you, that's all." Jake hugs me again. He's so full of honesty, I don't dare not believe him. "He's been so off these last three months or so. As a matter of fact, he's been an absolute fucking nightmare. Doc's even threatened his arse with euthanasia a time or two. I was hoping when you guys finally reconciled, he would pull the stick out of his arse!" I blush, the images flooding my brain from last night are running wild and out of control.

"Where's Charlie?" I ask, a little flustered, feeling my face redden further.

"She's upstairs. I didn't tell her you were coming over until security buzzed you up. She kicked me out of the bedroom and locked the door. She blames herself, Kara," Jake confides apologetically, handing me a key. "See if you can talk some sense into her. Upstairs, last door at the end of the landing."

I put my bag on the sofa and make my way upstairs. The long hallway is lined with glass and wood doors, and I speculate how many of them are packed with clothes and accessories.

I look at the large black and white pictures as I pass, and am stopped short by the one of Charlie, as she is now, with a woman who looks almost identical to her. It's like looking at a mirror image, possibly seeing her as she will be in twenty years' time. I stare at it with narrow, probing eyes, wondering if it's an aunt, since their mother had passed long ago.

Muttering from the end of the landing piques my attention and encourages me to turn. A door opens, and Charlie walks out in a robe. Her face instantly drains of colour when she sees me. Even from this minute distance, she looks clearly horrified.

"Hi," I smile. Her features sadden, and she starts raising her arm over her face. We approach each other, and I stall a little, but she grabs my arm and quickly marches us back down the landing and into the room. As I look back, I can see her eyes flash over the spot I had just been standing on, before she closes the door.

"Please, don't cry, it's not your fault. If it wasn't me, it would've been some other woman. You can't blame yourself for someone else's actions." I run my hand over her hair. It's a strange feeling to play the comforter again, but it has to be done, whether it sits well with me or not. I'm impressed with myself that I've hugged two people in the space of ten minutes and not gotten the feeling of anxiety with either of them.

Her sobs against my chest leave a damp spot just above my right breast. I'm beyond caring - I just want her to be comfortable in my presence. I don't want her hurting when I'm not. Well, that isn't entirely true, but neither of us would be able to move past this if she pitied me, or blamed herself, whenever we saw each other.

She eventually let's go, putting her finger on the damp patch. "Oh, Kara, crap, I'm sorry. I'll get you something else to wear." She guides us into an adjacent room, of which the contents alone make my eyes water.

How on earth can someone own so much clothing?

Although between the house and the hotel, I'm not too far behind myself.

Sitting on a stool next to the dressing table, my eyes rake over the watches and gem-encrusted jewellery on the top in astonishment. She hurries back with a green silk blouse and smiles at my expression of awe.

"Sorry, this is the nearest green I have to your t-shirt. Oh, that belonged to my mother, given to her by her mother, and her mother before her...you get the picture." I tentatively touch the bracelet. It's one of the most beautiful things I have ever seen.

"It's stunning. Sloan gave me a bracelet in the hospital, it also belonged to your mum. I'm honoured to wear it." I hold out my wrist to show her, and she nods, approvingly.

Taking the blouse from her, I turn around for some privacy. Lifting the t-shirt over my head, I hear her breathe in harshly, no doubt seeing the new scars gracing my back courteously of Deacon's beating and being thrown against a wall like a rag doll. I quickly slip the blouse on and turn. They actually look much better now than when I was first admitted, or so I'm told. Even though they no longer hurt, the reminder is permanent. Still, her reaction is better than the one I got from her brother when he first saw them properly in the hospital shower.

"Did he hurt you really bad?" she asks, clutching her robe.

"I don't know. I don't remember," I reply quietly. I'm not comfortable lying to her, but there's no other way around it. If I had my way, I would make myself forget again, except you can't forget evil when it's staring you straight in the face with a sneer.

Years ago, after the event, one of my many psychologists said my memory would come back in time, and that my mind was currently blocking out all that had happened to me, not just the rape, but everything that came before. This could join them as far as I'm concerned. It could stay blocked out for all eternity with the rest of the untold depravity. But that isn't the case this time. And it's impossible and pointless to wish, because even years' old memories are coming back with fierce determination now. I shall always remember because my mind hasn't given me a reprieve like before, and everything in the darkness eventually comes into the light.

"Come on, let's go shopping," I announce a little too happily, and partially disturbed with myself. Shopping isn't my thing; it's Charlie's. But that is why I'm here - to build bridges and heal with her.

"Your brother ordered me to spend. I think he will have a

coronary if I don't!" I say, faking shock.

She gives me a pained smile that doesn't reflect in her eyes, before going to get dressed.

Watching her leave, I doubt even retail therapy will make her crack a smile today.

Chapter 16

YESTERDAY, I HAD a lucky escape.

Today, I'm not so fortunate.

We have been walking around the stores for hours, and my feet are screaming. Jake and Devlin trail behind, carrying the multitude of bags.

Regardless of Sloan's explicit instructions, I've been sparse with his credit card. Although, when Charlie dragged me into Armani, I couldn't resist buying some shirts that took my fancy. I'm thankful she is with me, because as much as I'm familiar with the contours of his chest and shoulders when they are pinned up against me, I wouldn't have a clue of what size shirt to wrap them up in.

We are deciding where to go for lunch, when my new phone rings from inside my new bag. "Hi," I answer shyly, knowing only one person could be calling it.

"Hi, baby, are you having fun?"

I let out a small chuckle. Shopping isn't fun; it's annoying. Especially, when the sales assistants look at you and deem that you either have no money, or a lot of it. At this moment in time, I'm not quite sure which category I fall into.

"I'm okay. You'll be pleased to know I bought a dress, some heels, and a jacket that I don't actually need. And, you've also bought yourself some new shirts! Say thank you – graciously!" I giggle.

He laughs. "That's great, baby, thank me! How's Charlie?" His voice grows sombre. "Is she okay?"

"She's good. We talked a little. Well, I mainly talked, and she mainly listened. It's hard, but I think she'll always blame herself if something happens involving him. Anyway, we're going to have some lunch and give Jake and Devlin a break from sitting outside dressing rooms."

"So, how's Dev been treating you? If he says anything untoward, call Walker, he'll straighten the little shit out."

"Okay. What's the deal with them?" Walker had already told me what he was like, but I didn't know much about him.

"Ah, sorry, I forgot you don't know. He's John's nephew. He got into trouble some years back in the army, and John put him on the straight and narrow. Why?" The sound of rustling papers echoes through the line.

"Nothing. He doesn't act all tough and military-like. He doesn't even look like it, actually." The sound of Sloan's belly laugh pinches my eardrums, and I wish I was with him right now.

"No, he was more intelligence than front line. He's just very much in touch with his kinder side. I guess being the only boy with five sisters doesn't help. It made him a very good fighter, though. He has a belt in something or other." I hear tapping in the background like there's someone at his door.

"Oh, right. Do you think he would teach me some moves if I asked him?" I query nonchalantly. The direction my life is heading at the moment, the more I learned how to defend myself, the better.

Sloan's long, silent pause makes me twitch. It tells me he probably isn't impressed with the brilliance of my new idea.

"I'm sure he would, my love, but you don't need to. I'll always be with you, or someone else will. There's no need to learn self-defence."

I sigh a little too loudly, then hear someone on Sloan's end clearing their throat. "Am I keeping you from something?"

"No, not at all. Ken and I are just waiting for a client to arrive." He's all business now. The slight hum of a male voice tells me I'm loud and clear in his office.

"Am I on speakerphone?" The sound of a muffled male laugh tells me I am.

Good job I didn't thank him for a wonderful night!

"You are, my love. Call me when you want to come home, I'll have George come and collect you." The sound of happiness in his voice is tangible, and I wish I could bottle it up and listen to it over and over.

For a single moment, it feels like the last four months have never happened. Except, we both know better since my nakedness exhibits the reality.

"Actually, I was going to spend some time with Charlie this evening. Maybe watch a film. A little more girl bonding will do us both some good right now."

"That sounds great. However, call me when you want to come home." His tone is commanding, and a tingle sweeps over my body. I stay on the line and visual my thoughts of telling him that I love him.

Would it be unprofessional to say it when he has me on speakerphone and his business associates with him?

He takes a breath. "Oh, and baby?" His voice kicks through my haze. "You refused me the other day, but go buy another dress...for me."

"Ah, you do cross-dress at weekends!" I giggle, and his companions do, too.

"Quite! Seriously, nothing too formal, but preferably something that's ridiculously sexy and easy to remove!"

I gasp that he has the audacity to say it in company. Evidently, Ken and his client are, too, since there's only silence behind his laugh now.

"Are you still there?"

"Hmm, I'm still here." *I think.*

"I love you."

"I love you, too. I can't wait to see you later."

My arms are laden with clothes outside the dressing room.

I have found the perfect LBD; strapless and knee-length, much like the dress he bought me for our first date. I have even managed to unleash the hidden co-ordinated side of myself and bought a green sash that matches my eyes. While waiting for Charlie to hurry up, I admire it on the hanger, but still feel nervous about the price on the tag.

Eventually, the door opens quickly, and she stands in front of me in a simple, pale blue, summery shift dress. It's elegantly cut and is more of a business dress than a day at the beach. She bobs her head up and down, and I have to agree - she wears it well. Very well, in fact.

A little stab of jealousy hits me, knowing I will never be able to carry off half of what she wears.

Thinking back to the first time I saw her, I smile a little. A smile only I will understand.

I thought you were the biggest bitch walking when I first met you.

Suddenly, she spins around quickly, shocked and upset.

Oh, shit! I slap my hand over my mouth.

"I'm sorry. I didn't know you then, but you were fairly rude to me. Even you have to admit that," I add quickly, keeping my tone light.

She slaps both hands on her hips, waiting for...I have no idea. My hand is still over my mouth, since I've shocked even myself with my outburst. Her upset expression slowly gives way to a smile, then she laughs.

"I know you did, that was the whole idea!" she says, unzipping the dress and letting it pool at her feet, leaving her in only her simple white underwear. I should be embarrassed at such a brazen display, but considering I have been sitting here for so long my behind is numb, I'm past caring.

"Sloan already told me. After we left the ballroom, he said he liked you, and wanted to get to know you. I admit, I really wasn't for it. Like I said before, he doesn't do longevity or permanence, and suddenly he decides he wants to try his hand at love?" Her expression and tone are both suspicious, but I'm not insulted, because I feel the same. After all these months, I'm still waiting for a plausible answer I know I'm never going to get.

"Anyway, I asked him to give me your number so I could meet you myself, but he wasn't having any of it. In the end, I had to resort to sneakier tactics," she says gleefully, dropping herself into the seat next to mine. I turn towards her and grin, today is definitely becoming more interesting.

She nudges my shoulder. "Did you ever find out how I really got your number?" I move my head slowly. As though reading my mind, she giggles. It's girly and full of fun, and I find myself waiting impatiently for her to answer.

"Walker?"

"Nope, Jake. I threatened to make him sleep in the spare room. He cried to Sloan about it. He was being pathetic; can you imagine? Still, I wasn't happy at all. We've kind of been on and off for years, but I didn't want him finding out about us like that, but typical big brother, he already knew. Said it was about time we came clean. So that's how I got your number, nothing too drastic, but enough to put the fear of God into Jacob." She winks and finally proceeds to put her own clothes back on. I stare down at the pile of stuff she has chosen.

"Now, let's eliminate!"

I groan.

Shopping definitely isn't my thing.

Standing in front of the flat screen, Charlie holds a DVD box in either hand. "So, we can watch girls chasing guys -" she holds up one box, "- or guys chasing girls!" She holds up the other.

I'm sitting on the floor with my back resting on the sofa. "Is there a third option?" I ask, hopeful, but she shakes her head. "Okay, girls chasing guys, it is then." I point to her left hand.

I pull a few cushions from the sofa and get comfortable. Charlie crowds in next to me and does the same. We are surrounded by sweets, wine, and ice cream, and it hits me that I've never had a real girly night in with anyone other than Sophie, and very rarely, over the last few years, with Sam.

Samantha.

My heart begins to hurt just thinking about her. No one has heard from her. I need to know she's okay, that Deacon hasn't found her again. I hope she's trying to get clean. I have to know - she's as good as my sister.

Shaking her from my thoughts, the film starts to play, and I rest my head back against the sofa.

"Deacon hurt me," a voice whispers in my subconscious. I yawn and raise my hand to my mouth. Rubbing my eyes, I see that it's past midnight, and I have obviously fallen asleep.

Oh, shit, I didn't call him like I promised!

Fumbling for my phone, Charlie grabs my hand. "He knows you're still here. Security don't let anyone come up unannounced. *Ever.*" She lets go and tangles her fingers in mine. She studies me for long, silent minutes, judging whether or not to tell me what she needs to finally release.

Eventually, she does.

"When I was fourteen, I was staying with Sloan for the weekend when he was at uni, and Deacon came into my room..." The tears spoil her small voice as they threaten to leak from her eyes. She stares at me anxiously, and I don't know what to say to her.

Do I tell her about my past? The times I had woken up sore and disorientated? God, even Sloan doesn't know the half of it. Do I dare tell her, knowing she might tell him? I fight my inner turmoil and decide it's better to just listen.

"He said he would kill me if I told anyone. I was so frightened, he hit me and put his hand over my mouth so I couldn't scream." The sobs tear from her throat as she cries into my shoulder. I wrap my arm around her - one little girl lost, trying to soothe another.

My rage simmers just below the surface, while she continues to recite what he did to her. I want to lash out at the way we've both been hurt, but I can't. It's too raw, and I remember far too easily what it's like to have free will violently ripped away from you.

"Sloan found me after he ra..." She doesn't finish, and I silently release my own tears as she fills the room with hers.

I can't even begin to imagine what must have gone through his head the moment he found his little sister - who was only a teenager at the time, just like I was - in that state. I shudder at the graphic visual my mind creates. It's a mixture of her words and my own damning past, and I now see why he's filled with hatred. Just like me, she will always live with it, but unlike me, she didn't have to live in silence.

For a split second, I close my eyes and remember.

I'm no longer alone in my cubbyhole hiding.

At long last, I have a true friend who understands my pain completely. Because Charlie is right there beside me, holding my hand under a shroud of darkness, praying not to be found.

Chapter 17

THE STREETLIGHT OUTSIDE floods through my bedroom window as the door slams. I jolt upright, disorientated, still half asleep, to see a figure lounging at the foot of my bed. I grab the covers and pull them up to my neck, trying to hide.

The man slowly comes closer and pauses, before he snatches away the duvet covering me. He throws it to the floor, and I scramble up the bed until my back hits the headboard.

Gripping my foot, he drags me back down as I kick out, hoping to hurt him. Instead, he twists a hand around my ankle, causing it to burn.

"Are you going to be a good girl?" he asks me sadistically. I start to mumble and sob, but he ignores my whines and protesting. He climbs on top of me and starts to lift up my night vest. I tug the hem back down as he continues to lift, until the sound of tearing ripples around the room.

"Mum!" I scream out, hoping she will come and save me. Time passes slowly as I wait for my door to open, but it remains shut.

My shorts are slid down my legs as the man leans down to my ear. "Call all you want; she won't help you. Nobody will because they don't care! Now stay still, little one, this will only hurt for a second."

A painful prick on my arm sweeps through my body, until I feel light and strangely fuzzy. I've never felt like this before. I raise my hand, and the feeling is completely weightless. My limbs are being moved, but I don't seem to have the ability to stop them. Or the ability to call out again.

I feel like I am drifting.

"The first time always hurts, sweets, but I can't promise I'll be gentle," he says, pressing inside me, taking away my innocence. The man's silhouette looms over me again, stealing the light, until I'm hidden by his shadow and consumed in his pain.

The sound of sobbing haunts the apartment, as the light of dawn penetrates the darkness outside.

I shuffle towards the window, remembering the past, hugging an oversized cushion for post-nightmare comfort. The sun is trying to break through the clouds outside - the promise of a new day. Only, underneath the exterior, every day is the same.

I glance in the direction of the muffled sound of tears, and walk aimlessly along the landing, until I stop.

Charlie.

I want to go in there, and comfort her, and tell her that everything will be okay, but I'm no fool. I know nothing can erase the horror that she lives with daily. I know this because, I too, exist in the same place she does. A place where soap and water don't wash away the dirt and the shame. A place that is alive inside your mind. A place that forces you to relive it when you least expect it.

Rotating on my heels, I turn back towards the sofa, when the sound of breaking glass alerts me to the presence of someone in the apartment other than us. I grab the phone and steady my finger over the keys. It's stupid to think I'll even be able to dial the first number, but a false sense of security is vital right now.

Edging stealthily towards the kitchen, a man mumbles and swears to himself. I tilt my head around the door, and let out the breath that I'm holding so fervently.

"What the hell are you doing, Jake? You frightened the living shit out of me!" I scream at him.

"Sorry, Kara. I didn't know you were awake," he replies, picking up the broken glass.

I ease onto a stool and watch him. My eyes might be on him, but my mind and hearing are elsewhere. The sound of painful memories is audible, holding everything in their path hostage, including me.

"I think she needs you," I say quietly.

He shuts his eyes and dips his head down. "Yeah...yeah, she does, but I don't know what to do anymore. There are times when she shuts down completely if I do something or say something. Most of the time, I don't know what it is I do wrong. It's getting worse, even more so lately."

And there's the painful truth, Jake brings the darkness out of her, like Sloan brings it out of me. And while I can't speak for Charlie, it's because deep down, I feel unworthy of his unconditional love.

Jake raises his head towards me. It's a stare that tells me he's informed. "Maybe you should go in." He says it so softly, I barely hear him. I move my head from side to side slowly.

"No, that's your job. If you love her, you comfort her. My own experience will only make it worse. What she needs right now is to be held by the man who loves her." He nods at my words, but I understand what he's saying - he can't turn her darkness into light, the same way he can't undo the past that still torments.

"She finally told you then? What the bastard did?" He stares at me, like he's wondering if he should say whatever is on the tip of his tongue.

"Yes, she did."

"Does Sloan hold you, when you do...*that*?" He points in the direction of the bedroom.

Running my hand over my brow, I shake my head timidly. "No, because I don't do *that* out of choice. I've spent the majority of my life trying to block *that* out, but he makes me remember. And the reason why I remember, is because each time he holds me, it feels natural, and I have to wonder why. He seems to know my past, or at least has an understanding, although I have never fully told him. I don't even know why I'm telling you." He quickly turns away with an expression filled with guilt.

He definitely knows something.

A door creaks open, and small footsteps beat on the hard floors and down the stairs. Charlie stops just inside the kitchen. Her eyes are red and swollen as she stands there, somewhere between broken and defeated. I take in her small frame, as she looks at us both apprehensively. Jake walks towards her and scoops her into his arms. She struggles a little in protest, then finally relents. I silently excuse myself from the room.

Hunting down my bag, I text Sloan to let him know I'm more than ready to come home. Dropping the phone down, I run up the stairs into the bathroom, and dress in the loaned shorts and t-shirt, making myself as presentable as possible.

I silently pray he doesn't recognise the aftereffect of my latest nightmare, and Charlie's damning confession when he eventually arrives.

Hard knocking on the door, followed by feet approaching, rouses me awake. I open my eyes, realising I've been snoozing on the sofa. Sloan, Walker, and Tommy are standing in front of me, staring at me. I look over each of them, and then make eye contact with the same man who was sitting in my flat with Sam all those months ago.

Tall, well over six foot, he is just as attractive as I remember. He also looks just as guarded, too. He watches me closely, and starts to move into the small space separating us.

"Hi, I'm Jeremy. Most call me Remy or Jer. Take your pick." He holds out his hand. I look at Sloan, wanting him to confirm he's safe, and he nods.

"Hi, again," I reply, ignoring his hand and shielding my eyes from the sun flowing into the room.

Jake and Charlie then enter, and I'm grateful the sound of pain no longer fills the void. I glance innocently around the room, as Charlie takes a seat beside me on the sofa and squeezes my hand in silent contemplation.

She looks like a completely different woman from the one I had witnessed earlier. I cast my sight around the room, then give her a small smile. She rolls her eyes and laughs, as we take in the empty ice cream tubs and wine bottles.

Walker looks astonished, surveying the mess. "What? No beer?" he asks sarcastically, and I laugh out loud.

Thinking up a witty retort, my attention is diverted when two big hands come under my arms from behind, and I'm momentarily airborne. Ready to voice my disapproval, I smell the familiar masculine scent, and the unmistakable feeling of the man I adore under my thighs. He sits me across his lap, and his eyes start to narrow at my exposed, bare legs. I shrug at his silent questioning of why I'm not properly dressed and where my clothes are. He shakes his head grudgingly, but lets it go.

"What are you all doing here?" Charlie asks, as she picks herself up and starts collecting up some of the litter.

"Missing you obviously," Jake says affectionately and only to her, pulling her in tight.

I wait for Sloan's verbal intervention. She might be a grown woman, but she is still his little sister, and no doubt he doesn't want to see her in a state of undress being mauled by a man, close friend or not. Strangely, he doesn't even flinch at the spectacle.

"Actually, Remy came to tell us about...well, I guess it can wait until later," Tommy says, eyeing Sloan before turning back to the flat screen, remote in hand. Taking a good look at him, the first thing that screams at you is the wild red hair. Not ginger red, it's a darker shade with hints of brown. He's smaller than Walker, but still a large guy. He turns and gives me a smile, and I reciprocate.

I twist to Sloan, who palms my cheeks and starts to move my hair back. "My landlord left another message about the flat again. He said he has a new tenant coming in next month, so I need to clear my stuff out by the end of next week." He smiles, but the moment is lost when his features harden, and he frowns, recollecting something.

"Will that rapist bastard be there?" he spits out venomously.

Danny.

How could I forget his abhorrence for my old landlord's son?

I fidget in his hold, but this only makes him grip tighter. "I guess," I say, not wanting to meet his eyes. "He apologised for what he did. I think I'll be okay on my own," I grumble weakly.

"Fuck, no! If he's there, then you're not going alone. Right, who's got some free time this week?" he shouts out to anyone listening. Charlie's hand shoots up - *God bless her* - and I smile, although I know she's going to be shot down in flames any minute.

"No fucking way! Get your hand down, Charlotte!"

"Excuse me, dear brother, but I'm doing it for Kara, not you. She's my friend, and if you don't let me, I'll just drive myself over there, anyway!"

His chest heaves. "Why do you women insisting on doing everything the hard way?" he asks, annoyed. He's pissed off, and he rubs his hand across his face while his jaw twitches. I lean in and kiss his chin.

"Maybe you're just lucky," I whisper in his ear. Walker and Tommy titter between themselves, confirming I said it in more than a whisper.

Sloan's hand trails up my thigh and stops just before the juncture of my legs. The clearing of a throat stops him immediately, and he peers up infuriated at whoever has the audacity to interpose his groping.

"Come on, Foster! I came to talk to you about serious shit, and instead, you drag me all the way out here, and now you're making out with your woman, deciding who's clearing fucking house!" Remy shouts in frustration. "If it means you'll give *me* some time, I'll help her move! Besides, it might be the best course of action, especially if *he* thinks she trusts me."

Sloan moves, so my back is nestled tighter to his chest. "I don't like it, Rem, think of something else." His tone is firm, with a hardness that induces a cold sweat to ripple through me like wildfire.

"Let her do it by herself then," Remy replies sarcastically, shrugging his shoulders.

Sloan's hands pinch my flesh, and his jaw hardens and twitches all over again. His eyebrows arch at Remy. "Fine! But remember, *she* is an extension of *me*, and if anything happens to her, you'll deal with me. Got it?"

Remy rolls his eyes exasperated and nods.

"Have you got it, Jer? Fucking say it!" Sloan shouts at him.

"For fuck sake! Yeah, Sloan, I've got it! I'll get a van hired, and then give you a call for a day next week sometime."

"Do you have any preference, baby?" I shake my head in response.

"No, just as long as it's not Thursday. I have an appointment, remember?" I give him a look, and he nods.

Thursday is going to become my new shrink day, I think. It's going to become the day I lose myself in the past while trying to forge a future.

Remy gives me a small smile. "Okay, I'll get it sorted, and organise for a charity shop to come and pick up whatever you don't want."

Remy doesn't wait for the *thank you* on the tip of my tongue and saunters off into the kitchen.

"I'm proud of you," Sloan murmurs into my neck. I know he's referring to my willingness to see David, but one session isn't something to be proud of just yet.

"Don't speak too soon," I mutter, as he kisses my cheek.

Chapter 18

"HEY, WHAT YOU up to today?" Sophie's voice carries over the line.

It's just gone one o'clock, and I've spent all morning doing the usual when I have nothing else to do – cleaning. The worst part about being on unnecessary sick leave – the loneliness and boredom.

"Huh, same as every day – nothing. Marie's still refusing to let me come back to work, so I'm bored shitless. Why?" I reply, far too honestly, as I run my hand over the wall of glass that makes up the living room window.

The day has brightened considerably since I drew the curtains back this morning. The light patter of rain outside has dried up, and the sun is forcing its way through the pale, grey clouds above.

Sophie lets out a tiny squeal. "Good, meet me at the pub for lunch. I'm taking half a day off. Maybe we can hit Oxford Street?"

I lean my head towards the glass and allow my forehead to graze it. That would make shopping the top of the agenda for two days running – three, if I hadn't managed to talk Sloan down from the ledge.

I turn and look over at the kitchen, remembering the way he intoxicated me before leaving for work this morning. It took nothing more than a touch of his lips and a swipe of his tongue to make my senses take a leave of absence. Five hours later, I'm still trying to pull myself back together.

"Sure, but I need to call Devlin. I promised I wouldn't do the solo thing considering what happened last time." I wait for her response. Again, there is long, unwelcome silence.

"No, that's fine, understandable really. Except, he can't sit with us. I have stuff to tell you!" Her voice radiates excitement, and I guess it has something to do with a tall, fair-haired, handsome doctor we both know.

"Stuart?"

"No! I'm not telling you anything until you meet me. Now get calling Devlin and get your cute behind over here!"

"What you're already there?"

"Of course, I am! Have been for an hour. Hurry!"

"Soph, how much have you had to drink?" I squeal out, worried that my best friend is currently on course to sign up for AA meetings.

"Not enough!" she mimics my tone.

"Do you mind if I call Charlie to join us?"

"No, of course not, she's more than welcome. See you soon!" she says with an inkling of a slur, and I laugh to myself. My afternoon isn't going to be a long one. She's just as lightweight as I am, and that means there will definitely be no shopping of any kind!

I scroll through the contact list on my new phone, looking for Devlin's number, when my old phone starts to ring from inside my bag. I lean back slightly, as though it may jump out like a Jack in the Box and cause me harm. I roll my eyes, there's only one person who would be calling that number. And trust me, he has inflicted plenty of harm against me. Grabbing the handset, I stare at the number I don't recognise. I hesitate to call it back, but my gut tells me to leave it well enough alone.

Dropping my old phone back into my bag, I fist my new one and slide the screen again. I wait, tapping my foot, as I dial Devlin's number with no luck. Scrolling down the list, I hit Sloan's office number.

"Good afternoon, Emerson and Foster, Gloria Truman speaking." Gloria's warm, motherly tones sing out on a happy note. Something tells me she has the art of that greeting down. I bet she's having the worst day ever.

"Hi, Gloria, it's Kara. Is Sloan available?"

"Oh, hello darling. Sure, give me a minute, I'll put you through," she replies.

"Erm, Gloria?"

"Hmm?"

"Are you having a good day?"

She sighs out an exasperated breath. "I work for Sloan, Kara. My answer is the word he hates!" The answer is no, just as I thought.

"Just asking! Bye." She bids me farewell, and the classics start to play, until he finally answers.

"Foster?"

"Hello, Foster; Petersen here," I greet him shyly. I know I should have gotten over it by now, but he brings it out of me unknowingly.

"Hey, my love, Gloria didn't say it was you. What's wrong, are you okay?"

"I'm fine. I just wanted to let you know that Sophie called and wants me to meet her for lunch, but I can't get in touch with Devlin." I start to climb the stairs to collect my things.

"Okay, I'll get John to come and pick you up."

"No, seriously, you don't have to go to that much trouble, I'll drive myself. I'm sure he has more interesting things to do than babysit me." I stop in the doorway of the bedroom, the smell of him fills my nostrils to capacity, while his voice fills my hearing.

"Baby, it's no trouble. You know he adores you; he has for a long time."

And there is another open, one hundred per cent honest revelation. He isn't even trying to hide it now, and I know I should be chomping at the bit to find out the truth, but a promise is a promise.

I bite down on the inquisitive side of my brain, which is currently screaming a hundred and one different things to me, hoping I will relay them. But I don't and I won't. I trust him, regardless of how unwise it may transpire to be.

"Thank you," I say.

"I love you. Call me later on when you're both finished, and I'll come and meet you. I want to take you somewhere."

"The Savoy?" My eyes widen, but I know it's definitely not The Savoy.

"You're obsessed! No, not that place. Somewhere better. It's huge and secluded, and the owner has an amazing swimming pool..." he rambles on, listing all the beautiful, amazing things inside and outside his mansion. The last words out of his mouth are *woodland trail*, before I cut him off.

"I don't have a swimsuit or hiking boots, genius," I laugh out. I'm pointing out the obvious, but I know I will not be wearing either inside his house.

"Don't worry, you won't be needing them, smart-arse!" My body clenches in all the right places as invisible water laps at my back. "I'll be expecting your call, my gorgeous girl."

"Don't you worry, Foster, you've just guaranteed it. I love you. Bye," I whisper, trying to calm myself down.

My hand shakes on the screen as I find Charlie's number. She picks up after the fourth ring. "Yes?" she answers sharply, sounding flustered. I frown, hoping I've not interrupted something I shouldn't have.

"Hi, it's me. Are you okay?" I query, noting her laboured breathing.

A huge sigh ripples over the line. "Fine, but I'm going to kill Ken! I swear he does it on purpose!"

"Okay," I say slowly, misunderstanding. "I'm meeting Soph for lunch. Want to join us?"

"I'd love to, but I'm too busy sorting out the idiot's office! Why I have to work for the most inept man on the planet, I have no idea!"

"What, you're at work?" It flies from my mouth before my brain has a chance to engage. "Sorry, I didn't mean for it to sound like that." I correct myself quickly.

"Yes, of course I'm at work! What do you think I do all day - shop? Granted, I only work part-time, but yeah, I do actually make a half honest living for myself. What did you think I did? Live out of big brother's pockets?"

I screw my face up, because that's exactly what I thought she did - half does. Oh, I don't know. I stay mute, knowing any response I give will be the wrong one.

"You so did! I work for Ken at the office." And finally, the penny drops when Gloria walked me around. "Trust me, it's days like today when I could murder Sloan for making me do it. He says it will keep me honest and in touch with reality, whatever that means! Anyway, like I said, I'd love to, but I really can't," she confirms, exasperated.

"Okay, well next time then?"

"Absolutely, I'll see you later," she says, before hanging up. I stare at the handset in wonderment. The idea of her actually working for a living never occurred to me. It also conjures up a variety of different images of what she must be like in a working environment, especially with big brother in the CEO's seat. I laugh to myself uncontrollably.

In the bedroom, I pick out a jacket and pull on my boots, and wait for the concierge to call up.

As I make my way downstairs, I hear my old phone ringing yet again. And, yet again, I let it go to voicemail. Finding the courage to listen, I dial into my messaging service and wait for the outstanding new voicemails to come through. I don't have to wait long.

You have two new messages.

One of two.

"You can't avoid me forever, sweets! Kara, I need to speak to you,

calling me fucking back! I mean it, if I don't hear from you..."

He hangs up.

Two of two.

"You've had your one and only chance! He's coming, mark my words!"

You have no new messages.

Maybe not for now.

I shudder and shake the ranting from my head. I knew I shouldn't have given in to temptation. I had deleted all the old ones before listening to them. It was a stupid schoolgirl error to listen to these.

The phone starts to vibrate again, and it's the same number as before. Intrigue gets the better of me, and I answer, but don't speak.

"Kara, are you there?" my mother asks from the other end.

I let out a breath. "Hi, Mum, I'm here. Where did you get the phone from?" I ask, since she has never had one. Anytime I've wanted to speak to her over the years, I've had to jump through Ian's hoops first.

"I got it a while ago; I just didn't have the heart to call you. Look, I can't stay on the line for long, but you can get me on this number. Sorry, I don't know what it is, I had to get yours from your dad's phone when he was asleep."

"Sorry, Mum, but I don't understand," I say, realising her call is more goodbye than hello.

"I'm leaving Manchester. Franklin is back, and I can't live like that again. You were right all those years ago, I should have left with you. I put him first, and I lost you. I never should've let you walk out of here alone." I slouch against the wall, hearing my mother say the words I have longed to hear for many years.

"It's okay," I reply. Except, it's not okay, and it never will be. There were times I needed her, and she thought of me last. I was too guileless at the time to expect anything different.

"No, it's not. I should have protected you, and I didn't. I'll make it up to you, baby. I promise I will. Look, I'll call you again when I have a place to stay. I love you, baby. I'll call soon. Bye." The line goes dead, and my eyes fix on the rug in front of me, as I toy with the idea of calling her back. Lost in my own head, the sound of the suite phone ringing brings me back.

"Hello?"

"Your chauffeur awaits!" Walker states perfunctory and hangs up. I put the receiver down and pad into the hallway.

Standing in front of the mirror, I double-check my appearance, making sure any tell-tale signs of unhappiness are banished for the short term. The last thing I need is Walker making observations, and then subsequently reporting in. Satisfied my expression is not giving anything away, I start to collect my things when the phone rings again.

"I'm out front on double yellows. If I get ticketed, you're paying!" John laughs and hangs up.

Yeah, right! I had flouted those rules twice, and I never got a ticket! I bet he could talk his way out of anything if he was required to.

Engaging the security system, I leave the suite and wait for the lift. Not because I want to, but because it has permanent CCTV, whereas they are intermittent on the stairs. Who would have thought the lift would prove to be more secure than the stairs? But I knew that was subject to change in the next few months. I overheard Walker and Sloan talking about ramping them up so there wouldn't be any more blind spots, and movement could be tracked more accurately throughout the building.

I really do have to stop with my eavesdropping, one day it's going to get me into some serious bother.

I walk out of the lift and into the foyer, greeting everyone as I go by. These days I even get a smile from James. It's a far cry from the first time I showed up here, and he wanted to turf me out on my arse.

He and Laura are manning the front of house as I pass, and she quickly waves. I am starting to like them both, truth be told. They have assisted in making these last few months liveable. Most likely at the insistence of Sloan, one of them comes up and checks on me throughout the day, making sure I have everything I need. They even book out their boss's preferred table in the hotel's restaurant, just so I have something other than the suite walls to look at, day in day out.

"Good afternoon, Kara. Nice of you to grace us with your presence on this fine day!" James says dramatically. His eyes gleam with honesty, while Laura shakes her head beside him.

"Afternoon to you, too!" I counter, just as enthusiastic, heading to the entrance.

"So, is Mr F taking you to lunch?" he asks, keeping in step with me as I walk towards the front door.

"No, I'm meeting Sophie. Why?"

"Hmm, nothing. Only my boss had this," he pulls out a black velvet box and hands it to me, "delivered to me, with explicit instructions that you are to bag it and forget about it until later. Understood?"

"Yes," I confirm suspiciously, as I take it and bag it. "Thanks, James."

"You're very welcome. Have a nice day." I wave him off as we both head in opposite directions.

"Has Mr Happy quite finished giving you whatever it is the kid has been buying now?" Walker asks with mock annoyance, his hip leaning against his huge car. Although alongside him, it looks normal. Me, it's a tank.

"Yes, any ideas what it is?"

"Nope." The word rolls off his tongue, but the sneaky grin validates he knows damn well what's in it.

"Buckle up, honey, let's go," he says gruffly, as I climb in and pull on my seat belt. I risk a look, and he catches me.

"Thanks for doing this," I say gratefully.

"Well, at least someone is. I'm gonna skin Dev's arse when I find him! I'm wasting Marie time being with you." I nod; I know exactly what he means. I'm a bit irate when anyone interrupts my Sloan time, but I think he forgets he and Marie are the biggest culprits behind it.

"I hear you, better still, I even understand you for once."

He laughs and hesitates with his hand on the brake. "I bet you do. Lifts have eyes and ears, my girl," he says gleefully, pointing to body parts, and my face flushes red.

"Yeah, I'm well aware. Trust me, my ear still aches from listening to Marie tell me all about it, so thank you for that."

"No problem, just doing my bit to keep you honest." I can't help but laugh because he really has no qualms about invading our lives at all. Then again, he's like Sloan's father, whereas Marie is like my mother. It would be strange if they didn't have an opinion on what was recorded in that lift the other day.

He slows the car to a stop at a red light. "The Swan?"

"Huh-uh," I reply while dropping Soph a text to say I'm nearly there.

My head darts up as an ambulance siren starts to wail loudly behind us, and Walker manoeuvres the car to allow it to pass. As he pulls back into the line of traffic, my eyes fix on a black Mercedes behind us, and I huff out.

Why?!

"John?"

"Yeah, honey?" He looks shocked that I'm finally using his actual name.

"Black car behind us. I'm pretty sure it's the same one that followed us yesterday." I turn to him, and he's checking his mirrors.

"Don't worry, honey, it's only Remy." His eyes shift slyly.

"Oh? I thought Devlin was-"

"Two pairs of eyes are better than one," he cuts me off quickly.

He drops his speed to less than thirty, irritating the shit out of the drivers behind us - if their horns are anything to go by. He keeps the same pace, flicking his eyes between the mirrors and the road ahead.

"Fucking bastard!" he mumbles, barely audible under his breath. I quickly turn my head, pretending I haven't heard him. He fiddles with his phone affixed to the dash. When Tommy answers, he brings it to his ear.

"Car behind us, it's black," he whispers, obviously hoping I don't hear.

Do they think I'm stupid? We both know it isn't Remy! Not to mention it's a little coincidental that the Range Rover has disappeared, and this is now the vehicle of choice. I'm also more than positive it is the same car that was outside the office, and that it *does* belong to Deacon.

My breathing is silently erratic, but Walker is a vision of calm. Twenty minutes after first spotting the car, he pulls up in the pub car park. He walks me to the entrance, and I stop, my mouth gaping.

"John, what are you doing?"

"Well, apparently, I'm having my afternoon wasted by spending it with two wine spritzer sipping females. But since I'm not that desperate to indulge in girl talk, that will, without a doubt, be centred on the kid and the doc, I'll get a pint and sit by the door with a paper until the kid shows up." He gently pulls my arm, whilst looking behind us. His eyes narrow and I refuse to look. I know what's there.

"I'm sorry, I'm taking you away from Marie today."

He looks down at me and lightly brushes his finger over my cheek. "I wouldn't have it any other way." He encourages me to walk inside. "Besides, could you imagine what she would do if I went back and told her about this?" He's right; the thought of Marie venting her wrath on him is far too easy to envisage.

I shrug my shoulders. "Why would you tell her? It's only Remy, right?"

Staying silent, he crosses his arms and gives me a stern look.

"Hmm, that's what I thought," I murmur.

I spot Soph as soon as I enter. She is sat by herself, and she stands and waves me over. My eyes narrow when she sways a little.

"Kara?" John asks, wanting to know my poison.

"White wine spritzer, what else? And get a pint of lemonade for madam. Thanks, John." I slowly walk over to Sophie, who is all smiles.

"I didn't think we were going to have company. How am I supposed to tell you stuff with GI Joe sat here?" I laugh. *GI Joe?* That's a new one.

"He's not going to sit with us. He is going to stay here until we are finished, however. Let's just say we had an *incident* and leave it at that."

"Hi, Soph, how's Stu?" John asks from behind me, holding three glasses between his hands with ease.

"Ask him yourself!" she replies flippantly. She really does push it sometimes, more so than I ever do.

John places the pint of lemonade, and her eyes cross. He grabs the half-consumed glass of wine before she realises what he's doing and holds it away from her. "I think you've had enough." She opens her mouth to protest, but he stops her.

"Don't. There's nothing attractive or more disgusting than a paralytic woman, who doesn't know when to quit! And I would ask Stuart, but you see more of him than I do, so I'm asking you."

"He's fine!" she spits out.

In an attempt to show him she doesn't care that he has just taken away her favourite tipple, she downs a quarter of the lemonade and slams it back down, splashing liquid on the table. I look from her to John and give him a weak smile.

He grazes his hand over my face again. "I'll be right over there." He walks away with a paper from the bar and selects a table that gives him a full, unrestricted view of both of us and the entrance.

"So, *incident?*"

"Oh, it's nothing. Anyway, come on, tell me about Stuart."

With a dreamy glint in her eye, she starts gushing about how great he is, and thanking me for introducing them. I smile remembering back to our teenage years, the times she tried to hook up with someone at school, and how she would wear the same expression of infatuation, but this time, it's different. It's more than just infatuation, it's…deeper.

I give her a serious look. "Are you in love with Stuart?" Soph bites her lip nervously and nods.

"Please don't tell him," she pleads.

"Why would I? He won't want to hear it from me!"

"I know. I just need to find the right time. I almost spat it out the other night when he-"

"No! Please, don't! I do not want to hear about you two playing doctors and nurses. Now, let's talk about something else."

"Kara, please? You have no idea what it's like not to be able to have this conversation with you when I know I finally can!"

"No! I'm not talking-" I quickly look around and lower my head "-sex with you. Not at all!"

"*Please?*"

"No!"

"Fine!" she huffs and takes another large mouthful of lemonade, before swapping it with my wine. "Tell me about his relationship with the redheaded bitch ex."

"You really had to go there, didn't you? How do you know about Christy?"

"Stuart told me," she says with a wicked smile.

Oh, I bet he's told her!

"There's more chance you know more about it than I do, then!"

"Possibly, but I want to hear it from you."

"Actually, I don't know what she is – was - but he finally confessed they had *that* kind of relationship. Ugh, God, even the thought of her makes me want to throw something!"

"Fuck buddy, friends with benefits, mattress warmer…town bike!" She giggles uncontrollably.

"You can shut up now!"

"Okay! You know, *that night*, when Sloan hot-tailed it out of the club after you, she looked like she was ready to break down and cry! When he came back in, she tried to put her arms around him. When he refused, she started mouthing off, calling you all sorts! You could see him change instantly, and he threw her off – I mean, really threw her off. I don't agree with violence towards anyone, but I'm surprised her arse mark isn't permanently shaped into the floor with the force that she hit it!"

I grimace. "Well, it's safe to say she hates me. Seriously, the highlight of my week was a run-in I had with her the other day. I bumped into her in the ladies at Sloan's office. It wasn't pretty, even more so, because not less than thirty minutes earlier, Sloan took full control of her father's company at a cut-price. Let's just say she's going to be finding it financially hard in times to come."

"Oh, shit! I think you maybe need to be more cautious with regard to her in future. Just because she no longer has money, doesn't mean she still doesn't have connections," Sophie says objectively.

"I know. It probably didn't help that I told her I would be his in every way she never would be. When I came out of the ladies, she was giving him a mouthful in the corridor!"

"Fuck! Really? What did he do?"

"He was unimpressed and amused." I take a sip of my wine and gaze at her. She's thinking, and so am I. I know she likes Sloan, but we've never really talked about him in-depth.

"What?" she asks, as my stare becomes far too focused.

"I was just wondering what you think of him. I know it's not something we've ever really discussed, but honestly, what's your opinion of him? And don't just tell me what I want to hear!"

She gives me a look of incredulity and leans back. "My opinion, for what it's worth, I think he's perfect for you. You complement each other beautifully. You're like the light to his dark, tacky but very true. Even Stuart thinks so."

"Don't you mean he's the light to *my* dark?"

She shakes her head. "No. Never. When you were hospitalised, he was intense. Stuart and John said they had never seen him act in such a way. He all-out refused anyone seeing you unless he or John had final say. Even *I* had to ask for permission! I know you probably don't want to hear this, but there's a real darkness inside him. Surely you of all people have witnessed it."

I stare at her. She's right; I have witnessed it. His hatred of Deacon and what he has done overrules every rational thought when it comes to the safety of myself or his sister. Walker sitting alone in the corner with a broadsheet is testament to it.

Still, people in glass houses shouldn't throw stones, because I'm also concealing truths. But remembering the things Deacon did to me in that dirty place, I will not stop Sloan, not unless he becomes a danger to himself. He can dictate and order as much as he likes, because I've learnt well that I'm strong-minded, but not strong bodied. I can't fight against Deacon, and in an attempt to keep myself safe, I have to learn to trust.

I have to trust Sloan when he tells me not to see the constants from my old life alone. He knows Sam and my father possess a danger towards me, and they threaten everything that may consist of a future for me.

For us.

"Look, this is getting a little too deep for my inebriated brain, so let's talk about shit instead!" Sophie giggles, easing my mind instantly.

And that's exactly what we do for the next hour or so, until Walker calls time on our party of two.

Chapter 19

STANDING IN THE pub car park, my attention is drawn to two things: Walker, trying, rather unsuccessfully, to put a playful and sleepy Sophie into his car; and the spot where Sloan nearly bared my flesh for all to see in the back of his car. My phone starts to ring, and I dig it out of my bag.

"Hi, guess where I am?" I quiz him.

"Not a clue, my love. Harrods, exercising the plastic, making me proud?"

I laugh. "Guess again!"

"Are you...naked in a suite at The Savoy, wearing nothing but a smile? Wait, no, scratch that! If you were, I'm sure the bank's fraud squad would have called me, since I never go there for obvious reasons. One minute, let me think! Are you three sheets to the wind on cheap vino?"

"Maybe! Actually, I'm just looking at the spot you almost gave the pub patrons a free show."

"Don't be getting any ideas, Petersen," he says firmly, while I level my gaze on the precise spot we were parked in that day.

"Oh, I have plenty of ideas, Foster."

Deep breathing commences on the other end of the line, until he breaks the silence. "Is John still with you?"

"Huh-uh," I reply.

"Get him to drop you off at the club."

I sigh subtly. "Okay, I'll see you in a bit." I hang up, my good humour gone. I press my lips together; I don't want to go to the club. As a matter of fact, I want to forget he owns it entirely, and never, ever, set foot inside that bastard place again. I plod over to Walker, who has just slammed the rear door shut.

"Jesus, she's hard work!"

I nod and roll my eyes, watching Sophie in the back seat as she holds the seat belt to her chest and smiles sleepily.

"Sloan wants me to meet him at the club. Do you mind taking me?" I ask dejectedly, and Walker puts his hands on his hips.

"Are you okay with that?"

I shake my head. "Not really, but he asked, and I will never refuse him anything, so..." Coming closer, I stare at John's cropped hair, focusing on a small scar on his temple.

"Honey, listen to me." He gently cradles my cheeks. "He said nothing happened between him and Christy since you, and I believe him. I don't know if he said anything, but I knocked him out in the suite after he kicked you out. He's lucky I didn't kill him – he's lucky Marie was there." I harden my emotions, not ready to let him see me cry over the past once more. Sensing my need to be released, he lets go and looks at the back seat again, to Soph, who is now half-asleep with her head up against the glass.

"Right, we'll drop madam off home. Actually, I'll take her to Stuart's, let him deal with her, then I'll drop you at the club. Okay?" I smile and pat his arm.

"Thanks, John."

Standing on the uninhabited dance floor, I feel physically sick. This is the last place I want to be right now. It's also the first time I've been here since the night Christy taunted me for her own personal enjoyment, and Deacon battered me for his. Needless to say, my discomfort is back in abundance.

I look around uneasily, seeing the exact spots that bitch wore me down and finally broke me. My eyes flit over the VIP, and my stomach flips, as I latch onto the sofa that I had seen them sitting on together. I squeeze my eyes because as hard as I may try, nothing will erase the memory of her tongue lapping at him. He might have placated me with his words, but a small part of me will always be hurt by what I saw that night.

I walk towards the bar where Remy is putting bottle after bottle into the fridges that line the wall. He turns when he sees me approach.

"Hey, Kara, he's in the back. He shouldn't be too long, but do you want me to get him?" I shake my head and study him as inconspicuously as possible. He seems to forget that I'm here, and that makes it easier to gain my own perspective of his character while he works.

"Have you been here all day?" I query, already aware he wasn't following us earlier.

Turning around, his eyes narrow. "A few hours. Why?"

I smile and shrug. "Just wondering." With a suspicious look, he turns back to the fridge.

"Remy?"

"Yeah?"

"What car do you drive?"

He shifts and smiles. "A Lexus. Why? You thinking of upgrading?"

"Rem, how many of these do you need?" Sloan's timing is faultless, as he calls out from an open door which leads into the back. Seconds later, he appears carrying crates of alcohol. "Hey, baby, I didn't know you were here already."

I smile as he walks behind the bar. His defined forearms are visible due to the rolled-up sleeves. His shirt hem is peeking out of the bottom of the waistcoat, and his tie is slack around his neck. He pauses carrying the crate of lager, puts them down, then turns. With his signature smirk firmly in place, he stalks towards me.

Picking me up, he jogs us into the centre of the dance floor, puts me on my feet and twirls me around. "May I have this dance?"

"No," I murmur, wondering what he will do.

Pressing me into him, he grins. "Tough shit, it's mine!" He spins me out to the side and back again, before plastering my body to his and pretending there is actually more than silence surrounding us.

"Are you guys staying or going? I need to lock up," Remy shouts over to us.

Sloan stares down at me thoughtfully. "We're going."

Remy salutes him with one finger, as Sloan picks me up and carries me towards the back corridor. The sun beats down on us, as he throws the rear fire door open, and pushes me up against the wall outside. My arms are all over him the minute he lodges his leg between my thighs to hold me up.

"Now, tell me about these ideas you have." He starts to fidget with my shirt buttons, and I become flustered and move his hands away.

"No, someone will see! Besides, I'm sure you'll remove these later for me!"

"You worry too much." His mouth takes charge of mine, and I struggle to breathe, until I break him off.

"One of us needs to, because you don't seem too bothered! What happened to going slow? We have more sex now than ever!"

He raises his finger to my lips and traces them. "I don't want to go slow. I want everything, and I wanted it yesterday. I don't want to wait for anything any longer." He straightens me up meticulously and guides me towards the car. "Let's go home. I have something for you."

"Hmm, cystitis!" I mumble, as he unlocks the car and climbs in.

"I heard that! Might not be a bad thing, it means I can keep you at home in bed and kiss you better!" He chortles.

Quick thinking bastard!

It isn't lost on me that I'll never be able to keep up with the way his mind works when it comes to us.

Throwing the door open for me, I slide inside. Studying my bag on my lap, he gives me a grin.

"I think it's time we went home and started to make some new memories there." He starts the car, and I gaze at him, not really understanding what he's saying. "Baby, the house, we need to make new memories that will make me want to live in it permanently. Open the box in your bag." He nods at my handbag, and I fish it out. I quickly open it and pull out two sets of keys.

My mouth opens in anger. "Why the hell is one set goddamn car keys again? Shall I just pull another Kara out of my arse to drive it?" I scream at him. "God, I'm no longer allowed to drive the one I have already! I feel guilty even looking at it."

"Don't be upset!" he counters sharply. I open my mouth again, but he puts his finger over it. "Just hear me out. Eventually, the house will be our home, and in winter the roads can be dangerous. You need something that will easily get through the snow and ice, and God forbid, something that will be able to sustain impact should the worst happen. Obviously, I'm aware you're too little for a normal 4x4, so I got you a smaller one. If it makes you feel any better, we'll sell the BMW."

"Okay," I say slowly, allowing him to win this particular battle. "How small?" I look at the symbol on the back of the key, not realising Range Rover produced anything that I would ever deem small.

"It's an Evoque. It's pretty sweet. Still, it's bigger than what you're used to, but come November, you'll need it." He looks nervous, before he quickly adds, "Anyway, I'm thinking we'll go get something to eat, then go home and make some new memories. Sound good?"

"Hmm, thank you," I accept graciously, although my jaw aches from the grinding he hasn't noticed. He looks stunned that I haven't back chatted, but heaven knows I want to. Biting my tongue is proving extremely difficult!

Witnessing the vacant expression spread across his face, I smile that he is at a loss for words, due to the lack of mine.

Chapter 20

DUSK IS FALLING, and the lights flicker on on the driveway as we pass, each one illuminating, capturing the movement. Sloan effortlessly glides the car to a stop just in front of the house.

I climb out and admire the structure, still amazed by its beauty, and the fact he genuinely detests being here so much. He stands next to me, and I dig inside my bag, looking for my new door key.

Holding it out, I look up at him. "May I?"

He laughs. "Of course. You really are taking this gracious thing to the next level today. Speaking of which," he says, grabbing my hand. "Let me show you the car." He moves us towards the row of high-end cars and bikes lined up along the side of the house. We stop at the last one, and my breath catches in my throat.

"I didn't know what colour you wanted, so I picked out this stone colour. It's got a black and cream leather interior, and every gadget you are probably never going to use!" He's still telling me what else is on it, but just like the last time he presented me with a vehicle I would only ever own in my dreams, I am again, very distracted.

He's right, though; it is smaller. *Just.*

Pulling out the car key, I unlock it and climb inside. Everything is cream or black, and it has that new car smell my senses are becoming far too accustomed to. I'm lost in my own world of happiness, when Sloan loiters outside the door and swings my body around so that he is positioned between my legs.

"Please don't be angry. I bought it with the best intentions," he whispers, leaning in further.

"I'm not. I love you. I love that you do these things for me."

"We can make a new memory right here, if you like?" he suggests friskily, shifting his eyes to the rear seats. They turn glassy, and I know he's giving what was a fleeting thought some serious consideration.

I squeeze my eyes, trying to gain control over the sparks beginning to flare to life inside me.

"You're thinking about it! I'll give you a choice; here or in the pool?"

My body clenches like a vice. I wrap my legs around his waist as he slides his hands under my backside. "T-the p-pool," I stutter, succumbing to the constant visceral need to be his.

"I like that idea." He lifts me out of the car and shuts the door. Before I can activate the locks, we're already at the front of the house.

"Key, baby." I unlock the door, and he kicks it shut, then engages the security system.

Moving down the hallway, with me still in his arms, he pulls another key from his pocket. He unlocks the door, and the vast space drowns in light as we enter.

He drops me on my feet, and I slowly move around the water's edge. Soft music fills the space, and I look around for the invisible speakers but only see Sloan on the other side, fiddling with a docking station. I smile as he slowly walks towards me, stripping off his jacket and tie, and dropping them on the floor.

"I don't suppose those pesky personal shoppers of yours bought me a swimsuit, did they?" I ask, knowing there isn't a chance in hell I'm getting in the water in anything but my own skin and very little else.

"Don't know, don't care," he answers cockily, as he unbuttons his shirt and discards that, too. He gives me a smirk that induces my insides to melt, and I suck in some much-needed air.

With only fractions between us, he runs his hand through my hair, dragging out the bobble. "Strip, now." My body quivers at his commanding tone.

This is another first; openly stripping for my man.

I slowly divest myself of my cumbersome clothing, until I'm down to my underwear. "Are you sure there isn't a swimsuit languishing in the bowels of that room upstairs?" I ask again in vain.

He shakes his head, as he drops his trousers and boxers to the floor collectively. I gasp audibly when he takes himself in hand and slowly strokes from base to tip. "Naked, baby." He continues to stalk towards me, predatory and maybe a little scary.

I slowly unclip my bra and hold the cups over my chest. The straps fall down my arms, and I hug the material to my front, prolonging whatever it is I'm trying to achieve without success.

"Drop it!" His command echoes around the large space, and I comply immediately. I let my arms drop to my sides and watch the fabric fall to earth at my feet. I don't look up, as his feet slap against the tiles, edging closer.

"Eyes on me," he says, his toes stopping a little away from mine. My heart rate is soaring, and my body feels out of control. I'm doing a good job at hiding it, but I know as soon as he touches me, it will be game over. I will give him what he wants without hesitation. I may question repeatedly, but for as long as we both live – together – I'll never hold back on anything.

I slowly tilt my head up, and my desire laden eyes meet his. The glassy ripple effect of the water's surface reflects, and I look into them deeply, losing myself further than I already have within various tones of blue.

With a single finger under my chin, he brings my head up fully, until my neck feels strained and my back arches, pushing my chest into his. Never removing his eyes from mine, his other hand gently squeezes my shoulder, and slowly, carefully, glides down my back, until it stops and grips my behind.

I let out a small moan that destroys the beautiful quiet, and he drops his head to mine. "Open." My lips part, and he seeks out solace in the wet heat of my welcoming mouth.

Allowing my body to grow lax under his strength, I press further into him. Raising my leg up to come around his hip, I rest my heel on his arse, and he moves his hand from himself and cups me. I drop my head back and bring my hand around the back of his neck; the urgent need to devour is potent.

With a quick movement, my other leg is now wrapped around him. He walks us around the pool to the other side, where there are steps and a ramp that slants down into the water.

Smirking, he pushes a finger inside and back out, never wavering in his stance. "Always on."

Pulling his finger free, he holds my flesh open, and I feel his tip at my opening. The arm under my bum lifts me, and he carefully lowers me onto his engorged length. I let out a keening sound as he fills me to the hilt. I dig my hands into his shoulders, using him as ballast to lift and lower once again. He appears surprised and stills.

"Hang on. Do not move."

Slowly, he walks us down the incline and into the water, before turning and lowering me down on to it. Twisting my head to the side, the material that covers it is soft, and, unexpectedly, provides traction. He gently brings my face to him and leans into me. The water laps at my aroused breasts, just like I imagined it would when he tried convincing me days ago.

"*Sloan...*" I breathe out, wanting him to move and take me to the edge of desire and beyond.

"Still want a swimsuit?" he asks with a confident grin. I shake my head, and he covers me perfectly.

In a moment of over-exuberance, I remove my hands from him and drop them to the non-slip material, using it as leverage to move under him.

Sensing my need for release, he slowly starts to thrust, not all the way, but enough that I feel the change begin to take effect. Working me continuously, he sucks on my nipples and grinds his body into mine for long, welcome minutes, until I feel him pulse and throb deep in my heat.

"Oh, shit, I'm not gonna last like this!"

"Me neither. Oh, God!" I gasp, enjoying the sensation beginning to tear through me like fire on dry tinder. He picks up his speed and slides in and out, each time touching a part of me that makes me burn deeper.

He roars out my name, and I relish hearing it leave his lips. My nails dig into his upper back while he holds my legs further apart, and his pushing eases. Eventually, he stops, and I wrap my legs around him. His head drops to my neck, and he nips and sucks on the curve that meets my collarbone.

"I'll never look at this swimming pool the same way again!" he laughs, the sound making a wave of echoes around the hollow space.

"No," is all I can say.

This has just become yet another place in the house that will carry a good memory for him, and one I will always associate with his ability to make me feel.

I close my eyes and allow my body to come back down to earth. He moves gingerly, and I feel his softening length harden once more. I shiver from the sensation of it deep inside my hidden walls.

"Cold?"

"No," I say again, and he smiles and lifts me.

"That word has never sounded so good." He pulls out of me, finds his footing and picks me up. "Come on, let's finish this upstairs with a bottle of something chilled." I giggle and secure my wet body to his.

At the door, he flicks off the lights and locks it. "How's that for another first conquered, baby?"

"Unforgettable," I whisper.

"Damn right!"

I stare up at the ceiling; the trees cast random shapes all over the room. I turn to watch Sloan. He's snoring lightly, and I feel content I finally have a life that no longer exists in the darkness.

This extraordinary man has brought me out into the open. He's given me something I never expected to be tangible or even in my grasp.

Love.

Yet it is so much more than that. It buries deeper than anything I could have hoped for.

When he first entered my life, I was suspicious. It didn't matter how much he turned me on - or unknown to me at the time - how he had helped Sam, he was just another rich man, and I was just a girl with nothing, except a shell of a life.

In such a tiny space of time, he has turned my world on its axis.

Gone is the girl who roamed the shadows, waiting for life to pass her by because it was safer that way. In her place, is the girl who I might have become, had I not been subjected to things I should have been shielded from.

I cover my hands over my mouth to avoid him waking and hearing my desperate cries. The mournful tears of a child, still very much alive inside me. I might have thought I had survived, but I haven't. I died all those nights ago, yet the memory never will. I carefully climb out of bed, slip on my robe, and lightly pad out of the bedroom.

In the kitchen, I wait for the milk to boil and pull out my phone. It's three o'clock in the morning. There's nobody I can call at this time who will be awake, but I need someone - I can't talk to Sloan. One day, I hope I can reveal every horrifying detail of my life. Except, just like before, I can't rationalise being able to, because once he realises just how damaged and defiled I truly am, I know there's a possibility he may leave me. And I will have to deal with the heartache of watching him walk away for the final time. But I know I have to. Objectively, we have a relationship built on deceit. How far his deceit lies, I have no idea, but mine is something I will have to come clean about eventually.

I open a new message and text David to ask if he has availability to see me tomorrow. His reply comes back within ten minutes with an offer of eleven. I reply, accept, and apologise for the lateness of the hour. He responds, saying it's part of the service, and we will speak tomorrow.

Pouring the milk over the chocolate powder, I know I really do have to start speaking more than I have already - and it needs to be for longer than half an hour.

I dig into my bag and pull out my notebook. I've taken to carrying it with me at all times, not because I have urges to write every five minutes, but because I can't risk having Sloan, or anyone else, finding it.

Blowing the top of my mug, I wait for it to cool, then start to write.

"What are you doing?"

I raise my head and look up. Standing in a pair of low pyjama bottoms, he folds his arms across his chest. His displeasure is unmistakable. Turning towards the clock, I realise I've been down here for nearly two hours. I thumb through my book, shocked to find I have written page after page of truth and pain.

"What is that?" he hisses, his eyes flicking to the book. I sigh out and close it.

"What does it look like? It's a notebook." I drop it in my lap and hold it tight, fearful he may snatch it from me.

He doesn't say a word. Instead, he shakes his head and marches to the fridge. He pulls out a carton of juice and necks it from the container. Slamming the door shut, he leans back against it.

"And what's in the notebook, Kara?"

"It's none of your business!" I retort, as I get off the stool and walk the long way around the island. He grabs me as I try to get by him. His hands grip my arms with such pain and force, I flinch.

"Well, I say it is my business. You're my woman, for fuck sake! Or has that fact escaped your notice? I've been lying alone upstairs for two fucking hours waiting for you to come back. Did you honestly think I wouldn't feel you move?" he shouts.

My body starts to shake; I'm raw and frightened. "You're hurting me!"

He lets go instantly and steps back. With his hand over his face, he looks distraught. Of all the things I could ever have said to him, I unintentionally pick out the first thing in my head, and it's one that causes him pain.

Holding my book out to him, I allow him to take it. Broken, I slowly move past him and climb up the stairs.

I pull out a bag and start to throw some stuff into it, making sure I only pack whatever I know was paid for from my own pocket. With the bag half-full on my arm, I shuffle into the bathroom to get my pills and toiletries. He hasn't come up here yet, and I'm grateful. The only bad sign is that he's most likely downstairs, reading my book and all the depravity etched into the paper.

"What are you doing?"

I spin round to see him at the door, his hands on his hips. Stepping away, the back of my knees graze the toilet.

"I thought I'd save you the effort of throwing me out for the second time." He scrubs his hand over his face, and his confusion slays me.

He hasn't read the book. I bet he hasn't even opened it.

Tears pinch my eyes that I really have no idea what a relationship entails. I have no real premise on how to put it first, or how to conduct myself within it when trouble comes knocking. I'm in the motions of doing what I promised I wouldn't; I'm trying to run again.

"What's in this notepad, baby?" He holds it up between us. "And do not lie to me!"

I sag to the floor, and my knees hit the marble, hard and unforgiving. Unable to take much more, I mentally shatter, and the barrier is breached. Strong arms lift me up from the cold and wrap around me. I fight back in protest, but it's no use. My back touches down on the bed, and he makes quick work of removing my shoes and clothing. He pulls the duvet over me and scoots around to the other side.

Opening my eyes, my notebook is on the bedside table; the pen sat innocently on top of it. My body is pulled back, and Sloan coils himself around me, caging us together.

"Baby, talk to me."

But I can't, not in the way that he wants me to.

"It's my memories." My words are a whisper, carrying over the stillness like an impending death sentence.

His chest puffs out, and he inhales deeply. "Oh shit, I'm sorry. Baby, I promise I will not read it unless you want me to."

I stare, unseeing, unable to fathom why he isn't ripping the bloody thing apart. I know I would be, and therein lies the crux of the matter we both circumvent frequently, reluctant to address. The reason why, when my world constantly folds in on itself, he continually takes it in his stride.

My heart breaks in self-pity, and he pulls me closer. I sob out softly as he strokes his hand over my stomach. He seems to know there are no words that can bring me back from the precipice at this moment.

"Get some sleep, we'll talk in the morning," he whispers.

"I love you. Always. Even when I'm trying to run," I tell him, slowly and quietly, keeping the emptiness from my tone.

"I love you too, my love, and I'll always be right behind you."

Chapter 21

MY EYES BLINK open. The sore redness of them hurts when I rub. A feeling of loneliness hits me, and I shuffle around.

I'm alone.

The bag I packed last night – or, this morning - is still laying on the floor in the same place I had left it. My clothes, that Sloan stripped me out of, are gone.

Twisting the knob, hot water cascades to the floor, and I rotate back to the sink and start to brush my teeth. Last night comes back to haunt me, and I race back into the bedroom with the toothbrush sticking out of my mouth.

My fear subsides when I see my notebook still sitting on the table, the pen in exactly the same place. I wonder if Sloan has read it, and meticulously repositioned them to make them appear undisturbed? Unable to hypothesise any further, I pick them up, put them in my bag and go back into the bathroom.

With my hair balled up in a towel, I wrap the robe around myself, and make my way to the landing and down the stairs. The house is deathly silent as I slowly descend each step and walk down the hall. I look into each room as I pass, but he's nowhere in sight.

Confused, I enter the kitchen and sit alone at the island. I gaze at the fridge and replay the look on his face when I refused to give up the contents of the notebook this morning. Tears fall against my freshly washed cheeks, and I pull the robe tighter.

Where on earth is he?

The clock in the hallway starts to chime - ten o'clock.

Oh, crap!

Laced with panic, I dash back upstairs. Running into the dressing room, I grab the first pair of jeans my hands touch, a sweater, and a pair of flats.

Moving hastily into the bedroom, I grab my phone and slide my finger across it. No new messages or missed calls. I have no time to think about where he is because I am going to be late for my appointment if I do.

Back downstairs, I spoon some coffee into a travel mug and pour the water. Leaving it black, I lid it and hurry out into the hallway. I look at the multiple sets of keys on the table and bile pushes its way up to my mouth. I'm going to have to drive the baby Range Rover since my car is at the hotel.

Shit, I'm actually going to have to drive that thing into the city!

Outside, I unlock the car and notice the Aston is still in the same spot, but one of the bikes is missing. My eyes widen at the thought, and worry grips me as to what state of mind he is currently in - considering the way things were left last night. Horror consumes me, but I can't allow it time to manifest.

Climbing into the car, I text Devlin to let him know I have an appointment in the building next to the office, then I call Gloria to ask if I can use one of their parking spaces.

Starting the ignition, I stall before I've even moved. I know now my hazard lights are going to be making a regular appearance today. I slowly drive up to the security cabin and wait for the guard on duty to open the gates. He gives me a nod, and I motion for him to come around.

"Have you seen Sloan this morning?"

"Yes, Miss. Mr Foster left a few hours ago with Mr Fox."

"Mr Fox?"

"Tommy." He gives me a look that tells me I should already know who he's out with. I feel like the village idiot.

"Did he take a bike?"

"Yes, Miss," he replies in his usual unimpressed, yet polite way.

"Okay. When he comes back, can you remind him I have an appointment at eleven?" The guard nods. "And please, it's Kara, not Miss."

The guard smiles. "Yes, Miss."

I shake my head and drive away.

The drive into the city isn't too bad. Despite the fact I've stalled at literally every set of lights and every give way sign, I've managed not to incite any serious chaos. Of course, traffic is still ridiculously heavy, but what else is new. Parking in the space Gloria indicated, I make my way up to the street level through the bowels of the car park.

As I exit, a black Mercedes is stationary on the street opposite, glinting in the sunlight. It's a terrifying thought that Sloan isn't with me, and it's still here. Clearly, they are not following him, they are following me, which validates my theory. I gulp in a deep breath, knowing that until we find out who's in it - or rather confirm who we know is in it – I'll never be free of my constant companion.

With that scary prospect in mind, I move quickly through the mass of people to the adjacent building and ring the bell. Margaret buzzes me up after I confirm my name and appointment time.

As I take the stairs, a greying man crosses my path. He has a baseball cap pulled low, and dark glasses obscuring his partially lined face. It may be warm outside, but it is by no means so hot that he needs both. The small, yet somehow, familiar grin he gives me makes me shiver. And not in a good way. I watch as he passes by and leaves the building, never looking back. I hope my mind is playing tricks on me, as I move into the empty space he has just vacated.

I greet Margaret the moment I see her. She is a beacon of light this morning; arranging flowers and fluffing up the cushions.

"Ah, it's so nice when it's sunny and warm outside. Makes everything feel better, don't you think so?" I gape at her. It would take a hell of a lot more than that to make me feel anything remotely resembling better this morning. My mind is still in turmoil from the events of the early hours of dawn.

She hands me a coffee, and I thank her. David then appears from his room and motions me inside. I stop as I feel the vibration of my phone in my pocket. I apologise and dig it out. Sloan is calling. I switch it off and enter, clutching my notebook.

"How are you today, Kara?"

"Oh, I'm fine, sort of. I'm sorry about the early morning text. I couldn't sleep, and I had a rough couple of hours afterwards."

"I'm sorry to hear that," he says, his eyes observing my book. He picks up his own pad and pen as I sit opposite him. He looks pointedly at my lap, waiting for me to unburden myself of my newest, untold strife.

"These are my memories. Things that I remember. I don't know if I will ever be able to talk about them, but writing them down makes me feel like I've released something, you know?"

"I do. If you would allow me to read them, I might be able to get a better understanding of what has happened in your past. May I?" I stare at him, and then back down to my lap. This book is detrimental to my future, both the good and the bad.

He doesn't push the subject while I re-evaluate my thoughts and weigh up the pros and cons. Finally, I acquiesce and hold it out to him. He doesn't snatch it or make any kind of haste. Instead, he gently slides it from my hand to his.

My heart thumps against my breastbone as he opens the first page, skim reads it, then moves on to the next.

I place my hand over my mouth, as he takes his time to work through to the end of my words. When he has finished, he passes it back to me, and I drop it on the table. I take another long draw of my coffee and lean back.

Waiting.

"I think we need to start with the past. Tell me about the most apparent memory you have."

The biggest stand out moments in my memories are the ones that happened before and after the event. These were the memories I had pushed aside, but am now trying to keep hold of. Ones I had clawed back from the black hole. I take a look around the room and open my mouth.

"My cubbyhole. My hiding space." David starts to jot down his notes, but I ignore him and concentrate. "I spent more time in there than I did in my actual room. When my dad was drunk or angry, I used to hide in there so he couldn't find me. I was too young to realise that he always knew where I was."

David's eyes narrow. "Why is that your most significant memory?"

"Because it's where everything started and ended." I slowly close my eyes, the unshed tears tormenting them.

He lifts his brows. "Make me understand, Kara."

I take a deep breath. "There were times I would wake up and feel…different. Times I couldn't remember leaving the cubbyhole but waking up in my own bed. Sometimes I was naked and sore. The last time, my arms were bound above my head, and I was in pain…and then afterwards, there was a man. A man who saved me." I let out a sob and rub my eyes.

David gives me a sympathetic look and passes me a box of tissues. "If you feel you can, tell me about the man who hurt you. What do you remember?"

I shake my head in both upset and amazement, proud that I'm kind of staying strong and verbalising things I dared not speak of to anyone for a long time.

"Not much. He was a shadow, a ghost. I never really saw his face, just his voice and h-his l-laugh," I stutter, recalling the way he had spoken to me before he did *that* to me. Before he took away everything that was pure and true and destroyed my faith in love. "He hit me, a lot, and he tied me down and r-ra..." My tears run away with abandon. Other than explaining to him about my assault at our initial meeting, this is the first time I have ever voiced my hidden truths, and it's causing me absolute physical pain because this will not be the first and only time I speak of such horrors. A second will be on the horizon in the foreseeable future, with a man who might not be half as compassionate.

The clock chimes singularly, and I realise I've been sat here for nearly sixty minutes, yet it only feels like ten.

David gives me a cautious look. "Do you want to leave it for today and pick up on Thursday?" I shake my head, wanting to continue, proud that I'm doing well at the moment.

"Okay, whenever you're ready, tell me about the person who saved you."

I smile. He's one of only a handful of good memories that I have in my life.

Him, and Sloan, of course.

I slowly recant what I can honestly remember the night the man saved me. The way he looked after me and took me to the hospital. I tell David how the man made me feel calm, and how only three people – men, actually - have ever made me feel such a way. The one who saved me, a stranger outside a restaurant, and Sloan.

David writes down bits here and there, and we move from the night of my making, back and forth from my childhood, to now. Eventually, the conversation stops, and David closes his book and tents his hands at his lips.

"So, Kara, how do you feel?"

Tearful.

Heartbroken.

And very bizarrely, I feel refreshed, like a weight has been lifted from me.

"Erm, good. I've never really spoken about any of that stuff before. I just made myself forget, so I didn't have to." I hold back my tears, but they will be making an appearance in his presence someday soon - of that I am certain.

"A lot of people do different things to help them deal with trauma. Soldiers who have seen battle and death tend to let it fester away inside, rather than speak of the atrocities they have borne witness to. People who have been attacked and abused prefer not to speak about it because they feel it is something they have done to deserve it, or that blocking it aside will allow them to go on. Except, I find that it merely holds them prisoner until they release it. None of the above is weakness or failure, it's the human spirit that makes us feel and connect. I'm sure you understand that." I nod my affirmation at his words of accuracy.

"Kara, if it is acceptable to you, I would like to keep our appointment on Thursday. I think you have done exceptionally well today. When you do come back, I think we need to delve further and see what you can recall from your childhood."

"Okay. But just so you know, I wasn't going to cancel Thursday. I just needed something after last night."

"What happened last night, if you don't mind me asking," he queries.

"Nothing bad. I woke up unable to sleep and started writing in my book. Sloan got frustrated when I wouldn't tell him what was in it. Don't misunderstand, he would never hurt me. He just wants me to share every dirty, sordid detail of my life, but I can't do that with him. I know it's inescapable, but it's something I'm trying to put off." I let out a breath mixed with a sob, amazed at my ability to be comfortably open with this man.

"Why can't you tell him? You've managed to tell me."

"Because he'll leave me. Who wants to love a victim of abuse?" David's brows arch, and he gives me a look that tells me he knows more than he should, just like everyone else seems to.

"I think the next time we meet we also need to talk about the way you see yourself. Maybe you should ask Sloan how he feels. I think he might surprise you." David stands and veers around the chair. Reaching for my jacket, he holds it out to me.

"Is Sloan a patient, too?" I ask, my curiosity piqued. David sighs, but doesn't respond.

It isn't a coincidence that the shrink Sloan found me is right next door. It also isn't a coincidence that he seems very much at ease with both Margaret and David. And it definitely isn't a goddamn coincidence that said shrink is asking me to be open because Sloan *'might surprise me'*.

"I'm sorry; I shouldn't have asked that." I pick up my book and tuck it inside my bag. "Thank you for today, I feel loads better. I'll be back on Thursday." David holds his hand out, and I take it. Mine tenses, but not nearly as much as it did the first time. I smile and impart my goodbye.

As I enter the waiting room, Sloan's familiar, messed-up dark hair is in front of me. His back is to the door, so he doesn't see me until I pass him en-route to Margaret's desk.

"I just wanted to make sure my appointment for Thursday is still booked in."

"Of course, it is dear. We'll see you then."

I turn with a smile, and Sloan fills the space in front of me. He reaches for my hand, and I lean into him. "I'm sorry, my love."

"So am I. I didn't mean to be so vague this morning. I'm just scared that if, *when*, you read it, you'll see me differently," I confess, walking down the stairs with him, knowing David would be proud that I have just voiced my biggest concern, or part thereof.

He kisses the top of my head. "Kara, how many times do I have to say it? I love you. I don't care what has happened before."

I don't reply.

Because he will.

The sun is bright and high in the sky as we hit the pavement. "Where were you this morning?"

"Shit, I'm sorry. I shouldn't have just left you like that. I just needed to clear my head, and Tommy called, so I asked him if he wanted to go for a ride. I couldn't sleep when we went back to bed."

"Oh."

"There's no '*oh*' about it. I fucked up. When I came back, Tim said that you'd left for an appointment. I thought it might be here, but I wasn't too sure, until I pulled in downstairs and saw your car. When did you make the appointment anyway, I thought you were coming back on Thursday?"

"I still am coming back on Thursday. I did it last night. I just needed to talk, so I text David as soon as I got out of bed."

"Well, knowing David, I bet he loved that!" I spin round and look at him.

He *is* one of his patients.

"Baby, don't give me that look. Of course, I *was* one of his patients; I was for a long time. I told you I let someone in once and then they were gone. I lost them, and he's helped me over the years." He gives me a guilty look. I'm not sure he even knows what his expression is right now, but it's there, and for some unknown reason, it tugs at me on a level deep inside.

I clamp my hand around his as we enter his building. He doesn't lead me up to the lifts. Instead, he guides us towards the back of the foyer and into a small café.

"Oh, this is nice." I glance around the empty tables and sit at one by the window. He joins me with ham and cheese on white, and a caramel latte. I give him a wide eye.

"Sophie told me what you preferred when you were in the hospital. I feel pathetic that I should've already known."

I smile. That girl thinks he's the bee's knees, even if she does believe there's a darkness festering away inside him. Except, I could no longer think it, I knew it was fact. His name had been on the books of the same shrink that mine currently is.

He takes a bite of his egg mayo and subtly looks around. "What do you think of, maybe, eventually, having a counselling session together?"

I almost spit out the mouthful of coffee and froth. "I think you're wishful thinking right now. The last thing on my mind is us going into that room together!"

"Fair enough. I just thought I'd ask. But, consider it, alright?" I nod and pick at my sandwich.

He takes another swig of his drink, and I can see his wheels turning. I know it won't be long before I'm reprimanded for coming here without backup. He leans back in his chair, assessing me, clearly wondering how to word it. Then he says the magic words.

"And another thing, you drove here alone."

I drop down the sandwich, not giving a shit. "You seem to have forgotten that *you* disappeared this morning without letting me know where you were going! I text Devlin to let him know. I called Gloria to make sure there was somewhere I could park. Forgive me, but I think after this morning, and the fact you were out doing God knows how many miles an hour on a bike, you have no grounds to give ultimatums here!"

He opens his mouth, but I continue.

"I called David of my own free will. Do you even understand how hard that is for me? To come here, without any outside pressure, and talk about shit that causes me to regress? You have absolutely no right to make me feel bad. And I won't. Today I did something good for myself, and you've just made it feel worthless!" I get up and stomp out of the café, towards the lifts. Screw my anxiousness.

I board the first one that arrives and press the minus first button to get to the car park. Deactivating the car locks, I slide inside, slam my hand on the wheel and breakdown. My heartbreak fills the cabin, and I no longer have control.

Suddenly, the door opens, and Sloan lifts me out and hugs me close to him. The need to push him away is great, but the need for him to hold me prevails stronger.

"I'm saying and doing all the wrong fucking shit today, aren't I?" I nod against his shoulder. "Baby, can we have a do-over?"

"A what?" I pull back and wipe my nose with my sleeve, much to his expression of mixed amusement and acute concern.

I don't care.

"Can we start again? A clean slate. The moment we drive out of here, anything that has already happened today has gone."

"Sure," I reply half-heartedly, as he gets into the passenger side, knowing no such thing would ever exist inside my world.

I reverse the car out of the space, mindful of his Aston on my near side. After flashing my security card at the barrier terminal, it creaks and begins to ascend.

"Sloan, I don't want a do-over. I want to remember today, because it's the first time I have willingly given up information to someone. As much as it hurts, I have to start living – and not through you. I have to do this for myself."

His hand grips mine as the barrier is almost up. "Okay, I'm proud of you. I always will be."

I drive up the ramp, and the sunlight spreads over the windscreen. I pull out of the side street and look to my right. The man I had passed on my way into David's is stood next to the Mercedes. I give way to an oncoming bus and then edge out. Looking back in my mirror, the man continues to watch as I become lost in the sea of traffic.

Chapter 22

"MARIE? I CALL out, frowning as the front door handle opens in my hand. I quickly rush inside, dismayed that she's failing to heed her own advice and not lock the door. "Marie?"

"Stop shouting, I'm in the kitchen!" her raised voice drifts down the hallway. I lock the bolts in triplicate, smiling to myself that Walker has finally managed to battle through and come out triumphant on the subject.

I stick my head around the architrave to find her bent over a cheesecake base, a bowl of topping in her hand. Not noticing me, her tongue sticks out a little as she thickly layers the cheese over the biscuit in meticulous fashion. Her concentration is second to none. I used to love watching her do this when I lived here.

"Hey," I whisper, as not to shock her into making a mistake. She pops her head up and smiles.

"Hey, honey. How on earth did you manage to escape prison today?" she asks sarcastically.

"With difficulty," I deadpan. It took every power of persuasion I had this morning to convince Sloan to let me drive over here unmanned. The argument brewing between us was thick and, bizarrely, rather than allow it to fight its way free, he compromised. He was getting better at that lately.

"What do you think?" She twists the rotating cake platter around to show me, then she levels off the last bit.

"It looks amazing, but you don't eat it," I say confused.

"No, but I had a request to make it, so voila!" she states proudly at her creation. I narrow my eyes at her, and she gives me a nervous grin.

"Request from whom?" I ask suspiciously, and she shrugs her shoulders and smiles. "Fine, don't tell me then." I shake my head, knowing my beloved kid has commissioned her to do it. It also makes me query why. He's good at keeping secrets, although I don't think I'm that far behind in him in the deceit stakes, regardless of my good intentions and the self-sacrificing reasons for my concealment.

"Long shot, but have you heard anything from Sam?" I ask from my spot at the breakfast bar. Marie gives me a look, one that shows her disapproval that I can still care after all is said and done. I raise my brows, and she waves her hand a little.

"No, but did you really expect anything else?"

"I don't know...maybe." Marie flicks her brows up. "Okay, I guess not, but I can live in hope," I grumble. "So, when can I come back to work? I feel physically fine. There's no need for me to be sat staring at four walls day in, day out," I comment, staring at, but looking past my favourite dessert sitting innocently on the worktop.

Marie turns the instant the last letter flows from my mouth. "Kara, you're not well enough yet," she says, in that pre-conditioned, brainwashed tone I last heard in the hospital. She looks quickly, then turns away again.

With her back to me, I shake my head. Those men have really done a number on her, making her believe things that have yet to materialise - *if they materialise.* As much as I want to throttle something at this moment, I can't scream and take it out on her, because I also know what it's like to be coerced and moulded to the Foster/Walker way of thinking.

"I understand," I say softly, and with great disappointment. Her reaction makes me wonder if she has already had this conversation with Mr Unreasonable.

She rotates slowly and sighs. "Kara, I-"

"I'm sorry; I shouldn't have put you in that position. I know what they're like." I raise my hand in surrender. "I just need something else to do than play the dutiful little wife."

"Honey, I'm clearly stating the obvious, but one day that's precisely what you will be, sooner rather than later if he gets his way." She passes me a coffee.

"I know, but I just can't stand it. You'd be amazed at what I would do not to be cooped up in the house or the hotel. It's like being a rich man's prisoner!"

"Really? Tell that to the hundreds of girls out there looking to bag a rich footballer! And dare I ask what you've been reading?" She frowns at me and pops her hand on her hip, tapping her foot.

I smile innocently and shrug. "Sophie's book from the hospital," I mutter, flushing with colour and dropping my head. "And maybe a few more like it..." I finish under my breath.

"Well, don't you be getting any ideas. I'm too young to be a grandma!"

"I'm not. Although you might want to have this conversation

with him whom you think walks on water. I'm sure he has an opinion or two on this pointless subject." I smile involuntarily and bite my lip to conceal it, already aware of what his personal views are on the matter of our future procreation.

Sons – no daughters!

"Well, just make sure it's safe!"

"I should be saying the same to you! You're still young enough to have a family. I'm surprised Walker isn't here already, telling me to leave because he hasn't seen you in the last hour!"

"Very funny, missy. Anyway, who is the adult and who is the child here?" she says, very motherly, hammering the point home. Sometimes, in the past, when she used this line on me, I would laugh. At seventeen years older than me, yes, she could very well be my mother, but her outlook on life was always positive and youthful.

Settling down, she has just unknowingly brought up the true reason I pressed the subject with Sloan on coming over here today. "Speaking of mother's, Lorraine called." I lift my eyes, not wanting to witness her reaction.

"Lorraine? Your mum?"

"Hmm, she called the other day and said she was leaving him - finally. She didn't say where she was going, but I'm pretty sure it will be Newcastle. I think my aunt still lives there, but they hadn't spoken in years up to the point of my leaving. Not quite sure when that changed." Although it might not have changed at all. I'm making assumptions of which I have no grounds to base them on.

"She finally said sorry for letting me down and putting him first. I really don't know what to think. Honestly, it could just be another one of Ian's ploys, using her as bait to call me out." I sigh. I have long since turned off my old phone, but I know I'll have to switch it back on again soon, since my mother only has that number. It's just unfortunate that it's also the only number my father is in receipt of, too.

Marie sits and puts her arm on mine. She stares at me, waiting for me to pull back. Instead, I put my hand over hers and rub.

"Honey, it's your life and your parents, but please proceed with caution. Until you can be sure that what she's telling you is true, you can't trust her. I'm sorry, I have no right to say it, and although I love you like you're my own, she brought you into this world."

"But you're the one that raised me properly." I squeeze her hand, concerned that after all these years we are finally having the conversation of which we've both skirted the subject on many times.

"Honey, regardless, she will always be your mother. She's made mistakes of catastrophic magnitude, and I know what it's like to be in a position where you have to choose. Believe me, I choose *him* more often than not, and I still couldn't make it work."

"Have you ever heard from him?"

She shakes her head. "No, the last I heard he was in Peterborough with his new fiancée. She's welcome to him!" I watch as she walks away.

My phone beeps and I pick it up to find Sophie has text me. Sliding the message open, I scrunch my nose up.

OMG! Nd dres nw!

I stare cross-eyed at the message, until Marie takes it from my hand, equally confused.

"I swear she gets worse with these bloody texts. One of the girls from work types in letters and numbers. It takes me hours to reply since I end up having to look it up on the internet!" I laugh; I'm not quite that bad. I dial Soph's number, and she picks up instantly.

"Oh, my God!" she squeals. "Stuart's taking me out tonight, and I need a dress! You have to come shopping with me, like now!"

"Seriously, you don't need a dress. I have more than enough that are still tagged. I'm at Marie's, come over."

"No, I can't take one of yours."

"You're not, technically they're Sloan's."

She remains silent. "No, I'll just go buy one."

"Fine, but they're all designer..." I wait, already knowing she will never refuse. Long seconds drift by, and she momentarily breathes, until she finally opens her mouth again.

"Well, if you insist! I'll be there soon."

I hang up and pour a glass of juice. Sliding open the patio doors, I tiptoe into the back garden. Pulling up a chair, I ease into the seat, enjoying the late summer sun. A short time later, Marie comes to join me.

We sit in silence, enjoying the quiet, when Sophie finally comes around the back gate. "I've been at the front door for ages! I thought you might be back here." She waits beside me and starts to tap her foot. "Come on, I need to get back and get ready! How far in the middle of God's green nowhere does he live?" She's impatient, and I smile. She has yet to see the house, having been only to the hotel over the last few months.

"Two minutes," I say, heading back into the kitchen to locate my bag. I perch my backside against the table as I call Sloan.

"Hey, babe, everything okay?"

I smile. "Yeah, but why do you always assume something is wrong?"

He's silent, until he says, "Just erring on the side of caution, you can never be too careful."

I nod my head, even though he can't see me. "True. Anyway, I'm just calling to tell you that Sophie needs a dress for tonight for a date with Stuart, so I'm going to let her pick one out of my disgustingly vast collection."

He laughs. "Oh, I have to remember to thank the good doc for his discretion."

"Eh?"

"It's a surprise. Just make sure you're both ready by seven-thirty. George will be picking you up." He sounds so happy, whereas I'm getting that crazy butterfly feeling in my stomach of something both good and bad on the horizon.

"Sloan?" I query, knowing he won't tell me.

"Baby, all will become clear later tonight. Can you curb your enthusiasm for an argument until then?" I can hear the smile in his voice.

I laugh; he knows me all too well. "Why not!" I reply flippantly.

"You also need a dress for tonight, my love. The one I requested you to buy? Wear it - for me." I close my eyes, visualising the dress and him peeling it from me. My eyes flutter with undeniable bliss at the thought.

"Kara, are you still there?"

"Hmm, I'll see you later. Love you."

"Not as much as I do you."

We hang up, and I turn to see Sophie inside the doorway, a smirk on her face.

"Don't say a word!"

"I wasn't!"

"Apparently, I'm also going to this thing tonight, so we'll go to the house and get ready. George is picking us up around seven-thirty."

I collect up my things, find Marie and tell her goodbye, before heading out with Soph a few steps behind.

The lush, green countryside whips around us as I drive through the narrow roads. Sophie has been uncharacteristically quiet for the entire journey. I don't expect it to last long when she finally sees the house.

Turning into the private road and pulling up at the gates, she turns and raises her brows. I grin, waiting for her to comment as Tim opens them. He nods his greeting as I drive past.

"Oh, my God!" She finally squeals beside me, as I slowly drive down the gravel to the front of the house. I park the car alongside the other handful of vehicles and chance a peek at her. She is wide-eyed, looking up the façade of the property. I vividly remember what it was like to see this place for the first time, too.

Holding the front door open, she marches in and does a full one-eighty, before edging down the hallway, looking at every painting the walls house.

She rattles the pool room door, and I open it for her to see inside. The room illuminates before her and she baulks.

"Holy fuck!" she spits out.

I give her a ridiculously quick tour of the downstairs, then lead her upstairs. The look of absolute awe is permanently etched on her face as she quickly peeks into each room, and each time it's met with an expletive of some description, forcing me to chuckle.

Standing outside the dressing room, I push the door back, and wait for the sharp breath and profanity to resume. Surprisingly, she is speechless as we enter and slowly pivots to take in the contents.

"All my stuff is on that side." I point to my dresses, eveningwear, and everything else in between. I leave her looking around as I pick out the dress I was requested to buy and hang it in front of me.

"Oh, my fucking God!"

I turn around laughing as soon as the words ring out clearly in the room. She's standing at the island; her eyes rake over everything shiny on display. I watch, remembering my initiation was far different from hers, and I took to curling up in a ball on the floor.

"Jesus Christ, that's a frigging Rolex! An Omega!"

I chortle again. "Quite finished with the effing and jeffing?"

"Babe, I can't believe this place, and that all of these are yours! You really weren't kidding when you said there will be something in here, were you?"

"Nope." I shake my head. "Trust me, he has every angle covered.

If there's nothing on these rails that you like, I will be very shocked." Her eyes broaden as she looks over my handbags.

"You know, I'd just like to say, if you ever get bored of him, let me know well in advance. I'm not against slutting myself out to have a designer handbag like this!" She picks up Sloan's latest Chanel acquisition and sniffs it deeply. "Now, that really is what money smells like!"

I leave her to get it on with the leather, turn to my side, and dig into the drawers. I look in confusion at the black satin underwear set laying on top along with a receipt baring yesterday's date.

Tentatively touching the expensive scraps of material, I hold them up. Jesus, there's nothing to them! They're going to accentuate *everything*.

Sophie breathes against my neck. "I guess this is what he wants to take off you later. Shit, look at how much they cost! Doesn't miss a beat, does he?" she mutters to herself.

And no, he really doesn't.

Chapter 23

"SOPH? ARE YOU almost done?" I shout at the bathroom door. Silence is her reply. "Sophie?"

She's been in there for ages. The only thing that has stopped me from banging down the door, is the fact that it isn't the only bathroom in the house.

Slowly, it opens, and she appears on the other side. For the first time in the seven years we've known each other, she looks...worried. Dropping her head, she refuses to meet my gaze. Unable to understand what has suddenly got her terrified, she passes me the price tag. Confused, I take it from her.

"If I'd have known it was that expensive, I swear I wouldn't have put it on," she says, ashamed. Narrowing my eyes at the label, they widen when I see the figures. She has seemingly chosen, quite possibly, the most expensive dress in here.

"No, don't think about it, it's yours now, and you look gorgeous! Much better than I would've," I say, meaning every word. She is a vision in red, with her highlighted hair flowing around her shoulders and her make-up smouldering. "Besides, it's a better red dress than that thing you wore for the school dance all those years ago! Just remember not to throw alcohol down it!"

She brightens up and steps out. I turn back, but her hand grabs mine. She waits for me to scream murder at being touched, yet it never comes.

Moving us towards the mirror, she smiles. Gliding her hand lightly over my cheek, caressing my simple, barely-there make-up, she nods her approval. I do a quick flick of my eyes to my back. Charlie had already said the marks were barely noticeable, but I still feel self-conscious that others may see them and question.

Sophie turns me. "Nobody will notice, I promise." She throws her arm around me and hugs me tight. "We look good!"

I laugh out loud. It's the same line she always uses.

"We do!"

George brings the car to a stop outside Oblivion. I breathe in my dissatisfaction that, yet again, I have to endure this place. Sophie tugs my hand, and I hold it firm.

"It's okay, babe."

I nod, unable to stop my eyes watering.

"Hey! Forget her, this is your man's bir…night!" Her eyes shift nervously, and I wipe mine, unable to think of anything other than the obvious.

Sophie cups my face and slides her thumbs over my cheeks. "He loves you. Never forget that."

The door then opens, and she squeals when she sees reporters and the like vying for some attention. Laughably, everyone is just walking past, not giving them a second thought.

"How do I look?" she asks, wide-eyed again.

"You look great! Stop worrying," I say, although my tone lacks conviction due to my own internal distress.

"Do you think Stuart will like it?"

"Ask him yourself," I reply flatly, seeing two familiar figures sauntering towards us.

Standing alongside Sloan, in fitted jeans and jacket, Stuart looks like a completely different person outside the shapeless scrubs I have become accustomed to seeing him in. Sophie sucks back an audible breath beside me.

"Oh, shit," she utters, the same instant he motions for his date to get out. I cover my mouth as she constantly mutters to herself to breathe, before tottering towards him on her five-inch platform spikes, hands flailing out beside her to keep balance.

Stuart links her arm through his, winks at me, and guides her towards the club entrance.

Shuffling over the seat, a hand darts in, and the fingers wiggle. I hesitate and sit back, curious how he will react.

Folding my arms over my chest, I wait. Seconds later, a mass of dark hair ducks under the door. He smiles radiantly, and I hold firm. Knowing he isn't going to get me out, he gets in.

Slamming the door shut, he slides me over the leather and onto his lap, rubbing his hand over my knee. Slowly averting my eyes, midnight blues see through to my soul. He turns back to the window and sighs.

"You can't sit in here forever."

"I know," I whisper. "It's just…"

"Baby, she's gone."

I sigh sadly and touch his face, as the car illuminates from the cameras flashing outside. "It's not just her, or this place, it's…"

"I know you hate this side of me, but I didn't do it this time!"

I purse my lips, unable to respond. He's right; I do hate this side of his life. The philanthropist side, the side that does good, and the side that may, unfortunately, shine a spotlight on mine.

"Come on, let's do the walk of shame, beautiful, then I might give you some champagne..." He grins, and I cave.

"Okay, but I want more than that!" I counter playfully. Pressing a tender kiss to my lips, he pulls back, thinking.

"Don't worry, I have a full schedule planned for tonight." Gently moving me, he opens the door and climbs out. His hand reaches for mine, and this time, I grasp it firmly.

Walking towards the entrance, Sloan ignores the reporters, who are bizarrely congratulating him for some reason, and quickly ushers me inside.

Entering the club, something isn't right. There is nothing to indicate what's actually going on here tonight.

"How many functions do you hold a year? And how come it isn't at the hotel?" I start my line of enquiry, and he brings his hand to his mouth.

"It varies," he says, still touching his face, confirming he's withholding something. "And the club has a greater capacity than the hotel."

"And what's tonight in aid of?"

He quickly looks around the room, spotting the guys. "Ageing," is all he commits to, before taking my hand and pulling me along with him.

"Oh, right. Well, it's good that every charity benefits, including the elderly."

"No, it's not that. I admit, I'm leading you astray intentionally, but all will become clear shortly!"

"I don't understand. Are we here so you can schmooze clients out of their annuities?"

He chuckles. "No, but I am going to schmooze you! I told you, all will become clear by the end of the night."

A waitress passes by, and I snag a glass of whatever she is touting around. Sloan takes the full tray from her, gives her his best smile, and takes off with it towards Tommy and Parker.

"Drinks are on me, boys!" he shouts, feet from them, turning surprised heads as he passes.

I shake my head at this completely new side of him. Making my way over to them, I watch as they toast, down a glass each, then pick up a second.

Smiling, I realise I may never know all the sides of Sloan Foster – although I'm willing to risk a lifetime to find out.

I look around the club, seeing the bodies packed in. There has to be hundreds of people here. Looking at a few, this isn't the usual *impart-with-your-money* gig. Gone are the tuxes and ball gowns. Instead, we have jeans and jackets, and chest exposing, thigh-skimming dresses.

"Little lady! How very nice to see you tonight! Looking good as always!" Parker says. I give him my best *seriously* expression, and he laughs.

"Yeah, evening, little lady!" Tommy shouts, taking my glass and putting it down on the table. I adjust subtly to see if anyone has heard my new nickname amongst men. Indeed, as sods law would have it, a few people have turned at their spectacle.

"What's with the little lady moniker? It's embarrassing!"

"Well, you're little, and you're the boss's lady. We can call you flavour of the year if you prefer?"

I snort. "You can keep calling me little lady, thanks."

Tommy winks. "Yeah, that's what we thought." He drains his glass.

Sloan moves around my back and wraps his arms around me. "Could be worse, they could call you the little wife instead!" I close my eyes as the trio begin to high five each other. It's clear they have all lost their minds - or have had too much to drink already.

"Congrats, half-brit!" Devlin shouts behind us, and Sloan gives him a look that could smite him.

There's something I'm missing here. Looking around the room, everyone who passes is congratulating him, and he seems to be growing more nervous by the second because of it.

Easing away from his arms, I stare at him keenly. His eyes dart all over the place, until he grins and salutes with two fingers to the other side of the room. I narrow my eyes when I see Marie. She is dressed in a stunning black and red number – one which she doesn't wear for work. Moments later, Walker's large arms come around her waist. Looking at him, he's also in smart jeans and a shirt, as opposed to the usual t-shirts and combats that seem to be his staple wardrobe.

I pivot back to Sloan, but Stuart and Sophie approach, stopping me. She starts to open her mouth, but Stuart puts his hand over it. He leans into Sloan and whispers something to him. Curiously, I nudge Soph. If put in a tight spot, that garrulous tongue of hers will answer anything. We both start to back away, until it's thwarted.

"Oh, no, you don't!" Sloan pipes up, dragging me back from her. Doc laughs and pulls his date far away from me.

As I stand watching, Charlie and Jake enter the room. She looks immaculate, as always, in a little cerise, strappy dress - that is flowing around her legs - and killer heels. Giving me a small smile, she marches towards Sophie. Studying them, they are in deep discussion, pointing in my direction.

"Do you know all these people?" I ask, wanting to get to the bottom of what's really going on.

"No," he confirms amused.

"What are you hiding from me?" I ask suspiciously. The triad at his side snigger, and I tilt my head at the troublesome foursome. "I *will* find out."

"That's a given."

I glance at the women staring at the entourage of men surrounding me. I turn to look at them, noting that, although they have seen, they are more interested in what I'm doing.

"There's a lot of women very attractive women here tonight," I comment, feeling pale, ugly, and inferior in comparison. Sloan raises his brow, giving me his own *seriously* expression. I quickly turn back to the threesome behind me. "Looks like you boys have some admirers."

Parker laughs out loud. Just like the others, he looks impeccable. His crisp, white shirt and slack beige tie highlight his mocha colouring perfectly.

"Kara, they're not here for us, babe! Obviously, they missed the memo that the ultra-successful and obscenely wealthy Mr Foster is off the market permanently. That said, it's a good job I'm young, hot, and have an abundance of energy to dispel. I'm also appealing by association, which means that cheeky looking blonde is mine!"

I look away, embarrassed by his crassness.

"Oh, don't be embarrassed, little lady. I'm not as bad as him!" he says, nudging Tommy's arm.

Tommy laughs and grips his chin in his fingers. "Fox by name, fox by nature, honey!"

"Why? Because you're red or secretly cunning?" I query logically, while Sloan laughs raucously beside me.

"Both... And neither. Think about it!" Tommy grins as Parker throws his arm around his shoulder.

"Come on, Foxy, let's go give them our condolences...and something to cry on." They walk away as I stare and wonder.

I gasp, finally realising.

Sloan strokes my cheek as he continues to laugh at his friend. "Let's dance, my gorgeous girl."

I tug his hand a little. "I'm really not trusting you tonight!" I grip my hips and tap my foot.

"I know, it's the fun of the game." He laughs, starting to walk backwards. "Okay, how about you call this," he motions his hands down his jeans and shirt, "my birthday suit." He quickly grabs me up in his arms and swings me around, before carrying me onto the dance floor.

"Your birthday suit? It gives that expression an entirely new meaning." I laugh. He's out of his ever-loving mind.

"Maybe, maybe not. Just know that by the end of tonight, you'll be wearing yours and nothing else!" He breathes in, extremely satisfied. I dig my hands into his shoulders and pull back.

"Still very delusional, I see," I chirp with a smile. "It's nice to know some things haven't changed!"

"No, I told you before, when it comes to you, I'm merely fucking honest!" I laugh, as he paraphrases that memorable night which is clearly etched on the forefront of my mind forever.

The DJ changes the song, and the upbeat tempo seems to have everyone gravitating towards the dance floor. I look down at my heels, wondering if I should just kick them off and have done with it, when I feel his eyes on me and stare up.

"That reminds me..." With one hand on his hip, he looks me up and down. Appraising my appearance silently, he slides his free hand down my leg at a snail's pace, causing every nerve ending to tingle with excitement. He glides his hand over my emerald heels, and then brings it back up. Pulling me close, he tangles his fingers in the green silk sash at my waist and squeezes my arse for everyone to see.

His lips skim my neck delicately. "You know, for she who doesn't like to shop, this is one very stunning, sexy dress, Ms Petersen, but tell me, is it easy to remove?" He stands in front of me, chin between his finger and thumb. I sway a little, trying to rein in my giddiness.

I shrug my shoulders innocently and bat my eyelashes, countering his lively demeanour. "Oh, I don't know Mr Foster, define *'easy to remove'*?"

Moving around to my side, his hand glides down my waist. "Zips?"

"No."

He lifts his brow as he takes two steps behind me, then trails his fingers down my spine with determination. "Buttons?"

My breath catches in my throat. "No."

He smirks and comes around to my front, skimming both hands up my stomach and brazenly holding each breast, giving them a little squeeze.

"Ties?"

"No." I grin, and he places his lips over mine briefly.

"I'm tired of hearing that diabolical word, tell me what it does have!" he mumbles against my cheek.

"Just a hell of a lot of stretch!" I press myself into him and stare into his dark, desirous blues.

"Good, I'll be testing it later!" Changing his stance and putting his thigh between my legs, ensuring I feel it in the good areas, he tilts his head to my ear. "What's under it?"

"The lingerie you bought yesterday." He closes his eyes momentarily, then opens them, to reveal they are now glassy.

"Good girl, I knew you'd get the message." He moves us slowly on the floor, ignoring anyone else present.

I chortle. "I couldn't have got it any better if you'd have dressed me in them yourself."

"Baby, if I'd been left in charge, you wouldn't have got one leg in!" I throw my head back and laugh, raising a few eyebrows around us.

"True, you do have a penchant for stripping and shredding."

"Absolutely! Don't grow too attached to them, they'll be in the bin by morning."

Breathless, I push away and pick up a glass of champagne. Unyielding arms reach around me and I still, feeling the electricity fire, as his hand grips mine around the glass. "Round two is five months overdue, we'll be doing that again later, too!"

Collecting myself, he doesn't allow me an inch as he continually strokes me. I'm on the verge of demanding he gets us out of here now, when he turns me slowly.

"You should come with a warning."

"Me?"

"Yes, you."

His mouth thrusts itself over mine again, and I grip the back of his head with one hand while holding the glass out of the way with the other.

"You're insane, Sloan Foster!"

"As long as I have you, I'll always edge on insanity."

My feet are slightly sore by the time Sloan carries me off the dance floor, much to the amusement of an older couple who have been watching us for a while. The man winks at him, and Sloan laughs.

Raising my head to peer over his shoulder, Sophie and Charlie are floating around the floor together, glasses of champagne in either hand, while Jake and Stuart wait on the side lines, watching their dates.

I giggle and sigh, understanding I'm no longer walking through this life relatively alone anymore. With the exception of Marie and Sophie, I've been given a second family; a ragtag group of ex-army boys, an amazing doctor, a second sister, and a man who can take me to places I've only ever dreamed about.

The sound of laughing causes me to shuffle out of Sloan's hold, and he lowers me down, as Marie and the man who bonds them all together approach.

"Let go of her, birthday boy! You've monopolised her long enough!" Walker taunts light-heartedly.

Birthday boy?!

Oh, my God, I feel sick. Pressing my hand into his chest, I look into his eyes, and he stares at me with an encouraging look, daring me to see the truth.

Birthday suit? I think, as my face muscles contract a little. "Oh, shit, today is your birthday, isn't it?" I ask, horrified, thinking back to scouring the internet, vaguely remembering something about August. "Oh, my God, it is!" I bring my hands to my face and start stepping back, mortified and teary that I didn't know. He tugs me close and runs his hands the length of my face.

"Today is the best birthday ever, because I finally have you. Don't be angry that I didn't tell you."

I smile, but it's guarded, because I am hurt. I'm angry with myself that I should have known and didn't.

"Please don't do that. Don't cut yourself up over it."

I shake my head, feeling pathetic. "I can't help it!" I say, trying to keep out the pleading, teary tone. "I should've known. It's also a very sorry state of affairs that there's nothing that you don't already have that I can possibly give you." And that's what hurts the most; that I haven't actually got him anything. Something that would be from only me, irrespective of cost. I turn to Marie and Walker, they both wear saddened expressions, realising I honestly didn't know.

A long pause devours the surrounding area, and for a minute, it's just him and me. Two lights in the darkness.

"That's not entirely true. There are actually three things you can give me that I don't already have." He leans in, holds my head and slowly kisses me, then pulls back and does it again.

"Forgive me. I love you."

"Always," I reply, as Walker gently slides my hand into his.

"Let's dance, honey." He slowly guides me back onto the dance floor, while I continually glance back, watching Sloan escort Marie, but he never takes his eyes from me.

Settling into Walker's large arms, my mind runs away with itself, thinking back to every birthday I've never celebrated, unless put under duress by Sophie and the girls.

Why didn't he tell me? I feel like such an idiot.

"Honey, he wanted it to be a surprise." Walker's deep voice punctuates my hearing. I bristle uneasily, not because I've verbalised my thoughts, but because I'm so disappointed in myself right now.

I lift my head and sigh. "Why is he surprising *me* on *his* birthday?"

He laughs. "Not a clue, honey. You know how he is! You're the centre of his universe. Everything he does is with you in mind."

"I know, but I'm angry and upset that he didn't tell me. And also, that I don't have anything for him. What do you give the man who has everything?"

Walker stops us moving and pulls me in close. "You give him you. All of you. Anything less will never be enough." Walker rotates and stares directly at Marie and Sloan. Sloan's head shoots up when he sees us looking, but Marie pulls his chin back down.

One song melds into two, two turns into three, and when three threatens to become four, a throat clears, and we both stop to find Sloan with his hands on his hips, Marie by his side.

"I would like to dance with my woman now," he says, grabbing the end of my sash and pulling me towards him. Walker opens his arms wide, and Marie fills the space I've just vacated.

"After this dance, we're leaving. I have something amazing planned for-" The sound of clapping stops him, and we both turn to see a cake being wheeled out.

"You've got to be kidding me!"

"Happy birthday, kid!" Walker pats him on the back.

"You two are disowned!" he laughs.

Wrapping my arms around his neck, I ease into his chest, listening to his heartbeat. "Happy birthday, baby," I say, slowly peppering his cheek with soft kisses.

"Come on, let's get this cake cut and get out of here." He rubs his hands up and down my back, silently comforting me.

Devlin passes him a knife and wraps his arm around me. I smile up at him, and he winks, then unexpectedly, the crowd breaks into song.

"Oh, it just gets fucking worse, doesn't it!" Sloan mutters to himself, as the first line of *Happy Birthday* kicks in. "You're all fucking disowned!" he shouts to anyone in the inner circle.

I grin; the issue of not knowing doesn't seem so bad when the event brings him so much discomfort. More so when the guys incorporate 'half-brit' into the verse and everyone roars with laughter. I cover my face with both hands, burning with embarrassment for him. He laughs it off as he comes back, and Devlin passes him a microphone.

"To the best birthday ever." He holds a piece of cake up to me, and I take a bite, as the crowd coo and applaud. "Let's get out of here!"

"Okay, let me just find Sophie and Charlie." I pull away and edge through the crowd. As expected, I find the troublesome two leaning over the bar.

"I'm sorry; I've been dying to tell you! I almost blurted it out in the car!" Sophie grabs me, and she and Charlie cocoon me between them. "Stuart's been on edge just in case I couldn't hold my tongue!"

"It's fine. Probably better that I didn't know really."

"Kara, he made me promise! Do you know how hard it's been for me?" Charlie exclaims. She leans over the bar and speaks to the bartender, and he hands her a bottle of champagne. "Here, go celebrate!"

I take the bottle and hug it to my chest. Sophie pulls me to the side away from Charlie and starts fussing with the top of my dress. "Well, I think it's time to take the birthday boy home and give him his present of hot, sweaty, birthday sex! Call me in the morning and tell me how it goes!" My mouth opens in horror, but before I have time to verbalise my thoughts that I have no idea what the difference is, she literally shoves me away.

The loose soil shifts under my now ballerina clad feet, as I move blindly outside. I have no idea what he's doing or where he's taking me. He carefully manoeuvres me by the waist, keeping me close to his side.

A gentle breeze picks up and forces his scent to wash over me, infusing my senses deeper. I close my eyes beneath the fabric; absorbing him, wanting him. Falling deeper in love with him, understanding he will always be the opposite side of me - the completing side of me.

"Sloan, considering today is your day, shouldn't I be the one leading *you* down the garden path?"

He chuckles, and the warmth licks my temple as he leans in closer. "No, because my only desire is to please you. And my birthday wish is to create another unforgettable night together," he says softly as his full lips sweep over mine. Gently, he unties the blindfold, and I blink away the dark spots in my vision.

I tilt my head around and make out the house behind the thick trees. This is the woodland trail he was trying to sell me a while ago. The clearing we're occupying is set up with a cast iron gazebo, flowing with pale silks. Lanterns illuminate the growing darkness and cast shadows around the vicinity, while music softly emanates from an unknown source.

"This is amazing, but I feel guilty that you seem to be making this all about me. I didn't even get you anything."

"Kara, you've given me everything these last five months. You're my past, present, and future, all rolled into one." I bite my lip, not knowing how to address that statement. "Look, don't think about it. When the time is right, I will explain, but tonight is just for us." He pours two glasses of champagne and passes me one.

"Earlier, I said there were three things you could give me that I don't already have. Those three things are a wife, a family, and a future. You're it for me. There will never be anyone else who completes me as wholly as you do." Unable to respond in a way I deem satisfactory, I cling to him like the world is ending.

Evening descends into night as we laugh and dance the hours away. With my arms secure around his neck, he picks me up and carries me back to the house.

Setting me down on the kitchen worktop, I scan all the baked stuff Marie has been conjuring up in secret.

"I'm going to do this a little differently."

I scrunch my nose up as his scent invigorates me again in as many hours. "I don't understand."

"No, but I do. And since it's my birthday - as you so eloquently put it - I'm going to play with my present...and eat my cake as I see fit." He cages me in and brings my head to his. His kiss leaves me borderline breathless, and I feel my lungs expand, as he slowly picks me up and takes us upstairs.

Carefully reaching around me, he grips the dress and slides it down my body, gazing intently. Standing in nothing but the underwear he had bought for himself, he towers over me in only his shorts.

"Now, where to start?" he murmurs rhetorically, deep in thought. My breathing stills in anticipation, then he hooks a finger under the centre of my bra and drags me to him. His hardness grows between us, and I glide my hands up his muscled back.

Picking me up under the backs of my legs, I cinch them hard around him. Lowering us to the mattress, he licks a line across my stomach, and my body spasms instantly under his controlled action. He comes up further and sucks my satin covered nipple into his mouth. Pressing my bum into the padding, I arch my back at the feel of it, and close my eyes to prolong the sensation. A light nip on my hardened bud brings me back. He swiftly slides his hands over the full cups and feels around my back to unfasten it. He clearly fails to find it, when the material is torn from behind me.

Holding it up, he grins. "I honestly don't know why I bothered. I have no control when it comes to you. I guess you could say these gorgeous garments are wasted on me. I guess I'll just have to buy some more!" He lobs it on the floor and sits astride my stomach, while his look gives way to a darkening expression.

A long time passes, with each of us just studying the other, until he gently sucks away at my breast. My body flourishes under his, until he pulls me up and we're nose to nose. His hand clenches in my hair, and he lowers us back down.

"Make a wish," I ask him softly

"I would, but it's already come true," he whispers, before smothering my neck with his lips.

Staring up at the ceiling, I give myself over to the raptures. I close my eyes and my body arches under his skilled mouth. As he moves down slowly, I savour every moment, never wanting this to end.

Relaxing back down, I make my own wish, and long for it to come true.

Chapter 24

BLOWING MY BREATH out in a whistle, I knew this was a very bad idea.

If only I'd been given the unavailable and unthinkable option of doing this alone. I should've coerced Marie into lying for me, so I could finally lay the demons of the last few years of living with Samantha to rest.

I should've refused when Remy said he had a van ready, and a charity shop sorted to deal with the removal of my unwanted furniture.

Except, it's pointless, because I didn't do any of those things. And now I'm here, still fretting over what I should and shouldn't have done.

My knuckles whiten around the door handle as I grip it excessively. The queasiness in my stomach deepens, and the acid audibly churns. I don't want to do this, especially not with Charlie here. It's been months since I've crossed this threshold, and I fear what I may find on the other side.

Remy moves closer. "We can't stand out here all day, Kara. Sloan will call at some point, and I don't know about anyone else, but I'd rather not have to deal with him when he's irrational. And trust me, when it comes to you, he won't be anything less. *Ever.*"

A chill runs down my spine when his hand comes over mine. I quickly shift past him and rub my sweaty palms over my denim-clad bum, hoping he doesn't see, as he pushes the door open.

A musty, old smell hits me first. I don't recall it ever smelling this bad - if at all. I take a deep breath and enter, quickly moving to open the windows in both the living room and kitchen as wide as they will go. Fresh air circulates throughout the space, and I stand in the middle of the room, not quite believing what I'm seeing.

For the first time ever, I actually want to cry, and I don't care who bears witness to it.

Looking around the room, my eyes pull in all directions, unable to concentrate solely on any one thing. The sofa is destroyed, knifed and shredded - the foam padding is poking out through the lacerations. The coffee table is upended, and the legs have been broken off. The television screen is kicked in and smashed on the floor. I shiver and pray that Sam had not been here at the time of this destruction. I pull out my phone and dial her number.

Nothing.

Hugging my mobile to my chest, I notice Charlie is clearly in shock, loitering in the doorway. I stare up at the ceiling and squeeze my eyes shut. I don't want her to see this, to know that on some level deep down she may have been right, or at least thought she was. I might have nothing, but I'm not some gold-digging bitch who will latch on to any man who offers the right price.

Tears spring from my eyes and a warm arm wraps around me, rocking me until the tears subside. I ease against her and rest my head on her shoulder in defeat. I open my eyes, fearful of what look might be levelled at me, but surprisingly, her face is soft and sympathetic.

"Do you want to keep anything in the kitchen, Kara?" I stare at her, trying to fathom why she isn't disgusted by the person I really am. I might have the designer clothes and fancy diamonds now, but underneath, I'll always be the poor girl with nothing. I shake my head in self-pity.

"Okay, I'll get them to clear that first. Be back in a minute." She goes off to instruct Devlin, Tommy, and Remy.

Left alone in the mess and destruction, I head down the landing. Standing outside Sam's old bedroom door, I push it open hard. As expected, the room is a mess. Everything is either broken or torn to shreds. Walking deeper inside, I notice all of Sam's stuff is gone. Hope blooms in my chest that she had cleared out long before whoever did this came to visit.

"Is everything in here to go as well?" Charlie asks from the doorway, and I nod shakily, desperate to get this over and done with. I turn, and my reflection casts in the mirror, but it isn't my likeness that hooks my attention, it's the words scrawled above it.

You can run but you can't hide. I fucking own you!

In the corner of my eye, I see Charlie staring at the graffiti. "John will find her, Kara. I promise he will." Only we both know he won't. I'm hearing this promise of finding those who don't want to be found a little too often lately. And each time, it lacks conviction.

"Come on, you don't need to see this." She gently tugs my arm to leave. "Come on," she urges. "Let's clear out your room."

I dally in the doorway of my former bedroom. Charlie is in front of my old dresser, studying the few photos I keep on there. One is of

Sam and me when we were just kids... Kids who didn't know anything about pain. We were completely innocent and carefree. Eventually, we would learn the hard way.

With a little smile, she then picks up the next picture. It was taken when I'd been admitted to hospital. Sam had her arm slung around me. The picture doesn't carry particularly good memories at all – it was a reminder of how harsh life had once been. To the unknown eye, we looked like friends posing, only I know she was holding me up since I was so broken, I couldn't even manage my own weight.

I study at it with glassy eyes, smiling a little when I see the Manchester University sweater I was wearing. I sigh thinking of the stranger who had saved my life and taken me to the hospital that night. He had left it behind, and I never had the heart to destroy it. That same sweater still hangs not less than two feet away in the wardrobe. It's morose, but the true, undisclosed reason I keep it, is because it brings me peace and tranquillity.

Charlie's thumb grazes over the picture, her face seeing something ghostly and familiar. She turns and looks at me, something piecing together inside her mind. She scans me up and down apprehensively, before a look of understanding ripples across her eyes. A chill runs the length of my spine under her scrutiny.

"What?" I enquire, desperate to know what she's thinking. She shakes her head, seemingly to clear her thoughts, before picking up the frames and carefully stacking them in her hands.

"Nothing, nothing at all!" she says, plastering on a fake smile. She then walks towards my wardrobe, reaching to the top to pull down one of the bags I store up there, still avoiding my gaze. "I'll take the drawers, if that's okay?"

"I guess I'll take the wardrobe, then." I grab the handle and open the doors. I gather up an arm full of clothes, still on their hangers, and throw them onto the bed. I quickly pull them off and fold them up.

Thirty minutes later, the wardrobe is empty, apart from the sweater I'd kept for all these years. My fingers stroke over the worn fabric and my vision is assaulted with images and feelings, remembering things I'd kept securely locked away. Things I made myself not remember. I fist the hoodie in my hand and sink onto my old bed.

"Where did you get this?" Charlie asks. Her tone is neutral, but her eyes are anything but.

"It was given to me years ago," I reply, hoping she won't push for more because I know I won't be able to expound the truth. Although she's probably already aware, on some instinctual level, that I, too, have been abused, I don't want to disclose anything further to her. No good would ever come out of two victims comforting each other while trying to right a few wrongs.

Charlie's hand reaches for the sweater, and she starts to examine it. Twisting and turning it around, looking at the label, the neckties, and finally, the cuffs. I watch with curious, narrow eyes. My mind turns over with a question I don't know if I'm strong enough to ask.

And if I do, will I be able to deal with the potentially damning answer?

"Why did you keep it?" Her eyes narrow.

"It helps me to remember." I take it back, unzip it and drag it over my body. Needing some space from her, I walk out of the room.

Looking around the flat, the life I had worked so hard to build for myself now resides in a few black bags and recycled supermarket boxes. Every room I pass is now empty, and all my remaining personal things have been packed away. Entering the living room, that, too, is now bare, as are the kitchen and bathroom.

As discussed with Remy, everything - apart from my personal belongings - were to be donated or skipped, and at some point, a van had arrived, and the majority of my furniture was now gone. Everything was divested and devoid of life. The flat is finally an empty shell, and seeing it so unembellished induces me to shed a solitary tear.

"Sloan just called," Charlie shouts to me. "He's going to be here shortly to pick you up. Rem will stay with you. I'm going to get a ride home with Tommy and Dev." She puts her jacket on. Her narrow eyes work over my upper body again. I'm still wearing the sweater, but the urgent need to ask her what's so interesting about it is deepening.

"Did someone clear out Sam's old room?" I ask, she nods. "Did they find *anything*?" I pray to God they didn't unearth any drug paraphernalia she might have hidden well – too well that even she forgot about it.

"No, nothing. Looks like she left when she said she would. Are you going to be alright here waiting for him?"

"I'll be fine. I have something I need to do anyway." She pulls me into her arms and cuddles me tight. Even though I don't feel the prickle, I remain stiff until she eventually pulls back, pats my arm, and starts to walk away.

"Hey, Charlie?" She turns around, and I hold my arm out a little. "What's so interesting about this? You've been acting weird ever since you saw it in the photo." She drops her head to the floor. "Seriously, what is it?"

"It's nothing. Just that Sloan had a sweater like that once...when he was at uni." Her voice is uncertain, nervous, as though she is debating whether or not she's doing the right thing by telling me this.

"*Once*?" I ask inquisitively, my mind slotting together a puzzle that I'm positive will destroy me if it turns out to be true.

"Yeah, he said he lost it. It was his favourite." She shrugs as though it doesn't mean anything, but to me, it means *everything*.

And, in my mind, it has just shunted my world further into the darkened abyss.

Feeling like I have just swallowed shards of glass, I have no idea how I manage to ask the next question. "When did he *lose* it?"

"Years ago. I don't know, maybe six or seven. I'll see you later, Kara." She then turns quickly on her heel.

I run into my bedroom and slam the door behind me. Ripping up the carpet, and then the loose floorboards underneath, I stretch, until my fingers grasp the object of my attention, all the while my mind swims with the latest of his innuendos.

You're my past, present, and future, all rolled into one.

So clear as day, the flowers, the dress, the shoes...the card.

My mind rewinds back, plucking out another unmistakable comment.

That wasn't the first time I ever saw you, Kara.

Oh, my God! He'd said it!

He fucking said it!

Using my sleeve to wipe the built-up dust off the top, I sit back on the bed with my box in my hands. My breathing begins to falter, and I hesitate. In the space of a few minutes, my entire world has shifted on its axis. Regardless of what he says, I *know* he was there that night.

Did he save me?

My mind starts to race with questions I'm too terrified to ask. If he was there, is he with me now because he feels indebted to stay and repay me emotional recompense for what happened to me? Or, does he really want to be with me because of who I am, and not as a result of what he saw back then – *if he was there?*

The shadow of doubt lurks towards the forefront of my mind. Confusion consumes me, and bile starts to seep higher in my throat while my next thought engulfs me.

Oh, my God, did he rape me?

Acid floods the recess of my mouth, and I dry heave onto the carpet. I grip my chest, as I drop and kneel on the floor, trying to catch my breath. A swift knock brings me back to reality, and I straighten myself up. Opening the door, Remy is leaning against the frame.

"Ready to go whenever you are." He looks relaxed and unfeigned. His eyes squint slightly in horror when he sees me, no doubt seeing my paleness and red-rimmed eyes. He reaches out to me. "Are you okay?"

I nod. "I'll just be a minute." I close the door with haste, forcing him out of the room. The lock clicks into place, and I pick up the box from the bed. Lifting the lid, I quickly scan the contents. Satisfied, I shut it and stuff it into my holdall. I close my bedroom door behind me for the final time and go in search of Jeremy.

"Hey, Kara. Good to see you again." Danny greets when I enter the kitchen.

"Erm, hi," I mumble.

Danny seems weary in Remy's presence, and I have no doubt he most likely recognises him. Remy walks into the living room and relaxes his large frame against the wall. He watches every move Danny makes with acute suspicion.

Coming closer to me, Danny looks away from him. "Kara, are you sure about this guy? He's been here before...with that other weirdo," his says, his voice laced with concern. Whether it's for my benefit or his, I can't quite say.

"It's nothing for you to worry about, Danny. Take care of yourself." I drop the keys in his hand and walk away for the final time. I manage to get down one flight of stairs, needing to escape when I hear heavy steps behind me.

"Hey, do you know what happens if you run off, little lady? I get my arse tag teamed Sloan and Devlin style. Stay close, I actually like having full function in my arms and legs!" He makes light of it, but I know he's serious. I slow down my pace and walk next to him, trying to disentangle myself from my own head, and him who fills it completely, along with every other cell of my being.

Sloan...

What the hell am I going to do about him?

I don't need to know for certain that I own his missing sweater, because I know it on an intuitive level. I feel it in my gut. Each time I've worn it in the past, I've felt at peace. Bizarrely, it's the same kind of peace Sloan brings out in me each time he holds me, and when he kisses me, and when he professes words of affection to me. If it is true, it means I've had a piece of him with me for years and never known it. That means he has seen me at my best, and my absolute worst - as far down to rock bottom as anyone can go. But none of that matters anymore.

Now I need to be strong and ask him for the truth, and the skeletons I know he doesn't want to disclose. My heart breaks, realising we may never recover from it, but I have to know – my future depends on it.

But what I will do with the truth after he gives it to me remains to be seen.

Remy assists in pushing open the heavy door. The communal entrance is never locked like it's supposed to be for residence safety; and seeing the state of the flat I've just left for the last time, I'm glad I'm leaving.

Except, am I just escaping one world of pain, and possibly entering into another that is yet to materialise?

Inevitably, I know when it does, my world will shatter.

Remy's hand twists my elbow painfully, and I feel the tingle of awareness run the length of my limb, from wrist to shoulder. I twist abruptly to see what the hell is wrong with him. His face is tight and hard. His eyes are black, and he's not even looking at me. Following his line of sight, to see what's holding his undivided attention, my heart stops.

Deacon.

Chapter 25

"STAY CLOSE TO me, Kara. Play along, don't do anything and don't say anything. Don't treat me any differently than you did when you first met me months ago," he orders, straightening his shoulders discreetly. A mask of indifference slides over him, and watching the transformation before me, it's not hard to pretend.

"Remy, I'm scared," I confess hesitantly, unsure what I'm to do. I'm not entirely comfortable with him, and I can't say I fully trust him, either. No matter what Sloan and Walker might tell me, somewhere inside, my subconscious tells me to be wary and alert.

"Just stay behind me, honey. Come on, the sooner we get rid of him, the sooner we can get you home safe." He places his hand on the small of my back and guides us towards the enemy.

Deacon's face lights up like Christmas when he sees us approach. "Ah, Kara! You've done well, Jeremy. I didn't think you'd be able to do it, but you've impressed me this time." Deacon circles us and Remy's hand moves from my back to the inside of my arm. His hold is vice-like, and I'm completely on edge, aware this could turn dire at any moment.

"She's with me, Deacon. I have to return her to that bastard shortly. If I don't, he will hunt us down. Just a bit longer, *brother*," Remy says. I stare up at him, and note he wears his mask well, but is it just a mask? In the far depths of my soul, something is prodding me, awakening me, telling me their friendship knows no limitations.

Deacon stands inches from me. His hand tugs at my chin, and invisible fire flares through me. I'm itching to kick him and run, but I dare not move. Right now, it is irrelevant whether I trust Remy or not, because I'm trusting him to get us the hell out of here. *Soon*.

"Okay, okay," Deacon replies. "I can wait. I see the bruises have gone, Kara. Next time I'll have to remember you can take so much more. Next time, your little slut friend won't be there to save you. She can run, but she can't hide. Neither of you can. *I fucking own you!*" he sneers in my face.

I remain solemn and dignified, although my heart is breaking beneath the surface, listening to him talk about Sam. The only positive that has come out of his mouth is that I know she's still alive. Wherever she may be.

Deacon begins to shuffle on the spot. It's not nervousness, it's something else. He spears me with a thoughtful glare. "How are your weekly chats going, Kara? Do the puzzle pieces fit yet?" he goads, and my body starts to tense.

How does he know about my shrink?

The sound of tyres approaching breaks Deacon off, and he spins around just in time to see Sloan's Aston halt a few feet in front of us. The door opens, and he climbs out. Striding towards us, his movements are as graceful as a panther on the prowl for its next kill, but powerful enough to show Deacon he's not leaving here without me. My heart pounds frantically; thankful that he is finally here, but terrified how the situation might escalate further.

"Deacon," Sloan hisses between gritted teeth, once he's within earshot. Deacon's face twists into a wry smile, satisfied he now has the person he wants to hurt most in the world at arm's length.

I stare into Sloan's eyes; his game face is firmly in place. He glances down my body, his eyes huge and recognising when he sees the sweater. And any uncertainty I had washes away.

Eight years of wondering who, and now I know.

But in what capacity, I still have to brace myself for.

I pull away from Remy and stand beside Sloan. His arm slides around my waist, and I lean into him for moral support and security. His hand caresses my chin and gently touches the spot Deacon had only moments earlier, erasing his filth.

"Oh, isn't this sweet! If I'd have known it was this easy to call you out, I would have done it sooner. A *lot* sooner, if you know what I mean, brother. Two birds, one stone. How's my little Charlie these days? Does she still cry herself to sleep at night, dreaming of me?"

I start to edge away from Sloan; my fists bunching at my sides. I feel his eyes burn into me, but I don't allow it to deter what I'm about to do. To hell with the consequences of my actions, I seek vengeance.

"You son of a bitch!" I scream, as my arm swings up from my side. My fist connects with Deacon's cheek, and his head is thrown back on impact. Remy quickly moves behind him and grabs his arms, holding him back in a death grip, as he frantically tries to get to me. Sloan, in turn, stands sentry in front of me, protecting me; shielding me.

Deacon spits watery blood onto the ground, and his black, lifeless eyes stake me on the spot. "The next time we meet, I'm gonna fuck you so bad, you'll beg me to end you!" He scrubs his hand over his face and then sneers at me. "And you still can't hit for shit, you little cunt!" My eyes shoot open at his parting shot.

"You come near her or Charlie again, and I'll fucking kill you!" Sloan shouts at him, and every muscle touching mine tenses before the last word has even left his lips. He's ready to fight this out by the look of it.

Remy remains quiet, but the expression he's giving us from behind Deacon speaks volumes. It's a look telling us to leave. *Now.*

Deacon struggles against Remy, and the sound of heavy metal hitting the ground reverberates around us. A gun lies ominously on the concrete, and Sloan glares at it.

"You want to shoot us, Deacon?"

"Oh, I'm gonna do a lot more than that. Just watch your back!" He frees himself from Remy, straightens up, and then turns back to me. "And you, you'll be mine again. Just you wait." He picks up the gun and puts it back in the holster beneath his jacket.

"Hey, Kara? Has that shrink of yours delved to the bottom yet? Do you finally know what secrets *he* hides from you? Why don't you ask your knight in shining armour what he did? Look at your wrists. The scars you bear, yet try so hard not to remember! Ask that fucker what he did eight years ago!"

My head moves between both of them. I'm anxious to hear the truth - I've waited a long time for it - but I know whatever comes out of Deacon's mouth will be prevarications, knowing lies will work in his favour to slide a wedge between us

Still, there is no smoke without fire, and between these two men, the truth of a past that has decimated me is dying to be heard at long last.

Deacon stands with a devious grin in place, staring at us. Above all else, he's intentionally goading Sloan, who's moving towards him with a predatory pace. Remy is caught between them both, appearing physically sick. I look into Sloan's eyes and place my hand on his chest, digging my fingers into him.

Remy finally snaps out of whatever trance is holding him mentally hostage, and steers Deacon towards his 4x4, blocking the driver's door when he's inside. Sloan's body is still rigid, watching undeterred with his fists rounded and hard, until Deacon starts the car. The roar of the engine and the fading sound signals his departure.

Remy jogs back and grabs Sloan's face hard, but he's still watching me like a hawk. "Hey! Hey, he's gone! Don't make this worse than it is. His time *will* come." Sloan finally faces Remy and nods in confirmation. His strong, handsome features look ashen and beaten, but his eyes are still wild with anger.

"Is everything done here?" he asks, through gritted teeth.

"Yeah, we're done. We still need to talk, though," Remy tells him, looking down at me again. "In private. I'll come by your office tomorrow."

"Call me first," he replies.

Rem slaps his back and makes his way towards his car. He gets in and tips his invisible hat at me. I mouth *thank you,* and he salutes before driving off.

When I turn back around, Sloan's eyes are fixed on my torso. His lips press together tightly, and he stares for a long time, clearly struggling to find the right words.

Unable to take the silent treatment any longer, I walk towards his car, deposit myself in the passenger seat and wait for him. He hasn't moved, and I'm trying to judge whether or not Deacon's venom has just prematurely started the chain reaction that is inevitably going to change everything.

Again.

I sit and wait, mentally walking myself through how I will find a way to broach the subject of the sweater. *His* sweater.

If I asked, would he tell me the truth or feed me bullshit to keep me sweet? If I pressed harder, would he snap and spill his demons? Or would he push me away with ambiguity to keep the truth eternally buried?

I watch as the car door opens, and he gets in. He doesn't look at me at all. It's almost like he is trying to forget my presence beside him. His hand curls around the steering wheel, and he starts the ignition.

We cruise steadily through the afternoon traffic. In the twenty minutes we have been in the car, he still hasn't glanced in my direction, not once. I'm actually upset that he's avoiding me when I haven't done anything wrong. He's the one harbouring eight years of secrets and lies – *we both are* - and they have defined us in completely different ways.

The more I allow myself to think about it, the more it compels me to query everything I assumed I knew accurately. What had he done eight years ago? I already knew he had entered my life without my knowing it – he has inadvertently confessed to that little indiscretion. Now, I'm sitting next to him, wearing his *missing* sweater, and he hasn't said two words to me since Deacon rocked the foundation and departed. The tension between us is too thick to push aside.

I openly stare at him. Studying him, noticing every little movement. The way the vein in his temple bulges; the tick in his jaw when he grinds his teeth; and the determined grip on the wheel. I can even see the power of his shoulders, flexing angrily under his jacket.

He's fighting himself internally, mentally trying to retain his cool control. I've witnessed him do this many times previously, but today, he's fighting a losing battle.

Because today, Deacon has won.

He effortlessly glides the car into his reserved space next to my Evoque. He exits immediately, still not acknowledging me or even asking if I'm okay.

Heading straight to the lifts, he boards the first one that arrives. He turns to face me; the torment and pain are evident in his handsome features. I remain unmoving in the desolate car park as the doors close, before finally breaking down with my head in my hands.

Curling up in a ball, the haunting sound of my newly fractured heart echoes through the wide-open space.

Outside the suite door, the silence envelops me. It's uncomfortable and unwanted. At least if he was venting his anger at seeing his sweater after all these years, he is still expressing some sort of emotion. The handle turns in my palm, yet I'm still debating whether or not I'll be welcome when I cross the threshold. My holdall is slung over my shoulder. My box of memories is burning a hole in my hand. Opening the door fully, I tiptoe inside.

There's no sound, no movement. Nothing.

I lock the door behind me and pace into the living room. Dropping my bag beside the coffee table, I lower onto the sofa and clutch my box as though my life depends on it.

Once upon a time, it did.

The sound of water flowing upstairs shuts off, and I sigh subtly, chewing on my thumbnail.

I'm not completely naïve and stupid to acknowledge that there's more than a fifty per cent chance I might be calling Marie shortly to tell her I'm homeless again. I square my shoulders and repeat in my head that I can make it alone. I've done it for this long, and I would again if I had to.

I curl my legs underneath myself on the sofa and open the box. To an outsider, it's a box of junk, none of it is actually worth anything, but to me, it's priceless. Tipping it up, I empty out the contents and rummage through the tat. Just like I remember, the last item is a badly torn piece of scrap paper, buried deep beneath everything else.

I twirl it between my fingers, repeating the numbers scribbled on it over and over in my head. I stare at the number as a whole. A phone number I've possessed for eight long years. A number I had wanted to call for as long as I could remember. A number I could never bring myself to call because I feared where it would lead to. The number held the answers to my questions. Questions, of which, I'm positive I already know the unspoken answers to.

When I had finally regained consciousness at the hospital, a nurse had given it to me. She said it was the number of the man who had brought me in. He had requested that I call him, but I never did. I didn't want to remember. I didn't want to run from every man I would ever meet, because of the one that broke me in more ways than I knew existed - up until that point, at least.

Laying in my hospital bed for days after I woke up, the numbers became permanently embedded in my brain, as I deliberated what would be in my best interests. In the end, I knew nothing good would come from it, and so I boxed it away along with everything else I didn't want to remember in the short term. But at the same time, regardless of how much I pushed, I didn't ever want to forget either.

The sound of bare feet slap on the floor, and I turn in their direction. The paper is still lodged between my fingers when Sloan appears at the foot of the stairs. He has changed into sweatpants and a t-shirt, and is rubbing a towel over his hair. His eyes go straight to the sweater and then to the paper in my hand. I take a deep breath, because he suddenly seems indifferent; harder, colder. He makes no attempt to approach me, just studies me unnervingly.

I take off the sweater, fold it, and gently place it on the coffee table. I carefully position the paper on top of it and throw all the other bits of worthless shit back into the box. I re-lid it, put it back inside my bag, and zip it up.

Crossing my arms over my chest, I wait for him to fabricate his explanation, but he just stares resolutely.

"When are you going to be completely honest with me?" I ask quietly, feeling utterly ashamed that I'm asking him to do something that I also refuse to. "Today, I managed to piece together some of what you hide from me. Those," I point towards the table, "are yours. You gave them to me the night I was brutally raped and beaten within an inch of my life."

Outwardly, I'm composed, but inside, I'm falling apart.

"It's not what you think," he answers softly, his eyes trained hard on the floor.

A laugh escapes my throat. "*It's not what I think?* Sloan, I don't think you fully understand exactly what happened to me; what I went through. For months afterwards, I secretly wanted to die. I had nothing to live for. All I had were memories, *nightmares, shame...* I forced myself to not remember, but some things just don't want to stay hidden." I step towards the window and stare out of it. Anything is better than to look at him right now. "Please...just tell me what happened? I need to make sure I can eliminate you. *Please,*" I plead. I hear him move behind me, and I'm in two minds whether or not I should face him. Making the decision, I slowly rotate.

A stray tear leaks from his eye, and he finally answers me. "I didn't rape you. I would never hurt you, Kara. *Never.*"

"So who did? Come on, I know that you know!" I scream, but he remains defiant in the face of my anger.

"I can't tell you! There's so much more to this than you understand. I just... I can't! Not now."

I look away and curl my bottom lip into my mouth. It's a preventative measure to stop myself from crying, because I know once the dam breaks, I won't be able to stop the flood.

"Well, I guess I have my answer then."

I tilt my head up and start walking back towards the door. He watches me, all the while never taking his eyes from mine. He stands there motionless, undoubtedly damaged from a past that binds us together in the most debauched way possible. I can tell from his expression he's still fighting the inner battle that is tearing him apart. He's judging what to do for the best – for both of us. But it makes no difference because his choice is apparently already made.

And so is mine.

"Just tell me one thing? Is that your sweater?" His face and neck harden, and his eyes zone in on the offending garment. He isn't going to answer me, and I've had enough. "Just answer the fucking question! *Is. That. Your. Sweater?*" I bite out between my teeth.

"YES!"

My lungs draw in a shallow breath. I close my eyes, absorbing the shocking, yet predictable truth that I already knew was fact.

"And was that your mobile number eight years ago?" He doesn't respond, instead, he walks into his office. My leg shakes until he returns, and he throws an old mobile phone onto the coffee table.

Finally, I have some of the answers I've waited nearly a decade for.

"Thank you." I mean it, because for the first time in eight years, I can put a little bit of the mystery together, and a little piece of my past to rest. It's not what I wanted to hear, because a few simple words have just altered any future we might have had together.

I pull my bag over my shoulder and shift back around to him. "Obviously, you still can't find it in your heart to be one hundred per cent honest with me, and sadly, that means I can no longer be with you."

He starts shaking his head rapidly, coming out of his rigid state. "God, no, don't walk away! Not again. Baby, please don't do this!" He moves in front of me; his hand caressing my cheek.

Any other time, I would have drifted in closer to feel him, but this is not the time. I can't allow myself the luxury of having him this close, not while he still conceals secrets that have brought me unimaginable pain and suffering, and definitely not while he still doesn't trust me enough to unburden himself of them.

Again, I'm dealing with double standards, but I can't divest my heart of pain until he does the same.

Still, I refuse to feel guilty any longer because he knows my darkest secret.

He's known all along.

"One more chance – tell me the truth. Please, *I'm begging you,*" I implore. His hand drops instantly, and he steps back. It's exactly what I expected him to do – he would rather I walk away than close the lid on the last eight years forever.

Finally, I have my answer.

I tug on my bag strap and walk towards the door. Stopping in front of it, I hear his sobs of pain deepen. The fight to do what's right is killing him. I know this because it's killing me, too. But being denied the truth has done me in for eight, long, fucking years. It has to stop at some point, and that point was now.

"Goodbye, Sloan." I place my keys on the table, fighting back my own tears.

Closing the door with a soft click, I break down on the other side, where he can't see.

Chapter 26

WALKER IS WAITING just inside the open front door when the taxi pulls up. I get out, and hesitantly walk towards him. He appears downcast, and I purposely evaluate his expression. His eyes - normally hard and unforgiving - are consumed with sympathy and something else that might even resemble guilt.

He knows.

There's not a shred of doubt in my mind that he was with Sloan that night.

Clearing my head, I don't say a single word as I walk past him into the house. I find Marie in my old bedroom, changing the sheets.

"Hi," I greet softly, and her eyes meet mine. I break down instantly, my knees hitting the floor hard. Her arms are unyielding while she rocks me gently. My tears don't subside; if anything, they become stronger and more determined.

"Honey, I promise I didn't know. When you called to say you'd left again, I thought you'd just had a little tiff, but then Sloan called John and... I'm sorry, baby, I really am. I know how much you love him."

The sensitive, delicate skin around my eyes is sore, burning with salty tears. My body is weak, boneless and mentally shattered from the emotional battering I've endured today. Not even the hardened solitary existence I forced myself to live in for years can help me now.

I'm broken. Irrefutably.

"He wouldn't tell me! I asked him, and he said he couldn't. All he confirmed was that the old sweater and mobile number I'd been given at the hospital were his. He wouldn't tell me..." I cry harder into her. She embraces me the only way a mother can and allows me to fall apart inside her arms.

In my peripheral vision, Walker is loitering cautiously at the door. He doesn't look at me, just motions for Marie. She kisses me on the head and leaves me alone.

Using the bed as leverage, I scramble to my feet. Subdued and pathetic in my abysmal state, I seem to have reverted back to the girl who woke up in that hospital bed screaming.

My phone beeps from inside my bag, and I fish it from the

bottom. The screen lights up fiercely, and Sloan's name is all over it. I reject the call and chuck it on the bed. It lands face down. *Perfect.*

Picking up the pillowcases, I start where Marie had left off before I had interrupted. I manage to get one pillow covered when raised voices drift into the room.

"I don't care, John! I don't want to hear any more! I told you this is fucking bullshit! She has a right to know – it happened to her!" Marie's voice raises in ways I don't recognise. She's a pacifist; she absolutely detests confrontation. She said it was one of the reasons why she never questioned her ex-husband about his suspected infidelity for years.

"What was he supposed to do, angel? Leave her there? You didn't see what that bastard did to her. He pumped her with so much shit, she was barely fucking breathing!" John's voice raises in defence and defiance.

The screaming continues back and forth, but all I can concentrate on is his last sentence.

"One of you needs to start telling her the truth. She deserves that much!" A long pause. "No, don't fucking touch me, John! I don't need comforting! I need to know that my daughter will be able to have some kind of life away from all this shit one day! That she will be able to close her eyes and not see the past. No, I mean it, don't!"

I close the door as quietly as possible until the mechanism clicks into place. Sitting with my head in my hands, the heated argument goes on and on, and after hearing the words of denial in various different guises, I grow tired, and ball up on the bed.

I want to drift away to a place where I can dream, where everyone is free, and pain doesn't exist. It's a beautiful lie I long to believe.

Once upon a time, I did, but after today, that dream is dead.

The vibrations running through my hand nudges me from my sleep. My fingers stretch out and seek out the object of disturbance. I open my eyes slowly and bring the phone to my face. I don't know why I even bother. The man just doesn't know when to quit. He's demonstrated that on more than one occasion.

Only this time, it isn't him.

Private number.

"Hello," I answer, getting up.

"Hello, is this Miss Kara Petersen?"

I wrinkle my nose curiously.

"Yes, speaking. Who is this?"

"Sorry to disturb you, Miss Petersen, but I'm calling from St Mary's. I'm a colleague of Doctor Andrews, he asked me to contact you urgently. Do you know a woman called Samantha Jones?" the woman asks.

"Yes, Sam. She's my...my best friend, but she moved out of the city a few months ago. I'm sorry; I don't understand. Why are you calling me?" Except, I do know. Gripping my chest, nausea overcomes me. Whatever has happened to Sam can't be good if the hospital is contacting me at this hour – any hour, as a matter of fact.

"Miss Jones was brought in earlier this evening severely beaten. She has sustained multiple fractures to her skeleton, and there was some internal bleeding that we've managed to control. Some of her organs are also ruptured. Due to the severity of her injuries, she is currently in a coma. I'm very sorry, Miss Petersen," the woman says sincerely.

Oh, my god!

The phone slides from my hand and drops to the floor. My knees buckle underneath me, and my body follows in quick succession. The woman is still speaking, and I bring the phone back to my ear, my mind in freefall as my world comes crashing down for the second time in six hours. All I know is I have to see her.

"I'm on my way over right now."

Hanging up, I run downstairs, praying Marie hasn't gone to bed. Fortunately, she hasn't. Even more fortunate, Walker is still here.

"I need to get over to St Mary's. A nurse or a doctor, I don't know, but someone just rang and said that Sam's in a coma. She's been beaten, and God knows what else!" I rush out, verging on tears. My eyes narrow involuntarily in Walker's direction, and I'm pretty sure if I were to look at me, I would think I was pinning this on him.

"I'll take you," he says, lifting from his chair and grabbing his jacket. Marie rises and pecks his cheek with what could be classed as a small, grudging smile. It isn't their usual full-blown passionate style I've become accustomed to recently, but I guess it wouldn't be after what I had heard earlier.

I freeze at the end of the bed, staring at a woman I no longer recognise.

Gone is the girl with long, blonde hair, and pretty cherubic features of my childhood, in her place, lays a woman who has been dealt a shitty fucking hand in life.

The parts of her body that are visible are heavily bandaged. White gauze wraps securely around her head, and I can see the bruises already fully formed on her face, neck, and shoulders. The machines keeping her alive resound with an intermittent beep, indicating that she's still breathing. But only just.

The door opens, and Stuart enters. His look goes from consummate professional to sympathetic friend in an instant. Only I'm not his friend - Sloan is, regardless of my association.

"I'm very sorry, Kara. I didn't know who else to call when I recognised her." His eyes study Sam's medical notes on the clipboard. "Have the police talked to you yet?"

"No, you did the right thing; and yes, I've already spoken to them. Not that it was much use. I haven't seen her in months, and she has never returned my calls. I have no idea what she's been doing or doing it with. She said she was going back to Manchester, but obviously didn't." My mind races at my own words.

Where has she been?

"Any ideas how she ended up like this?"

He shakes his head. "No, unfortunately not. One of her neighbours rang the police when they heard screaming coming from the house. When they got there, she was already unconscious. Apparently, they never saw anyone go in or come out. That's all I can tell you." These were facts I'd already been informed of. I pinch my nose, attempting to block the tears that have built up to monumental levels behind my eyes.

Stuart pulls out a pen and starts making notes, looking from his patient to the machines, writing sporadically. I'm a little detached from the whole situation, when his hand grazes my arm lightly, and the fine hairs stand on end at his partially foreign touch.

"You know, you can talk to her. We like to believe that coma patients can still hear what's going on around them. Maybe you should tell her how you feel." He gives me a weak smile and leaves the room. I watch him through the blinds, conversing with Walker. They nod at each other intermittently, no doubt discussing some new revelation I'm not entitled to know about.

I look back at Sam and approach the side of the bed. I plop down in the empty chair, assaulted by the turmoil inside my head. My mind is numb as I think of things to tell her. I want to tell her how I feel, how much I love and miss her, but they won't come out. All those things needed to be said when she was well and conscious. A sob escapes me when I realise this might be it, and the opportunity might never arise. I may never get a chance to make our relationship right again.

Switching off the lights, the rooms falls into partial darkness. I take her hand in mine and prepare to do something I haven't done in years. Inhaling, expanding my lungs to capacity, I begin.

"I wish you were awake. There's so much I need to say. Things you need to know. Things I need to say sorry for. Firstly, I'm sorry I couldn't protect you from the life you had before I left. I didn't leave because I didn't care, I just couldn't sit there and watch you turn into our parents. I never wanted that for you. I love you so much; I hope you know that." I swipe the back of my hand over my cheeks.

"I also have so much to thank you for, too, because I'm in love with Sloan. So much so, I would die for him. I haven't told anyone how much I love him, not even he knows. Sadly, I just don't know if I can trust him anymore." I lay my head on the bed and curl my fingers in hers, wishing she would reciprocate the motion.

"Remy helped clear out our old place and Deacon showed up. He said we can run, but we can't hide." I shiver. He did this to her, but how to prove it? I absolutely hate him, and for a moment, I hate how weak she had been to get caught up with him.

At the same time, I can't help but think that, somehow, I was the cause of all this. Initially, I thought he was inciting Sloan, but after the poison he spat at me today, now I have to question everything that has come to fruition already.

Somewhere inside, I know this started with me. My only fear is that, eventually, it may also end with me.

"He said something about what happened *that night*. He said Sloan had something to do with it. I don't know what to do. I wish you would just open your eyes and tell me which direction to turn, which path to take." I finally concede and bring down the walls, as I cry for a woman who was as close to me as a sister for the majority of my life. I let my hand run up her arm as far as I can reach and then back down again. She doesn't respond; she's nothing. Her mind is in a completely different world, whilst her body remains vacant and hollow in this one.

My eyes drift shut, and I remember our childhood. The days we talked about running away, but never got further than a few streets.

The times we sat on the swings at the park and imagined that if we got high enough, we would be able to fly away. The moments of pain, and the times we would comfort each other from the disharmony and fallout of whatever abuse one of us had suffered that day.

I close my eyes and regress, until the door slams shut, and my body jack-knifes up. A lone presence invades the room. The small space is dark, and I struggle to gain a visual. I whimper, terrified it might be Deacon coming back to collect whatever he has left of her. I hastily reach over to flick the lamp on. Light drowns out the dark and the irritation in my sleep-deprived sight.

I breathe a sigh of relief.

Sloan.

He rests against the tiny wall separating the window and the door. I lift my head and turn to Sam, then back to him, giving him a look that tells him to have some respect for her, regardless of how inconceivable it might be in that convoluted brain of his. He seemingly reads my thoughts perfectly and takes up the seat at the opposite side of the bed.

As he sits, I drink in his appearance. He looks like he hasn't slept in days, but it's only hours ago that I last left him. His jaw works tirelessly, studying Sam, then me. He looks guilty, and my heart breaks for him. He obviously thinks this is his fault when at the same time, I know it's mine.

"I'm sorry," his rich, velvet whisper trails over Sam's unconscious form. "I'm sorry I didn't do more for you... And God forbid, for her. I'm sorry this is happening to you again." Tears stream down my face when I see the hurt and defeat spread across his.

"No! You have nothing to be sorry for. This is all me." His eyes shut sadly. It's all the confirmation I need, to know that I'm right. "Somewhere all this started because of me…"

His eyes expand wide, and I stare into them intently. They are the darkest I've ever seen them. A mixture of pain and sorrow ripples over their glassy surface, and I debate whether or not to say what is garnering supremacy inside.

"And I know this will all end with me, too. Deacon made that much clear today."

His body clenches violently. "No, I will not let him hurt you! No matter what happens, he will *never* put his hands on you like *that* again!" His voice resonates a whole new level of determination.

"Again?" My head shoots up, and my hand drops on Sam's, clutching as the words ring out mutely. Sloan gets up, moves to the window, and tilts the blinds.

"Yes, again."

I remain quiet, but I need to know what he hides. It scares me to death, but I don't have a choice anymore.

"Please, tell me," I whisper, as my memory pulls out some of Deacon's last words, and he definitely wasn't referring to beating me in that dirty room.

You still can't hit for shit, you little cunt!

Sloan scrubs his hand down his face agitated. I watch, captivated, at this strong man wilting before me. He turns back to the observation window, his attention piqued by whatever is happening outside.

"No, not here. Come on, we have to go." He holds his hand out for me.

I stare at him across Sam's lifeless form. I've waited my whole adult life for the puzzle pieces to fit together flawlessly, and finally, it's going to be a reality. I move around the bed, accepting his proffered hand and edge towards the door.

Walker is still speaking to one of the doctors, but ends the conversation abruptly when he sees us. His legs move with purpose, crossing the distance quickly. Sloan blocks my view, and his face is twitching all over at whatever Walker is whispering in his ear. Sloan nods at him and coils his hand around mine, almost restricting my circulation.

"Let's go, *now.*"

I'm virtually running to keep up with his long strides as he hurries us down the corridor. I'm about to ask what's going on, when the reason why presents itself.

"Sweets!" The shout comes from behind us. I spin around perfunctorily at the excruciating sound of the childhood nickname I despise vehemently.

My father loiters shadily at the end of the corridor we've just come from. Sloan shakes his head in disapproval and tugs my hand to move in the opposite direction, but I'm immobile. I look between my father and the man I love, and make a decision that may have serious repercussions. Sloan growls when I slip my hand from his and slowly, reticently, move towards my father. Ian has a smile on his face, his arms outstretched.

The loving father he isn't.

"Ah, sweets! I knew as soon as I heard Sam was here that you would come. I was right!"

His deviant smile sends torrents of pain through me. It's the same look that has drawn me in and spat me back out so many times in the past. One day, I would learn to walk away from the bastard, I just don't know when.

Taking in his appearance, his thin, drug and alcohol abused face, is in need of shaving, and he looks like he hasn't eaten in weeks. Long gone is the man that towered over me, who scared the living shit out of me. In his place, is a fragile man, using any power he still thinks he possesses.

"She's more family to me than you ever were. Of course, I would be here for her. What are *you* doing here?"

"Well..." he begins, cradling his chin between his thumb and forefinger, appearing to be considering his response. "You haven't returned any of my calls." I quickly turn to see Sloan's fists ball at his sides, yet his expression is strangely nonchalant. "I hoped you had seen the light, sweets. Frankie is on my back, and I can't hold him off any longer."

I laugh in astonishment. "You really don't care about anyone but yourself, do you? I was fooling myself all these years, thinking one day it would be better, but it never will, will it?" I turn to walk back to Sloan, only to find him now standing by my side. His arm comes around my shoulder.

"Come on, my love, let's go home. Nothing more can be done here tonight," he says, never breaking eye contact with my father.

"So, you're the rich fucker that's making her think she's better than me, huh? Well, I've heard all about you, so how about we make a deal? If you give me what I want, I'll keep *him* away from both of you. How does that sound, *Sloan*?"

I'm instantly pulled behind Sloan's back as he levels off with my dad. "I don't make deals with heartless bastards who sell their daughters down the fucking river! Don't you remember what happened the last time?"

I spin around to Sloan in question instantly, wanting to know what had happened the last time, and when exactly that was. Sloan gives me a stern stare but doesn't comment.

Slowly looking back, Ian's face screws up, clearly remembering whatever the words insinuate, and simultaneously, realising he no longer has the ability to make me do whatever he wants me to.

"Frankie won't be happy!" My father says mockingly, bringing his gaze back to us, but I'm not quite sure who it's aimed at.

Standing in the face-off between them both makes me see the truth that has been there all along.

I have power.

"Goodbye, Ian. I hope you have a nice life, because I sure as hell will." I curve my hand around Sloan's, caressing his skin, and he counters without hesitation as he leads us away. The tension that was there begins to dissipate, and I can feel the pride radiate from him at my resolution.

My father, on the other hand, is incensed.

"This isn't over! You hear me? He'll fucking get you! He always did!" I curl my fingers tighter into Sloan's hand as he begins to turn back to my dad. I shake my head, and his eyes close slowly, reigning in his resentment. His hand squeezes mine in both security and affection, and I return it with ease.

For me, it's a way to express my anger at my father's words. For him, it's a way to express he's still mine after today's latest episode of chaos.

Chapter 27

THE HOUSE IS imposing and ominous, coming out of the darkness and into the light, as the car manoeuvres down the long driveway. I know, by his own admission, Sloan has serious undisclosed issues being here, but I'm so happy not to see the hotel suite after this afternoon's confession.

Approaching the door, a small bout of electricity tingles across the small of my back. His large hand rubs lovingly as he steps behind me. Walker, who is waiting for us to arrive, places his hand on my shoulder, leaving no aftereffect. With each new revelation, my aversion to being touched lessens. I can only think it's the acceptance of my past that is now allowing me to move forward.

Albeit, very slowly.

Sloan pushes the door, and Walker enters first. He disappears into the house, leaving us waiting just inside the doorway.

Covering my body with his, he holds me close, his lips touching my forehead. It's painful to admit, but I need him. And not because he makes me feel safe, but because I'll never love anyone as much as I do him. He draws back and looks me over. Concern etches across his brow, and his words of enquiring if I'm alright, remain thick and unspoken, hanging precariously in the air around us.

We are both abundantly aware that our entwined, fucked-up past has the ability to destroy us and what we have created. That can never happen. Although it's abundantly clear after today that even the smallest truth can tip the balance.

I shuffle closer into him; his lips are just too tempting to be left alone any longer. Realising what I'm about to do, he also starts to shut down the minute space, and his hands draw me in until I mould against him.

"All clear!" Walker shouts. I gasp and jump at the verbal intrusion, and more so at the gun he's waving around haphazardly, indicating towards the hallway. "Oh shit, sorry!" he says jokingly, looking between us with smugness, rather than shame.

"Give me that!" Sloan grabs his hand and takes the gun from him. He does something with the hand bit, and something drops out of it, then he passes them back to Walker. I'm dying to ask what he's just done, but think it best not to know too much about where he learnt how to use a gun and why.

The house is cool when we enter, and a ghostly silence shrouds the expansive hallway. I shiver as hot arms instantly snake around me, and his hands rove shamelessly over my body.

"*Sloan...*" I breathe out, longing for his touch, wanting to feel him inside me. To move so fluidly within me, that it takes us to a place greater than love, and somewhere I never want to leave. Instead, I subject myself to endure the separation, and step away from him.

Sex will not get us anywhere tonight.

I leave him in the hallway and walk into the living room. Easing myself onto one of the leather sofas, I notice the sweater and paper I'd left with him at the hotel earlier, are folded on a small lamp table next to me. God, this afternoon feels like a lifetime ago. Sloan enters, and I watch him intently, curiously, wondering how he will react if I wear the hoodie again. Something sparkles in his eyes, and I feel confident he won't object.

His hand reaches for it, and he holds it out to me. He smiles brightly, but he can't pull the wool over my eyes. Although the look of pain and hurt from earlier has vanished, the fear marring him is evident, and it has been since I broached the subject this afternoon. I lift my arms, and he helps me into the sweater. It's snug and comforting; a security blanket of sorts.

"I like you in my sweater. I didn't have the heart to bin it earlier. God, I wanted to burn it...*so much*. Anything to forget how I came to give it to you." I put my finger on his mouth, stretch up on my toes and drop a kiss onto his lips.

Would I ever tire of kissing this man? Of wanting him? I hope not, but now isn't the time to procrastinate. Now is the time for answers, and I shall have them. I walk away from him and rotate slightly. My body saying what my mouth isn't able to.

He grips his hips and breathes out resigned. "This is going to be a long night. Drink?" he offers, padding out of the room and into the kitchen with me in tow a few steps behind. He removes a glass from the cabinet and shakes it a little in offering again. I decline; I need to hear his story in complete sobriety. He pours a glass and comes back to me. His wary eyes glint under the overhead lights. Downing the liquid in one, he coaxes me to him and kisses me hard, the taste of Shiraz overwhelming my taste buds.

"Come on." He's literally dragging me towards the stairs, but suddenly, he releases my hand. Eagerly, he takes the stairs two at a time, while I follow behind, a little more lacklustre.

When I agreed to come back here tonight, this isn't the side of him I expected to get. At least with the man from this afternoon, I already knew where I stood.

The bedroom is empty when I enter, but I hear him moving around the bathroom. The sound of running water forces me to seek him out.

Oh shit!

He's half-naked; his t-shirt and socks are strewn at his feet. The bath is almost full when he starts to remove his belt. His jeans hang open, exposing his ripped abs, and the line of dark hair that disappears under the material. He strolls towards me and shakes his head.

"Too much clothing," he mutters and starts to undress me. Slapping his hand away, he gives me a thoroughly frustrated look.

"No, this isn't going to assist with anything - especially us. You promised me. We need to talk - seriously for once," I tell him, but my eyes fill with lust, betraying me.

"No, this will assist us perfectly," he counters. "I don't want you to run from me. If I have you naked in the bath, surrounded by me, you can't run."

He's thought of everything.

"Fine!" I acquiesce.

His hands fumble furiously to strip me of my clothing. Letting his jeans and shorts drop, he sets his hands on my shoulders, and we stand bare in front of each other. God, I want nothing more than to lose myself in him all night. My constant desire for him clouds my common sense.

He leads us towards the bath and climbs in. His arm comes around my middle, and he lifts me easily, lowering me down to him. He sinks deeper, coercing me further, until he positions me between his strong thighs. My body complies far too easily, and I know it will always be impossible to refuse him anything he wants, regardless of the situation.

And he knows it too.

I wiggle, trying to get comfortable, and his growing erection digs into my lower back. I giggle to myself when a desirous groan escapes him.

"Behave!" he admonishes playfully.

"Sorry," I reply in haste, but I'm not. I'll never apologise for feeling attraction this strong.

I settle into him; my back relaxing against his chest. His thighs clamp around mine, caging me into position so I can't run, as per his request.

No words are spoken as he strokes me delicately. Easing my mind and body, I force myself not to move. My skin is instantly inflamed under his touch, and I let myself relax and just enjoy the feel of him - at my back, around my legs, his hands on my stomach.

He pours water over me slowly, before murmuring something in my ear I don't understand. My eyes snap open the moment I hear him say he's ready. My fingers entwine with his, and I'm more than ready to listen. I only hope my poor heart will still be beating by the end of it.

"I had just turned nineteen and was in my first year of university, when one night changed everything. Charlie had come up to stay for the weekend, and I was out with some friends. I had left her home alone since she wasn't legal... She called me... Fuck! I remember it like it was yesterday. Her blood-curdling scream sounded out over the phone, but the line went dead before she managed to speak. When I got back home, I found her in the bathroom, covered in blood. She'd been beaten beyond comprehension. Her phone was lodged in her bloodied hand, and she wasn't breathing properly. She was fourteen. I didn't know what to do. Panicking, I called Stuart - he was still a med student back then. He managed to get her breathing properly, and staunched the flow of blood before we got her to the A&E. We sat there all night waiting for someone to tell us what was happening. Finally, a doctor allowed us to see her." His voice falters, the impending tears evident in his tone.

"It broke my heart to see my sister destroyed, not knowing who did it to her. At first, we thought she'd been beaten from an attempted break-in, until it was confirmed she'd been raped. As her only next of kin, I had to listen while the doctor spoke of the various levels of external and internal tissue damage she sustained during the assault. I sat through his detailed notes of how violent it had been, all the while my sister lay only a few feet away, fighting for her life. I wasn't a medic, so I had no idea just how bad it was, until Stuart explained it better."

I freeze, because at last, I understand why he's so overly protective of Charlie, and lately, of me. He views us as damaged women, and while the thought heats my blood to boiling point, it simultaneously soothes me, knowing he will always try to protect those he loves.

"When she finally woke, the police questioned her about the assault. At first, she refused, saying she couldn't remember. But she was lying, I could always tell when she was lying. After a private discussion with Stuart and a psychiatrist, she finally told the truth. I can still remember the sound of her voice when she eventually admitted who did it to her." I stare at him, mesmerised, as his beautiful blue eyes begin to darken, becoming truly devoid of all emotion. "It was Deacon, and he raped and beat her for hours. *Hours!*"

My hand covers my mouth in shock. I already knew Deacon had raped her by her own confession, but for hours? My heart sinks for Charlie, for myself, and for every other person the world over, who has ever had the power of free will cruelly snatched away.

"I'm so sorry..." I whisper. His eyes narrow, and something I can't describe nor understand takes control of them.

"After hearing that, I lost it. I smashed up half the house and stormed out. I was fully intent on killing the son of a bitch. And I would have; I wanted to. Instead, John followed me and calmed me down. We decided to make a plan of action to bring him down, but he vanished not long after and we lost him. The only logical lead we had to go on, was that we knew he couldn't stay hidden forever. He had become privileged to having whatever he wanted, materially and financially, so we waited until he showed up again. And he did-"

A knock on the door halts him.

"Kid, Kara? I'm off!" Walker shouts through the unlocked, closed door. I stiffen, embarrassed that he knows I'm in here. Sloan doesn't answer, and instead, strokes his hand over my stomach, pouring water over me again. Walker's footsteps drift further away, until it's silent once more.

"So, what happened?"

He takes a deep breath, and his hands crush my waist almost painfully. Do I want to hear what happened next, especially if this is the reaction I get from asking?

Unfortunately, I do. It's pivotal to everything. I breathe deeply when his mouth opens.

"We got an anonymous call one night," he begins. "Deacon was at one of his dealer's houses. Apparently, he went there a lot. At

first, we didn't think much of it, but it led us to him. *Eventually.*
When we arrived, it was a full-on party, everyone was either drunk
or high, and the house was a mess. We searched around, but
couldn't find the rat bastard, except something else was brought to
our attention..."

I turn in his arms, looking at him expectantly. His hand strokes
over my face with such reverence, that I freeze immediately,
knowing exactly what he's going to tell me. My body starts to shake,
as I try to escape the confines of him and the bath. The water sloshes
over the side in a small tidal wave at my ineffective attempt to gain
emancipation. The sound of the water slapping on the floor
punctures the quiet beauty of the room.

"No, no, no, no…" My mind is moving, but my body isn't. He
has me in a tight spot. One hand is firm around my waist, the other
is still tenderly stroking my cheek.

"You need to hear this, baby. This is the truth you want from me.
I'm going to give you what you want, and pray to God that it doesn't
spell the end of us. I've carried this torture inside me every single
day for eight, long years, I can't do it any longer. Please tell me you
won't hate me when you've heard everything."

I stare deeply at his stunning features; his lips are tight, his fallen
expression heartbreaking. His face is prematurely lined, full of fear,
and I close my eyes and capitulate. My body lowers, but the sound
of the water stilling doesn't ease me, it only adds to the tension
further. My eyes are still shut tightly as his muscular chest resides
against my back again. Strong arms cocoon me, and for the first time
ever, I don't feel safe inside them.

"The party was all over the house. We searched every room,
anywhere he could be hiding, doing something he shouldn't. We
didn't find him, but we did find something else. There was one room
that was locked. Open your eyes," he requests softly, his fingers are
light on my chin, tilting my face to his. Staring into his midnight
irises, they radiate love and desire above all else he keeps locked
behind them.

"John picked the lock. It was so dark we couldn't see who was in
there. The room was empty, and we were just about to leave when a
small cry came from the cubbyhole." I hold his concerned gaze,
while he tells me his version of my life story.

"Inside was a girl, curled up in a ball, asleep-"

"With a book and a torch, and ted beside me," I whisper, cutting him off, as the past comes back to haunt me. His mouth curves slightly and his arm tightens further. His lips press against my forehead, and he kisses me gently.

"She was probably the most fragile girl I had ever seen. I picked her up and put her into bed. She grumbled at me, something about being safe in the cubbyhole, but I didn't think anything of it. Once she was sleeping peacefully again, we left, making sure we locked the door behind us. Needless to say, we didn't find Deacon that night, but over the coming days and weeks, he was making regular appearances at that house. Tommy and Parker tailed him for hours, trying to find out what he was up to. He wasn't using any of his bank accounts, nor his credit cards. We assumed he was dealing to stay afloat and to keep off John's radar."

He holds me firmly, but I feel empty. For the first time in my life, I am loved, ostensibly and unequivocally, and yet I feel...nothing, just cold.

"Was he?" I ask, not really caring either way. I just want him to finish his recollection of my darkest days.

"Of sorts, yes. Although we could never pin him down. Then, one day, John and I tailed him to the local high school. He was sat on the benches watching the football team practice. We stayed and watched him; followed him. It became obvious he wasn't taking in the practice game at all, his attention was fixed on something else entirely." His face pitches into tight lines and his colouring pales significantly.

I shift uncomfortably, this wasn't sitting right with me. I remember the many times I had sat on those goddamn benches, or under one of the old oaks after school, not wanting to go home. For years I'd blocked this shit out, never to be remembered, never to be spoken of again. But just hearing those few words, it all comes rushing back.

"Go on," I encourage pitifully.

"A girl. The girl from the house. *You*," he emphasises. His eyes fix on mine, and I shudder under his stare. "He was watching you!" Tears choke his voice, and he grips me in his arms.

Trying to be strong, I ask the question of which I already know the devastating answer. "Did Deacon rape me eight years ago?" My voice is exceptionally calm considering, and I let the question hang heavily between us. Surprisingly, I'm even composed in waiting for the response that he doesn't want to give me.

"Did he?"

"Yes," he murmurs.

One word. A whisper. A truth. A dirty secret he has carried with him for so long.

My blood boils furiously, coursing through my veins with a vengeance. I search his face, trying to decide where my newly forming anger will now lie. He doesn't move and doesn't speak. He doesn't do anything but watch me. He's waiting for me to crack, to break down and to push him away. He's waiting for me to run – and I want to, I really do. It's the one thing that is standing out clearly in my mind's eye right now.

Yet I don't do any of those things.

"Thank you," I tell him honestly. I carefully rotate again, so he can't identify my pain and the way it is slowly consuming everything beneath the surface of my skin.

Every muscle in his chest tightens uncontrollably against my back. I link my little finger through his and tug it. He has been quiet for so long, it wouldn't surprise me if he closes off entirely from the revelation.

A small snort of disbelief blows through my hair. "Baby, shout at me, hit me, scream in my goddamn face! Say something - anything! But don't say fucking *thank you!*"

"It's not your fault."

"No, it *is* my fault! I couldn't save you from him! If I'd just stopped him after what he did to Charlie. If we had got him, instead of allowing him to roam freely. If I'd had him arrested for what he did. If I..."

"That's a lot of *ifs*, but I don't blame you, not at all." I scoot back around, kneeling in front of him. "You *did* save me. You saved me in more ways than I can ever thank you for. You didn't rape me, he did. And one day he will pay for it, but the time isn't now. Promise me you won't go after him. Promise me!" I brush my hand over his face, down to his chest. "I couldn't bear to lose you...Not again." I press against his lips, dragging mine gently over his.

The water is chilling around us, and I let out a small shiver. Instantly, he stands, bringing me up with him. He climbs out of the tub, lifting me over the edge. Steadying me, he wraps a towel around my body and one around his hips. He carefully carries me back into the bedroom, lowering me onto the bed and settles in beside me. On his side, he strokes away a few wet tendrils of my hair.

"Sloan?"

"Hmm?" He runs his finger down my temple, all the way to my chin.

"Sam and Emily? That was him, wasn't it?"

"Yeah, it was. The morning after the first night you stayed, Remy called to say he had battered another girl. You heard my response."

I shift towards him, and he holds me tight. "Months ago, you said you had stopped letting people in. Was that because of him, too?"

He nods, staring up at the ceiling. "Remember when I told you I had someone once, and then they were gone? That was you, Kara. I wasn't lying when I said the effects had been long-lasting." He pulls me closer. "There's more I need to tell you, but there will never be a good time to talk about it. I need to tell you about the night he did...*that*...to you." Tears glaze his pools, and I raise my hand to catch an escapee fleeing down his cheek.

"I know, but not now. Now, I just want to hold you."

Bringing his arm around me, his nose strokes mine. I can feel his love for me radiating from within. The feeling of security is finally resurfacing again. I love him, and I know that even though I should be, I'll never be angry with him for concealing the truth. I want to be, so desperately, but I cannot. He saved me that day, he gave me the courage to run away, he gave me Marie, and I may never be able to repay him for it.

I only hope my love for him will prove to be strong enough to save him from himself, should the time ever materialise.

"Eight years. Eight years of forcing John to follow you, to find out how you were doing. That's how I know things about you I shouldn't. The real reason I had your number and address, even if George hadn't have taken you home. I love you, Kara Petersen. Always, from the first moment I saw you, I think. I'll never stop loving you for as long as I live." His warm breath feels good against my forehead, but not nearly as good as hearing him open his heart to me.

"I love you, too. More than living, more than breathing, more than I've ever loved anyone in this life. Because that's what you did back then, you didn't just save me, you gave me a chance to live."

Chapter 28

THE TENDER CARESS upon my skin is both gentle and hypnotic. I stretch gloriously, my whole body inexplicably sated along with my mind. Rubbing my eyes, his careful touch is maddening, stroking up and down my bare thigh repeatedly.

God, I need him. I need him to erase the memories, to erase the memory of Deacon's unwanted touch that has plagued me throughout the night. I need him to create new memories with me, the same way I did with him.

Last night had been cleansing for me, there's no other way to describe it. Although I had accepted my past and all the things that had transpired in it long ago, hearing him confirm my suspicions helped to alleviate some of the uncertainty I've carried around with me for such a long time.

Like an invisible noose around my neck; some of it slackened.

Except, inside, I know I should be running for the hills as fast as my legs will carry me, escaping this pain that imprisons me, but I've lost all ability to. A life without him present in it is internally agonising, too unfeasible to imagine. I already know first-hand what it's like to live with love lost, I doubt I will survive a second bout.

My back is tucked into his chest, and I relish the fluid movement of both his breathing and the sensation of his skin on mine. I roll over to face him; he's on his side, his arm propping his head up. I lick my lips intentionally, openly ogling him like I'm seeing him for the first time all over again.

He is magnificent, and I can tell he has been awake for a while. Whereas I'm still groggy and disorientated, he looks fresh and alive. His dark hair is a sleep-induced mess, and my fingers itch to run through the strands. I clench my palms together, desperately needing to slide them over every part of him. Laying inches from me, watching me, his own fingers never stop their perusal of my flesh.

He slowly arches a beautiful, dark brow at me. "See something you like?" His eyes lower to my fists, still rounded through sexual frustration and the indisputable chemistry that we share.

His sly grin tells me he knows exactly what I'm thinking, and without a second thought, I nod quickly and reach out to him. His breathing halts, then comes out laboured when my hand lands on his abdomen. I let my touch linger briefly, deciding which direction to head in.

North or south?

My heart decides for me, and I elevate myself to match his current lounging position. He allows my outstretched palm to familiarise itself with his body all over again. Painfully slow, I move up his stomach, stopping at his navel, circling the conclave with my finger. His chest inflates faster, deeper, and I'm quietly confident the devastating truths of last night might bind us closer together, as opposed to tearing us apart.

Goosebumps prickle his skin under my fingertips, but I never deviate from the task at hand. Drawing the perfect lines of his muscles, I flatten my palm over his chest, shift closer and rest my head on the opposite side. I watch, enraptured, as my hand moves up and down, feeling the reverberation of his heart, passionate and wild under his ribcage.

Tilting my head further down his chest, my tongue darts out, and I drag it over his nipple. It puckers instantly, and the first sharp hiss is followed in quick succession by a second. Peeking up innocently, my mouth starts to curve in triumph at my achievement.

"*Baby...*" The word rasps from his lips.

Suddenly, I'm up and over his body, and my legs are quickly being adjusted on either side of his hips. I sit tall above him, admiring him stretched out beneath me, his arms beneath his head. He smiles lazily, in the way that only he can, and I know there will never be anyone else, except him. He was made for me in every sense.

I wiggle a little on his groin, and his semi-hard shaft presses unforgivingly at my centre. Both anxious and desperate to grind my body on his, I nudge up a little and lean over; my hands linked inside his, just above his head. Dropping my head down, I taste his full lips with a ferocious hunger. The need to devour and savour is potent and all-consuming. He doesn't respond immediately, and I'm positive he's still in turmoil over last night's truths.

"Please..." I murmur into his mouth.

A sound of annoyance resounds from this throat, but his lips part invitingly. Feeling victorious, I take full advantage of my position and devour his mouth. Our lips move together in a dance fuelled by our shared passion.

His hands cup my backside, and his talented fingers move tentatively between my cheeks. I gasp when his finger drags up and swipes my anus. Withdrawing slightly, I sit back on him again, effectively ending his playtime. His hands roam from my behind to my waist, finally settling on my hips. He pushes me back a notch so I am once again in the perfect position for him to slide inside me at any given moment. Rising up so that we are chest to chest, his hands fall to my thighs, massaging them.

"Baby, I don't want-"

"Shush, I don't want him to come between us. Tell me nothing has changed, *please*." I shut my eyes against the impending tears, knowing everything *has* changed, and ultimately, his feelings towards me might have, too.

It's too painful to acknowledge that this might be the breaking point that eventually leads to the true death of us.

"Open your eyes, my love," he murmurs into my mouth, his hot breath washing over my lips. I comply, my tears flowing freely. "Don't cry. I can't stand to see you cry." His thumbs brush over my cheeks, and he kisses away my hurt.

"It's not that I don't want to, I do. I just don't want to hurt you. You're still raw from last night, and I don't want it to overshadow how much I love you. I want you so much, it hurts. I want to feel everything, but I don't want the memory of what he did to taint what we have together." His strong arms hold me securely, and I bury my head into his neck. I cling to him dearly, but still can't get close enough.

"Tell me you don't see me any differently. Tell me we're still the same. I feel like I'm losing you." I cry as the tsunami of emotions keeps on coming. I dig my fingers into his back, aware I'm probably hurting him, but he's still too far away. I want him to take me and claim me, and prove to me I'm still his.

A soft sound of incredulity escapes his throat, and he holds me away from him. His action causes a ripple in my heart that threatens to eviscerate me.

"Kara, I've been in love with you for eight years. I've known what Deacon did to you for eight years. And I've spent all those years planning, turning fate in my favour, praying one day we would find each other again. What was said last night doesn't change a goddamn thing for me," he says resolutely.

My tears start to subside, and I gaze keenly at him. His beautiful, sinuous mouth begs to form a smile. His hands skim down my body, pausing briefly at my breasts before settling on my hips again. His thumbs move in slow, deliberate circles as he waits patiently for my answer. I can't give him one - he has rendered me mute.

Realising I don't seem to be able to form coherent speech, he continues. "Last night I stayed awake, watching you. I ran a million different scenarios through my head to make you stay. I was positive you would leave me this morning, that there was a chance I'd be waking up alone." He kisses me deeply before retreating. "But yet here you are, thinking I don't want you. God, I love you so much, I can't think straight at times. I don't see you as broken or damaged. You're the strongest person I've ever met; resilient, resourceful, determined. You're one of life's survivors. Never think that what he did has any bearing on what we have, or how I feel. It doesn't. I've loved you for eight long fucking years, and now that I finally have you, trust me when I say I'm not going anywhere, and neither are you. You belong to me. You've always belonged to me. You've just never known it."

Dumbstruck, I listen absentmindedly at his declaration of undying love. I'm so conflicted about the past and the present, I don't know how to answer.

Naturally, my body responds for me in the most elementary way known to man; by grinding down against his. His length slides against my folds just where I want him, and I close my eyes, luxuriating in the feel of him against my centre.

"Make love to me baby, prove to me I'm still yours," he requests. My eyes shoot open, and I focus on his; primal and animalistic. They have darkened considerably in the last few minutes, and his face is filled with desire. I glance down between our bodies, staring at him hard in between us. "Claim me," he bids forcefully.

The familiar tingle of yearning creeps up inside. I fix my hands at the back of his neck, allowing my forehead to fall against his. I'm mesmerised when he begins to stroke himself. I'm almost over the edge just watching him. A bead of semen glistens on his tip, and he catches it with his thumb and brings it to my lips. My tongue springs out instantly, and I suck it into my mouth. His palm and fingers are flat against my cheek and temple, caressing softly, as my mouth claims his thumb - the same way I plan to do with another appendage shortly.

He growls possessively. Instinctively, my hand joins the foray, and I slowly move my fingers down my stomach, and into my sensitive folds. I open my eyes to see the intensity in his, as he watches our combined act in awe.

"So fucking beautiful," he says into the void between us. I smile, delighted that I can still affect him this way. I love watching him lose control and knowing I possess the power to assist with it. His hand pumps his shaft furiously as my fingers circle my aching centre in a fevered motion. My body convulses as the fire inside burns stronger than ever before.

"Oh, God!" I moan out, grinding my body on his, lifting my hips. I let out a guttural cry, and his eyes penetrate mine with such passion, I reach fever pitch in record time.

"Wait for me...together," he says huskily. His face cultivates a lazy, wicked grin, as he continually strokes his hard length, and semen begins to protrude from the tip.

"*Sloan!*" I cry out.

"Let go, baby!" he demands. I work up and down on my hand, my fingers deepening and stretching; my movements completely attuned to his.

"Fuck!" he gasps out, his lips finding mine, kissing me fiercely.

A spurt of hotness warms my stomach, and the sensation of his moist hand on my breast makes me delirious. His deft fingers roll my nipple continuously into a hard point. The onslaught of stimulation is pure ecstasy, ensuring my climax goes on and on.

"Oh God, don't stop. Please, don't stop!" I strain out against his mouth, the moment I'm able to formulate rational speech again.

"Never. I'll never stop, my beautiful girl. Fuck, you amaze me!"

My body falls back against his, perspiration slicking both our bare flesh. Placing another pillow behind his head, I slowly stretch over him, his hands run roughly through my hair. My legs straddle his hips harder, and I circle mine over him.

"I want you inside me," I request breathlessly, my persona taking on the other side of me that only he will ever see. In one fast move, I pull him back up with me. "I want you to devour me."

I take his thumb into my mouth, sucking it hard, tasting him all over it. He groans out, and his hands grip my thighs abruptly. Spreading them further, and pulling me closer towards his waiting hardness, his fingers snake up the inside of my leg until he teases me. I elevate myself higher to watch his administrations, to see the moment we connect so perfectly. I'll never be ashamed to admit how he makes me feel.

His fingers are extraordinary on my sensitive flesh, and I almost buck off of him, when he slips two inside me. He presses on the outside of my pubic bone contemporaneously with his other hand, and I moan with abandon at the pleasure he's bringing out again. It takes all I have not to drop back on to him. I move my hips in a circular motion, working against his hand as he kicks my body into a frenzy. His look of appreciation is encouraging as my body spasms, and I contract and release around his fingers. I keep my eyes open, watching him as he watches me come undone, knowing the eye contact pleases him.

No words are spoken as the headiness fades away. He slides his hands under my thighs and arse, and lifts himself up to me. Our eyes never leave each other while he guides me down onto his hard length. Moving my hand down, I massage slowly as the last inch of him fills me completely.

He then lifts me up and lowers me back down again. It's the simplest of actions and makes me feel like I'm in seventh heaven. He repeats it over and over, each action controlled to perfection. My thighs harden around at his hips, and effortlessly, I find my rhythm again. One of his hands curves over my backside and strokes my anus, while the other begins to tease; his fingertips massaging my nub constantly.

The sensation is unbelievable, and his body stiffens in all the right places and mine follows suit. I clamp his shoulder hard as I slide up and down, riding him with everything I have. My skin shines with perspiration at the fullness inside me. His fingers penetrate both entrances attentively, and I pant profusely, knowing inside my heart what he's about to do.

"Oh, that feels too good!" I drawl out, unsure how I'm still able to speak. His smile widens further and he leans forward; the shift in position pushing me back over the edge.

"The best is yet to come," he breathes into my neck, and I freefall over the edge. There's no time to catch my breath when he pulls out, rolls us over, and positions me on my front. "Trust me?"

I peer over my shoulder to look at my stunning man licking his lips. He sheaths himself with his hand and swathes me. I nod, albeit timidly. Yes, I do trust him; I trust him more than I do myself right now. I hear a drawer open and close, and wonder what he has just removed.

"On all fours," he says huskily, and I obey, eager to feel him do something that is considered taboo. "If this is uncomfortable, tell me to stop and I will." I nod and take a deep breath. "Kara, look at me." I turn shyly to see his beautiful face; a combination of arousal and concern openly displayed. "I will never hurt you or force you to do something you are not comfortable with."

"I know. I love you, and I want to give this to you." I'm more than ready to have him fill me in a different way.

He slowly kisses and nips my shoulder, then instructs me to lift my behind up. I obey enthusiastically. His lips tenderly kiss either cheek, before the cold, wet sensation of lubricant smears into my flesh, and I gasp. Light kisses trail up my spine, causing me to shiver in anticipation of the unknown. His hand teases my nipples, and I breathe out, completely comfortable with his gentleness.

"Remember, relax and if you feel-"

"I know. I trust you," I tell him justly.

The wait is agonising, but then his tip nudges my rear entrance. Exhaling smoothly, I relax my body, but murmur a little when he begins to slowly slide inside me. One hand is braced beside me, the other is massaging my core, assisting in readying me further. The feeling of full and completeness is intense, as he presses a little deeper, pausing each time, waiting for my reaction. I hiss as he slides in, and he stops and breathes deeply, but I push back, indicating to continue. By the time he is fully seated, the discomfort is waning, but I won't lie - it hurts. I breathe out and urge myself to relax again. Although it doesn't stop the foreign sensation, the burn is starting to gradually wither away.

"Baby?" I rotate a little and smile at him the best I can. I dip my chin to ensure him I'm fine, willing him to move, hoping he doesn't identify my current discomfort. I want him to do this to me. I want him to claim me every way possible, and I know he reciprocates that particular sentiment.

"We'll go slowly."

He withdraws a little, then pushes further back in, building a gentle rhythm, each time deeper than before. His talented fingers continue their familiar exploration of my sex, and I love the way he replicates the speed of himself in both areas. Eventually, the pace is faster, and I rock back to meet his thrusts, completely forgetting the pain that has now subsided. The fullness is exquisite, and I quickly grow acclimatised to the sensation of him filling me to the hilt.

Tension spikes inside, and I relax further, deeper. My impending climax starts to bear down on me fast and furious. Clamping both sets of muscles, he growls loudly.

"Oh, fuck!" he moans behind me. "Fucking amazing. You were made for me and no one else."

Smiling to myself, I press back when he slides back inside. It doesn't take long before I am screaming out his name, loud and clear, begging him for more. I'm completely submissive whenever he makes love to me, but this act is on a different level entirely.

This is absolute ownership.

"More!" I gasp wantonly. Taking my lead and giving me what I desire, his speed increases, and the power of him is mind-blowing.

"God, I'm gonna come!" His voice is thick with desire as heat engulfs my rear. I milk his fingers internally, not stopping until my release is finally abated. He growls my name repeatedly, coming hard and fast. His fingers leave my core and come up to my mouth.

"Suck them, my love, taste how fucking sweet you are!" I curve my lips around them, sucking my way down them and back up seductively.

He pulls me tight into him, still impaling my rear. He leans back against the headboard, bringing me with him. I shift a little, and his length twitches inside me, priming itself again. I chuckle softly when he takes a sharp breath. I lift off gingerly and twist around to look at his beautiful face.

"How did I ever get so lucky, my love? So goddamn beautiful and all mine. *All. Fucking. Mine.*" He punctuates every word seductively, cupping my face. "Always mine."

Bringing my arms around his shoulders, my damp skin clings to his. His steady breaths soothe me, and I count the rise and fall of his chest against my cheek.

"I love you, Sloan Foster. More than living, more than breathing, more than I've ever loved anyone in this life. There will only ever be you." I repeat the words I have voiced previously. His hand rubs up and down my back languidly. "I'll always be yours."

"I love you, too. You're my miracle, Kara. I cherish every day that I have you in my life. I'll never let you leave me again. You're it for me; you're home." His fingers link through mine, and he secures us together. I kiss him, never closing my eyes, taking in every little thing that flickers over his.

"Mine," I growl quietly, throwing his words back at him.

"Yours forever, *Ms Petersen*."

The water cascades down on us. The droplets hit my sensitive flesh, then finally, the shower floor. It holds my concentration just as equally as the glorious, male specimen, standing naked in front of me does. Facing each other, his midnight blues electrify me with each stolen glance.

He raises his open palm to me and places it over my chest, just above my heart. A thousand unspoken words spear me repeatedly. He doesn't need to say the three words I love to hear to know the truth of how he feels. I know it, because I feel it, too.

Manoeuvring around me, he quickly shuts off the water. I hold back, standing in the cubicle alone, squeezing the excess water from my hair, when my beautiful boy holds out a towel.

Admittedly, I was surprised when he carried me in here, and that's exactly what we did. There's no need for me to question it because truthfully, I don't need to – we belong together. We're two halves that make a whole.

"Come here, let's get you dry," he says, wrapping my overly sensitive body tight.

"Thank you," I reply timidly, not for the towel, but for everything. He's my saviour, and the love of my life. He's the air that I breathe, and all the elements that surround and invigorate me.

If only I felt strong enough to articulate precisely that.

He carefully holds my waist and lifts me to the vanity. Standing in front of me, his hands on my thighs, he studies me, seeming to ponder whatever is running through his beautiful head. I nibble my bottom lip in anticipation. His hands leave my legs and brace at either side of my behind, as he leans in closer.

"There are still lots of things we need to discuss," he says, turning to grab another towel from the cabinet near the bath. He carefully starts to dry my long, damp strands. "But right now, the one thing I want to talk about are your memories. The ones I don't already know about." He stops and looks at me. Hesitation streaks across his face, then his eyes drop to my wrists and the faint white marks that adorn them. "Will you tell me about them?"

I sigh sadly in retrospect. My injured wrists have never really been topic of discussion, there are on the same emotive page as *that* night. Except, he knows all about that night, and it's a natural progression for him to ask about my other experiences - whether good or bad - that I've sustained in my short life. The only problem is, my scars are a result of that night, and I don't know whether he really doesn't know, or he's simply playing dumb in an attempt to make me verbalise and open up at long last.

Weighing up my options, I stare blankly at his damp hair. I raise my hands up, keeping my wrists held out so his downturned eyes can continue to analyse them. I cup his jaw in both hands, lifting his face to mine. I can see his pain, and every ounce of worry he is now feeling from asking me to speak of something so painful and guarded.

"I won't lie to you; I'm remembering most things lately, and that's what makes it so hard to talk about. I remember the beatings, the starvation, the drugs. I remember everything. But these? Deacon kindly gave me these scars. I woke up in the hospital with them, but the absolute horror of what he did, I subconsciously choose not to remember. Weeks afterwards, they slowly started to punch their way through, and I made myself block them out. It took eight years, and the love of a good man to make me remember." Never breaking our visual connection, I pull him closer and kiss his forehead. "We need to go to Marie's. I'll get dressed." I jump down from the vanity and edge towards the door.

"Baby?" I hear the questioning in his voice. He's standing there, still holding the towel he had been using to dry my hair. He looks lost and confused.

"She's as good as my mother, Sloan. She has spent the last seven years taking care of me, risking imprisonment and God knows what else. Although she knows about the rape - or parts of it, at least - she doesn't know the rest. She deserves to know the truth, and I will not have her hearing it from Walker. I love her, and I owe it to her." I linger against the door frame, and he moves towards me. He slings his arm around my shoulder and kisses my neck.

"I know you do, my love," he says, guiding me into the bedroom.

Chapter 29

WE PULL UP outside a house in a part of the city I have never been to before. Sloan deviated on the drive over, and now we're here. Wherever *here* is. The tree-lined street appears to be middle class, and I wonder where he has brought me. I study the house, trying to gauge who it might belong to, when the outside lights flicker on, and a shadow moves behind the half-glass front door.

Undoing my seat belt, my door clicks, and Sloan is already holding it open for me. He is looking up and down the street unnervingly. He's been on edge the entire drive over, making it one of the most uncomfortable journeys of my life. I know that the situation with Sam and the presence of Deacon looming over us is the cause of it. We all know his unwanted attention will be upon us again at some point. It clouds his judgement, and for good reason.

He clutches my hand like his life depends on it, as we walk the short distance from the car to the house. The front door opens on cue and Marie waits on the other side, looking anxious and simultaneously relieved. She practically runs towards me, and I hold onto Sloan for balance as she threatens to become one with me.

"Thank goodness!" Her eyes skim over me, checking for anything untoward. I peek at Sloan, who merely grins, but never releases me. The two people I love most in the world flank either side of me as we enter the house.

In the living room, I study the collage of pictures on the wall. I have no idea who this house belongs to, but all the pictures are of Sloan, Charlie, Walker, and the rest of the guys he is close to.

"Whose house is this, Marie?" I call back to where she and Sloan are now standing a few feet behind me, whispering to each other.

"Oh, it's John's place. Didn't Sloan tell you?" she says, staring at him in disbelief. I shake my head; she knows better than that – the man never tells me anything.

Shouting emanates loudly from another room, and she twirls in the same direction and rolls her eyes. After muttering something about useless men, she absconds down the hall, dragging my man behind her. Intrigued, I follow the direction of all the swearing and general banter.

"God damn it all to hell!"

"Shut the fuck up, arsehole, and clean that up! Don't treat this place like your pigsty. This isn't your fucking house!"

I peer into what I now know is the kitchen, and see Walker and Devlin at the island, throwing random pieces of food at each other, while Tommy and Parker duck to miss the carrots flying past their heads.

"I told you, if Marie sees you doing that, you're a dead man!" Walker tells Devlin, who sticks out his tongue like a petulant child.

"She has to see me first, old man!" he says, pushing up his glasses, the same instant Walker cracks him over the back of the head.

"Hi."

The quartet turns instantly in my direction and air their hellos with embarrassment. Devlin's expression turns from pure jubilation to sadness. He approaches with haste, then hugs me fiercely. My body is stiff, but relaxes as his hold becomes familiar.

"God, I'm so glad you're okay, little lady. I'm sorry about your friend. I know she isn't the best, but she didn't deserve that."

I nod against his shoulder as loud steps enter the room. I turn to see Sloan and Jake behind me. I smile shyly, but Devlin doesn't let go of me.

"Run along, boss, we've got stuff to catch up on!" Devlin says teasingly. He releases me, but still keeps a tight rein on my hand. "So, he told me that you want some kickboxing lessons?" I nod enthusiastically. "Well, I'm going to start teaching Charlie, so I'll teach you, too. We'll have fun." He swings my hand out with his and walks us over to the table, which is set to capacity.

"Thanks, Devlin, I really do appreciate it." He pulls out the chair behind me, pushes me in, and then sits next to me.

"I know you do. When he mentioned it, I wasn't too keen on the idea. In my opinion, women shouldn't have to fight, but since Deacon has made his presence known tenfold, it's sensible to know how to defend yourself. Anything is better than nothing." He looks completely past me as he speaks, and I feel a rush of electricity skim over my leg. Sloan sits on the opposite side, wearing a humorous expression that is bordering on hysterical.

"Well, don't let me interrupt this little reunion," Sloan tells Devlin coolly.

"It's okay, boss. My woman and I are catching up. Anytime you want to go find your own, feel free," he says, waving him away nonchalantly.

I grin, although my cheeks burn crimson. A laugh erupts from the other side of the table, which has now been occupied by everyone else present. A small hand on my shoulder shocks me, and I turn to see Charlie's welcoming smile. I rise immediately and pull her towards me tightly.

"Hey, let me breathe here, Kara. Anyone would think you missed me!" I hear the smile in her voice.

"I have. I really have!" Releasing her, she puts her hands on her hips and glares at Sloan. He huffs and stands, waving his hand over his chair with a bow. She thanks him sarcastically and sits.

"You know," Walker says, waving his fork from the head of the table, to where Sloan is now taking another seat next to him. "He may be lord and master of all he surveys, but you women sure can put him in his place. What do we think he would do if we talked to him like these two-" he glances to Marie on his left, and her eyebrow raises in silent challenge, "-three, do?"

"You? Nothing. The rest of us? Balls on a stick!" Parker replies zealously from next to Marie, high-fiving Tommy on his left. The table erupts in laughter, and even Sloan is amenable to the banter. I smile, loving the side that rarely makes an appearance in public.

Jake clears his throat. "Seriously, John, they're not that bad. We know all we have to do is slide them a credit card, send them out shopping, and it's peace to all men! We might all end up bankrupt, but at least it will be quiet!"

"Hallelujah, sunshine!" John raises his glass, and Jake copies him.

Marie huffs out. "We don't all like to shop, Jake," she says, pointing between us. I give out a timid smile as all eyes turn towards me. I don't dare look to my right, I can already feel Charlie's eyes burning proverbial holes in my head.

"*Sloan!*" she shouts indignantly across the table.

"Yes, my beloved sister?" He feigns blamelessness a little too well. The smile he's trying to hide spreads across his face without a hope in hell of concealing it.

"You've had me buying and collecting all sorts for months, and she doesn't really even want any of it?" Nobody answers her, so I turn and shake my head.

"Sorry Charlie," I apologise for her brother, who is remaining rather tight-lipped across the table. His and Walker's shoulders are bouncing up and down, as they silently laugh between themselves that she has only just caught on.

"Thank you, Kara. I stand by what I said before by the way, *you are* better than the rest of them." I smile inwardly the same moment the table turns remarkably quiet.

Feeling uncomfortably aware, I break the silence. "So, has anyone heard anything on Deacon?" I figure I might as well throw it out there, considering everyone, bar Stuart, is here, and he is probably the real reason why.

"No," Jake responds sharply. "Remy said he's been lying low, even he keeps losing him. All leads have dried up. Again."

"Really? I fail to believe that you boys cannot find him, especially considering he doesn't seem to have any issues finding me." I voice my true thoughts.

Jake quickly drops his head down. "It's not as simple as that," he mumbles.

"Huh! Well, what about Sam? I mean when, *if*, she wakes up, she might be able to tell us something. Let's face it, either she found him or he found her, but either way, she'll know something."

"Hey," Parker says from the other end of the table. "We don't even know if he did that to her. With all due respect, she is a prostitute and habitual druggie, it could've been anyone."

"True, but we all know it's not." I almost laugh out. "Sam is many things; prostitute, druggie, slut, call her whatever you want, she was already gone when she met him. But she went further on that downward spiral with him. Trust me, he did that to her. I know it, because I saw what he did to her when he took me."

An eerie silence overcomes the room. Obviously, nobody wants to talk about what he did to me. The table is uncomfortably quiet again, and eight pairs of eyes look anywhere, but upon me, until Marie clears her throat.

"What about Ian, honey? What's going on with him?" I sigh; she's always been sympathetic to my situation. I shrug, not really wanting anyone to hear about my dysfunctional father, who cares more about where his next fix or pocket full of cash is coming from above all else in his life.

"He was at the hospital last night, shouting off as usual. I used to think his threats were idle and empty, but now I'm not so sure. I mean he keeps saying he's in trouble, but why is he still...*breathing*." My eyes work around the table, and sure enough, all attention is thoroughly centred on me. Knowing I need to explain, I take a deep breath.

"You see, what you all have to realise is that his relationship with Frankie goes back decades. They grew up together. Even when Frankie left Manchester and got married years ago, my father was still running for him. He has been my whole life, and if something didn't go right, well it didn't matter how many miles separated us, we knew about it. So, if my dad's in so much trouble, why is he still giving him time? Something's just off about it." I can see the knowing looks pass between the men at the table, each one questioning and answering wordlessly.

A sob resounds from beside me, and I turn to Charlie, who is tearful and looks visibly sick.

"What?" I ask.

Walker throws down his napkin in anger and grips Marie's hand. Sloan gives him a weak smile, puts down his knife and fork, and temples his hands under his chin. His features pale significantly and pain clouds the mask he fights so hard to keep intact daily.

"That's what we need to talk about; Sam, Deacon...and Frankie. We're all involved in some way or another." His voice sounds strained, and he releases a deep, drawn-out breath. I know whatever is said next is going to alter the equilibrium.

"Franklin Black is Charlie's father, Kara. I'm so sorry. I wanted to tell you, but I hoped I would never have to. That's why he left Manchester for years."

I slam my fist onto the table, fighting the tears behind my eyes. "And Deacon? What does he have to do with Frankie?" I spit out, mentally slotting together a few stray pieces of the puzzle that has been unsolved in my mind for years.

"He's one of his boys," he whispers out, in a tone that is not dissimilar to shame.

The room is deathly silent. Everyone seems to be looking at Charlie or me. A small hand finds mine under the table, and I clench my fingers around hers, secretly consoling each other. A phone vibrates on the table, and Jake picks it up, studying the screen.

"Rem's on his way over." He throws the phone back down and drains his beer. His eyes are fixed on Charlie, who is now openly crying into her cupped hands.

My heart is slamming against my rib cage, it's out of control, and so am I. All I can think of is running. I rub my hand over my chest, hoping to alleviate the pain that is threatening to make me regress.

I stand abruptly, knock the chair back, and race towards the front door. I'm almost halfway down the street, tears streaming down my cheeks, unable to see clearly, when I'm pulled back and falling.

"I hate you, Sloan Foster! I hate you so fucking much right now, you have no idea! I could handle knowing about your old friendship with Deacon. I could even handle knowing he is one of that man's brutes! But Franklin? You fucking lived with the man! He was your stepdad! You knew all this time, and you didn't say anything. Not a fucking thing! I can't do this, please don't make me, *please*," I beg him. My body wilts in his arms, and I can feel myself giving up with each moment that passes. Kneeling behind me, he holds my wrists to the point of cutting off my circulation. "I can't deal with this, I can't. It's too much. I can't fucking breathe!" I scream out in his face.

My mind throws me back to the past that is filled with hatred for *that* man. My father was the walking dead because of him - his entire life has existed in Franklin's hands. I had endured starvation, because of *that* man. I had been beaten by my own father, multiple times, because of *that* man. And I had been sold, however many goddamn times I can't properly remember, all because of that fucking man!

"I didn't tell you because you have no idea what it was fucking like for us! That man is the harbinger of death! He brought us nothing but pain! I didn't want to tell you because I knew you had suffered the same. I was protecting you! I never wanted you to go back there. I didn't want you existing inside memories and nightmares!" He shakes my wrists, letting out whatever hatred is in his heart through his hands.

"Protecting me? By omitting the truth? That isn't protecting me, it's keeping me in the dark, the same place you've always kept me! Let go of me!" I scream at him again.

I look at him through watery lashes. He's hurt, heartbroken, and balancing precariously on the edge of sanity. On the other hand, I'm conflicted, and I know it's because of the connection we share in this truly fucked up life, and it's one that binds us in the most unimaginable way possible.

"We need to talk," I manage to get out, in my snotty, teary state. "*Privately*," I add for emphasis. The things I had to tell him were not up for an open, round the table debate. I didn't want anyone else hearing them. *Ever*.

"Yeah, I know." He stands, picking me up with him, and carries me back to the house.

The hardest thing in life is being honest. I have done my fair share of trying to hide who I really am, and the shame that has moulded me this way for such a long time.

Now, time was up.

I can't hide anymore.

I sit back in the chair, recanting the absolute worse times I remember with vivid clarity. Walker and Sloan stare, clearly distraught from each word that passes over my lips.

"...I cowered in the corner as he called her every name under the sun, before battering her repeatedly. It was Christmas Eve, and the deal they had been planning for weeks had turned bad. The next day, when my mother should have been making dinner, she was in the hospital, lying to the doctors, telling them she had been robbed on her way home from work. My father, on the other hand, had gone to the pub with his fistful of blood money from Frankie, while I stayed home alone and cleaned fragments of my mother's blood from the walls. I was eleven. I should have been playing with the toys that Santa never brought, but instead, I was forced to play the adult."

Sobbing erupts again, but I can't look at Marie, because I know I'm breaking her spirit. I mentally thank myself that I had spared her the majority of the more, raw, sordid details, but still wish I had told her this years ago. She deserved to know, considering the way she put her neck on the line for me, but I just couldn't. The less she knew, the safer she was, but that just isn't a viable option anymore.

"There was a complete week I remember when the only meal I had every day was lunch at school because we had no money. Then there were the beatings, times I couldn't really walk the next day, and my teachers tried digging a little deeper, but never quite managed to delve below the surface. I could go on and on. Looking back, there are so many things I should have done, but I was a child, I didn't know any different. The only good thing that it has done, is that it's made me stronger, or had, whichever way you want to look at it."

My heart continues to break as I watch tears stream down Marie's face, and Sloan and Walker's looks of shock. Just airing those simple facts, the ones that nobody, not even Sam, knew about, is genuinely terrifying. I haven't cried this time; I've remained strong.

I've held it together while I described some of the events that had moulded and destroyed me in equal measure.

"Remy's here," Jake calls through the closed door. Walker stands, pulling a heartbroken Marie up with him, and ushers her out. Jake skulks outside, waiting. "He's found Deacon." Then he's gone.

"*Sloan*," I say, fear consuming my voice. His hands rub up and down my back soothingly.

"I know, baby. John will get him." His determination is clear and concise, and I tilt my head to look at him. Just how far would he go to end this?

"No, I don't want you doing anything that might endanger yourself. Please, *promise me*," I plead. He sighs annoyed and tilts my chin up.

"He'll always be a threat to you. I can't live with that. Not knowing if, *when*, he'll show up again." He tucks my head into his neck and rests his chin on my crown. "I can't take the chance that he'll hurt you. I couldn't live with myself if he did that again. Please just...trust me. Please."

Trust has been the one word I have always had difficulty believing in. I let down my walls because I trusted him, and it took me to two places. One I never thought I would live in, and one I never thought I'd be out of. But I know I have to trust him again now. I nod numbly at his words. He's right, and while I couldn't care less about Deacon, the thought of never seeing Sloan again, *that* I couldn't live with.

We move as one from the office, and his hand slides further down to my lower back, finally resting on the curvature of my bottom. I don't attempt to pull away; the thought never even crosses my mind. I'm right where I want to be.

In this precise moment, I am home.

Albeit, right now, it's a truly fucked up one.

"Every goddamn time! Don't you guys ever get sick of this?" Remy says when he sees us. A few sounds of agreement and chuckling float around the room. "Seriously Sloan, for as long as I've known you, all you've done is screw random women, and now one comes along, and it's like you're joined at the fucking hip. Come up for breath for, Christ sake!"

Remy divests himself of his thoughts and his jacket, and I watch each movement he makes carefully. He seems wired tight tonight, and my distrust of him is growing more determined. His whole demeanour is suspicious. I cling to Sloan's waist a little tighter, as Remy's dark, secret-filled gaze filters to me and remains. I'm more than uncomfortable in his presence, and the little glimmer of wickedness in his eyes tells me to be cautious and alert.

Sloan turns my face to his, no doubt he's still wary I might chance running out of the door again. I want to, I really do. All I can think of is Frankie Black and Deacon. I've hated them both long before Sloan had entered my life. Frankie had destroyed my family, and Deacon, unbeknown to me at the time, singlehandedly destroyed me.

"You okay, my love?"

"Fine, really." I slap a fake smile on my face and lie credibly. *For once.*

"Ignore his crap!" Sloan says, kissing my nose, seeing past my pretence. But that is easier said than done, especially when it causes bile to scorch my throat, hearing about the Sloan of yesteryear. Yet again, it forces my mind to fester, even more so now I know the truth.

I seat myself at the far end of the room. Remy is watching me, and I notice the stiffening of his body from my position. Walker looks from me to Remy, and back again. His eyes silently question my demeanour, and I hold his gaze, hoping the voiceless words that I don't completely trust Remy will emanate loud and clear. Studying me with curious intent, Walker finally gives a little head jerk in recognition, and I release my breath in a silent, controlled blow.

"So, what do you know, Jeremy?" Sloan moves towards him.

"He's holed up in some shithole bed and breakfast. Not heard anything about Samantha though, but I imagine it's his handy word. I heard she's bad, that she might not make it. It wouldn't surprise me; it's not the first time. But let's face it, she's good at orchestrating shit, but not good at taking it." My mouth falls open, not by his words, but the context of them. He was the one who helped Sam remove me from the devil's lair, but now I have to query whether it was Deacon who put her in a coma or Remy.

Sloan gives me a hardened, sympathetic look, and I turn away, so I don't have to see the fake pity in his eyes. I'm aware he despises her. I'm also aware in my heart of hearts that she might not make it, but unlike everyone else, I'm not ready to give up hope just yet.

Life made us what we are: fighters, survivors. And I know down to my last breath that she will do both.

I sit in the corner alone for the rest of the night, dwelling on what might be. There are a lot of *ifs* and *buts* running around my head, and I bite down on each painful choice I know I shall have to make in the foreseeable future. I know Deacon or Frankie, or both, will call me out at some point, and I just want it over with. This all started with me, and I vow it will also end with me.

Slowly descending the stairs, I sit at the bottom and pull my knees to my chest. Observing the guys talking between themselves, I wish I had joined Marie and Charlie instead.

After the conversation became too close for comfort, they choose to catch a late showing at the cinema. Obviously, Charlie still has unaddressed issues, because she has never really fully embraced what Deacon had done to her. These men haven't allowed her to. While it's admirable that they have cocooned her, protected her, all they've done is damage her further.

I, on the other hand, have had many years to come to terms with the abuse I suffered. And although it was only recently I learned the truth – or part of it, I dealt with it my own way - abandoned and alone.

Entering the living room, I pace to the window behind me. Night fell long ago, and I stare at my reflection in the pane. The images of the men behind me are outlined perfectly, but all I can focus on is Remy. He's watching me keenly, but the rest don't seem to notice. They're too engrossed in discussing how to deal with him, who conveniently, they have trouble locating.

Of course, it's very convenient, isn't it?

I rock slowly on my heels as I come up with my own plan of action should Deacon - or Remy - try to take me again. Devlin is the key, and he's going to give me what I want.

"Devlin?" I don't turn around because I can see his silhouette perfectly reflected in the glass. His head jerks up in open invitation for my imminent question. "How soon can we start?" I twist in a perfect circle to face him.

"How about tomorrow?" he suggests, swaggering towards me with complete ease and confidence. I like this about him - his empathy with women. Being raised the only son in a house full of them, he's never once made me feel inferior. I wonder if he has been told of my past, and what Deacon had done to put his vicious mark on it permanently. I wonder just how much they all know, since they seem completely comfortable discussing him in front of me now.

"Tomorrow's good for me. Sloan?" I look at him, and his head lifts and his features contort a little. He looks between us and dips his chin in acknowledgement, but he's not happy.

"So, tomorrow then. Anything I need to bring?" I ask brightly. This is the first good news I've had in a while. I'm finally going to do something for myself.

"No, just wear something comfortable. T-shirt, jogging pants, good trainers. I'll pick you up around eight." He turns with a mischievous smile and a wink.

I look back to the window, and my eyes are instantly drawn to Jeremy, whose toxic gaze would burn me alive if it was possible.

Chapter 30

"MORNING," SLOAN GREETS quietly behind me as I pull a plate from the high cabinet.

It's been almost a week to the day since I had my heart broken all over again. Sloan has tiptoed around the issues that came to light that night, and as much as I really want to delve deeper and pull out the demons *that man* has chained up inside me, I can't.

The morning after the night before was rough.

I've avoided Sloan entirely, ensuring when he enters the room, I leave. I've also thrown myself into my sessions with David, and other than that, I've pretty much not left the house. My training with Devlin didn't start as planned since John needed him to go on some business up north. I have basically spent the majority of my time pottering around the house and the vast gardens, reliving his birthday night, and subsequently submerging myself and my overactive brain in the pool. I'd like to say the miles and miles I have swum over the last six days have washed away the bad crap, but typically, they haven't.

"Will you drive me to see David this morning?" I ask him. He is dressed in another immaculate suit, so I know he's going to the office today. He doesn't respond, merely nods his head.

"Kara, you know the answer to anything you ask will always be yes. Seriously, it infuriates me that you think I would ever tell you no." I nod and slide away from him. A frustrated noise ripples around the kitchen, and I turn back as he slams a mug down on the marble top.

"What?" I bark out. I knew it would eventually come to this point - the point of no return.

"We need to talk about this; about what was said last week, and other things I still need to tell you, which you keep brushing aside!" He slackens his tie and unbuttons his collar. "You've holed yourself up in here for a week. You haven't seen or talked to anyone! It isn't healthy, and God forbid that I'm actually worried about you!"

"I'm fine. Honestly, I am," I mumble quickly.

He shakes his head. "No, baby, you're not fine. You're so far from fucking fine! How many times do I have to say I'm sorry? I'll say it again – I. Am. Sorry! I'm sorry I didn't tell you about Frankie. I just couldn't do it. It would've broken your heart. What a fucking excuse that is! It was inevitable and unavoidable. I was fooling myself when I thought I could keep it from you forever. You would have found out eventually, and yet I still thought that if I could just-"

"Just what? Protect me from him? Impossible. Look, we're just going round and round in circles with this. You can't change your past, the same way I can't change mine. I just need time to process it." I reach out to him, and for the first time ever, he backs away. I drop my hand in defeat. I'm going to lose him, and I shall have no one to blame but myself.

He stares at me, but I know I need to say what has been plaguing me since the moment we met. It has been even more prevalent from the second I left John's house with a head full of new revelations and assumptions.

"Why are you with me?" He cocks his head to the side, a look of *what the hell* spreads over his face. "Seriously, what do you see in me? I remember all the women who approached you at the events, the way Christy and her friends looked at me. Why?"

He scrubs his hand over his cheek. "What, you think I'm with you for sympathy? To atone for Deacon's vile actions? Is that what you think this is?" His voice is rising, and in turn, so does mine.

"Well, isn't it?"

"No!" he roars out. "The moment I reached into that fucking cubbyhole you were mine! You wormed your way inside me and refused to leave. You were the only pure thing in my fucked-up life. For years growing up, everyone looked at me and Charlie like we had it all! Like we had some perfect, gilded life. On the outside, maybe we did, but nobody knew what we had to live with. Go and take a good look at the bedroom doors, see the old screw holes in the backs of them for yourself. We locked ourselves in every night, so that Frankie couldn't beat us! Even my mother was too terrified to go to sleep! Talk to John, ask him why my mother hired him! Ask him about the first meeting they had when she could barely walk or talk, and you couldn't see past the fucking bruises!"

"Sloan-"

"Kara, please let me say it, so that at long last you will finally understand, and we can get past this lunacy inside your head! I fell in love with you the moment I picked you up. Before Deacon did that shit to you, and before I knew what part of Frankie's business your father was into. *I fell in love with you!* You were just fourteen, and I was nineteen. I didn't give a shit what anyone thought, and that night when I left you at the hospital, John made me leave. I walked away because I didn't stand up for what I believed in, but by God, I will not walk again. Not now, not ever!"

He reaches for me and grabs my arms. "Baby, it doesn't matter what may have happened before, as I said last time, I wanted you before *him*, and nothing, not him, your father or that bastard Black, are ever going to change that. Understand?" I nod and rest my head on his chest. His heart is beating a mile a minute.

"I'm sorry I've been such a bitch to live with this last week." He holds me tighter, and I ease myself into him without any indecision.

"I've barely seen you because you've avoided me. Trust me, I haven't seen anything remotely bitchy. Most days I was lucky if I saw the back of your head!" He pulls back and pushes the hair from my face with both hands. "We leave in ten minutes. Go grab your bag and anything else you need." He places a tender kiss on my lips and lets me go.

"Devlin's back, by the way. You might want to call him to arrange a session. I know Charlie's itching to learn how to throw down Jake." I stare at him as he shakes his head incredulously, like even the idea is entertainment worthy. I shake my own head. "What?"

"How do you do that?"

"Do what?"

"Act like this last week never happened? I acted selfishly, allowing my own insecurities to manifest until I almost pushed you away. Now you're acting like it never existed. I don't understand," I mumble.

"Baby, you've just answered your own question. You allowed yourself to believe something that wasn't there. I get there will be times when you start to wonder, but when that arises, promise me, in future, you'll talk to me, rather than thinking up all kinds of stupid ideas."

"I guess I just never thought I'd have someone like you in my life. I'd grown accustomed to being on my own for so long that... Oh, I don't know, can we drop it?" I turn towards the window as the car eats up the miles from the house to our final destination.

"Okay, we'll drop it for now. But the next time you feel the need to go off on one, please speak to me first, rather than try to block me out." I give him a small smile and turn away.

Eventually, the beautiful green countryside gives way to the motorway, and sometime later the imposing concrete structures that make up the London skyline appear on the horizon. Manoeuvring through the streets, his building eventually comes into view.

Picking up my things, I climb out of the car and shuffle around to the other side and wait for him.

"I'll walk you in, but then I need to leave." He looks at his watch. "I've got a meeting in fifteen. Shit, it's probably going to last all day, maybe even into the evening. I'll get Devlin to come and pick you up and take you to buy some appropriate clothes for kickboxing." I laugh; I can't help it. He doesn't share my amusement.

"I can wear my yoga pants and a t-shirt," I reply, as we exit the car park and edge back up the ramp to the street level.

"No, you need something that will give you more protection." I stop, and he halts in front of me. He gives me a determined look that dares me to challenge his authority. And challenge it, I shall.

"And what would you suggest? Chainmail and a full armoured suit?" I suggest flippantly. "I don't know, maybe I can loan one of those metal knight things they have on display in museums! They might even throw in a lance, too!"

"Kara, don't! Don't get pissed because I don't want you getting hurt. It doesn't work like that. You forget that Devlin and I spar together sometimes. Trust me, after a while he will forget that you're half his size and half his weight, and he will go at you full throttle. And trust me, it will hurt! I want you home in one piece, not one of many!" I shake my head and walk off in front, listening to his huffing and puffing behind me.

My finger jabs the buzzer, and I wait for the security door to open. It doesn't. This is the second time I've pressed it, and the third time that Sloan has looked at his watch. He's going to be late for his meeting.

"Have you ever had to wait this long?"

He gives me a quick head shake. He then pulls out his phone and brings it to his ear. "He's not answering," he says, looking up at the structure.

"Seriously, just go to your meeting, I'll be fine. If he doesn't answer, I'll get Devlin to come and pick me up."

"No."

"Sloan, it's the middle of the day! What do you think is actually going to happen on a crowded street?" He grinds his jaw.

"Fine! But in another five minutes, if he doesn't answer, come and get Gloria to get me out of the meeting," he compromises, but he's displeased. I watch him march back to his office, until he eventually disappears into the building.

I sigh and turn back around, repeatedly pressing the buzzer. I'm about to turn away when the door opens, and the same man who I passed the other week walks out. He gives me the same smirk, and a chill ripples through me.

"Hello, again," he says; his voice familiar. I slowly turn away, trying to fathom where I've heard that voice before, but a second later, the word *sweets* drifts over the atmosphere in a ghostly whisper. My head shoots up and he gives me a sardonic smile, then he tilts his head and lowers his glasses in salutation. I fall back against the wall, the air caught in my lungs.

The living, breathing spectre of Franklin Black approaches me and runs his finger down my cheek. "I'll be seeing you again, sweets." My heart is thumping out of control as he stands in front of me. He narrows his eyes and cracks his neck from side to side. "Give my love to Sloan. Tell him I'll be seeing him again soon, too." He then turns and walks down the street, never once looking back. I watch as he disappears into the crowd and becomes lost.

Panic rises from deep inside, and I run down the busy pavement towards Sloan's building, pushing people out of my way. I dart into the disabled toilet and lock myself in. The tears are streaming down my cheeks, and I tuck myself into the tiny space between the wall and toilet as my mind paints a vivid picture of times gone by, in which Franklin Black and his thugs take their pound of flesh, while still offering the world.

The constant knocking on the toilet door shocks me back into the present. I gaze numbly as the handle moves up and down - whoever is outside is trying to get in. I hold my bag to my chest, praying they leave me alone.

"Open the door!" Someone shouts from the other side. I shake in my tight space, distraught and fearful that he's really coming back for me again. I close my eyes and start to count. I make it to thirty-four, before the sharp twist and snap of metal rings in my ears and the door flies opens.

Two of the building's security guards are stood in the open doorway. They look around the small facilities and then to me, before one turns to the other. "Go get Mr Foster," he says. The other guard looks bewildered, not moving an inch, unsure what is actually happening here. *"Now!"* The guard quickly moves and is then out of sight. The remaining guard enters the room and reaches for me.

"Don't touch me!" I scream. He halts, perplexed, not knowing what to do with the crazy, desolate woman sitting on the floor in tears before him.

"Just calm down, okay. No one here is going to hurt you," he says pathetically. I need more than goddamn words right now. What I need, nobody can give me. I need to be free, and I will only get that in death. I've known that for so long, and for so long, I thought I could escape it. I never will.

"Kara?" I hear him before I see him. Sloan comes charging into the toilet, bypassing the guard, and reaches out to me. I allow him to pick me up and console me. He moves us into a larger space and slides down the wall, still holding me tight.

"Mr Foster?" The guard addresses him with a confused tone.

"Leave, now! And lock the door behind you," he says firmly. The guard nods and does as requested. The turn of the lock signals the silence.

Sloan rocks me back and forth as I allow myself to fall into the start of my newest mental breakdown. We stay in the same position for a long time, until my legs start to cramp, and I have no other choice but to move. I slowly ease my head from his neck and look up.

"What happened? Was the session really that bad?" His concern is undoubtedly heightened. I shake my head.

"I didn't go," I confess pitifully, knowing this is the start of the latest overbearing behaviour that I'll be on the receiving end of from here on out. "Franklin was there. He passed me in the doorway. He said he would be seeing you soon." I break down again. He pulls me tighter to him, cradling my head.

"Son of a bitch!" His hand grips my hip hard, and he fumbles in his pocket and brings his phone to his ear. "John, we've got a serious fucking issue. I'm in the ground floor disabled toilet with Kara." I shuffle around so we are face to face and he puts his phone away.

"Was John there the night Deacon raped me?"

"Yeah, he was. Tommy and Doc, too. They took care of you until we got to the hospital." He stares emotionless into my eyes.

"That's why they all looked at me funny that night with Emily."

"Yes, it is," he confirms, stroking my face tenderly.

I take a deep breath. "The day I went to meet my dad..." I hate bringing it up, but it has to be done. I need to understand just how deep this actually goes. "The way he looked at Walker. Did he meet him back then?" I ask, replaying the way my father wilted in fear at seeing the bulk that is Walker edging towards him.

Sloan cups my cheeks and brings my face to his. He kisses the tip of my nose, before pressing me back a little. "Yeah, he did. John knocked him out on his front step. A woman was screaming at him to stop. I presume she was your mother. Baby, I'm sorry. Jesus Christ, I'm sorry for all of it. This was never meant to be your life. I never wanted this for you. When I left you in that hospital, Stuart and Walker tried to convince me that I'd saved you, but I didn't. If I had, you still wouldn't be dealing with it all now."

I wrap my arms around him and hold tight. "It's easy to play the blame game. Everyone can have a part." His hand drifts up and down my back comforting.

"I suppose. The truth is I'm amazed you're taking it so well. Anytime I try to broach it with Charlie she goes mental at me. I've been trying to get her to talk about it lately, considering eventually she's going to learn the truth about you, but she just won't. She prefers to compartmentalise it, so she doesn't have to acknowledge it."

"But that's not her fault, it's yours. You, Walker, and Jake. Between you, you've never allowed her to deal with it her own way. You've constantly protected her her entire life, and what he did to her is no different. But whereas I grieved for the loss of a part of myself alone, you guys rallied around and made her look past it, but not completely. Sorry, I don't mean to be harsh, but at some point, you all have to take responsibility that she may be eternally damaged, because she hasn't been allowed to mourn the part of herself that was taken; the part of yourself that you only get once."

He's about to answer, when Walker calls through the door. Sloan stands us up, wraps his arm around me and manoeuvres us to the door. Walker is on the other side, looking grim.

"Okay?" he queries hesitantly.

"Am I ever?" I deadpan, in my post-teary, red-eyed state. He gives me a small smile.

"How long until it's over?" Walker turns to Sloan, referring to his meeting.

His eyes widen, and he shakes his head from side to side. "I don't know. It could go on all night at the rate they're arguing upstairs. Nothing is ever easy, is it?"

Walker chuckles singularly. "Not for us, kid. Look, I'll take her to mine." He slaps Sloan's back, and waits outside the toilet to give us some privacy.

Rubbing his hands up and down my arms, Sloan studies me. Silently, he pulls me close and kisses my forehead hard. "I love you," he breathes against my head.

I smile and grip his arms. "And I, you. Don't be too long."

Moving us outside, he pushes me into Walker, who clenches his arm around me. "We'll see you later." We both watch, motionless, as Sloan walks away into the foyer, towards the lifts.

No words are spoken as we exit the building. Climbing into the car, I wrap the seat belt around myself and stare straight ahead.

"Sloan asked me to ask you about his mother this morning. Will you tell me?"

Firing the ignition, he turns to me. "Not today, honey. It's not a bedtime story you ever want to hear. I will tell you…one day."

I feel my heart crack. "I'll hold you to it."

He squeezes my hand. "Don't worry, I won't forget. Come on, how about I buy the three – no, four - lovely ladies in my life dinner. Call Charlie and Sophie, we'll pick them up on the way."

A chill hits my shoulder, and I drag the duvet closer. Just as I'm nearly comfortable again, an unmistakable draught runs the length of my front. I turn, drowsy, at the sound of shuffling, and gasp.

"Shush, don't worry, my love, it's just me," Sloan murmurs, climbing into bed, coaxing me towards him.

"I thought you would've just gone back to the hotel; it's closer."

"I couldn't; you weren't there. It's been a long time since I've bunked in this room." His hot arms snake around and position themselves over my abdomen.

"Yeah, it's another first for me."

He chuckles briefly and breathes content against my neck. I drift my finger up and down his arm, loving the way the fine hair stands on end under my caress.

"John called David. Apparently, Margaret wasn't well, and he had a patient in who ran over schedule. That's the reason why he didn't answer today."

"That's good. I was worried. You'll just have to re-arrange, my love." A soft kiss on the back of my neck causes me to mellow.

I nod against his chest, but guilt rocks me. I've long decided today was the last for me. Until I can live freely, I can't see any other way around it. Franklin's presence in the same building was just the icing on the proverbial cake.

I twist and turn on the bedside lamp, and the room softly illuminates. Sloan looks exhausted. "Bad day?"

"Hmm, you?" His finger trails over my cheek and nose.

"I've had worse," I say with a little smile.

His brow tilts up as he leans over and switches off the light. "I know, my love, but I promise they're going to get a hell of a lot better."

Chapter 31

"THAT'S SO UNFAIR!" I scream across the room at Devlin, who is bouncing up and down on the balls of his feet. He's edging across the mats, punching his fists out in front of him, smiling triumphantly. I, on the other hand, am sprawled out on the floor where he's left me, after knocking me over for the hundredth time.

Needless to say, I admit I was wrong, and Sloan was right; I do need more protection.

It's the third day of his *training*, as he likes to call it, and I have more bruises than I believed was physically possible. Every limb aches alarmingly, and I'm thoroughly pissed off. I didn't think it would be this exhausting, but he has reiterated, more than once, that there's going to be pain.

Lots of it.

He wasn't lying.

I find my footing and pick my sore body up off the floor. Brushing down my behind, I can feel the discomfort starting again already. It's yet another dark mark that Sloan is going to have a fit about.

He was ready to rip Devlin a new one when I arrived home last night, barely able to walk properly. Silently, he picked me up and carried me upstairs, only putting me down when we reached the sanctuary of the bathroom, and the bath he had already run for me.

"I'm going to fucking kill him!" he said, as he started to peel my clothes off my body. "I told him to teach you how to defend yourself, not bring you back home black and blue. The little bastard! Wait until I get my hands on him!"

To say he was seething is an understatement.

"Who said anything about fair, crybaby? Now get your arse back over here and let's go again!"

Defiantly, I tap my foot, weighing up my non-existent options. The sound of water flushes, and Charlie all but crawls back into the room. She feels my pain, and over the last three days we've comforted each other more than once when Devlin has taken it upon himself to get one over on the both of us.

"I can't take anymore! This is not what I signed up for!" she shouts at him, but he just laughs and tells us to get our arses over to him, *now*.

We both look at each other and Charlie appears deep in thought. "I wonder how many of those laces we would need to gag and tie him to something." I grimace at the past visual in my head, but the punchline never comes - she is completely serious.

Trudging over to him, he's basking in his own glory. "So, ladies, had enough yet?" His delighted expression makes me want to smack him. With my hands on my hips, holding myself as upright as I can manage, I scowl at him.

"Oh, come on, little lady, don't be like that!" Devlin cajoles, like a parent consoling their sulky child. I ignore him and start making my way across the room to collect my things.

"I swear you enjoy seeing us suffer. Just you wait until Sloan and Jake get their hands on you. You'll know what suffering really is!" Charlie says to him. Her slow steps resonate directly behind mine.

I reach for my bag and lob it onto the bench. Taking a seat next to it, I rummage around inside until I find the object I'm seeking. I swipe the screen to read the text Sloan has sent me. A single cream rose fills the panel, and I smile at his thoughtfulness. Dialling his number, I wait for him to answer.

"Hi," his voice breathes life into the other end. "Do I need to come and get you?"

"Please," I reply. There's a long pause until I hear him breathe.

"Do I need to come and kick Devlin's arse?" I murmur in the negative. "Okay, my love. I'll be there shortly. I love you." I shall never tire of hearing him say that.

"And I you," I reply, quietly confident.

Charlie hobbles over, slumping down next to me. She rests her head on my shoulder. "Is my brother coming to pick you up?" she asks wearily, and I nod. "Okay. I was going to drive you, but I'll head off now. I'll see you tomorrow – if I can move, that is." She bends down and hugs me the best she can, given the current soreness in her own body. I have no doubt it's as shattered as mine.

Devlin follows her out to make sure she gets away safely. He hasn't taken any chances these last few days, knowing his neck will be on the chopping block should anything befall either of us.

A short time later, he jogs back over to me, rocking on his feet. His triumphant grin is still fully intact, and I swallow down his unwarranted enthusiasm. "Same time tomorrow. I promise we'll start on the good stuff. Come on, I'll wait outside with you until he arrives."

"No, you don't have to," I tell him. It's a beautiful late August day, the sun is shining, and I just want some time alone to gather my thoughts. The last time I felt this raw and battered had been an awakening. The fear of my past was slowly subsiding, and I wanted to be alone to process and to procrastinate a little.

"Go on, I'll be fine," I say, as we stand outside the gym.

"Okay." He leans in and kisses my cheek, which leaves no lingering effect. "Call me if he's late, I'll be right back for you." I wave him off, and he climbs into his car and drives away.

I let my mind digress, watching the world pass me by. Life is good at the moment, really good, and I'm grateful that someone up there believes I am worthy to be included in it.

Quickly glancing at my watch, it has been over half an hour since I called him, and panic is starting to get the better of me. I'm fully aware I'm foolishly sabotaging myself by sitting here alone. There is no one here to protect me now.

My phone vibrates in my pocket, and I flick the screen.

Sorry got caught up. On my way now.

I drop it back into my bag and gaze around again, but this time, something seizes my attention. Further down the street, a black 4x4 is parked ominously. I visually examine it from a distance, it's too familiar. Shielding my eyes from the strong midday sun, the dark paintwork glistens under the rays, while acid churns thickly in my stomach.

I scan the street to see how many people are milling around, but in this part of the city, they are few and far between, even at midday. Devlin had told me the reason he could lease the gym so cheaply is that the area is run down. I shiver, mentally kicking myself for making such an impulsive and reckless decision to let him leave.

The vehicle's engine kicks in, and it slowly begins to crawl down the street. It stops a decent distance away, but I can vaguely make out a shadow through the dark tinted windows. I clutch the phone in my hand, chastising myself, and coming up with some sort of plan should my worst nightmare materialise again. I will never forget the night Deacon conspired to intercept me and succeeded. Even though my body has healed, my mind never will.

In my heart, I know my entire life shall exist in pain of some description.

It's the only thing that has ever been a real constant in my life.

Again, the vehicle starts to slowly roll forward. Stopping directly in front of me, I tense every muscle, mentally prepared for whatever is about to ensue. Time ceases to exist, as I wait with bated breath for whoever is in the car to show themselves. It never happens. Instead, they just remain inside, watching, waiting.

The distinct sound of a powerful engine punctures the relative silence. In the distance, I see the Aston hurtling down the street. Admittedly, I'm not fond of his speed driving, but he could put his foot down at hundred, and it still wouldn't be fast enough right now.

Aware that within minutes I will no longer be alone, the unidentified driver throttles the car engine. It pulls, straining against the biting point of the clutch. Slowly, the window rolls down, and the driver makes himself known.

Deacon.

My heart fails to function as I come face to face with my worst nightmare all over again. He stares me down, taking quick glances in the mirrors. Sloan is almost upon us, and I've never been so thankful.

In the last remaining seconds, Deacon narrows his eyes, blows me a kiss and mouths *soon* at me, before the tyres protest against the tarmac, and he speeds off. I slump to the ground and breathe out in fear.

The Aston stops directly in front of me, the door slams open, and then I'm inside Sloan's arms. *Safe.*

"Hey, what's wrong?" I search his face for some sign he may recognise the vehicle that is now fading into the distance in a cloud of exhaust fumes. He twists in its direction, and his jaw ticks and tightens.

There's nothing I can say because I'm too consumed with how soon, '*soon*' would be.

"Son of a bitch!" he spits out through clenched teeth.

I can barely hold my own weight, until Sloan assists. After putting me in the car, he now has his phone to his ear - and he's raging mad. It doesn't take a genius to work out who he's going to let rip at. I only hope the poor guy forgives me, because this time, it absolutely is my fault.

"What the fuck, Devlin! I told you to make sure she wasn't alone. I get here, and Deacon is driving off. Where the fuck are you, you little bastard?" he shouts into the phone, then pauses, listening to whatever Devlin is saying. His head bounces and then he responds. "I don't care!" he grits out. "She doesn't get left alone ever again. Do I have to remind you what the hell is happening right now?" he shouts yet again, and then quickly searches my eyes. I sigh, seeing the clear mask of concealment drop perfectly in place. He's keeping secrets again.

"Fine. It's done, but next time..." He ends the call and turns to me, then his hands run over my cheeks and neck. "God, I'm sorry. I should have been here. I shouldn't have-"

"It's okay. It's my fault, I told Devlin to go. I didn't think, I'm sorry." I drop my head in my hands, the stress of the day and the torture of Deacon's words carve at the hollow crack in my heart even further.

"It's not your fault! Don't ever say that. I don't want this for you! Not being able to live fully or do something you want to because he might be there. I don't want you to live like this for fuck sake!" He lifts my head up with his knuckles.

I ease into him; he is my solitude, my saviour, my first and only love. I could stay with him like this for the rest of my life. But then I remember. I remember Deacon's words that indicate I may not have him for the rest of my life. I may not live past next month, if evil personified gets his way a second time.

"Deacon... Just before you got here, seconds really, he said 'soon'." Hot tears spread across my cheeks before I realise I'm crying.

"Don't think about him. I won't let him hurt you again. I won't!" His words are laced with sincerity, but his eyes are sad. We both know he's making a promise he might not be able to keep.

"Let's go home, you can show me some of your new moves," he insinuates, wiggling his eyebrows suggestively.

His way of distracting me is impeccable, even though we both know *soon* will come eventually...and quite possibly destroy everything.

Chapter 32

"HEY BABY, LET'S get hot and roll around!" Sloan winks, and the heat in my body explodes. We've been in the gym for an hour or so together, with nothing but the sounds of our breathing and grunting for company.

I watch him as he begins looking around for whatever objects he can improvise with. He walks towards an empty area at the far side of the vast space, and pulls out a few mats and positions them on the floor. With his hand cradling his chin, he looks over at a weight bench, then turns back to me. A boyish grin spreads over his cheeks, and he moves towards it, quickly dragging it back into the space.

He edges closer, grips my face in his hands, and his thumbs massage my temples. I close my eyes, loving how he can calm me with a simple touch.

Tapping my cheek, my eyes shoot open. He smiles at me before pulling me into him. My body is plastered against his, hot and sweaty, as he takes what he wants. Pillaging my mouth like never before, my moans escape me as he works his talented tongue over mine. I sigh into him and close my eyes. His lips claim me roughly, moving down my chin and neck before he sucks my nipples through my sodden vest. My need to get him away from the perspiration drenched garment is strong, but as I push, he pulls. Looking up at me, his sparkling blues, alive with need, tell me the only thing I'm pushing is my luck.

Continuing to work down my body, he kneels in front of me, and his hands slowly glide up my thighs. His thumbs drag up the insides until they find my aching heat. My lids lower desirously, and he slides his thumbs as far as they will go, pausing just before the act becomes obscenely indecent.

"Come on, baby, I want you under me, in more ways than one." The promise of his words turns me on immensely, more so than I already am. I can't see past the sexual fog clouding my rationality.

He stands firm with his legs spread and faces me head-on. "Right, punch me." My brows arch questionably. "Seriously, my love, punch me." Seeing my hesitation, he runs his hand over my cheek, letting it stroke lower until he squeezes my breast. I melt into him and allow my eyes to flutter shut momentarily.

"Kara, you're doing it again."

"Doing what?"

"That!" He waves down my body. The one that is silently calling for him, like a siren, meant only for him.

"I can't help it!" I look away, and he brings his hand around the back of my neck.

"You're letting me take control. One little touch and you submit far too easily. Don't get me wrong, I'm not complaining, but I don't want a simpering wife who will give me whatever I want with a flick of my finger. I want you to challenge me every day for the rest of our lives and keep me on my toes. After chasing you for eight years, it's the only thing I know how to do efficiently. You might be good at running, but I'll always be a few steps behind."

Smiling, I close my eyes and let him take control. I listen to his steady heartbeat and the way he sighs as I wrap my arms around him. He holds me close, and I know that I don't need to know how to make a relationship work, because we already do. A small pat on my backside sobers me, and I stare up at Sloan innocently. He grips my cheeks and kisses my forehead, before moving away from me. I bring my arms around myself, suddenly feeling exposed, but unable to explain why.

"Now, let's start again. No more distractions from you!" he laughs. "Punch me!"

"I can't hurt you," I whimper.

"Okay, but the only way I'm going to get you under me, is if you attack. Now, punch me! Think of something that burns you like never before. Think of something that has made you cry. Think of anything, just punch me!"

Oh, hell!

I inhale and think of the only person I can to focus my anger on. My fist takes on a mind of its own as it lurches around from my side and connects with his jaw, imagining it's someone else's.

"Holy fuck! That's hurts!" I scream, clutching my hurt hand, bending over to catch my breath. Sloan moves quickly, as he plays doctor and feels around for any signs of damage, forgetting about himself.

"Nothing feels like it's broken. Might be a little sore tomorrow, though."

His eyes search mine for clues as to what I'm thinking, but he already knows who piqued my pathetic attempt at rage. He silently kisses my knuckles and resumes his stance. On my tiptoes, I reach up to kiss him, but he holds me back slightly until he shakes his head and sighs, knowing I will always be unable to be anything other than compliant with him.

He slaps my behind again, and I yelp. Cunningly, he takes advantage of the situation, and before I know it, I'm falling to the floor, looking up at the ceiling and him.

"I knew I'd get you underneath me," he says slyly. I wiggle, but he shifts his knee to hold me in place. "Baby, if you want to be fucked on a dirty floor, I can accommodate it. Although I would prefer to have you in our bed. Come on," he says, picking us both up instantaneously.

"No," I whisper alluringly. "Here. *Now.*"

He drops me so my feet are back on solid ground and rotates me in his arms. His strong chest twitches against my shoulder blades, while warm breath fans my ear. His arm crushes my waist, and I feel his hardness at my backside.

My breath lodges in my throat as he moves us towards the weight bench. My hands fumble over the worn leather, and my fingers curl around the padding. Shifting behind me, with his hand on the middle of my back, he presses down until my behind is raised before him.

"Perfect." The word rolls off his tongue, and I squirm, desperately trying to press my thighs together to suppress the moist heat that is now generating copiously.

"Stay in that position," he commands. His hand leaves my back, and his retreating feet slap against the wood floor. Silence envelops the room and, although I'm still fully clothed, I feel naked.

Exposed.

I glance at the door and then drop my head down, awaiting his return. Arching my back up and down like a cat, anything to assuage the dull ache growing in my spine, I moan gently when the stretch hits the right spot. Watching the door again, I begin to straighten up, needing to find where he has gone.

"Beautiful." His voice echoes hauntingly from the other side of the room - the side I haven't looked at. I cock my head and beam at him. "I love watching you; always have, always will." I approach him slowly. He is sitting on a stack of large mats, his knees raised up, his arms outstretched atop of them.

"How did you get back in here?" I question suspiciously. I heard him leave but never return. I drop myself down to the floor on my haunches, a few feet in front of him, awaiting his response.

"I never left. I would never leave you if I didn't have to."

My lips press together, savouring both his words and him. I crawl forward, shutting down the space that separates me from the one thing in my life that I know is certain and true. I halt in front him, drinking him in, conceding I'll never be able to quench my desire for him completely.

"Take me, right here, right now," I plead, sucking on my lip, hoping I will get my wish. The way his mouth tugs at the sides makes me happy.

Crooking his finger, I slowly resume my crawl towards him. My breathing is heavy and laboured, as the final few inches became a memory. He hauls me into his lap, and I move from side to side to get comfortable. His eyes close, and his head falls back. He lifts me up abruptly and brings me down on his groin. I moan breathlessly when his hardness hits my sensitive apex. I rub myself against him, desperate to feel the passion that only he can stimulate inside me. Gliding my hands up the back of his neck, I tug a little at his hair when he rocks me again. I really want the clothes gone, but truthfully, this is one of the best experiences of my life. I had read about this, but obviously, I had never experienced it. Until now.

After all these years, I am finally conquering another first.

"I love you," I whisper against his lips, our noses almost touching. My eyes are wide, and the world tilts a little further into the unknown the moment he opens his. His blues are glorious, glowing with sincerity.

Moving further forward, he claims my lips with a vengeance. I take what he's willing to give, but am still left wanting more, unable to decipher what *more* really is. Touching my forehead to his, I do what my body is screaming for. I move up and down on him, pretending we're bare. My heart aches observing him. He is losing control while still fully clothed beneath me. I'm not ignorant to what he's experiencing because I'm lost with him.

"Baby, I'm not gonna last!" he moans out. My thrusts become faster, harder. Encouraged by his confession, my body starts to quiver when the early signs of arousal beat down and begin to culminate.

"Good, I'm right here with you." I kiss him hard, taking full advantage, my tongue requesting and gaining entrance, while my hips gyrate autonomously.

His lips are unforgiving against mine, and he manages to salvage control of the situation. He licks behind my upper lip - which seems to have a direct route to my sex - and the moisture between my legs increases. He moves his tongue in and out, while I shamelessly move up and down on his hard, covered shaft. It's heady and sublime, and minutes later, a growl escapes the confines of his throat, and I close my eyes, as his guttural cry calls to me and claims me.

My body twists and the rustle of fabric grounds me. I slowly open my eyes, my mind and body still lost in sensation, to find him staring at me with such intent, a shudder ripples the length of my spine.

"On your hands and knees," he rasps out, thick and deep. I conform immediately as he expertly slides my shorts down, lifting each leg gently to remove them. I yelp, a little surprised when his inquisitive fingers tentatively probe my rear. He doesn't stop his perusing, but he doesn't infiltrate, either.

"Not right now. I just want to play while I screw you senseless," he says, positioning himself behind me, teasing me. He rubs his length up and down my folds until I cry out, begging him to enter me.

"Oh, God!" I breathe as he pushes, stretching me deliciously with each solid inch. "More. I want all of you." I throw my head back, making my spine arch, adjusting him deeper inside me.

"Fuck!" I feel him retract, and I'm about to beg when he slides back in. I keen loudly, encouraging him to do it again, over and over. And he does.

"Baby, I want to come, make me come," I whimper, while he devours me like a crazed animal on the dirty gym floor.

He slams into me hard with each thrust. His skin slaps against mine, and I push back to assist in taking him deeper. He has one hand locked on my shoulder for leverage, the other tantalising and teasing. His hand leaves my hardened nub and travels slowly up my stomach, seeking out my nipples, rolling them maddeningly. His hand continues to slide up, until I feel him stop at the front of my throat. He tilts my head up in the V of his finger and thumb, allowing his outstretched hand to cradle my neck as he licks long lines up the back of my spine.

"Look at how fucking sexy you are," he says huskily, slanting my head to the side. I have somehow failed to remember that mirrors line the walls, until now. I'm awestruck as he pulls out, then pushes back in, causing my body to move forward and my breasts to jiggle.

"I want you to watch us when we come together. I want you to look into your own eyes when I'm deep inside you. I want you to see what I see."

I gasp, completely mesmerised by the visual of us, eliciting my body to surrender further. It feels forbidden and voyeuristic, and I want more. So much more.

His hand ventures back south to the place silently screaming for him. His fingers glide through my slick folds again, teasing and tormenting with precision. My body starts to convulse and prepare for round two.

"That's it, my love, tell me when." I nod, unable to speak as the oxygen is snatched away by an invisible force. My mouth goes dry with the swelling inside me. The sensation alone heightens my pleasure, helping me peak.

"Sloan!" I cry in delight, watching both of us come in the mirrors as he rams home, chanting my name repeatedly behind me. He explodes into the raging fire inside me, but doesn't douse the flames.

My legs buckle, and my balance wanes. I press back until I'm sitting as comfortably as possible between his strong thighs; his hardness is upright and proud against my behind.

He rocks me slowly, whispering in my ear. He covers the side of my throat with sweet kisses and nips gently at my jaw. I close my eyes and lose myself in this perfect moment.

And I silently pray to whoever is listening, that this perfect moment will not be taken away from me again, and that history will not come full circle.

Chapter 33

THE SOFT PATTER of water rouses me. Reaching out my hand, the other side of the bed is empty. I groan, knowing Sloan is probably getting ready for work, while yet another day of roaming around the place and chatting with Charlie in between varying degrees of boredom awaits me.

I stretch and disentangle my naked self from the sheets. I feel a little tender from Sloan's recent ministrations, but still deliciously gratified and fulfilled. Climbing out of bed, I scan the floor for last night's discarded clothes.

As usual, they are already gone.

I let out a tiny laugh at his obsession with tidiness. If I had my way, everything would be all over, but Sloan, meticulous as he is, ensures nothing is out of place. Admittedly, everything in his life revolves around structure and discipline.

Well, almost everything. I guess chasing and virtually following my every move for the last eight years has definitely given him that.

A pained gasp forces me to turn, and I spin on my heels, facing him head-on. He stands there like a Greek God, with nothing but a towel as his toga, covering his essentials. The excess water runs in rivulets down his hard, ripped torso, disappearing into the edge of the material. I lick my lips hungrily, and his pupils dilate desirously. I'm breathless, shamelessly checking him out.

He raises an eyebrow. "Tempting doesn't even begin to describe you," he states, a sly look on his face.

He edges closer, until only the bed separates us. I look down at it and back to him, a silent invitation to stay and give it another unnecessary test run. He smiles beautifully, but he shakes his head. Stretching his hand over the bed, I accept, and clamber over it inelegantly on my knees to get to him.

"I would like nothing more than to stay and get hot and messy with you." I smile at his reply, still crawling naked. "Unfortunately, I have a meeting, and you, my gorgeous girl, also have work today." He kisses my nose in the most innocuous way. I scrunch my eyes up, not understanding.

"No, I haven't. Marie doesn't want me back yet, she told me so the other day when I called. Instead, I'm just squeezing you dry, like a financial leech, sucking the pennies right out of you!" I screw my face up again. I hate this. I hate not having my own money, not working. I've never depended on anyone for anything my whole adult life. I'd worked so hard to forge some kind of existence for myself, and now I've reverted back to nothing.

"Well, the temp she hired isn't particularly good, so she wants you back early."

He looks at me pointedly, his eyes searching mine before he provides the most amazing distraction ever, and yanks the towel from his hips. My eyes, already having had their fill of his damp, flawless torso, now drop lower down his cut abs and meet with his very hard and ready penis. My hand automatically shoots out to him, and he retreats back, holding his palm up. A command not to touch him.

"If you do, neither of us will be leaving this room. Please baby, shower. *Alone.*" It's evident in his eyes how conflicted he currently is. I agree under duress, not wanting to cause him any more undue stress. I kiss him hard before sauntering into the bathroom, chuckling quietly when he groans behind me.

I shut the water off and grab a couple of towels from the rack. After wrapping my hair and body, I plod back into the bedroom. Sloan isn't there, and I sigh disappointedly until I hear shuffling coming from the walk-in.

I watch from the doorway as he fumbles through the dresser drawers. He pauses and turns; knowing I'm watching him has become instinctual.

"I have something for you, but I can't find it..." he says frustrated.

He continues rummaging through the drawers, finally closing the last one, then throws his hands in the air, admitting defeat. I smile at his annoyance and move closer to him. He sits me atop the island, caressing my face in his hands.

"So very beautiful," he murmurs, then kisses me, sucking my bottom lip between his, making me simultaneously heady and feverish. "And all mine."

"What was it?" I lean back, breathless.

"Hmm?" His lips graze my temple.

"What you were looking for? What was it?" I laugh distractedly while regaining some semblance of self.

He pulls back, but his thumbs still circle my cheekbones. "It's just something I picked up. I know exactly where I put it, but now it's gone." His eyes narrow like he's just thought of something, but just as quickly, the look is gone. And yet again, he is keeping things from me, but it's the least of my worries today.

"I want to go see Sophie later on. Is that okay with you? I mean, I'll call Devlin to come with me, if you like." I suck in my bottom lip, wondering if I sound convincing enough. I hate lying to him. But truthfully, I know if I tell him I'm going to see Sam, he will most likely pop a vein. This way is far easier for both of us.

Forcing a wry smile, he replies, "Of course. I don't want to control you, just to know you're safe. I would prefer if you do call Devlin though. He's still avoiding me," he mutters.

"What do you expect?" I giggle, jumping down and turning to my side of the room. I pull out a white shirt and skinny black trousers. Simple and elegant. I subtly observe him remove a matching three-piece suit from the hangers.

"Well, I may have overreacted, but seeing your bruises...it just took me back, you know? It's not something I will ever forget, if I'm honest." I nod, knowing exactly what he's talking about. I guess it must have been hard to see me like he did all those nights ago, and all those years ago. I always thought I was quite lucky that I never really remembered most of the ghastlier details. A part of me knows I might not have made it through if I did.

"I understand." My hand slides over his face, and his stunning features ease from their pensive state. "Can you drive me to work, or do you need to be at the office?" His lips taste mine momentarily, never closing his eyes or looking anywhere except into mine.

"Of course, I'll take you, my love. I would never deny you anything."

I slip my shoes off at the foot of the stairs. Even though my fear of confined spaces is ebbing gradually, and my mindset is nowhere near as volatile as it once was, if given a choice, the stairs will always be victorious.

Taking each rung slowly, my mind flits around and halts, thinking of the last time I was here. Excluding the day I took it upon myself to get back into a routine, it was the day Sam set out to instil lies in Sloan's head. It was so long ago, but my heart is still heavy thinking about it. Regardless, I can't change the past. God knows there is so much I would erase if I could, but then I wouldn't be me. I wouldn't be strong and resilient as Sloan describes, although I believe he makes me outwardly appear that way because as I already know, I'm truly defenceless.

I stand outside the office door and hesitate. I feel like an outsider, like I don't belong. Whether it's because I know Sloan doesn't want me out of his sight, or the fact that so much as occurred in the last six months, I don't know.

Retrieving my security card, I wave it at the door release fob. It opens, and I slip inside. Looking around, I really do feel like I don't belong anymore. I hadn't realised how much it had changed in the time I've been on enforced sick leave.

"Sorry, can I help you?" a young, blonde girl asks, coming out of Marie's office. I smile at her, ready to answer, when Marie steps out, thoroughly engrossed in the documents she's holding.

"Oh, honey! I was positive when I said that I wanted you back he would fight me tooth and nail!" she says approaching me, arms wide. I fall into them and the familiarity of her. "If he had his way," she speaks into my neck, "he would never let you out of his sight. He would lock you away where nothing and nobody could ever hurt you again," she whispers.

And isn't that the unspoken truth.

"He only told me this morning, but he clearly doesn't want me here. I mean, he's trying not to be overbearing and stifling, but I need to have a life outside of his," I confess, easing from her embrace. I look back at the girl and then to Marie, who gives me a silent *we'll talk later* look.

"Hi, I'm Kara." I hold my hand out hospitably. Although I'll feel the grim prickle, she will think I'm a complete bitch if I don't. The girl looks at Marie with worry, then produces a truly fake smile and responds.

"Hi, I'm Nicki," she replies, taking my hand. Her hold is timid and barely scrapes my skin, which is itching to get away.

I peer deep into her eyes, seeing something all too familiar there. Marie clears her throat and passes Nicki the papers, asks her to process them, and she motions towards her office.

"It's so good to be back, Marie. I was going stir crazy with only my own head for company. Honestly, I don't know how I've managed it for so long!" I muse as I take a seat, and she closes the door behind us.

"I can imagine," she replies dryly. "You do know they told me to tell you no if you asked to come back, right?"

"I know."

"I actually told him months ago you needed to get back into a routine, and that I wanted you back. Needless to say, that conversation went down like a lead balloon! You know how he is, not that I blame him, if I'm honest. He can be too suffocating for his own good. John hasn't been far behind him in the suffocating stakes either, especially after what happened outside Dev's place. He wanted me to close down for a while, but that's not going to happen." She takes a sip of her coffee.

I slip into my own world, playing over and over my time with Sloan in the gym. The way our connected bodies reflected in the mirror. The way he held my head in position to watch the raptures come to life. The way he called my name reverently, as he...

"Kara!" I snap out of my daze instantly. "You know, you carry so much of your emotions facially, no wonder he can read you like a book." She shakes her head with a smile. "I'm happy for you, though. You deserve him; you do." Her look turns serious. "John told me *everything* by the way."

"Hmm, I thought he might've done when you were both arguing the day I cleared out the flat. It's strange to know that Sloan's loved me longer than I've known he existed. Maybe I should have called that number years ago. How different life might've been." I sigh into my mug, bringing my attention back to her.

"Have you heard from your mum lately?" she asks cautiously.

I shake my head. "No, and I haven't called her, either. I'm still undecided about it." I take a sip and give her a weak smile.

"Maybe you should."

"Maybe. Anyway, I'm told you're having issues with Nicki?"

"Oh, no, I lied to him. Well, I had to tell him something, otherwise, he would have dug his heels in. I had to have something better than you being proud to make him give a little. And it's not so much issues with her - she's great, actually - rather we seem to have more visitors than usual. *That* is the issue!" She smirks.

"Do tell?"

"*Devlin*. Devlin has taken a fancy to her. I'm actually thinking of keeping her on full time. She's a little raw around the edges, but nothing that can't be fixed." She looks at me cautiously.

"*What?* What about me?" I squeal, shocked that I'm effectively being replaced. "You can't just get rid of me! There are laws against unfair and constructive dismissal, you know. I'll take you to tribunal!" I say, smiling.

She sighs and levels with me. "Kara, we both know you won't be working for me forever. Hell, if Sloan gets his way, you won't be working full stop! These last few months have been the prime example. Each time I raised it with him, he said you didn't need to work ever again. I'm not stupid. One day, you will tell me you're leaving, and I figured this way, I'll have someone fully trained when the inevitable finally happens."

I nod in agreement.

Hearing that he has already been discussing it infuriates me abundantly, but deep down, I already knew it would happen. To someone who has no financial worries whatsoever, it's easy to say jack it all in, but for someone like me, someone who has worked hard to create a future, it's still difficult to relinquish and to become reliant on him for everything.

Closing my eyes in resignation, I know that in the not too distant future, he will ask me not to work. And I know when that predictable moment arrives, I shall fail in my mission to be independent. We both know that I'll never be able to deny him anything. Ever.

"Okay. How about I come in part-time. You can choose when, of course, and I'll train her. This way you only have to source a part-time wage." Marie weighs up the options, before agreeing and calling for Nicki to join us.

Nicki appears tiny as she shuffles into the room and takes the seat next to mine. I study her discreetly, watching every move she makes. She's skittish and unsure of herself, wringing her hands nervously in her lap.

"Nicki, Kara is going to train you up properly on a part-time basis. I know I said this was only a temporary position, but it's yours, full time, if you still want it?" Marie offers.

Nicki's face lights up, and she nods enthusiastically. "Thank you, I do," she whispers.

I watch as she courteously accepts the offer, and then wilts back into the scared little thing I saw outside.

It is disturbing and equally scary that in such a short space of time, I have met two women who are broken from something life has thrown at them. First Charlie, with whom my connection ran deeper than most would ever know, and now Nicki. It almost seems as though battered women unknowingly gravitate towards each other.

We sit for a while, chatting in general about how the business is doing, things Nicki was finding hard to grasp and new ideas she has implemented. I'm impressed by her tenacity, and also very sad that it's now blatantly obvious there's no longer a place here for me.

I smile to myself, now it was time for me to forge my own path. Being pushed out maybe isn't such a bad thing after all.

Chapter 34

"GIVE ME TWENTY, I'll be there," Devlin confirms.

Unbeknownst to everyone, he has been secretly driving me to and from the hospital to see Sam. I still haven't told Sloan about my visits, because I honestly just can't face the heartache of arguing with him over it. So instead, Devlin conceded to assist in my deception, on the premise that if we are caught, it's the first time he has taken me to see her.

"Thanks, I'll be waiting," I reply. I'm just about to put the phone down, when he speaks again.

"Is Nicki in today?" he asks cautiously.

I've witnessed his affection towards her grow over the last few weeks. Although she is still withdrawn and jittery around everyone, she has relaxed a little in his presence. It has got to the point where Marie gave Walker an ultimatum to keep him busy, just so he wasn't taking up permanent residence in the office. It also doesn't help that he's on bodyguard duty, and wherever I am, he isn't too far behind. And that means he's here on a regular basis.

"Yep, she's in. Look, I know it's none of my business, and I'm the last person who should be imparting relationship advice but ask her out already. It's clear that you like her and she likes you. She just needs a push, both of you do." I hear him groan uncomfortably down the line. "Think about it at least while you drive over here. I'll see you soon." I smile as he mutters at me before the call ends. I collect my things in anticipation of his imminent arrival and gaze out of the window.

"Kara?" I turn to see Nicki in the doorway, smiling timidly.

"Hey, do you need some help?" I ask. Her improvement has been amazing, but seeing her standing in front of me, reverting back to that frightened girl I'd first met, puts me on high alert.

"Um...no. Actually, I wanted to ask you something. It's about Devlin." Her eyes are trained on the floor, and I bite back the smile I feel forming on my lips. I straighten and motion for her to take a seat with me.

"Okay, what do you want to know about him?"

"Well, he just called and asked me out, but I didn't know what to say. I guess I just have some...issues, and he's...he's..."

"He's Devlin!" I say sarcastically. I admit I'm surprised. I didn't expect him to make his move quite so fast. Nicki squirms, but finally nods in agreement.

"You know, I was exactly the same as you when I met Sloan. All these guys have a tiny bit of caveman quality about them, but Devlin is easier to get on with. He asks about you a lot. Think about it, at least. He's one of life's good guys, and we all deserve to be happy." Her expression changes from worried to understanding.

She gets up, more confident than she had when she came in. "I will. Thanks," she replies optimistically, leaving me alone.

Pleased with myself, I stare out of the window again, checking my phone to see if Devlin is nearly here, but there's nothing.

Speeding resounds through the open window, and I huff out, counting as the noise gets closer. Devlin can be reckless in that goddamn car of his at times. If I thought Sloan was bad, Dev is ten times worse.

A black Merc speeds into the car park, and I stare with huge eyes, wondering if this is Deacon's *soon*. The door opens, and my father steps out, looking proud and self-satisfied.

"Oh, you've got to be fucking kidding me!" I hiss rhetorically, the moment he approaches the building. I yell out to Nicki, who comes running in, but I cut her off before she has time to speak.

"Don't let anyone in!" She looks terrified but agrees, running out equally as fast, when the entry intercom buzzes.

I wait.

"Kara, there's a man outside who wants to see you." Her voice cracks nervously from the doorway, no doubt because of the unnecessary pressure I've put her under.

"Okay, I'll deal with him, but don't let him in, under no circumstances whatsoever!" She quickly nods and turns to leave. "Hey, Nicki? I didn't mean to scare you, I'm sorry." She mumbles something under her breath and heads back to her desk.

Then, as expected, my old phone starts to ring. I glare at it, wondering why the fuck the man keeps doing this to me. He doesn't care about me. Never has.

"Yes?" I answer, watching him from my vantage point.

"Ah, Kara! You disappoint me, sweets. No hug for your old man?" he asks sarcastically, walking back to the car. "Frankie called, he said he wants to see you again." I squeeze my eyes tight, while my gut churns from his statement.

"Such a shame Frankie won't get that opportunity. Just leave me alone. You've done enough damage in my life. Can't you just leave me be?" I try to keep the pleading tone out of my voice, but it's easier said than done. Just the sound of his voice, hearing him call me that fucking name is enough to make me relapse.

I press my forehead to the cold glass, staring down at the car park, not seeing anything but the past I left behind in Manchester.

"I can see you!" Ian taunts. My eyes glare instantly and meet his. The bastard is pushing me, goading me, just like he has always done. Except now, I wasn't a child with no hope or future. Now, I was an adult, and I made my own choices. Choices he would never play a hand in again.

"What do you want? We've had this conversation over and over, and the answer will always be the same – I cannot help you!" I cry forcefully into the phone, never letting my eyes wander from his.

"Well, that's too bad, because I want to help you!" I snort at his laughable response. "You see if you help me, Frankie will make sure you stay safe. That is unless you want his little lap dog biting at your heels."

"What do you mean? What the hell do you know?" I want to ram my fist through the glass and down his throat.

"Ah, sweets, I know all about your little problem named Deacon. It could all be over in seconds. What will it be, you want to run down here and be a good girl?" His stance is consumed with arrogance, and I feel my heart breaking all over again.

Bitterly, I laugh out loud at the similarities between Frankie and my father. They both sold their daughters down the river and did fuck all to assist with the repercussions.

"Never! You have never helped me. I'm not even sure you even wanted me! What kind of father uses his daughter for his next fucking fix?" I slam my rounded fist down on the windowsill, and the pain shoots my wrist to my elbow. It's chilling, but at least it lets me know I can still feel something for him - even if it is rage.

I hear him inhale, but before he can respond, there's a rumble of an engine down the line. I look past him as Devlin speeds into the car park. He positions his car up against my father's in a way that means Ian won't be able to escape. Devlin's actions are a blur, and suddenly, he has Ian up against his own vehicle.

The call is still connected when I see - and hear - the power of Devlin's professionally trained fists beat against my father's skull. I should be screaming for him to stop, but I can't. I can't care for a man who had sold me to get high. A man whose actions had subjected me to a childhood of pain and abuse, both of which will never be forgiven or forgotten.

I'm wide-eyed as blow upon blow is delivered to my father's face. Eventually, Ian's body slumps down the side of his car, and he curls up in the dirt. Devlin stands over him, a man possessed, and even from my distance and vantage point, I identify the disgust for my father rolling off him in spades.

A small hand tugs on my arm and Nicki is behind me with unshed tears in her eyes.

Has she been watching the whole time?

I put my arm around her, never appreciating how strong I had become until this moment.

Devlin's fist bangs on the glass door to the office, and I rush to buzz him in. I raise my finger to say I'll be a minute, and lead Nicki into the ladies.

Passing her some toilet paper, I tell her about my father and why Devlin has just done what he did. I gloss over the parts of abuse and rape. She doesn't look shocked, and it actually worries me that she takes it so well. When we exit, Devlin is rubbing his knuckles gingerly.

"Can you give us a minute, Kara?" I look at Nicki in understanding, and she steps into Marie's office with Devlin following behind her.

I sit on the sofa and think back to my childhood, or the lack thereof. Sometimes I wonder if I would've been better off being taken into care at birth. When I was fifteen, the authorities tried to do just that. It resulted in my running to the other end of the country. Looking back, foster care might just be a dumping ground for unwanted children of despicable parents like mine, but not all foster carers are bad people – some just want a family. It's sods law that the good people of the world might not be able to have life beyond their own, while the heartless, uncaring bastards like mine, can reproduce at will.

Life really isn't fair sometimes.

Consumed in my thoughts, the door opens, and Devlin emerges with Nicki close behind him. She appears a little more relaxed than earlier. I hate that she had to see first-hand what part of my life is like. God, she's known me for less than two weeks, but unfortunately, she's now at risk, just like Marie is.

"Let's go," Devlin says tightly, guiding me towards the door.

The sound of our hollow footsteps resounding in the corridor, is the only noise alongside the electrical machines whirring and beeping constantly. The only indication of life being maintained.

As we make our way to the room, a nurse smiles softly as we pass. No words were exchanged on the drive over, and the strained silence is killing me as we get closer and closer.

"I'll wait outside," Devlin says, already heading towards the waiting room.

I enter and close the door quietly. I look over at Sam; she's never looked so serene in her entire life. It takes every ounce of strength I have not to buckle under the pressure of seeing her. It's the same every time I come to visit. The severity of her condition and the guilt I feel because of it, hits me like a bullet. It hurts so much that I couldn't lift a finger to save her, not just from Deacon, but from herself.

Stuart tries to keep me informed on a daily basis, and my heart wilts each time he texts to say she's still the same, and not showing any signs of progress.

"Hi," I greet her, enfolding her hand in mine. I sit next to the bed and put my bag down. "I'm sorry I've not been back for a few days. Things are difficult right now, but I guess you probably know that already." I wipe away an escaped tear with the back of my hand and refocus.

I inspect her face, happy to see that the bruising is finally abating. "I wish you would wake up and tell me what to do. There are so many things that I wish I could change, but I know I should never have left you alone with *him*." I stroke her hair tenderly, a part of me willing her to open her eyes, to move her fingers, anything to let me know she can hear me. But it's futile. The longer she stays in the coma, the less likely it is she will regain consciousness.

"So, things are going well with Sloan, and I'm glad I took your advice that day when you told me to give him a chance rather than sell the dress. You brought him back to me, and as much as I hate how you did it, thank you for making me happy, Sam. I love you so much, and I need you to wake up." My sobs echo in the room.

The door creaks, and I jolt back in shock to find Sloan watching. I wipe the wetness from my cheeks again, and he sits on the opposite side of the bed. Taking Sam's other hand, he starts to talk.

"The first time I saw you, you were high as hell. You had created such a commotion that night, that I was ready to kill you myself." I flinch at his words, which are so insensitive considering her current condition.

"You mumbled incoherently for Kara. I was at breaking point, knowing that she was one in the same person that we both wanted for very different reasons. But I owe you everything, Sam. I even owe you for lying to me, telling me Kara was playing with me, because if you hadn't have done that, I would never have realised how much I can't live without her." He smiles weakly at her, but it doesn't reach his eyes. I know he's lying, and I honestly can't blame him considering what we both went through because of her deceit - albeit under Deacon's control.

"I will thank you for every single day that I have with her, but that all means nothing if she is without you." I look over at him, tears clouding my vision. He veers around the bed, lifts me from the chair and sits, placing me in his lap.

"She'll wake up, baby. She will when she's ready to." He kisses my neck and secures his arms around me. "I'm going to get her transferred to a private hospital. She's not safe here, and you're not safe coming here. I wish you would have told me. You know I would never, ever, stop you from coming to see her." He sounds so dejected that my heart weighs heavy with guilt and regret.

"I'm sorry I misled you, but it wasn't done maliciously. I just couldn't tell you because I honestly didn't think you'd care. I know she's messed up, but she's family. She was the only one who was there for me. We were just two broken girls together; we held each other together. She can be reckless and think only of herself, but I love her. What will I do without her?" I burrow into his shoulder, and cry for her in a way I have never done before.

"Baby, you'll never be without her. Regardless of what happens, she will always be with, because part of her completes you, the same way that you complete me. I've already spoken with a specialist, and he thinks she's in a good condition to be moved. As soon as I can, I'll have her transferred. Is that okay with you?" His hand rubs my face, and I nod my approval.

Stuart had been in to check on Sam and had spoken to us about the different options available that might help her. I listened, but didn't really understand anything. I just want her cognizant and lucid. But I'm not a dreamer, and even I'm becoming more disenchanted with her chance of a full recovery as the days tick by.

"Where's Devlin?" I ask as we exit the room, and he isn't where I left him.

"He had to leave, so you got me instead," Sloan answers innocently, tugging me into him. His lips press mine hard, and I open to him automatically. I gasp when his tongue delves inside. Pushing at his chest, I feel the rumble of a chuckle breaking free.

"Stop it!" I say seriously. The last thing I want is to the give the nurses something to talk about.

"You're killing me, wounding me right here." He puts his hand on his heart in mock exaggeration. "Alright! He's taking Nicki out for a late lunch. Seriously, she apparently said yes. The silly girl must have banged her head!"

"Sloan!" His face drops, and he innocently fans his lashes at me a second time. I give up, knowing he and Devlin have a love-hate relationship at the best of times.

I tuck my arm into his, and we settle into a slow pace. I stop, still needing to tell him about what happened earlier today. Although I wonder if Devlin has already given up that nugget of information.

"My father turned up at the office today." I wait anxiously for his admonishment, but it never materialises.

"I know. I'm very aware of what happened. Dev already told me, and that's why he's taking Nicki out and I'm here," he says, putting a protective arm over my shoulder. "We'll talk about it later. Come on, John's outside."

Why is he suddenly being so reasonable?

"Aren't you mad that I didn't call you straight away?" I'm shocked he is so calm, given that I don't seem to be able to follow instructions, regardless of how simple and straightforward they are.

"A little, but Dev was already on hi-" He stops mid-sentence, and I narrow my eyes at him. He's no longer paying any attention to me, and is looking straight over my shoulder.

I feel his hand leave my body, and he fumbles in his jacket pocket. He quickly swipes the phone screen with one hand, and has it to his ear before I can even register what's going on.

"John, he's here!" Sloan ends the call and shoves me hard behind him. I'm about to protest at his unnecessary rough treatment of me, until I turn to where he's looking, and my world disintegrates.

So, this is *'soon'*.

Deacon saunters down the empty corridor wearing a Cheshire cat grin. His black coat sways out at the sides menacingly over his hulking form. The malicious smile he wears makes him look like the devil himself. He stops halfway, cracks his head from side to side, and smiles malevolently again.

"So, I heard a little rumour that your girl wants my girl moved. Well, guess what," he says, picking up his speed again, and in seconds, he is a heartbeat away from us. "Not. Fucking. Happening! I promise you this, Sloan, you take her..." He stops and pulls a strand of my hair. "Then I take *her*. Understand?" I pull back, tearing myself from his hold, and my yanked out hair lays limp over his fist.

Sloan's forearm tightens around me, and he steps in front of me, becoming a human shield, effectively blocking Deacon from my line of sight. "You touch her again, you fucking die! *I* promise *you* that. You did it before, but you won't get another fucking chance!" I don't recognise Sloan's voice as he and Deacon square up to each other. Deacon seems to relish the new, harder, Sloan. As a matter of fact, I would even say he's proud.

The sound of clapping begins to fill the uncomfortable silence, as Deacon's hands smack together over and over. The sound grates on me.

"Fuck me, little brother! I never thought you had it in you. But let's be honest – you couldn't protect her if you tried. You sit at a desk, turn papers and count money. You couldn't save her eight years ago, just the same way you couldn't save her when Sam came calling!" he taunts, shutting down the tiny space that's keeping them apart. "And when I finally touch her again, it won't be the second time, or even the third! I've had her more times than you can fucking count and more than she'll ever remember! It's amazing what a little injecting will do to render a bitch unconscious! Daddy didn't even protect her; the bastard gave her to me. *Repeatedly!*"

My brain stills and everything fails to function.

My breathing jars and halts at his words.

Then my heart stops completely.

The man in the room drags me by my hair and shoves me onto the bed. I claw at him, fighting with all I have, but nothing is enough. My clothes are ripped from me as he smacks me across the face. I close my eyes as pain strikes at my cheeks and nose. The blood in the back of my throat chokes me, and I open my eyes wide when I feel him agonisingly at my centre. I turn towards him, staring at my assailant through watery eyes as my body is debased and taken.

For the first time ever, I see his face clearly.

Deacon.

Silence envelops my body, and the darkness that lives inside comes out and claims me. The only thing that pulls me back from the precipice, is the sound of cracking bone reverberating over and over. When my eyes finally refocus, Deacon is clutching his bloody nose.

"Count the days, Deacon! Fucking count them, because you haven't got many of them left! Time is running out for you, *brother!*" Sloan is full of venom, and I cower behind him, unable to look at him.

One of the last pieces of my forgotten life has finally been aired, and I feel disgusting. Defiled in ways that are unimaginable. I hate myself, and I wouldn't hate Sloan if he felt the same way now.

I watch half-dead as Deacon leaves the way he came, still clutching his battered face.

"I'll get you, you little fucking bitch!" his voice echoes in the empty corridor. The words resound over and over.

I start tearing at my clothes in a bid to rip them off. I need to scrub my skin. I need to wash him off me. I need to forget what he's finally made me remember.

"Kara! Kara! *Don't!*" I hear Walker's voice fill the space that Deacon has just vacated. It's followed by the tug and pull of both him and Sloan grappling with each other. My back slides down the wall behind me, and I plummet to the floor, more broken and battered than I thought I could ever be.

It's finally real. Official.

I'm nothing but damaged goods; used, abused, defiled.

Desecrated.

Dead.

I was nothing then.

I'm nothing now.

"Don't you dare fucking touch her!" Sloan roars out, and I watch him trying to block Walker from getting to me.

"Get a fucking grip, kid! I'm not going to hurt her, but *you*, you need to calm the fuck down before someone calls security! Come on Kara, put your arms around my neck, honey. Let's get you home."

"Put her down, *now!*" Sloan growls out as my body is lifted.

"Sloan, I won't think twice about putting *you* down. Now is not the time to test me! Back. Off. Now! Come on, honey, put your arms around my neck." Somehow, I manage to do as he requests.

'...it won't the second time, or even the third...the bastard gave her to me. Repeatedly.'

The words resound over and over, and I know he speaks the truth.

My reality is blacker than the darkest night, filled with nightmares of the past and the voice of the man I love in the present. When my eyes refuse to remain open, the darkness wholly consumes me, and I know there's only one option left available to me now.

I have to run.

Chapter 35

LOITERING AT THE top of stairs, the dim light rises up from the living room, casting shadows from below.

The suite is uncomfortably quiet, apart from the murmuring of two male voices I know better than my own. My heart is broken, and I sway from side to side, lost in the past.

"You know, I thought when we found him there he was just selling. If I had known... If I had known what he was doing to her for all that time..." The words are barely audible, even in the deathly silence.

"We can't change it now. What's done is done, kid. She doesn't even remember, does she?"

"She didn't; she does now. This was never about Charlie or me, it's always been her that he wanted. I was just too blinded by my own love for her that I never saw it. I want him dead, John. Gone forever. It's the only way to keep her safe."

I feel physically sick hearing him say such things. To speak of ending someone's life, regardless of the fact it's Deacon's. This was all my fault. If I hadn't come back into his life, this wouldn't be happening. Deacon had stayed away for years. *Until now.*

Now I have to do what's right to protect him, because he's all that matters to me. I lower my foot onto the top step, but am stopped.

"If that son of a bitch finds out about New York... Well, we know what will happen."

"John, I think he already knows. He's probably known all along."

The final knife in my heart tonight twists mockingly. I can feel the walls that have been knocked down, quickly piece back together once more. Resolutely, I lower my foot onto the step again, and gradually, quietly, descend each rung.

"Does she know? Have you told her?"

"No, there just hasn't been the right ti-"

"What's in New York?" I cut him off. Both of their heads snap up, look at each other and then at me.

Sloan looks exhausted and pushes on his hands to stand. "It doesn't matter-"

"It does matter! It all matters! Can't you see that? We're all part of this in some shape or form. I will ask you again - what is in New

York? And don't fucking lie to me, not you!" I scream at him.

He stands rigid and straight, then crosses the room. Stopping in front of me, he raises his hand to my face. I instantly pull back, horrified. Pain blatantly envelops him, but I can't bear to look at him and I refuse to feel guilty for it.

"My mother," he finally answers dejectedly.

"But your mother is dead!"

"No, my mother is in New York."

Confused, I look between him and Walker, finally understanding this was the other part of the secret that he didn't want to disclose. My mind drifts back to the black and white portrait in Charlie's apartment, realising the truth that had been there all along.

"Oh, my God!" I mutter.

My body clenches; nothing but deceit and lies for all this time. I thought it easy of my own parents, but him?

My heart races as I try to run out of the suite, hearing his shouting behind me. His large hand slams the door shut the moment I open it. I spin around and give him my fiercest glare.

"I'm good enough to fuck, but not good enough to tell your secrets to! There is nothing that you don't know about me now. Nothing!"

"That cuts both ways!"

"No, it doesn't, because you already knew what I concealed and why! You've known for nearly a decade. You knew all this time, yet you let me break my own fucking heart, wondering how long it would take you to drop me once you found out how irrevocably damaged and used I am!" I bring my hands to my face to cover the shame of crying. "You even had the audacity to ask about my wrists when you knew damn well who did it!" I spin around to face him. "I should have known," I mumble, heartbroken.

I should've known better. I should've pried more when he left me for two weeks and was in New York on *business*. I should've done so many things.

Yet I did the complete opposite.

I trusted him.

I fell in love with him.

That is the biggest mistake I've ever made.

"Kara, I'm sorry I didn't tell you. I wanted to, but it wasn't my story to tell." He's pleading with me, and I'm reluctant not throw my arms around him and let him hold me. I need it right now - we both do. But I also need to know the truth. The truth that will never come if I give in to what I really want.

I hold my stance and refuse to back down. I stare at him vacantly, searching his face for some kind of indication of what he is going through. So much has happened in the short time we have been together; some of it good, quite a lot of it bad.

"And that's the problem, isn't it?" I hiss sarcastically. "Charlie's story wasn't yours to tell, yet it entwines us together in ways unimaginable. Your mother's story isn't yours to tell, either, is it! What the fuck can you tell me that is yours?"

He backs away from me, hesitantly removing his hand from the door. I contemplate making my escape, but realise if I'm going to walk away once and for all, I need something to take with me. It's selfish, but I have to, if only for one more night.

I shift away from the door, following his movements and raise my hand to his cheek. He leans into it and slowly closes his eyes.

"I love you," I tell him honestly. I would never lie to him about that. I love him more than I will ever be able to express. He completes every part of me. There are times that I'd felt hollow without him although I've never told him that. I've never truly expressed how he makes me feel whole and less flawed than I really am.

"I love you, too. More than anything. Please forgive me." His arms encircle me, and he grips my hips, dragging me towards him, until the only thing between us is our clothing. A shuffling sound behind us induces me to lean back.

"Sorry, I'll go. Marie's probably wondering where I am. Call if you need anything." Walker passes by us to the door. I wait for the inevitable clicks of it opening and closing before I capture Sloan's beautiful mouth with mine.

He bends slightly, picks me up under my thighs and I circle my legs around him. It's an action I have performed so many times, it's now second nature. Everything about being with him is the most basic form of human instinct. He pulls back away from me, earning himself my annoyed moan, before consuming me entirely in a kiss that takes my breath away.

Time stands still as he carries me upstairs and into the bedroom. His hands roam over every inch of my clothed back, and I take everything he has to give, returning it willingly, as we fight almost violently against each other to feel skin upon skin. I practically rip his shirt from his back in a desperate bid to feel his hard chest against my tender breasts. I ache to have him on me, over me, and more importantly, inside me.

For the very last time.

Reading my thoughts precisely, he lowers me to the bed. I look up at him and memorise perfection. He reciprocates with heavy eyes, unaware of my final intentions tonight. I'm aware that I carry a lot of my emotions facially, and I make myself block them aside.

On the outside, I obviously appear overcome with need. On the inside, I'm slowly dying.

"Tell me you forgive me for not confiding in you. I need to hear you say it, *please.*" He doesn't make any further attempt to touch me, just observes intently.

Putting up a smokescreen of losing his mother must have done something to him that I can't even begin to imagine. To make everyone believe such a lie, it must have been the hardest thing he and Charlie have ever had to face. Keeping her a secret... I don't even want to consider it.

"I do forgive you. I will always forgive you." I'm not lying. I only hope he can do the same when he wakes in the morning to find me gone. Yet I can't dwell on that, not now.

Now was for us.

I lean up on my elbows, and he follows my lead, bringing himself down to me. His lips start at my ankle and slowly make their way up one side of my body. He smothers me with such passion and intensity, I'm forced to question myself as to whether or not I'm making the right choice. Refusing to let my mind ramble and over-analyse, I shut my eyes firmly, focusing on the electricity we are generating, his wonderful mouth on my skin, and all the things he can do with it.

The urgent need to feel overtakes the slow build-up, and the fire stokes higher and higher. The heat between our bodies feels different than before. In my mind, it really does feel like it is the last time. I don't know whether or not he feels it too, but my fears are confirmed when he stops, his hardness ready at my slick opening.

"Don't leave me, Kara. It took eight years to finally have you in my life. I'll never let you leave. Please say you forgive me for everything I've ever done. For not protecting you from *him.* For not coming back for you when I first found you in that house. For leaving you at the hospital all alone. Forgive me, baby. Absolve me of all of it." His eyes glaze with tears he is desperately holding inside. I lift up, my hips flex suggestively, and tuck my head into his neck.

"I'll always be with you. I'll always be yours." I obliterate my own heart speaking words that are simple and true. I *will always* be his.

In some perverse universe, maybe I had always belonged to him. Maybe the first time he saved me all those years ago, my mind securely shielded his image away until the time was right to finally see him again.

I purr blissfully when he finally slides inside me. My soft, yet hard walls invite him in and hold him perfectly. It's another part of him that I need to memorise fully because there will never be anyone else. I watch him, and the way his face changes with emotions as he makes love to me. All is forgotten in the beauty of our coupling. My body accepts him gratefully, as he brings me to a natural high and holds me to ride out the low.

"Marry me, Kara. I love you so fucking much. Marry me!" he growls out, the moment his body reaches its pinnacle. He swells inside me, and I clench my muscles around him, wanting to scream out yes. Instead, I remain silent and become lost in the passion that is devouring me like never before; that I shall never experience again.

Laying on my side, memorising him for the final time, I know he is it for me. No one else will ever compare. He is the light to my dark, the night to my day. He is everything. It's a sobering thought that after tonight I shall live my life completely alone, for however long that may be.

I remain still and listen to his breathing gradually even out. His chest expands on each inhalation, and I gaze at him raptly. This moment should have been so different. He asked me to marry him, for God sake! What I wouldn't give to be his wife, to wear his ring, and to bore his children. To be his completely. I wipe a tear from my eye at the thought of never accomplishing my ultimate wish.

I creep out of bed when I'm sure he is dead to the world. Tiptoeing into the walk-in, I grab a small rucksack, filling it with only the necessities. I don't know where I'm going, and I don't care. I care about one thing, and one thing alone, and that is keeping him safe and well.

My decision to leave isn't just about hearing that his mother is still alive, it was made at the hospital when he threatened Deacon's life. While the bastard deserves to die, I can't have Sloan or Walker paying for my sins and those of my parents.

Standing nervously at the foot of the bed, I shift my weight from foot to foot and sweep over Sloan's peaceful sleeping form. He looks angelic, with the edge of the devil, with his dark, brooding looks. I smile sadly, remembering every time he has touched me, every single one from loving to possessive, gentle to forceful. But none of them make me smile as much as the way he touched me tonight.

Tonight should have been the start of a new life for me.

For us.

I should be tucked up in the arms of the man I love with his ring on my finger, dreaming of a future that I know I deserve.

Except, here I am, standing alone, drinking him in for the last time. I brush my thoughts away, knowing if I stay any longer, I won't have the courage to leave. I slowly stalk out of the room and down the stairs as quietly as possible. I pause, turning back numerous times, listening for any sound of life emanating from the bedroom.

There is nothing but haunting silence.

In the kitchen, I hunt out a pen and paper and write him a quick note. I feel like shit doing it this way, but I have to let him know I'll be safe, even if I don't know where I'm going to. I lay the paper on top of my notebook. The demons of my past are no longer a secret I have to hide.

Closing the suite door behind me for the last time, I run down the flights of stairs, past the concierge, and out into the night.

Running through the damp streets of London, the ground hits sharply at my heels. The pavement is unforgiving against my trusty, battered old trainers. I double over, bracing my hands on my knees, breathing hard. I twist around to find that I'm completely alone in a small park a few streets away from the hotel. I glance back, expecting him to be running after me like a man possessed, but he's not. I dig into my bag and pull out my phone. There are no messages waiting for me. My heart sinks, but this is the right thing to do.

Straightening up, I walk aimlessly into the cold, dark night.

I only hope one day he can forgive, and subsequently, forget me for what I have done.

Needing to tie up some loose ends, I head to one of two places that may give me sanctuary.

My feet feel sore when the hospital finally comes into view. I drag my tired and bewildered body across the street; every step is an effort. I have walked for what feels like miles. It might have been - I'm not even sure how I've managed to get here.

Keeping my head down, I move past the hospital orderlies and nurses. I pull up the hood on my jacket to cover myself as I head down the corridor to where Sam is sleeping. I manage to duck into her room unnoticed, and I bristle because if it was this easy for me to do it, someone else could, too.

I drop my hood and approach her with caution. Nothing has changed, she's still lifeless. I sit down next to her, and in the corner of my eye, a dark shadow of movement casts over the room from outside. Feeling vulnerable, I slouch my upper body against the bed and pour my heart out like never before, leaving no stone unturned.

Eventually, I tell her goodbye.

I open the door slowly, peering out of both sides, making sure it's all clear. I breathe a sigh of relief when it appears no one is around. Carefully closing the door behind me, I pull my hood back up and walk with purpose.

As I round the corner, I come face to face with the one whom I'm really running from.

Deacon.

He is leaning on the nurse's station, flirting with a young nurse. She flutters her eyelashes at him, and even though some distance separates us, I can see the menacing look in his eyes. I breathe sharply when he turns. Somehow, he knows I'm here, and he flays me with his unwavering glare. I double back on myself and begin to run down the empty corridors, willing for someone to magically appear and save me.

Running deeper and further into the hospital, the corridors all look the same All the while I can hear him behind me, but I don't dare look. I feel like my heart is going to explode as my feet pound against the sterile floors. The overhead lighting reflects off the tiles, blinding me sporadically. I run into the nearby ladies and pull out my phone. I still have no messages, and fear courses through me, as I find Sloan's number and hit call.

"Kara?" his sleepy voice mumbles on the other end. "Kara, baby, where are you?"

"I'm sorry. I'm so sorry," I whisper and sob as the main door to the toilets open. I hold in my tears the best I can, as the sound of metal scrapes against the doors and fills the room. "I left... I'm sorry. I'm at the hospital. Sloan, listen, Deacon... Deacon-" I don't have time to finish because the door is kicked in violently. It bounces back off the cubicle wall, and the devil fills the void.

"IS HERE!" he bellows. I shrink back into the tiny confined space, and my tears fall uncontrollably.

"KARA!" Sloan screams down the line, the same moment Deacon snatches it away. My hands fumble to reclaim it, but he holds the knife up to my throat.

"I told you she would be mine again!" Deacon says with finality, before smashing the phone on the floor.

He lunges towards me, and I fight against him, mindful of the knife he is holding far too close to my neck. My tears fall like a river, and the last thing I see are his black eyes, penetrating my soul.

Chapter 36

MY THROAT IS sore and dehydrated when I finally come back to reality. My mind is scattered as I try to piece together the events of last night.

In my stillness, my body feels like it has been used as a punching bag. There isn't an inch of me that isn't in some pain or discomfort. I look down at where my legs should be and can't see anything. The place I'm in is black. I squeeze my eyes shut, trying desperately to remember.

Sloan.

I remember Sloan.

Proposing.

I smile to myself, until the next memory comes back hauntingly.

Deacon.

The hospital.

Oh, my God! Where am I?

I shift around, even though I know it's futile in the dark space I'm imprisoned in. My body senses movement through the fog of pain that has overtaken my senses. I feel a bump underneath me and the drone of an engine, and guess that I'm in a car.

Where? I don't know.

Laughter assaults my ears, and I rotate my head slowly, the light gradually coming back. There's somebody next to me, holding my wrists together. I try to pull them apart, but they won't budge.

"Ah, someone's awake. How are you feeling, sweets?" My eyes fill with hot tears at the familiarity of the sneering voice. The light becomes brighter, confirming what I already know; Deacon has me bound and incapacitated.

"Don't cry just yet, sweets. Save it for later, when you'll really fucking need it!" He laughs satanically, and my tears keep on falling.

"Shut her up! You wanted to do this, remember? This isn't a fucking game! He'll never stop looking for her, and when he finds her, he won't think twice about doing time for ending you!" I turn my head to the front of the car, but Deacon forcefully grabs my chin and twists me to face him.

Staring straight at me, he narrows his eyes. "I wanna fuck with him, and then I'm gonna fuck with you. I'm gonna fucking tear you apart. You'll be unrecognisable when I'm finished with you!"

My sobbing escalates to a whole new level, and I cry uncontrollably at his words. I want to die. I don't want to remember again, because this time, I won't have the luxury of selective memory loss. I will carry it with me every day like an impending death sentence.

The car slams to a sharp stop, forcing my body forward and I hit my head on the seat in front of me. I reluctantly peer out the window; the street we have stopped in is a second home to me. I begin to struggle against Deacon's hold, but it's ineffective. He turns me back to him, and his fist flies at my face. The pressure on my nose and cheek is incomprehensible, and the sound of splintering bone and a hot trickle of liquid swiftly follows. I gasp when I taste my own blood seeping down my throat. My cries continue until Deacon threatens to put me out for good. I quieten down instantly, terrified I may not live to see the next hour, never mind tomorrow.

Deep inside, I know I won't.

Deacon's eyes fill with hatred, and he glares in a way that tells me not to do anything foolish.

Hope flourishes in my chest when he begins to lower the window, but it's soon eviscerated when the fabric comes up to my mouth to silence me. Between the crude gag and the blood still slowly trickling down my throat, I can't breathe, and I'm close to vomiting and passing out.

"Excellent timing!" Deacon says gleefully.

Walker's car pulls up in front of Marie's house, and he, Sloan, and Jake get out and scan the street, looking forlorn. The car we are in is shrouded in complete darkness under a line of trees. Even if they were to look this way, nothing would seem out of place or untoward.

I shift as Marie's door opens. She appears angelic with the glow of the light behind her. Tears fall from my eyes, and all I want to do is run to her with open arms and never let go.

"WHERE THE HELL IS SHE?!" she screams at the men in panic. "I swear to God if anything happens to her..." Walker approaches her, but she raises her hands in front of her.

Deacon's body starts to shake behind me. The bastard is laughing to himself at the scene playing out before us. I stiffen with each movement he makes, realising that he enjoys and gets off on the suffering of others. With that realisation, I don't hold out much hope for myself in his imprisonment.

"Where could he have taken her? He wouldn't have taken her home, would he? I mean back to Manchester?" Jake suggests, and they all turn to look at him.

Marie laughs out bitterly. "Clueless! All three of you are fucking clueless! Of course, he wouldn't go there. It's the first place he knows you would look! Have you checked the hospital cameras? What about his last known address?"

Sloan scrubs his hands over his face. From this distance - I don't really have a good visual on him, between my swollen eyes and tears – I can see he's breaking steadily. His intention to appear strong and composed is withering under the pressure.

The burning in my chest is growing stronger by the second, and I long for them to look in this direction, although I know it will be in vain. Deacon is too good at evading them.

He knows it, and so do they.

"We've looked all over, he's nowhere! She's gone! She's just gone." Sloan's voice cracks, and he tips his head up to the sky. Jake pats him on the back, most likely speaking words of comfort that will bring him anything but. I want to bang on the window and scream that I'm here, but I can't. Deacon has made sure of it.

Too much was left unsaid between us after his latest revelation, and my subsequent walking out. Everything was lies, and I didn't know what was real anymore. But I know more than anything that I have made the biggest mistake of my life. And it's one that I may end up paying the ultimate price for.

I raise my finger to the half-open window and trace his shape against the glass. Salty tears sting my eyes as I memorise him for what might definitely be the last time.

"Poor bastard!" Deacon pipes up behind me. I flinch when his fingers rub against my neck. "Sorry son of a bitch is in love with a dead woman! Because that's what you'll be when he finds you, sweets - fucked and dead!"

My body starts to shake, imagining all the debauched and horrible things he's planning to do to me. I'm in a world of my own making and one where he will decide my fate. Whatever happens, before that comes, remains to be seen. I am under no illusions that true pain and suffering at the hands of evil will be mine once again.

The window slides back up, and I shut my eyes. The last thing I hear before it closes completely, is Jake consoling Sloan, saying they will find me. I force myself to believe it, but I know I'll never see them, or him, again.

The car slowly moves off, and I drop my head down in realisation. This really is the beginning of the end. I take a final look at the man I love surrounded by those closest to us. My only hope is him finding me somehow, preferably before Deacon can commence with whatever evil he's longing to inflict on me.

I close my eyes in fear and devastation, and think of the man that has given me everything good in my life.

Groggily, I hear the engine cut out, and the driver exits the car. Deacon drags me out of the vehicle after him. The moment my feet touch the ground, clarity washes over me, and I realise my legs are not bound. I kick them out hard as my heart thunders against my rib cage. But my hopes of escape are dashed, when a large hand slams over my mouth and one braces my waist.

So, this is the way it ends, I think again, as I struggle against the brute force holding me back.

"Get her in-fucking-side, now!" I hear a stranger hiss somewhere behind me. The gag is ripped from me, and a hand covers my mouth. I bite down on the fingers, and someone lets out a strangled cry. I jerk violently, trying anything I can to break free of the death grip restraining me.

"Stop struggling!" A man shouts. I squeeze my eyes shut, recognising the voice, praying it isn't who I think it is. "I said, stop!" Only the man shouting isn't the one holding me, because I can see him directly in front of me now.

Remy.

He stands alongside another man who, with the exception of the disguise that covered most of his appearance weeks ago, I've not seen properly in years.

Those years haven't been kind.

His shadow casts over me again, looming with malevolence. I stop trying to fight back and finally accept, once again, I'm not in control. Remy wears a look that tells me everything I need to know. I know exactly who has me and why.

Franklin Black.

Whether it's because I'm finally here to pay the piper, or whether he does know all about his not-so-dead, wealthy ex-wife, alive and well in New York, is anyone's guess.

The arms that bind me harden further, and I know after tonight, I will remember everything - that's if I'm still breathing afterwards.

Frankie eyes me up and down, before looking over my shoulder at whoever is holding me. "She won't be very co-operative if you hurt her. That bastard has what I want. I don't want her looking any more damaged than she already does! Don't fucking touch her again, Deacon! Remember, she's leverage and nothing more!"

Frankie jerks my face in his hands and examines my battered features. "You don't seem surprised, Kara. Did he tell you? Did he?" he shouts. "Hmm, of course, he did." His eyes narrow, turning something over in his mind before he speaks again.

"Do you remember your childhood?" I harden my jaw and allow my eyes to close, as my sham of a childhood floods me and pulls out every bad part I had locked away in the recess of my mind. Frankie slaps me hard across the face, and my eyes dart open. He snorts and grins as he looks towards Deacon.

"Do you remember all the things that he did to you?" My face contorts, and I grudgingly glance at Deacon, who is openly laughing, enjoying the moment. My eyes capture Remy's, and he looks at his friend in disgust.

My body sags, and Frankie reaches out his arm and grabs me by the throat. He starts to exert such pressure that I can feel my windpipe closing, and black spots grace my vision. Slowly, he lets go and sneers.

"Remember, I always get what I want, Kara. What I want is to see that bastard you love so much six feet under. Except, we both know that isn't going to happen, and unfortunately, that means you will pay for his concealment." Frankie starts to walk away, but stops and turns to Deacon. "Try to play nice, Son." Then he gets into his car, never looking back.

And there is the real connection, Deacon *is* one of Franklin Black's boys - he's his bastard fucking son!

My body starts to slump as the full force of the situation, and the truth behind it takes hold. I shake my head, chiding myself for not putting two and two together before. All the signs had been there, and I was too blind to see them. But the one sign that was right in front of me, that I had missed, was at the hospital when he called Sloan *'little brother'*. I start to cry furiously at my own shortcomings, but my head is hit from behind, and I feel dazed and confused.

"Come on, bitch. I've been itching to get my hands on you

again!" Deacon's voice is thick in my ears, but my hearing is selective when he speaks up again. I struggle against him for the umpteenth time, but it's pointless and energy wasting. I shut my eyes and force myself to grow numb, to block out everything like I did when I was younger.

"Just kill me now. I'd rather be dead," I tell him, without a hint of emotion. Warm breath hits my neck, and I feel violated upon its contact.

"Don't worry, you may get your wish. *Eventually.* But first, you and I are gonna get to know each other all over again." These are the last words I hear, before something sharp pricks my neck.

My breath quickens, and I manage to let out a gut curdling scream before my body melts like liquid, and the world disintegrates in seconds.

Chapter 37

I SWALLOW BACK the acrid, stale air circulating around me as my eyes slowly open. The taste is vile and rancid, and it cuts through my throat and nostrils with each forced gasp.

Coming to, I'm back in that soulless room of Deacon's choosing. Turning slightly to my right, a dark piece of fabric covers the window, once more concealing the harsh reality of my fate.

A fate that is determined to claim me - one way or another.

Exhausted and disorientated, my eyes rake up as the sound of metal chimes out from my movement. I wince against my bonds, and the unforgiving chains cut into my skin, slow and deliberate, with each tiny jolt. My arms are shackled above my head, and my feet barely scrape the ground. My back touches the wall, so close that I can virtually smell the damp through the paper covering it. I've no idea how long I have been in this position, but my limbs are beyond numb. I lift my head further, and my neck cracks painfully, screaming against the adjustment. I'm aware that I'm still fully clothed, and that gives me little comfort, knowing that I haven't been raped again.

Yet.

A sigh resonates, and I tilt my head to see a figure sitting against the wall a few feet away, his arms resting on his knees. My face tightens, and I shake my head slowly as he stands and starts pacing up and down in front of me.

"What the fuck were you doing running away? John and Tommy were *this* close to getting him!" Remy says, defeated.

"Fuck you," I reply in a whisper.

He stops in his tracks and grasps my chin in his hand, coercing me to make eye contact. He doesn't say anything, but his expression is incomprehensible. I've witnessed this look a few times previously. He quickly glances towards the door before coming closer.

"Honey, I'm sorry." I can see his eyes watering in the dullness of the room, and I find myself softening towards him. "Why didn't you stay put and wait? You're fucking stupid, Kara. Franklin has been planning this for months. He wants his blood money, and you're the only way he's going to get it."

I absorb his words as my eyes fight the tears and darkness. "And

Deacon? Is this about money for him, too?"

"No, Kara. You're a smart girl, you know exactly what Deacon wants."

I let out a laugh of incredulity. He played his part well, and because of him, we're both at the mercy of the Black's.

The door handle rattles from outside, and Remy jumps back. Frankie strides into the room, each step echoes clearly and terrifyingly.

"Kara, Kara, Kara…" he sighs. "I hate to see you like this. All trussed up and nowhere to go." He lifts the back of his jacket and sits on the bed, contemplating. "I remember when you were this high. How you would run at me with open arms and hug me tight. I bet you don't remember."

I close my eyes and reminisce, plucking out that long-forgotten memory. I remember the little girl I once was. She who was easily bribed with sweets, giving life to the nickname that Frankie christened me with, that has stayed with me for nearly twenty years. I was everything I should've been at that age; young, unaware.

Innocent.

Two decades later, I finally see.

Frankie wrings his hands together and looks around the room. His appearance is more weathered than the last time I saw him properly, but he still has enough presence for everyone else to cower under his cold, dead stare.

I struggle against my bonds again, but the rough finish of the chain slices my skin, and the blood trickles down my forearm, forcing me to stop.

"It's useless to struggle, you're only hurting yourself."

"Let me go," I beg on a whisper. Frankie gets up and stands in front of me.

"I will. As soon as that ungrateful, ex-bastard son of mine coughs up my money." He slowly drags his finger down my cheek, and I feel the flames in my body stoke and threaten to burn me from inside out.

With a devilish smirk and grunt, he turns to Remy. "You stay here and watch her. I'm going to pay my old friend John Walker a visit." He stops at the door and turns. "Find Deacon. I need some visual evidence to present to them," he says, frustrated. The look on his face is that of desperation. "Now!"

I look into Remy's eyes, both of us knowing if Deacon walks in here, the next time we see each other, I might be changed forever. Never to be forgotten. Eternally damaged. His eyes fill with sorrow, and he whispers he's sorry, before following Frankie out sheepishly.

My sobs rack my hanging body, and I thrash against the chains holding me again until I hear a clucking of a tongue from the far side of the room. Deacon swaggers in, Remy hot on his heels.

"Don't cry, sweets. When I'm done with you, pretty boy will be the last thing on your mind."

His hand drifts over my face, down my neck, and finally stops at the swell of my breasts. He grunts and licks his lips. Locking eyes with mine, the sharp shredding of fabric echoes and he rips my bloodied, torn shirt from me. The tattered material hangs from my arms, exposing my breasts and bare stomach. He pulls out a knife and drags it lightly over my flesh, dipping it into my belly button.

"This is nice," he sneers, just before cutting my bra away.

"Deacon, don't! Your dad was clear on what he wanted."

Spinning around, I catch the malice spread across Deacon's face. "Well, do you see him here?" Remy grinds his jaw, knowing he has no power to help me now.

As Deacon continues to lightly graze my skin, I refuse to look at him, and instead train my sight over his shoulder at Remy, who turns away when my eyes capture his. He looks down at the floor, the walls, the darkened window; anywhere but at me. Is he ashamed? He assisted in bringing me here. I wonder whether Sloan knows his so-called good friend is privy to what's happening to me right now. I knew I was right to be wary, and I really want to hate him, but for some inexplicable reason, I can't.

"Do whatever you want to," I mumble, finding my voice. "I'm dead already."

Deacon, amused by my statement, comes closer, until he is within an inch of my bare chest. He looks down at them, before bringing his hands up and grabbing each one roughly. My stomach turns over repeatedly at his unwelcome touch, and I dry heave as he kneads my breasts.

"Just the same as I remember, maybe a little bigger. And since Daddy won't let me hurt you, let me give you a parting gift." He grins and starts to drag the knife again.

I harden my resolve just in time to feel the sharp point dig in and slice across my skin. I press my lips together, suppressing the scream building in my throat, as the blade cuts a red-hot path over my flesh.

I look down to see a gash from one side of my right breast to the other, just above my nipple. I stare up at the ceiling, fighting against the pain and tears. The chains cut a little further into my wrists, over the old scar tissue, but all I can feel is the searing pain escaping my wounded chest.

"Why the fuck did you do that?" Remy shouts. He marches up to Deacon furiously and shoves him aside. "She wasn't fucking fighting you!" They pull and grapple with each other, and a few fists are thrown in between, until Deacon slams Remy up against the wall.

"No, she fucking wasn't! And how disappointing is that! But I can't let her go back to him without something to remember our time together. This way, when he finally gets her back, he will remember everything I've done to her, because it'll be there, all over her body permanently. There won't be an inch of this bitch I won't have marked!" He laughs, and Remy pushes him back.

Disgusted, Remy takes one last look at me, sympathy all over his face, then the traitor turns tail abruptly and leaves the room. Deacon rotates and walks back towards me.

Now I'm all alone with the devil himself.

"Please don't. Please stop!" My nightmare wakes me instantly. I'm still hanging by my wrists, and I thrash against them, determined to break free, even though I know I'm wasting precious energy with each pointless struggle.

Deacon is at the other side of the room, holding a limp girl in his arms. He grunts something I don't understand before the door slams shut. The sound of nothingness indicates my doom, as the current situation doesn't look like it will be ending anytime soon.

"So, sweets, I tried to get my other little bitch last night, but it seems boy wonder has packed her off to New York with mummy dearest, so instead she got lucky. Since I'm not allowed to do anything to you that will jeopardise Daddy's plans, I figured I would use her for my own gain and make you watch. What do you think?"

"I think you're deranged!" I spit out.

He throws the girl face down on the dirty bed a few feet from where I hang, shattered and defeated, and rushes at me. Grabbing my jaw hard, he drags my head forward. His eyes turn dead, and he breathes in.

"Now, what will it be, Kara? Make your decision wisely!" He turns back and marches towards the girl, starting to position her unconscious body.

Tears careen in rivulets down my face at the thought of him doing that to her. I contemplate the best choice. I don't want to be the victim again. I can't tolerate the thought of him touching me that way. But whereas I had survived it once already, this girl might not be able to live with that shame.

"Please leave her alone! Do what you want to me, I'm dead already. You killed me eight years ago!" I cry, fixing my eyes on his dead, black ones.

He saunters over; the smile on his face grows broader and more exuberant with every step. He stops in front of me and fondles my breast, which is still exposed, cut, and covered with congealed blood.

"I was really hoping you would say that!" He grins and pulls out his knife, cutting off the button of my jeans. The metal fastener drops on the floor and rolls into space, echoing as it comes to its place of rest. The next thing I feel are my jeans being tugged down forcibly. I don't watch as he undresses me against my will. I have accepted what is going to happen, but I refuse to witness it.

I regress back to my teens and keep my eyes firmly shut. If I don't open them, I don't have to see. If I don't see, I don't have to remember. It all sounds so good in theory, but theory will not help me now - nor any time hereafter.

"Very nice. Very nice, indeed." The lecherous bastard breathes up at my face. I let his words roll over me. I don't want to remember anything.

I replay every beautiful moment of my life that involves Sloan. Each one assists in removing my mind from the present. Each one makes me realise I have to live through this.

Somehow, I have to come out of the other side again.

"Open your eyes, sweets!" Deacon commands viciously.

I refuse to give him the satisfaction. He might be able to control my body, but that's where it ends.

"I said open your fucking eyes!" he screams at me, and my head swings to the side as he starts to beat my mind and body into submission.

"Please stop," I whimper repeatedly until he does.

"Don't worry, sweets, I'm not gonna fuck you, not after he's had you. I'm gonna do so much better than that." I breathe a sigh of relief. I've just been granted a stay of execution from this vulture, desperate to feed on his carrion. My relief is short-lived when he sneers and laughs.

"Eyes down and fucking watch!"

Slowly opening my eyes, there is only him and me in this dark, lifeless place that connects us now. I feel his fists all over me. I cry out over and over as he continues to bludgeon me with his bare hands. There's not a place on my body he hasn't violated. My nerve endings are shot, and eventually, the pain subsides, until I'm unable to feel anything at all. His beating is long and cruel. The punches to my body, his knife sliding over my skin, and his hands touching me uninvitingly.

This is torture, in its most basic form.

"WHAT. THE. FUCK!" Remy's roar reverberates around the room.

I feel disconnected from myself, like a bystander looking in. I'm mentally and physically destroyed, and unable to stay awake. I slip in and out of consciousness while trying to remain focused on what is being said around me.

"You're a fucking dead man, Deacon! All Frankie wanted was money. He never wanted her hurt, never mind fucking beaten beyond recognition!"

"Well, I don't take orders well!" Deacon says gleefully, enjoying it too much. "Besides, no one will miss her!"

"You're a sick fucking bastard!"

I hear the men scuffle, followed by the sound of fists smacking flesh and bone. My eyes open a little, just in time to see Deacon's knife make contact with Remy's cheek, slicing him deep from temple to lip.

"Sick bastard? Now, now, Rem, let's talk about what *you* did all those years ago. Who the fuck tied her down for me? Yeah, that's right! You did it so fucking good she still bears the scars! Don't act like a fucking martyr now because rich boy's got you on the goddamn payroll!"

"You son of a bitch!" Remy spits out. My heart suddenly breaks for him, because a part of his torturous past has just been aired without his consent.

Deacon crouches down on the floor, where Remy is holding his bloodied face, breathing in and out in deep snorts.

"Know this, the next time we meet, only one of us will walk away, *brother!*" Deacon gives me one last look, then swaggers away.

The door slams shut, the same moment my sight and hearing finally fade out.

My naked body is freed from the chains, and I fall into my saviour willingly. My torso is sore, and the pain is excruciating, brought on by my open wounds. I lift my arm to cover myself, but the pain is unimaginable and lodges in my throat. Unable to hold it, my arm flops back down, landing on the mattress beside me.

"Please, no more. *Please*," I beg the person holding me. They don't respond, only cradle my broken body tenderly. Due to the lengthy beating I've suffered, I can't open my eyes fully, but recognise the man instantly. I stiffen under the injuries that Deacon has bestowed upon me.

"Kara, I'm sorry. Please forgive me. It wasn't meant to be like this. I'll make it right, I promise," Remy pleads. His hand continually brushes the side of my face, while he rocks me back and forth. He lays me down delicately, then his footsteps retreat further away. I hiss at the sensitivity in my arms and legs, while attempting to gain a comfortable position.

Laying alone, with only my breathing filling the void, I wonder where I go from here. I realise the vow I made to live through this is now diminished.

Letting the darkness in, I descend into a deep sleep, dreaming of midnight blue eyes and a future I so desperately want, but fear I will never have.

A light tapping on my face wakes me.

"Kara, can you hear me?" Remy asks apprehensively, his face marred with frown lines and pain, while the congealed blood creates a stark, weeping, red line over his cheek.

I nod and try to stretch, whimpering with each movement. I listen carefully to everything; it's the only sense I have left that isn't impaired from the violent assault I have endured. Carefully dressing me, he picks me up delicately, and his footsteps resound through the hollow space.

Pushing open the door with his back, daylight blinds me as he quickly moves us towards a waiting car. He sits me inside and gets into the driver's seat. Locking the doors, the engine comes to life, and he speeds off from the building.

"Remy?" I ask timidly.

"Yeah?"

"I'm sorry," I say, reaching up to touch his face.

Taking my hand, he carefully turns my wrist. "So am I, honey." He drops my arm back down.

Staring out of the window, I know I can't go back.

"What was that?" he asks with concern. I realise my inner voice was outwardly vocal again.

"I said, I can't go back. I admit I don't fully trust you, but I'm trusting you to take me away from here."

Leaving is the hardest decision I have ever had to make, but I know if I stay, I will always be looking over my shoulder for the rest of my life, waiting for the third time unlucky.

"Kara, right now I need to get you to a hospital."

"No, please, I need to leave. I need to disappear. He can't see me like this, it'll break him."

He pulls up at the side of the road and turns to me. "He's already broken. He will never stop; he doesn't know how to. Surely you must know that?" he says in disbelief. "He will find you, wherever you are."

I nod, insofar as I can. "I know he will; they both will. *Eventually*. But this isn't just to save him; I'm saving myself."

He grinds his jaw and starts the car. The silence is thick between us, until he speaks up. "North or South?"

"North," I say with conviction. I turn to him from the back seat. "Why are you doing this? Why are you helping me to disappear?"

A deep breath fills his lungs, and he lets it out, looking at my wrists. "Redemption." I nod my head slowly, continually, letting it in that neither of us will ever escape the pain of this life.

"Thank you, Jeremy."

"Get some sleep. I'll stop at one of the services so you can get cleaned up."

I turn back to the window, realising we both walk a different path, but it's one that will always lead to the same place of perdition. A place we are condemned to relive our past transgressions and those who have sinned against us until we are no more.

I rest back into the seat and dream of blue eyes, my heart shattering that I shall never look upon them again. I pray he will forgive me, and the ultimate betrayal of breaking my promise will lessen with the passage of time.

Time is void in my mind as the car eats up the miles of motorway spanning out in front of us. Rain clouds roll in overhead, threatening precipitation, darkening the world further.

With my head pressed hard into the rest, my breathing shallows, and tiredness overcomes me, as the signs for M1 North and every city and town in between, flash by outside.

The unearthly tug on my body is too strong to resist, and I relax, giving myself over to it with open arms. It pulls me down and cradles me beautifully. Letting the darkness in completely, I begin to descend into a deep sleep, realising any dreams of a future I once had are now just smoke and ash.

The light is eventually devoured, and I'm dragged back to the place I fear to tread inside my dreams.

Once again, I'm alone in the dark, hiding in my cubbyhole.

Through his eyes

EIGHT YEARS AGO…

"Just got the call, I know where he is. I'll pick you up in ten." The phone disconnects, and I slip it back into my pocket.

The picture on the table captures my attention. The nervous twitch in my eye works overtime. It has been constant since Charlie confessed. I look at her smile alongside my mother's, and know that I have to protect what's mine.

The truth can never be known.

I climb into the car, and John turns to me. "He's at some party being held by one of his dealers. A real piece of shit from what information I can source. Loser dad. He beats up his wife and kid. He's been there a lot over the last few months, I just can't figure out why."

"Good, let's get there quick. I want him gone." I stare out of the window as the car eats up the miles to the dead man walking. The murkier streets of Manchester come into view, and I consciously chew on my lip. It's either that, or crack my knuckles in frustration. I can't let John see how damaged I am by Charlie's admission.

"How's uni, kid? Any nice girls?" John asks, attempting to clear the thick tension swirling around the car. I cock my head over to him and raise my brows.

"Is that the best you've got, John? Seriously? Uni's okay, I guess. The girls are pretty much the same," I reply with disinterest. Turning back to stare out of the window, anything is better than making small talk with the big man.

I reminisce fondly of the security guy that my mother secretly hired when Frankie decided she had to learn how to take a beating like a man.

Son of a bitch!

I hate that the bastard can invade my thoughts so easily, wiping away everything else.

John's phone rings from the dash, and he presses it to answer. "What you got?"

"He's still at the house, boss. I can't pinpoint him, though. He disappeared from the main party a while ago, and nobody knows where he's gone. I'll stay outside until you get here." Tommy voices fills the confined space.

"Thanks, man. Ten minutes." John ends the call and turns back to me. "I don't like this. Something isn't right."

He's got that right.

Everything about Deacon Black is so fucking wrong.

Bodies are everywhere when we arrive. John parks up behind Tommy's bike, and the three of us make our way over the front garden into the house. Empty cans and discarded cigarette butts line the way. People are swaying, either high or drunk, making out with anyone who's readily available. I scrunch my nose in disgust at the sights and sounds swirling around me. There's no difference between this place and the uni parties.

Except, I'm not here to have a good time; I'm here for revenge.

We slowly walk through each room in the house. People fill every available space, and the smell of cannabis hangs thickly in the air. No corner will be left untouched as we search the scene for the devil incarnate.

Splitting up, John and I take the upstairs, while Tommy continues looking downstairs. My frustration is growing stronger by the minute, dashing any hopes of finding him tonight slowly start to filter through my head.

This is goddamn useless!

Looking at each other, John opens the first door we come to upstairs.

"Get the fuck out! Unless you like to watch!" a woman shouts at him. She is writhing up and down on some wasted arsehole, licking her lips suggestively. She turns her back on us, and returns to bouncing up and down like a slut with an audience. John slams the door hard and mutters about cheap, dirty whores.

The next door we come to swings open easily. The room is in darkness. Finding the switch, I enter and look around. Defeated, we leave and move on to the next.

There is one door left to try, and I look to John with hope in my eyes that this evening might not be a complete waste of time after all. Trying the handle, it's locked. John kneels down, pulls various tools from his pocket, and fiddles with the lock until it opens.

Pushing the door back tentatively, my surprise is piqued when I realise we're in a kid's room. White bows and flowers decorate the pink wallpaper. I feel sick to my stomach that any child should have to live with the shit that is happening here tonight. I have never been so thankful in my life that I didn't have to grow up like *this*.

John looks at me hesitantly, and I shake my head. I'm definitely not comfortable going through the room. I'm pretty sure Deacon wouldn't be hiding under some kid's bed.

Just as I'm about to close the door, a soft crying fills the empty bedroom, and I spin around to John, who is furrowing his brow at me.

We walk deeper into the room, and he flicks on the lamp. It's empty. I narrow my eyes in confusion, until the cry resounds again from behind a door in the corner. I stand in front of it and place my hand on the knob. John gives a quick nod, holding his gun low, and I open it.

The soft light of the room bleeds into the dark, confined space of the small cubbyhole. The shadow of a girl, curled up in the far corner, makes my eyes widen.

What the fuck? Why on earth is she goddamn sleeping in here?

I stare in disbelief, my eyes spying the old teddy bear, and book and torch beside her.

I look down at myself and then around tiny space, wondering how the hell I'm going to get myself in there to get her out without waking her. She mumbles softly, something about being safe, just as I manage to scoop her up in my arms. Gingerly, I carry her out, John pulls down the bed covers, and I place her inside.

We both look at her and then to each other. She can't be more than sixteen, virtually the same age as my sister. The subdued lamp lights her features perfectly, and for the first time in my life, I feel curious. I glance back at John, who's now wearing an expression of surprise.

"Interesting," he says, beginning to smile at me. I shake my head, because he can read me far too easily.

I really have to work harder on that.

"I wonder why she's in there?"

"The noise maybe?" I shrug my shoulders. I look around the room to see if there's anything else I can find out about her. I can't help but compare her sparse room, with its pink walls, devoid of posters or pictures, to that of Charlie's, which are covered with pictures of the latest fashion, old gig tickets, and posters of celebrities.

But this girl, there's nothing.

"I guess, but that wouldn't explain the big arse book and torch. I'd say she's hiding," John states, with a worried look on his usually stoic face. I'm about to tell him we should leave, when the girl murmurs again.

"Safe...cubby...safe." She then drifts back to sleep. I look to John; who no doubt shares the same expression I do. It's one of confusion and concern.

"Right. Well, it's safe to assume he's not here, so let's find Tommy and leave." I nod in defeat.

Tonight had been about finding that bastard, and fifteen minutes ago I would've hot-footed it out of here, but now? Now I'm interested to find out all about this girl, who seems to have subconsciously gotten under my skin without even realising it.

All in the space of fifteen minutes.

One week later...

"Hey, kid, you got lectures this afternoon?" Walker's voice penetrates my tender hearing.

I roll onto my side and notice the naked blonde lying next to me. I inwardly groan to myself. It's been a week since the night at the house, and I still couldn't get that girl out of my head. I have even gone so far as to get John to find out who lived there and who she is. I now had all the information I needed at my fingertips.

The blonde next to me stirs, and her eyes open slowly. A smile plays on her lips, and she scratches her nails over my lower abdomen. Annoyed, I climb out of bed, pick her clothes up, and throw them at her.

"Get dressed and get out!"

"Seriously?"

"*Get. Out. Now!*"

She blows her fringe from her face, grabs her clothes, and quickly dresses. "Fucking bastard! I should have listened to them! You are a fucking arsehole!" The door slams shut behind her.

"Hey kid, are you listening to me?" John shouts down the phone, irritated. This should make for a fun afternoon.

The sun shines through the window of my digs, and I pick up the stuff he has managed to extract on my girl.

My girl?

I shake my head at my inner thoughts.

"Yeah, come and get me. Twenty minutes," I confirm before hanging up.

Studying the school pictures of Kara Petersen, I'm finding it hard to believe that the tiny girl from the house is the same one on the picture in front of me. This girl looked relatively healthy and happy; her blonde friend had her arms around her. My girl is gaunt and vacant looking, even in her sleep.

My girl?

God, I really have to stop this. I have to stop thinking about her like this. She's fourteen. A child, for fuck sake!

Over the last seven days, I've had seven different girls become acquainted with my sheets. I'm not normally so easily swayed, but I'm so frustrated. I wanted to see her and couldn't. So what did I do? I fucked anything that offered herself freely. On one condition – she wasn't a brunette.

I jog down the stairs, but am pulled back by Stuart. He's in his last year of med school before he has to start his training, and we have become good friends over the last year. He helped when Charlie needed it. He has been professional and discreet, and I owe him big time.

"Hey, man. Party tonight, you coming? I heard Scarlett will be there." That girl is one of the biggest sluts walking, but if she could give me some relief for the night, I'll take it. I nod noncommittally, and he bumps fists with me, before saying he will call me later.

I sit on the steps of my digs and wait for John to arrive. True to his word, his car pulls up right on time. I open the door to see the big man wearing a grin.

"What the hell has got you all happy today?"

He winks. "You'll see."

We drive for ages, passing through the rough estate from last week, until we pull up at the high school. John steps out of the car first, and I follow behind, wondering what on earth we're doing here. We continue to walk to the football field where practice is in full swing, and I remember back to how high school was for me. Attending every day under the façade that life was perfect when it was so far from it.

Those were the dark years. *The Black years.* I grimace at the memory of the bastard, and how we now had to deal with his spawn.

"Look, over there," John says, tapping me, then pointing to the tiered wooden seating at the other side of the pitch.

Deacon is sitting alone watching the practice. He's hunched down in his seat, and we do likewise. Just like he doesn't want to be seen, neither do we. We stay and watch him until practice finishes. I'm just about to get up, when John pulls me back down.

"Wait, this is what you need to see," he says firmly.

I scrub my face in confusion until I realise the pitch is clear, but Deacon's eyes are still fixed on something opposite him. I cock my head to the left and see the object of his intention. My stomach lurches, and I can taste vomit in the back of my mouth. It's all so clear now why he spends so much time at that house.

Kara.

She's the reason why.

"It's not what you think, kid. She's a loner. She has one friend, the blonde girl, Samantha. She's another kid from a broken home, too. Parents neglect her, possibly some abuse, I'm not too sure. They seem to have more of a sisterly relationship," John confides, not looking at me, and I bore mental holes into the side of his head.

"And dare I ask how you know all this?" Do I really want to hear his answer?

"Well, I kind of made it my mission to find out about her. After all, I've never seen you soften against any girl the way you did when you saw her." He's now looking at me, reading me so perfectly.

Goddamn my traitorous face!

"I was just being kind," I mutter, chewing my thumbnail. I shift my eyes from him. I don't want him to see he is one hundred per cent correct.

"Huh-uh, and I'm the fucking tooth fairy, sunshine! How many girls have you screwed around with this last week, kid?" He really doesn't mince his words, and I turn back to him, scowling.

"Seven," I say through clenched teeth. He nods and arches a brow.

"How many have been little brunettes?"

Why? He already knows the fucking answer! "None," I whisper, almost ashamed that he can see through me.

"So, you see, I took the liberty of finding out all about little Kara, so that little Sloan would stop acting like a little whore! Your mother would be disappointed if she knew, kid. Don't make me call her." John's face hardens, and he stares at me unnerving.

His friendship with my mother went beyond employer and employee, they were friends, first and foremost. I used to think she had something going on with the young security guy, but I realised my imaginations were unfounded when John had eventually gotten married a few years after he started working for us. My mother was ecstatic about his news, and equally upset when she found out her friend had sought himself a gold digger.

I sigh, realising life is never going to be sugar-coated and easy for any of us, no matter how much money we could throw at it to hide the shit.

We stay for longer than necessary, following as Deacon stalked Kara from the field and then home. Hanging back on an adjacent street that gives us full view of her house, her friend, Samantha, is the one and only visitor.

In the last few hours, Deacon has disappeared again, but I've since decided I will let John seek him out and exact justice since my attention is now firmly fixed on her.

That night...

"What the fuck, Tommy? You mean you had him, and now you've lost him? Fucking find him!" I scream into the phone.

Two weeks of trailing my little brunette had caused my anxiety to pique to levels of rage I have never experienced before, not even with Charlie. I even ditched a few lectures to follow her. Everywhere she went, the bastard was there. She never saw him, but he saw her. I knew what he was planning to do. I saw it in his eyes. There was no goddamn way I would let him do to her what he did to Charlie. I couldn't save my sister, but I would save this girl, even if my life depended on it.

"Calm down, Foster! She's okay. From what I can gather, she's locked herself in her room again," Tommy replies.

And that is the real reason I'm so fucking worried. What teenage girl locks and double locks her bedroom door, even in broad daylight?

Something wasn't right.

I pull up the hood on my sweater and hop into the car. I know I'm breaking every possible traffic law as I speed towards the house. When I get there, John and Tommy are waiting for me, along with Stuart. I furrow my brow in confusion at his presence. The acid in my stomach begins to rise.

His presence isn't a good sign.

We enter the house, and John and Tommy push through anyone who gets in our way. We shoulder through the hordes of bodies until we reach the stairs. John gives me a worried look, but before I can ask, we hear gut-wrenching screams. My eyes narrow into slits as I run up the stairs, taking three at a time.

I'm stopped abruptly when I see Jeremy James, one of my oldest friends, standing outside the door. Grabbing his face in my hands, I look into his eyes. He's fucking high! Letting him go, his head drops down, and he starts to shake. The screams ring out again, and he mumbles incoherently. Realising he is guilty by association, I see red. Bringing my fist up, it's stopped by Remy's face. John pulls him away from me and kicks the door open.

Oh, my fucking God…

Deacon has Kara pinned down under him while he pounds into her. Her wrists are crudely tied to the bed head with cable ties, and blood seeps from them alarmingly. John holds me back as he launches himself at Deacon, yanking him from her tiny, broken body. Deacon raises his fist, but John sideswipes him, breaking his nose in the process. Blood drips from the bastard's face as he stumbles back, zipping up his jeans.

"You son of a bitch!" I bellow at him, rushing to cover her, noticing the blood between her legs and the bruises already starting to appear on her stomach, hips, and thighs.

"Say what you want, pussy! I'm fucking done here!" Deacon hollers out. He runs from the room with Tommy right behind him.

John throws his pocketknife at me, and I cut the ties restraining her while her blood stains the unforgiving plastic. I gently wrap her body up in the blood-stained sheet, protecting what little modesty she still has left. My heart breaks for her when her whimpers become painful cries. I quickly strip off my sweater and John helps me get her into it. I lift her carefully, trying to make her as comfortable as possible.

"Easy, don't move. I've got you; I've got you." Her body is shaking in my arms, she is both hot and cold, and it's then that I notice the used syringe on the bedside table.

I have failed her.

If only we had got him before he had the chance to do this to her. I fight back my own tears as I carry her down the stairs.

Stuart is waiting by the van, but John is nowhere to be found. "Hey, man, get the door! Get those blankets and layer them over the back." Kara wriggles in my arms, and a whimper leaves her puffy lips. I can see under the streetlights that her face is now beginning to swell up.

Son of a bitch!

"No, baby, we're not going to hurt you," I say, wrapping another blanket around her. "We're going to get you to a doctor, just sleep, okay?" I place my hand on her cheek, and she seems to quieten down a little. Her breathing evens out, and she appears to be falling into a deep sleep.

"Stuart, take a look at her. I think he pumped her with something. Where's John?" I ask him. He shrugs his shoulders as he ploughs through his medical kit.

I jump out of the back of the van and see John and Tommy at the front door of the house. They have a man up against the bricks by his arms. I run back, but halt when John punches the guy in the skull repeatedly until his body gives out and he slumps to the ground. A woman comes rushing out screaming, and kneels at the man's side. The bloodied man is pointing towards the van and John, who, along with Tommy, is already making his way towards me. He stops and turns back.

"She's your fucking daughter, you heartless bastard!" He then starts walking again. He doesn't stop as he passes by me - he doesn't even look.

Remy is slumped alongside the van, visibly shaking. "I'm sorry. I didn't know...I didn't know!"

John growls and smashes his fist over his face. "I fucking warned you!" John shouts, dragging Rem up from the ground. "I suggest you get the fuck out of here! Leave! Get yourself clean, and then come back and say you're sorry! Right now, it isn't fucking good enough!" John pushes him back, and he staggers away into the darkness.

John starts the van and presses on the accelerator harder than necessary. Stuart's in the back, forcing Tommy to play nurse as they tend to Kara. Stopping at red, I turn to John. His face is awash with fury, and I stare until he notices. He lets out a sigh.

"He knew. He fucking knew! He let that animal do that to her! How can a father do that?!" He turns back to the road when the lights change to green. I stare blankly out of the window, knowing I had also known and still it had happened to her.

"Don't do that! Don't fucking blame yourself, kid! It might have been a lot worse if we hadn't got to her." John leaves the van with the engine running, as he gently gets her out of the back. He runs into A&E with Kara in his arms, demanding someone treat her. Stuart leaves and comes back with a doctor he has been working with as part of his training.

We've been sat in the waiting room for hours until Stuart comes back in.

"She's going to be okay. Doc says there's no real damage externally, except for the bruising and swelling, and that should settle down shortly. Obviously, she will bear scars on her wrists due to the ties. Internally, he's not so sure. They are going to take her to theatre at some point tonight, pump her stomach, and operate if need be. I shouldn't even be telling you this."

"Thanks, Stuart," I say, crushed.

John rises and runs his hand through his cropped hair. "Has her father been in contact? We've been here for hours." Stuart shakes his head, and John kicks the table leg in frustration.

"I wonder what will happen to her," Tommy mumbles rhetorically in the corner. I look at John, and he shakes his head. I know right now that I have to take control of my facial expressions and emotions.

"No, kid. We've already helped her enough. She's almost an adult, and from what I've seen and heard of her, she's strong. Really strong. She'll make it. Now let's go!" He pats me on the back, then walks over to Stuart and shakes his hand. "Thanks, Doc." Tommy follows suit and leaves straight after him.

I approach Stuart, and he shuts his eyes and sighs before opening them again. "No, Sloan, I won't break confidentiality. What she does when she's released is not our concern. You saved her, always remember that." He pulls me in for a hug and lets me go just as quick.

I loiter outside the window of her ICU room. My uni sweater is draped over the chair, and she is sleeping deeply. She would never know who I am, and it's killing me, because, in the space of four weeks, I want her more than anyone else I've ever met before, and I can't explain why.

A nurse comes out of the room, and she gives me a small smile. A thought invokes my mind, and I quickly call after her.

"Do you have a pen and a piece of paper?" She nods. I quickly scribble down my number and hand it back to her. "When she wakes up, please can you give this to her and tell her to call it?" The nurse looks at the paper in suspicion and then to me, but eventually agrees. She turns and walks away.

I look back at the girl asleep in the room, and my heart heaves under the uncertainty of the future. A future that I want her to be a part of more than anything else. I banish the dire thought that I may never see her again from my head and walk away with a heavy heart.

Stopping outside the passenger door, John's looking at me, urging me to get in. Instead, I stand and look up at the sky.

The shocking turn of events has played callously on my mind for the last six months, and I make my final decision now, knowing this might be the only way to protect myself.

In order to preserve whatever little sanity I still have left, I need to leave Manchester, and *her*, behind.

Author Note

Ready for more? You can choose whether you want to delve into the past or keep with the present-day story.

Book 2.5, Aftermath, chronicles the missing eight years of Kara and Sloan's lives, while Liberated, book 3 will conclude their story. Both are available to download now!

Tormented is the second instalment in the series, and the story of Kara and Sloan develops and unravels throughout the first three books.

Finally, if you enjoyed this novel, please consider sparing a few moments to leave a review.

Follow Elle

If you wish to be notified of future releases, special offers, discounted books, ARC opportunities, and more, please click on the link below.

Subscribe to Elle's mailing list

Alternatively, you can connect with Elle on the following sites:

Website: www.ellecharles.com

Facebook: www.facebook.com/elle.charles

Twitter: www.twitter.com/@ellecharles

Bookbub: www.bookbub.com/authors/elle-charles

Instagram: www.instagram.com/elle.charlesauthor

Or by email:

elle.charlesauthor@gmail.com

elle@ellecharles.com

About the Author

Elle was born and raised in Yorkshire, England, where she still resides.

A self-confessed daydreamer, she loves to create strong, diverse characters, cocooned in opulent yet realistic settings that draw the reader in with every twist and turn until the very last page.

A voracious reader for as long as she can remember, she is never without her beloved Kindle. When she is not absorbed in the newest release or a trusted classic, she can often be found huddled over her laptop, tapping away new ideas and plots for forthcoming works.

Works by Elle Charles

All titles are available to purchase exclusively through Amazon.

The Fractured Series:

Kara and Sloan

Fractured (Book 1)

Tormented (Book 2)

Aftermath (Book 2.5)

Liberated (Book 3)

Marie and John

Faithless (Book 4)

Printed in Great Britain
by Amazon